NOT LIKE US

Doc Honour

Doc Honour

Copyright

Not Like Us...

*Cultural differences are a nuisance at best and
often a disaster.*

Geert Hofstede

*Just because they're not on your road doesn't
mean they've gotten lost.*

Dalai Lama

*To travel is to discover that everyone is wrong
about other countries.*

Aldous Huxley

*Human diversity makes tolerance more than a
virtue; it makes it a requirement for survival.*

Rene Dubos

Introduction

People often ask, "Where do you get your ideas?"

It's probably the most common question authors hear. Most of the time, the answer is completely intangible. Ideas come from shared experience, from strange correlations, or even from Sir Terry Pratchett's "inspirons" that sleet out of space into every mind, only taking root in those that are fertile.

In this case, however, I can actually point to a source.

I've long been bothered by the common sci-fi trope of "cohesive worlds," future universes in which each world is a singularity of culture, as if worlds could be treated like city-states. Even the best of sci-fi indulges in this unlikely fantasy. Trantor is a city world. The Dorsai are military mercenaries. Arrakis is a desert planet. (And so, not unsurprisingly, is its copy, Tatooine.) The Formic home planet is uniformly strange.

Our one real world isn't like that. It has deserts and forests and ice and ocean. People form monarchies, democracies, socialist states, and anarchies. I can't imagine any world, large enough to be a world, that would be consistent. When colonists spread out to fill a planet, human nature will make them diverge, splinter, try new things, return to old ways. Some sci-fi authors have acknowledged this. The weirs on the southern continent of Pern developed their own laid-back culture. The Stillness had high technology in the equatorial region that oppressed the mid-latitudes. Those who move to other locations change and become...

...not like us.

Carry that thought to its conclusions, and the results can be disastrous.

Doc Honour
November 2022

Illustration by J.N. Hinge

Time on Verdant

Imagine living on a world with a sixteen-hour daily rotation. Days are short, and so are the nights. People sleep for six hours, work for six hours, and have four hours for morning, noon, and evening time.

Imagine a year of 450 such days. Such a year is only 82% as long as Earth. Years pass fast.

Yet humans can and do adjust.

Months

Unober – winter solstice 1st
Duember
Tritember– equinox 23rd
Quartember
Quintember
Hexember – summer solstice 1st
September
October– equinox 23rd
November
December

Days

Hours, minutes and seconds are unchanged from now. A typical rapid 16-hour day consists of

3-00:	Dawn
4-00 to 7-30:	Work
8-00:	Noon
8-30 to 11-00	Work
11-00:	Sunset

All months are 45 days and have the same calendar. Every fifth year, an extra day (Holiday) inserts between December 45th and Unober 1st.

Work week						Weekend		
Newday	Twoday	Wentday	Midday	Thruday	Friday	Playday	Sitday	Endday
1	2	3	4	5	6	7	8	9
10	11	12	13	14	15	16	17	18
19	20	21	22	23	24	25	26	27
28	29	30	31	32	33	34	35	36
37	38	39	40	41	42	43	44	45

CHAPTER 1

Perhaps it is endemic to human nature that the most significant technology since the printing press, that which has come to change how humans see themselves, was at first suppressed and hounded by the forces of Law and Order.

—*The Making of a New Humanity* by Ellen Thranadil, Tileus Press 448 A.T.

Hot aluminum flechettes pinged on stones inches over Jake's head while he plastered himself prone behind the low wall. He felt tiny flecks of burning metal raining down on him. His eyes darted in all directions, frantic to find a way out. He didn't know how to do this. For star's sake, Jake was an engineer, not a soldier. Until today, his only contact with weapons was in the lab.

"Go that way," Zofia pushed him toward the right. "We can get behind the Mueller Memorial without being seen. That's our escape hatch. Hope the police haven't discovered it yet."

When the Solity Guards had discovered them in the Warrens an hour earlier, Jake and Zofia ran a mad race along narrow, winding streets. At one point, they dodged through an empty building littered with debris. An aircar shouted threats over their heads, though most of the time they were out of sight, a street or two away from where the aircar concentrated. Once they reached the grass and trees of Touchdown Park, they raced across the open sward through clots of people, thinking they were free. Just before reaching the memorial, though, needles came suddenly from behind them, which led them to dive behind the wall.

Zofia pushed him again. "Go."

Jake heard the whine of the aircar, still over the city. A loudspeaker shouted commands down into the Warrens. The guardsmen shooting at them here in Touchdown Park had surely called the aircar. If they weren't hidden before it arrived, it would be all over.

Jake made his decision. Heart racing, he slithered to the right. He crawled as fast as he could while staying below the wall. He heard Zofia behind him, urging him to move faster. The smell of the hot metal and the smack of darts on the stones stayed behind when he moved; the Guards still aimed where he and Zofia had dived for cover.

1

Forty meters of scrambling got him to the memorial. Jake stood up out of sight behind the monument. The wound in his neck throbbed. He pressed his fingers to it. Blood seeped out.

His heart pounded. He kept himself fit, but his race to escape was a completely different kind of exercise than he was used to. Fear kicked his adrenaline into high gear.

Zofia's presence gave him courage. Being together violated Solity's laws about fraternization, but she made his heart soar. She was bolder and freer than anyone he'd ever met. Now the two of them shared a rebellion against Solity, and she was suddenly even more precious to him. The extreme danger they were in worried him as much for her as for himself.

A group of grey city utility boxes hid behind the landscaping shrubbery. Zofia stepped past him to lift a hinged metal hatch cover and scramble down a ladder.

Jake followed, compressing his lean frame into the confined space. He slammed the hatch shut above him, quieting but not silencing the sounds above. Without the daylight, his eyes had to adjust to the dimly-lit vertical manhole. He found the ladder rungs mostly by feel, then stopped to catch his breath at the bottom.

Zofia ran along an underground passage with tile walls and utility pipes. Her feet splashed in occasional puddles.

Jake sucked in another good breath and raced along behind her.

The faint whine of the aircar arrived above the closed hatch. A loudspeaker amplified the threats overhead.

"Jacoby Palatin, Zofia Dobrunik, stand out with your hands up!"

Had it really been only three weeks since he'd met her?

CHAPTER 2

The totalitarian Solity of Verdant Prime was a natural successor to the four years of rigid shipboard control in transit from One Hope. Captain Mueller had a strong character that demanded obedience; after touchdown, he simply stayed in control while the colony established. The unusual fact was that Solity continued to strengthen its iron grasp on its citizens for another four hundred years, a feat accomplished by no other socialist government in all of human history.

—*An Annotated History of Verdant* by Ellen Thranadil, Tileus Press 442 A.T.

THREE WEEKS EARLIER: THRUDAY, 14 QUARTEMBER, 416 A.T.

A few weeks prior to his race to escape, Jacoby Palatin—his friends called him Jake—looked around with satisfaction at his antimatter lab, located in the heart of the General Defense building. The lab was a large room dominated by the floor-to-ceiling antimatter containment chamber at the far end. Workbenches strewn with equipment surrounded the chamber. The near end had five open office cubicles, his own being somewhat larger than the rest.

Well, it wasn't really "his" lab. Citizens in Verdant Prime owned nothing; everything belonged to the state, what they called "Solity," even the coveralls he wore. Solity told its citizens what to do through formal Assignments.

Jake's Assignment was to design and build an antimatter bomb, leading a team of three other engineers. He was proud to be part of Solity; it gave him purpose. Jake at twenty-nine Verdant years old had advanced rapidly in the six years since he received a doctorate in particle physics. Of course, he imagined much more useful things to do with his physics and engineering knowledge, but this was what Solity needed. Or so he was told. It didn't matter. Like everyone else, he had no choice.

"Indy, can you give me those results on the containment? And come here. Let's talk about them."

"Okay, Jake. They're coming to your desk holo in a moment." Indigo Westleaf was Jake's second engineer for the project.

Indy paused a moment with an inward gaze, using his implant to call up test data onto Jake's holo. Imps allowed audio and text communications through the InfoNet, hooked directly into sensory nerves.

For just a moment, Jake marveled at the technology. He touched the side of his neck, feeling the slight lump of the implant.

When they stood together, Jake smiled at the physical difference in the two of them. For all their similar engineering capabilities, Indy was at least twenty centimeters shorter than Jake. Not that Indy was all that short, but Jake was a tall man. Indy's hair was dark, while Jake's was strikingly dark red. The two had become good friends on this project, trusting each other, though Jake had deep knowledge of the particle physics Indy didn't have.

Jake ran his fingers through his hair, then extended one finger to point in the air into the graphs. "This looks good. The laser cage is holding the latest antihelium nuclei with a safety factor of..." He paused to read the numbers. "...about five times, right?"

"That's what I read, also. So, we don't need to worry about our little spark getting out." Indy glanced at the containment chamber. A glowing pinpoint visible through the glass hurt their eyes whenever they looked inside.

Jake continued, "Well, at least we're not going to accidentally blow up the city. It always worries me that antimatter can't be made fail-safe. It takes all our equipment operating to keep it safe; if something fails, it touches normal matter and we're done for. But all this apparatus doesn't get us a bomb we can use. The chamber and its support are far too large."

"Do you have any ideas how we can get a better laser cage with something smaller?"

"That's the question," Jake answered. "I've got a meeting with the director in a few minutes. Afterwards, let's get the team together for a brainstorming session." Jake sent a meeting notifier to the team through his implant, and Indy returned to his desk.

He heard the loud clack of the security lock releasing on the door. Director Berndt Denmark pushed it open, his forceful presence filling the room, his purple Administrative coveralls clashing with the Defense light green of Jake's team. Denmark was shorter than most with a swarthy complexion, and his penetrating dark eyes noticed everything.

"So, Jacoby my boy, how's the progress?" He had a gruff voice and a perennially dangerous edge to his smile. "We've been bringing you along for three years now."

Jake was still honored such a high-powered man had decided to mentor him. After all, Denmark was one of the eight members of the Solity Council, at the top of the whole country. However, he wasn't an easy man to satisfy; the director wanted others to be as driven as he. Recently, Jake had been feeling more pressure and less mentoring, which made him uneasy around the man.

"Slow and cautious, Director. We can contain the antimatter," Jake waved at the humming chamber, "but physics demands a large piece of equipment to hold it. The mechanism is still too big for a bomb."

Being with the director was a roller coaster ride, exhilarating one moment and threatening the next. Jake never knew what would happen when Denmark came to see him. The uncertainty demanded Jake's best.

"So, what are you doing to make it smaller?"

Jake felt the needle of anxiety. He used his implant through the local InfoNet to bring up a holo of different test data over his desk, a simpler summary. Jake manipulated his hand in the haptic sensor field to control the data display.

"Yesterday's data shows us the containment laser power needed." He pointed at a graph in the data. "The energy of the antimatter varies with temperature, so we're starting to pursue frigid conditions. Cold might reduce the size. We're also meeting this afternoon to explore other possibilities."

"Time is short, my boy. Very short. I've given you good advancement, because I've trusted in you. We've rewarded you with leadership, good perks and a nice apartment, right?"

Jake nodded.

"You should know we have other irons in the fire. War is coming, and this bomb is a key deterrent weapon. You need to work faster." After a pause, he repeated, "Faster."

Denmark's eyes bored into Jake's for a concentrated moment. Then, without waiting for a response, Denmark swept out, his expensive scent lingering.

Jake let out a held breath and rubbed the mole on his chin. He hadn't even been aware of how tight his muscles were until they relaxed.

The director's words about war made him think. He had grown up with the world defined by conflict. Verdant was a small world with only four countries. Yet ideological differences caused incessant clashes. In his short lifetime, Prime had skirmished with both Tileus and Rathas in various raids across the Vissensee Channel. The country of Winter was farther away and did not create immediate problems. Jake didn't know much about how people lived in those other countries; what he did know was they were not like us. He knew how Solity worked here in Verdant Prime. The administrators might be arbitrary at times, but mostly it worked. In contrast, the news media constantly harped on how little trust the citizens could place in those other countries. He spent a moment to imp the InfoNet about the current international conflicts. Jake found an article about Tileus trying to infiltrate its "true democracy" here into Prime. He also found surprising essays extolling the virtues of the Tileus democracy; they were marked subversive by Solity monitors. While he watched, one of them disappeared from this search list.

He could find nothing, though, indicating emergence of a new war. The international conflicts did seem to be accelerating, but not yet to the point of combat. Denmark must know things at his high level Jake couldn't know. He shrugged and returned to his work.

"Work faster," Jake muttered aloud. "Faster doesn't change physics."

ॐ ✳ ॐ

After the brainstorming session with his team, Jake worked to find designs for superconductor lasers. An hour later, he noticed his assistants were gone and he chuckled to himself. Sometimes, work got away from him. Whether he'd been affected by the director's injunction to work faster, or simply his own dedication, he'd lost track of time.

He got up from his desk and stretched his back, muscles stiffened from his fixed position. His stomach reminded him of dinner. Jake checked the lab before leaving, turning off unnecessary equipment. The containment chamber stayed on, of course, along with its backup power.

To clear his head, Jake decided to go to the local easygo. He would have some bar food for dinner; it would be fast with no need to cook.

Outside, the larger moon Bright was waxing gibbous and shed pale light on the wide plaza surrounding General Defense. The smaller moon Silver was a crescent in the west.

He looked up at the five carved stone figures of the defense monument. Each figure represented a branch of General Defense: Land Assault, Prime Navy, Aero Collective, Space Force, and Solity Guards. The figures upheld a globe of Verdant. The monument had been created over two hundred years ago, before other countries had split off, when Verdant Prime still controlled the entire world. At that time, the goal of General Defense was to protect Verdant from other worlds. Today, General Defense aimed at the other three countries—and, through the Solity Guards, at the citizens of Verdant Prime.

While he walked, he was bombarded with imp messages about Tileus. Some came in as audio reports to his inner ear. Others appeared in his retina as visual overlays. Perhaps his earlier search had triggered them. Some of the messages were surprisingly pro-Tileus and were marked subversive; others vilified Tileus for their anarchy. *Maybe there is international tension after all*, he thought. He told his imp to suppress similar messages.

Only a few people were in the easygo. None of his usual friends, but an intriguing woman sat alone at the bar. She was tall and sleek with long black hair reaching to her waist. Her yellow Technology coverall fit tighter than usual, so he could appreciate the curves under it. In her hand was what looked like a fizzy gin.

Jake had learned caution about meeting women. In Solity, fraternization between members of the opposite sex was illegal without approval. He had applied for fraternization twice before, once with Hama in secondary school and once with Imani four years ago. Both times, Solity had disapproved his application due to DNA mismatches. They never explained.

But meeting in public was legal. He'd enjoy some casual conversation.

"Do you mind if I join you? The place is pretty empty tonight."

She looked up with dark eyes and a friendly smile, a twinkle of surprised humor in the smile. "Not at all. I was hopin' for company." Her voice was feminine and a bit husky.

"There's always room for a new friend. I'm Jake." He spoke with the confidence of being good-looking, knowing he had even features, pale blue eyes and his striking dark red hair. He kept himself healthy by gym work and racquetball in the zero-G courts. Jake gave a hand signal, and the bartender brought his usual glass of white wine.

"Zofia," she said turning on the stool to face him. "I think I've seen you in here before." She flipped her bangs out of her eyes with an intriguing shake of her head.

"It's possible. I come in here when I'm wanting to get away from things."

"And what are you getting away from tonight?"

He shrugged with a smile. "Life. Solity. Problems."

She laughed. "Yah. Sounds like normal in Verdant Prime."

"And what are you doing in here?"

"Just relaxin' after a *hard* day fixing implant interfaces." She mocked the word by putting her hand against her forehead and rolling her eyes. "It's my Assignment."

"Interesting. I work in technology, too, but mostly I can't talk about it. Defense work." Jake took a sip of his drink and smiled. Zofia looked relaxed and comfortable.

"Defense? Well, that makes sense, for a light green." She waved her hand at his coveralls and laughed brightly. "Do you enjoy what you do?"

"It's challenging. I'm working with advanced particle physics. But, to be honest, I've always had a lifelong dream of doing something to end war, rather than contributing to it."

They talked for a while. He learned Zofia Dobrunik lived a simpler life than his. Because she did tech maintenance, her duties changed little day to day. She carried a test set to fix software problems in peoples' implants; she went where she was told and repaired similar issues all day. She rarely had to think about her work.

"I was pretty good at software in school. Earned some prizes. But I don't get to use it much in this Assignment; it's all rote work. I spend my time thinkin' about life," she told him. "For instance, have you ever wondered whether Solity really works best for us?"

Jake was taken aback by the question. "No, not really. Solity seems to work well. The other countries are the ones with problems. Weird forms of government. Religious. Tribal. Voting. I hear they have to buy things with money, whatever that is, instead of having it provided by the government. I don't think they could work as well as Solity."

"Maybe, but think about it." She tapped her temple with a saucy grin. "In Prime, Solity tells us what work to do. Where to live. We don't have any choice. It's like playing field soccer where the keeper tells everyone what to do, all the time." She laughed lightly. "Can't win a match that way. Bangit, we even have to get approval to date and to marry. Whatever happened to love?"

"Love? What an archaic term. Does anybody in Prime use it anymore?"

"Exactly my point."

They kept talking and got a second drink. They moved to a table, he ordered some chips and dip, and they shared the plate.

Jake found her philosophy fascinating but dangerous. Occasionally, when she said something particularly wild, he looked around to see if anyone was watching. Primary school had instilled in him a respect for the way Solity worked. She talked about different ways that might be better, of people choosing their own work, of men and women being together freely. Jake had never considered such things before.

Along the way, she bubbled with lively enjoyment of life.

He asked, "Yeah, don't you worry about a conversation like this? Solity frowns on people questioning its ways. It can even lead to arrest for sedition."

She laughed and put her hand on her heart. "Yes, it can. Maybe Solity isn't very concerned about someone like me, a lowly technician just doin' her job." Then her eyes twinkled with amusement. "Shoot, I like to live dangerously."

"Okay. Not something I've tried. I've always been too busy doing what's in front of me. Solving problems. My life has been challenging enough without adding danger."

Suddenly, the easygo door sprang open, and a dozen boisterous people surged in, most of whom Jake knew. They crowded around the bar ordering drinks.

"Hey, Jake!" hollered Beadie Ngumba. He dropped into the chair next to Jake and clapped him on the back. "Good to see you."

"Where've you all been, Beadie?" Jake turned to face him and gave him a friendly punch in the chest. Beadie wore the dark blue coveralls of Capital, blending with his dark skin. "This place has been empty, and you people look like you've been having a party."

Frayer Olsen, also in dark blue, grabbed the fourth chair at their table. "Oh, yeah. Party time!"

8

Beadie answered, "Oh, we got started in the distribution line and it just sort of grew from there. Who's your Technology friend?"

"We've just been getting to know each other. Zofia Dobrunik, meet Beadie Ngumba, the most capable capital distribution manager you'll ever know."

Zofia laughed. "Sounds like an oxymoron to me, but I'll believe it if you say so." She lifted her drink in salute to Beadie.

"So, why were you partying in a distribution line?" Jake asked. "Don't you Capital people just...control those lines?"

Beadie shrugged. "I'm not sure any of us can control it, but no. I direct a fair amount of consumer distribution, but what happens in the lines is whatever happens." He laughed at the recent memory. "We were queued up for some winter jackets. In the spring, of course; how silly can we get? Got the notices by imp, so we all knew they were ready for us. But one of my associates must have screwed up. The center had twice as many jackets as people in the queue."

Jake sat up in surprise. "Interesting. A surplus? It's normally the other way around, where distribution lines come up short."

"Yeah. We do our best, but it happens. The commissars tell us how many people need jackets. We pass the numbers on to Labor so they can set the production quotas. But it's months later when people actually get their jackets—and things change. Usually, we've underestimated the need. This time, well—"

"It's almost an impossible problem, isn't it?" Zofia chimed in.

"Yeah, it is. But how else could we do it? Someone has to figure out how many jackets to make." Beadie shrugged again.

"But how did the extra jackets lead to a party?" Jake was puzzled.

Frayer laughed, "Party time. Too many people, too many jackets."

Beadie laughed and nodded. "Somehow, the word got out about the extra jackets. There aren't many implants in the Warrens, but someone told somebody. Before the line was quite done, a bunch of light blues descended on us. Over the next ten minutes, the crowd grew to epic proportions, everyone pushing and shoving to grab whatever they could. Luckily, the distribution center only had jackets; it would have been a lot worse if there had been food...or liquor."

Jake raised his finger to make a point. "Still doesn't sound like a party."

"I guess the surplus led to a sense of abandon. People were dancing in the streets, waving jackets in the air." Beadie laughed out loud. "I found myself linking hands with a circle of twenty Labor people, dancing round and round like schoolkids."

Zofia leaned over to ask, "Why didn't the light blues from the Warrens get notified in advance about the jackets?"

Beadie shrugged. "I don't know, but they were happy to get what they got. We're still riding the high."

Frayer joined in again, somewhat more seriously, "The commissars who serve the Warrens often don't get the word. They get left out in the calculations, so production doesn't make enough." Then he shrugged. "This time, they got the goodies. And we got to party for a while."

Conversation moved on to other topics, the group quieted, and they split up into smaller groups, taking to the tables. Beadie and Frayer joined another table, leaving Zofia and Jake alone again.

Zofia said, "See? This is what I was talking about before they came in. It's practically impossible to calculate in advance all the needs and have production be responsive enough to meet them."

"Okay, but this is a special case," Jake said. "Great stars, the Warrens are just about a world of their own. It's difficult to get good information from them."

"True. But statistics are always fiction. Everything's a special case, where the general rules don't fit. The reality is production has a time delay, and the pre-calculated needs change during the meantime."

Jake was very uncomfortable with the discussion. He knew these thoughts were contrary to Solity's ideals, and talking this way brought danger. But what really made him uncomfortable was the ring of truth. He had seen many cases like Beadie's. Sometimes, excess led to a party. Much more frequently, insufficient supplies met those who showed up. He heard the stories, from Beadie and other friends in Capital, of the difficulties they faced. Riots, even. But still…Solity had worked for over four hundred years now.

Yet, while he walked home through the city streets to his third-floor apartment, Zofia herself kept playing in his mind. Strange ideas or not, he wanted to know more about her.

CHAPTER 3

Looking back, it is clear Director Berndt Denmark played a pivotal role in the development. The role he intended to play was certainly different, but without his ambition, the new technology would never have happened. After all, Denmark actually thought he was funding a form of mind control to enhance the totalitarian nature of Solity.

—The Making of a New Humanity by Ellen Thranadil, Tileus Press 448 A.T.

THIRTEEN YEARS BEFORE PRESENT: NEWDAY, 19 DUEMBER, 403 A.T.

In school, Berndt Denmark maintained top of his class year after year. He also gathered a cadre of followers who recognized his potential and wanted to be part of it. At each testing, his aptitude scores showed a strong capability for the kind of forceful leadership Solity wanted.

After graduation at twenty-three Verdant years, Denmark received Assignment to a powerful administrative position in the Department of Labor, evaluating citizen aptitudes and eventually making Assignments for others. His job was to predict Solity's need for each profession, then to select people with the right aptitudes to fill the need. He concentrated on making relationships among his peers and superiors, demonstrating his own gift for leadership.

One of his classmates stayed with him, Franklin Edobar, whose scores were only a few places below his own. Denmark fostered the relationship, using his inside information to keep Edobar as an assistant.

The two were as different as sea and land. Where Denmark used a harsh and demanding leadership style, Edobar gained support by caring for people. For over fifteen years, Denmark allowed Edobar to learn from him. The relationship worked for Edobar, too, because his own career rose faster than it otherwise would have.

Denmark's career grew rapidly, moving from Labor to Justice then to Capital. In each position, he learned more about how Solity balanced supply with demand while controlling the populace. Administrators like him created the hierarchical plans based on data supplied by commissars in every city and town. At each level of planning, the numbers got bigger—but the essence of the plans was to ensure each need was met with the appropriate quantity of supplies.

Decisions were at times necessarily ruthless. Denmark made them without qualms. He became a man of power, using people as pawns to achieve his own ends.

Fifteen years later, Denmark was a policy maker in the Department of State. His department received a panic request by ansible from the planet Branch. Ansibles used entangled particles to provide real-time communications across light-years of distance. Bandwidth was low, so messages were necessarily short.

Urgently need grain. War destroyed crops. Planet dying. Help.

Denmark sat straight in his chair in surprise. Through his position, he was privy to history knowledge only held by a few in Solity. He knew only four planets were still populated by humankind. Branch had been colonized fifteen years before Verdant; the two planets had similar histories and similar problems.

He called in Franklin Edobar to consult.

"Franklin, I've got a difficult message here. It looks like Branch held a final war and destroyed its ecology."

"Final? You mean like Earth?"

"What do you know about Earth?" Denmark asked.

"Just that it's gone. Long ago. Had a war and destroyed the planet."

"There's more. Closely-held information we weren't taught in school. Colonization from Earth started over eight hundred years ago. People on Earth discovered the repellor beam we use so widely now. At that time, one scientist named Einstein proved mathematically that nothing could go faster than the speed of light."

"But we go between stars faster than that now."

"Yes. Back then, repellor beams pushed spacecraft faster than ever before. When ships reached significant fractions of light speed, further subtle effects came into play. Radrashan physics modified Einstein's equations just like Einstein had modified Newtonian physics before him, removing the limitation of light speed. Humankind exploded into interstellar travel."

"Exploded? Where are they now? There are only four human worlds, right?"

Denmark nodded, his lips compressed in determination. "Right. That's the part we've kept quiet in Verdant Prime. The resulting technology growth also led to more powerful weapons of war. In less than a hundred years, Earth became the first human world to destroy its ecology in a worldwide war. However, it's not the only one."

"What?" Edobar seemed shocked.

"Humans have lived on seventeen planets. Unfortunately, a centuries-long trend has shown mankind keeps destroying its home worlds. Earth and twelve colony worlds are all gone. Given our current level of war technology, the cycle seems to take about four hundred years."

"Why weren't we taught this in school? It seems important."

"Because we don't want the Solity citizens distracted from their essential work. They can't do anything about it. The knowledge is restricted to our leaders, now including you."

Edobar sat, shaking his head. "This is terrible. And now Branch is in danger. Can we perhaps save Branch? Turn around the cycle this one time?"

"That's why I called you in. What could we do? Travel time to Branch is six months. How much effect could we have?"

"Assuming they have enough to last six months, we'd have to put together a huge fleet of ships to carry enough to feed even a fraction of their world. Then we'd have to keep the flow going until they could kick-start their ecology."

Denmark nodded, feeling bleak and hard inside. "Damn. We'd impoverish ourselves, and it's still likely most of them would die."

"Surely we have to try, yes?"

"Remember, Verdant can't be far behind Branch. The four countries on this world are already at each other's throats. Ever since they revolted against Prime two hundred years ago, the other three haven't had the steadiness of Solity. Tileus waffles back and forth with their popular votes on every issue. Rathas drives everything through their religious view on the world. And Winter has mostly dropped out of technology to live a simple life. Yet all four of us are building military forces, making threatening noises."

"If we banded together to save Branch, maybe the countries here could come together."

"No, that's brolshit. I just can't believe it. They're not like us, and we're not like them." Denmark ground his teeth and shook his head. "We can't save Branch. But maybe we can find a way to bring Verdant back together and keep from going down the same path."

Denmark took a plan to the Director of State and convinced the Solity Council. By this time, his gruff voice and forceful manner were well-known to the Council. They listened.

His strategy was to abandon Branch and save Verdant. If Branch were so desperate as to need food and seed, even a massive effort on Verdant would likely not be enough, and such an effort might doom Verdant. But if the leaders of Prime re-integrated the other three countries on this planet back into Prime, perhaps they could break the cycle and save their own planet.

Following the Branch incident, Berndt Denmark was Assigned to spearhead the plans for his strategy. He moved from Capital to General Defense and developed a ruthless team to foment war so Prime could retake the other three counties under its all-controlling wings. His plans began to bear fruit, and he was eventually Selected to the Solity Council, the highest level of government, to implement those plans as Director of General Defense. Denmark was dedicated to bringing each of the dissident "countries" back under Solity control. Doing so would save humanity.

His plan became a rift between himself and Franklin Edobar. Wishing the man good riddance, Denmark left him behind.

☙ ✳ ❧

FOUR WEEKS BEFORE PRESENT DAY: MIDDAY, 4 QUARTEMBER, 416 A.T.

Berndt Denmark, now fifty-one Verdant years old, looked out the window of his spacious fifth-floor office in the General Defense building. His dark eyes narrowed while he pondered the problems of Verdant Prime. Even while he advanced his long-term plan to bring Verdant together again, he also wanted to solve the problems in this country.

Outside the window, he saw the imposed order of Oriens city. Streets were clean, buildings were regular in shape and height, none more than five stories. Buildings had few architectural variation. Looking down from this height, people in coveralls of prescribed colors walked on the wide street and slidewalks. Occasional antigrav autocars slid down the narrow center lane.

He was pleased with Verdant Prime and its controlling Solity. He was still certain the same approach could save the other countries of Tileus, Rathas, and Winter.

Looking further to his right, though, he saw one of the lingering problems of Oriens—the Warrens, a ragtag assembly of dirty, random buildings. In contrast with the ordered streets around him, the buildings there looked like they had been dropped randomly from orbit. The disorder felt to him like a personal failure, an example of how his methods were ineffective. He wanted to fix everything, but knew he couldn't. He shook off the immediacy of this concern and turned away.

He used his implant to summon his operational assistant.

The door opened, and Shelton Overlock stepped in. "Yes, Director?"

While both wore the purple coveralls prescribed for Administration, the two were as different physically as a grizzly bear and a spitting cobra. Denmark was short and swarthy with close-cropped dark hair, while Overlock was tall, wiry, and blond. What they shared was a fiery intensity. Denmark's coffee-colored eyes were penetrating, noticing everything, giving him the persuasive personality that had carried him all the way to the Solity Council. He could smile with such dangerous charisma as to bring any resistance to heel. Overlock's blue eyes were cold as ice, almost frightening in their concentration, showing glimpses of a black soul capable of anything. When Overlock smiled, people cringed.

Denmark glanced around at the sumptuous furnishings of his office while he moved to one of two easy chairs. He motioned Overlock to the other.

"Shelton, I need you to search out the agitators from Tileus. They seem to be fostering a resistance force within our own intelligentsia. The proles do what they're told, but the intelligentsia get ideas…" Denmark's voice trailed off, and Overlock waited intently.

"They work against us, instead of just doing their part. Some strange concept of 'freedom' contrary to our collective. Solity works. We balance the collective needs with the individual skills. All provide, and all receive their due. 'From each according to his capability…'"

Shelton echoed the rest of the time-honored phrase in the approved manner, "'…to each according to his need.'"

Denmark nodded. "Right. But those other countries. We've never been able to bring them back into Solity. For a long time, we've let it go. They're on the other continent, and people here in Prime have had them out of sight and out of mind. It's been too long, way too long. I want to see the planet come together again in my own time."

"Of course, Director. Your plans are all working toward that goal, starting with Tileus."

"Yes. They are the most irritant thorn of all, constantly infiltrating spies and agitators even here in our capital of Oriens. I saw graffiti again yesterday in Touchdown Park, right on the Mueller memorial."

"It's been removed and cleaned, Director. I saw to it myself. I also made sure the active-duty Guards from the night before were appropriately punished. But I don't think Tileus agents did that. I think the Lazarite resistance were the culprits."

Denmark nodded. "It doesn't matter. The resistance wouldn't exist if they didn't have the example of Tileus. We need to turn that around. One of the ways we keep our own people in line is by using the threat of war. Do you understand that?"

"Yes, Director."

"We need our citizens to be so focused on the problems with Tileus that people don't notice our own weaknesses in distribution or production."

His eyes were out the window and his mind was connecting the past with the present. Was he still on track for his years-long plan?

He looked directly at Overlock. Most people would flinch under his gaze, but his operational assistant met it with equal force.

Denmark said, "So your primary task now, Shelton my trusted man, is to do something about the agitators from Tileus. But I don't want you to destroy them. I want you to keep them ineffective, while increasing the publicity about what they do. If you have to manufacture incidents, do so. I want the people of Prime to hate the agitators. I want them to hate Tileus

15

and their chaotic 'democracy.' I want our people to be ready to go to war against Tileus."

"I'll do so, Director. You can count on me."

CHAPTER 4

Early in the fifth century, problems became more violent in the socialist Solity of Verdant Prime. Population growth made it impossible for the government to manage successfully all the details of life for its citizens. As a consequence, an internal resistance movement—the Lazarites—arose to challenge the establishment. Given the antagonism between Prime and the other countries, it was a foregone conclusion Tileus would offer help to the Lazarites.

—*An Annotated History of Verdant* by Ellen Thranadil, Tileus Press 442 A.T.

FRIDAY, 15 QUARTEMBER, 416 A.T.

Jake was preoccupied at work the next day, thinking about Zofia. It had been years since his last request for fraternization had been denied by Solity. He was young enough to yearn for a relationship with a woman, but Solity made it difficult. One evening's conversation had him thinking about it again.

Indy waved a hand in front of his face.

"Hey, boss. Are you there? I've been asking you a question."

Jake shook himself awake. "Earthfire. Yeah, I'm here. Sorry. I've been woolgathering."

"Must have been pretty good wool, to take your mind off our technical challenges. You're usually all over them."

"It's a girl, Indy. Met her last night."

"Uh-oh. They'll get you in trouble every time."

"Could be. But I only met her the once." Jake took a deep breath and turned to the holo display. "Now, what was that question again?"

Franklin Edobar had learned about ruthlessness and the use of power from Denmark; it also convinced him Solity was corrupt to its core. He watched brutal treatment excused in the name of "fairness," unfair perquisites offered as "incentives," extreme punishment for failure, and even banishment and death for those who disagreed.

The area Franklin found most disagreeable was the national breeding program. People—citizens of Prime—were treated like cattle. The despicable controls disgusted him. Supposedly to ensure babies met genetic standards, men and women submitted to DNA tests for approval before they could "fraternize"—spend time together. Sex outside of marriage was

17

completely forbidden; even intimate touching between the sexes was illegal without fraternization. Solity enforced these laws with draconian power. He saw unmarried women submit to annual gynecological exams in which a broken hymen turned a young woman into a pariah. Young hormones sometimes still led people to illicit sex. When caught, they were physically lashed in public spectacle. The worst part was that citizens accepted all these controls as normal, just like cattle in their chutes on the way to a slaughterhouse.

Every time Franklin thought about it in any depth, he got a headache and his jaw pained him from clenching his teeth.

After his break with Denmark, Franklin had sought out the resistance movement—the Lazarites—within Verdant Prime. When he found them, thirteen years ago, they'd been rather ineffective. They had a cute name, based on a classic fictional character Lazarus Long, who espoused drastic liberal changes to society while living over two thousand years. But they did little more than talk. Solity had too many monitors and controls for them to act.

Franklin changed that. He designed an effective cell-based hierarchical network for their safety. The recognition Franklin got for the network propelled him upward, where he eventually become the leader of the entire organization. At the same time, Franklin grew into a position of power in the Department of Capital, from which he could surreptitiously route equipment and supplies to the Lazarites.

He was huddled at lunchtime with Delf Bendo, another Lazarite. The café hid in the Warrens, the only area in the city of Oriens where they could talk without being overheard through their imps. The implant tracking network had never been built to cover the area.

"I don't think we can trust these Tileus spies." Delf's anger came out of fear. The Solity Guard simply had too many advantages—as well as more weapons.

Franklin shook his head. He was often frustrated by the fear rampant in his members, but he used his personal magnetism to help them get past it. He filled his voice with assurance. "We're going to trust them, anyway."

Delf was still uncertain. "They're not like us. They don't have the same goals, and that makes them dangerous."

"True, but their goals overlap ours well enough to make them assets. The Tileus spies, just like us, want to bring down Solity. We can step in to lead the new country of Prime afterward. In the meantime, they have resources we can only dream about. Best of all, they're not tracked by Solity the way we are."

The Lazarites created information pamphlets, safe places, weapons caches, and discussion groups. Recently, they'd begun creating violent protests, embarrassing to Solity, to raise the awareness of endemic problems: supply shortages, freedom restrictions, general levels of depression. They needed the help of Tileus technology.

Extensive planning kept the protesters safe from the quick reaction of the Solity Guards. The government Sentinel Shield surveillance system included tracking and audio monitoring through imps, widespread public cameras, and more. Participants had to disguise themselves while also shielding their imps with metal collars. They used specified gathering and dispersal routes for individuals. Often, with the disguises, protesters didn't even know who stood beside them waving the other end of a banner.

"Franklin, won't our joining with the spies bring us more into visibility?" Delf asked. "Denmark's ordered his man Overlock to put maximum pressure on Tileus agitators. Overlock has the Solity Guard trying to catch or kill any they can find."

"Don't worry about it," Franklin said. "I know Denmark well. Remember, I worked closely under him before joining the Lazarites. I know how he thinks." Franklin shook his head again, this time in dismay. "Following Denmark was like swimming in a cesspool. I was too naïve for too long. I'm sorry to say I was so slow understanding how evil he is."

Franklin looked up at the door. "Here come our contacts."

A man and woman came in the door. Dressed in the light blue of Labor, they fit in with the Warrens. But when they entered, both of them scanned the place with their eyes, behaving like something more than mere Labor. Franklin also saw the two sniff the air with distaste. He had to agree the scent of raw food was strong in this Warrens place, distasteful like over-ripe perfume. He caught the eye of the woman and nodded an invitation. The two casually slid into the booth with them. The man quickly checked a reading on his wristband; Franklin recognized a signal strength readout for the imp tracking network. He knew the reading in this place was near zero.

"We're looking for pindel beer. Got any?" The man's voice was calm but sure.

Delf responded with the agreed password phrase, "It's out of season, but we can get some rotted rum."

The man nodded. "Okay. At least we know who we are, then."

"But no names, right?" Franklin asked.

Both newcomers nodded. The woman took over the conversation. "We understand you're looking for some cooperation. We've talked it over with our associates, and we're willing."

Franklin raised a hand in agreement. "Right. We have the organization to create protests and friction, but we have a difficult time getting anything onto the InfoNet because of the imp tracking. However, we've seen a lot of InfoNet traffic about Tileus ranging from straight information to downright subversive. Is that traffic coming from you?"

She smiled. "Yep. We've been pretty successful at it. Our imps aren't tracked by Solity's systems, though we can still insert things to the InfoNet. We've watched Solity proctors label our material 'subversive,' then eventually take it down—but we keep adding more. We have a chain of support people back in Tileus who create material."

Delf raised his eyebrows in admiration. "We can't do that. Anything we post traces back to who posted it."

The woman chuckled. "It might have to do with the fact Tileus designed and manufactures the imps." She winked.

Delf turned to Franklin. "Okay, you're right. They have resources we don't."

Franklin smiled. "Then let's get down to business. We have an event set for this weekend. We'd like to coordinate your InfoNet attacks with our protests. Let's talk about how to do that."

The Spring weekend afternoon was two weeks prior to graduation at Oriens University. Grey-clad students celebrated completion of exams in the park around the clock tower. Groups lounged here and there on the grassy lawn, some serious and some intoxicated. Relief filled the air, though with a touch of anxiety. Over the coming week, the graduates would receive their life Assignments based on their aptitude tests and the needs of Solity. They would report to those vocations after graduation.

Sam Entago was one of the new graduates. He sat with a few friends in the sun, laughing and joking. Blond and fair-skinned, Sam had many friends. It had been a long four years for him, struggling with secondary. Sam worked hard, but education had stretched him. He was glad he'd finished and could get on with life, with no desire for tertiary school. The aptitude test showed he would excel as a shopkeeper, and he hoped his Assignment would lead toward such a position.

"Wherever we go, whatever we do, let's keep our group together," said one of his friends, almost singing the phrases. They all agreed and raised their cups in salute.

Sam raised his face to the warm, blue-white sun and closed his eyes. He enjoyed the feel of the grass in his fingers. "I hope I get to stay right here in Oriens. I know this city, and I don't know anyplace else. I'm not into adventure." He laughed gently at himself. "I wouldn't know what to do in a seaside place like Millard or Timpi."

Even while he spoke, however, the sound of unwanted adventure arose in the streets outside. Dozens of people, most of them wearing light blue and yellow, emerged into the open area from several side streets. They were wearing hoods, carrying signs, and chanting a slogan:

"We want a say—Now is the day!"

Sam was astonished. He'd never seen a gathering like this in Solity—in fact, he had to dredge his memory to come up with the word "protest."

"Bold," one graduate said. "What is this?"

The activists spread out into the plaza, marching abreast while they continued the chant, weaving around the small gatherings. The clock tower, in the center of the plaza, was also in the center of their line. When they got closer, Sam noticed an ominously heavy bag on each protester's shoulder and rubber gloves on their hands. The signs shouted with an explosion of nasty exclamation points:

Stop Oppression!

We Want the Vote!

Choice Now!

Suddenly, Sam's imp was flooded with messages about Tileus and democracy. Hit after hit came to him, each on the heels of another. The InfoNet seemed to have gone as crazy as the plaza. One headline claimed Tileus was taking over Solity. Another shouted Verdant Prime was changing its government. A third extolled the virtues of the vote. The rapid barrage befuddled him. He had trouble thinking.

He looked around at the other graduates. His eyes wouldn't focus with the fusillade of information filling his head. Most of them also had glazed looks. The overload was hitting them all. They simply watched from their places while the protesters infiltrated toward the center of the plaza.

Then Sam saw one protester reach inside his shoulder bag. He had an alarming sense of what was coming.

"Look out!" Sam shouted.

The person—man or woman, Sam couldn't tell—threw an overripe tomato at him. He saw it coming and was frozen in disbelief. At the last moment, he instinctively ducked. He heard the fruit hit someone behind him with a soft splat.

His mind still consumed by the burst of imp messages, he raised up just in time for a rotten apple to hit him in the chest with a bruising thud.

The first tomato was a signal to the rest. The protesters all started throwing a harvest of rotten foul fruit. The clots of students dodged and ducked—and were hit—for about thirty seconds while the line of protesters swept past.

By the time the graduates reached outrage and rose to their feet, the agitators had gained the far side of the plaza and were disappearing into the streets on the other side. Sam watched one protester in yellow go into the nearest street. The woman tore off her hood and disappeared into the crowd beyond. Sam caught a glimpse of waist-long black hair before she vanished.

People in the plaza and street were now moving around in panic, far too late to affect what had happened.

The onslaught of InfoNet information ceased as suddenly as it had begun. Sam stood there, stunned, and looked down at himself. He had been hit at least three times and had received splatter from others. Foul-smelling waste smeared his coveralls, some of it reeking of death instead of rot. Apparently, not all the missiles had been fruit.

"Where did *that* come from?" he asked, waving his hand at the air.

His friend answered, "I don't know. It's the kind of chaos I might expect in Tileus, but not here."

Sam tried to wipe the filthy residue off his greys, shaking his head. "What can they possibly have to protest? Solity works."

An hour later in his office, Denmark was striding back and forth fuming with anger.

"What happened to the Solity Guards? They're supposed to respond within a minute anywhere in downtown Oriens. They never even showed up until the protesters were gone!"

Overlock was icy calm, but his glacier eyes were seething. "Apparently, the InfoNet overloaded their imps, and they couldn't coordinate."

"Unacceptable. Absolutely unacceptable. Who's to blame? I want heads to roll over this."

"Director, we never anticipated this kind of coordinated attack. We've never seen anything like it before."

Denmark stopped pacing to pound his desk with a hard fist. His production award rattled as it bounced. "This one was more than just the feeble Lazarites. I understand the InfoNet onslaught was filled with Tileus subversive brolshit. Have they joined forces?"

Overlock took a deep breath and his eyes narrowed. "It's possible, sir."

Denmark calmed while he stood for a long moment in thought, then fixed his eyes on his operational assistant with a new glint of purpose. The air in the room seemed to cool rapidly. "I told you to create incidents, Overlock. Was this one yours?"

"No, sir. Not mine at all. But I admire it."

The director nodded. A triumphant smile grew on his face. "And yet—as bad as it seems, this can work directly into our strategy."

Overlock's thoughts ran ahead. "How would you like me to handle this?"

"Before we decide, let's see if we can amp up the incident into something more." Denmark moved around his desk and sat down. He composed himself, then unlocked a side drawer and pulled out a small red box. The device was one result of a prior international incident with Tileus; activating the unit would connect Denmark's imp directly to his counterpart in Tileus, their Governor of Outside Affairs. He had met Welton Moller a few times in person and had respect for the man, even if he did serve a decadent democracy. The man had risen to the top in Tileus just as Denmark had done here. Denmark gathered his thoughts and waved Overlock to take a seat.

Denmark turned on the speaker and holo functions, then activated the unit. A short pause ensued until his counterpart answered.

"This is Welton Moller."

The holo showed a live image of the man's head and shoulders, looking directly at Denmark. Moller was a few years older than Denmark, with greying hair and a dark beard. His eyes were sharp and betrayed a hearty humor that also filled his warm country voice.

"Governor Moller, good to see you again."

"I gather this contact is urgent? May I have a moment to bring in another person?"

"I'll wait, sir." Denmark sat straight in his chair, giving the man time to gather.

After a minute, Moller spoke again. His voice had the echoing sound of a speaker on his end. "I've got my assistant here with me, Director. What can we do for you?"

"We've had an incident here in Oriens today, sir, that I believe needs your attention."

"An incident?"

"Something of international proportions, Governor. It might cause irreparable harm—irreparable—between us. We've had a violent protest here, a kind we've not seen before."

Denmark saw Overlock's skeptical eyebrows raise at the word "violent." Rotted fruits weren't very violent.

Moller asked, "Why would an internal protest in Oriens involve us, Director?"

"Coordinated with the protest, sir, was a widespread attack on our InfoNet and personal imps. The electronic attack prevented our police forces from being able to respond to the protest. The web-based attack was clearly done by Tileus spies here in Oriens."

After a meaningful pause, Moller responded, "And what makes you think the attack was done by Tileus, Director? Do you have some proof of our involvement?"

"First, we know Tileus has more advanced implant technology than you have yet shared with us. These attacks were of a nature our people could not have done. In addition, we have the very nature of the InfoNet overload, Governor. The messages overloading our web were all pro-Tileus, with exuberant posts about your democracy, voting rights, and your vaunted freedoms." Denmark's voice registered distaste on the political words.

Moller sighed. "But, sir, any such content could have been created by your own people. It doesn't take Tileus 'spies' to be aware of how restrictive your Solity is. If you have some proof, or some clear linkage to us, then we'd be happy to cooperate with you."

"Do you deny, Governor, the fact you have spies in our country agitating to overthrow our legitimate government?"

"Director, 'spies' is a very strong word, and so is 'agitate,'" Moller responded. "If you wish to discuss our citizens in your country, then we can also discuss yours here in Tileus. But I think such a question is for another day and another time. Again, if you have something actionable, please don't hesitate to call me. In the meantime, I believe I'll return to my duties here. Thank you for your concern, and for letting us know of your problem." He put a slight emphasis on the word "your."

The line went dead. and Denmark turned to Overlock with a pleased but wicked smile. "That was perfect, Shelton. It advances our cause nicely, to have one of the five governors of Tileus avoiding questions about their spies and agitators here in Prime."

Overlock agreed. "Yes, Director. We can make use of his avoidance in our propaganda."

Denmark continued, "So, put our web specialists on the electronic attack. Find out where it came from, what path was used. Get video from any cameras in the area. Have someone select segments which make the protest appear to be driven by Tileus. Doctor the videos if necessary. Couple them with the InfoNet attacks. And then, best of all, use all this information in your public releases about today's incident. Slant it all against Tileus and downplay the Lazarite participation." He grinned. "Work the people. Play up the damage. Get them to believe Tileus is evil incorporate."

His assistant nodded, his eyes sparkling with cold danger. "And what about the protesters?"

"Track them down if you can. Try to trace any imps that 'disappeared' from the network before and after the incident. Perhaps we can correlate them with known resistance networks."

24

CHAPTER 5

Negotiation works best when it is separated from emotion. This is why interpersonal negotiations are always so difficult.

—*A Practical Guide to Negotiation* by Ellen Thranadil, Tileus Press 426 A.T.

Following the weekend, Jake sat in the lab, still bothered by Denmark's injunction to work faster. The demand was contrary to the normal work environment in Solity; everyone did their part, but he never heard of pressure to do more. People did their required work in the required six hours each day. Doing more got you nothing. Doing less got you in trouble. He couldn't understand Denmark's willingness to violate Solity rules by demanding more. Yet Jake felt guilty for following the rules.

He also pondered the reports of an attack by Tileus spies right here in Oriens. The news reminded him of what the director had said about coming war. According to the news, Tileus agents posing as Solity workers pelted students at the university with bricks and filth, injuring several. Rumor, however, said the Lazarite resistance did it.

He turned back to his designs for superconducting magnets to reduce the size of the laser containment guns. Jake had thought about it all weekend; now his team members needed to work on it, too.

Afonso Patel was good at research so he assigned him a task to find suitable parts. He gave Minya Balan the challenge to calculate field strengths, part of her core engineering science. She went to it with glee, glad to be doing engineering calculations instead of documentation. His primary assistant, Indy Westleaf, was already hard at work creating the structures to hold a superconductor magnet.

Late in the day, the director came in again. He was brisk and direct.

"So, Palatin, can we make it smaller yet?"

Jake was surprised at Denmark's attitude. He was used to encouragement and help.

"We're working on it, sir. I think I have a design for a new magnet to reduce the size."

"You think?"

"It's only been two days, sir. Engineering takes time."

Denmark shook his head, a scowl on his face. "Five days, not two. You also had the weekend, my boy. Our enemies were at work this weekend. We

25

should be, too. We can't afford to waste the few days we have left. When can you give me assurance?"

Jake winced. "I have the theory, but we can't know whether it really works until we build a prototype. We'll have to get parts, build the new magnet, and then test it. That's going to take time and effort."

"How much time and effort?"

"I truly don't know, Director. The science is untried, and we can do nothing but take the next steps to see where they lead."

"I'm disappointed. Very disappointed." The director was still frowning. "Let me know of any obstacles, and I'll do what I can. I'll also arrange some more help for you. But damn, it's up to you to make the project happen."

Denmark's gruff voice had carried through the whole lab. When he finished, he captured the eyes of each of the workers in turn, emphasizing his imperative. Then he nodded firmly, knowing he had their attention, and turned to the door.

When Denmark left, Jake traded a helpless look with Indy.

"Does he want us to work weekends now?" Indy asked.

"Apparently so, but no one does that. Working extra days never gets anyone anything." Jake paused to think. "Other than avoiding his anger. Let's at least get back to design for this afternoon."

❧ ✻ ⚬

He saw Zofia again in the evening. Newday was the first workday of the week, generally quiet in the easygo, because people were still recuperating from whatever they did during the weekend. She was sitting at a table with Janus and Bricka, two Defense friends of his who were working on high-energy repellor weapons. Zofia's yellow coveralls contrasted with their pale green, and he thought she looked even better than he remembered. Jake joined them and poured a brew from their pitcher.

"Hey, everyone. Life going well?"

Janus answered with a laugh, "You bet. Our DNA tests came back compatible, so Bricka and I just got fraternization approval. We can date." He reached out to hold Bricka's hand. "We can touch!"

She glowed. "Yeah, we're looking forward to doing things together. We don't know yet where it will go, but we'll take it day by day."

Jake smiled with them and held up his glass in tribute. "Congratulations to you both." Then he turned to Zofia. "Nice to see you again."

She smiled back at him. "You, too."

Janus continued the conversation from before Jake arrived. "So, what are we going to do about Tileus?" He turned to Jake. "Did you hear about the news from the weekend?"

Jake snorted. "Who couldn't? It's been flooding the InfoNet for two days now."

26

"I find it unconscionable," Bricka said, "that Tileus thinks they can come into Prime and create problems. They must think differently than us, to do something like this. I hear they disabled everyone's imps in the area while they created that disturbance."

Jake was puzzled. "Disabled? I heard it was an overload of information."

Bricka waggled her hand in the air. "One or the other. It doesn't make much difference."

Janus added, "The Solity Guard—" he waggled his eyebrows while he added the popular but derogatory name for them, based on their bulbous black helmets with face shield "—the ticks—were late arriving due to the InfoNet problems. Even so, the news says they caught all the Tileus protesters, but they're still looking for the Tileus people who jammed the InfoNet."

Zofia had been silent through all this, but she gave a blithe laugh. "Not sure we can believe everything the news tells us. If the ticks arrived late, how could they catch all the protesters? I heard everyone got away."

Jake crinkled his eyes. "Why wouldn't the news be correct?"

She shrugged. "Maybe because Solity wants us to know what they want us to know. By the way, Jake, what are you plannin' for dinner?"

"I came in here thinking about bar food again, but I'd rather have something better. Would you like to go to the Tangled Tackle for seafood?"

Janus raised an eyebrow and laughed. "This wouldn't be an unauthorized date, would it?"

"No, no. Just getting something to eat. You guys could come, too, if you want."

Zofia laughed along with them. "Sure, Jake. Let's do it. I'm up for seafood." She turned to Janus and Bricka. "Going to join us?"

Janus shook his head. "No, we already have other plans." He smiled at Bricka, who giggled.

Jake and Zofia bid goodbye while they stood.

The Tangled Tackle was only two blocks away, so they walked. They had a pleasant stroll, with occasional antigrav autocars sliding by. Jake enjoyed walking downtown because of the quiet, but today his focus was more on the woman beside him.

Zofia walked with a delightful sway. "What'd you do over the weekend, Jake? I checked in the easygo a couple of times, but didn't see you." Her husky voice was made even more attractive by the contrast of the murmuring city crowd.

He shrugged. "I spent most of the weekend reading technical reports. My boss is putting pressure on my team."

"Oh, that's too bad. If we all just 'do our part,' there wouldn't be any reason for that kind of pressure, would there?"

Jake heard the emphasis, looked up and saw she was grinning. "Are you making fun of me? We each need to do our part, don't we?"

Her grin faded. "Yes, we do. But wouldn't it be more exciting if there were some *reason* for us to reach for more? For instance, what will your boss do if you don't meet his expectations?"

"Ouch. He's pretty powerful," Jake said. "He could make life miserable for the team."

"And what would happen if you really pushed hard and went over the top—you know, worked evenings and weekends, came up with something completely marvelous?"

Jake cocked his head. "Probably nothing special. That's what he'd expect."

She nodded with a serious look. "See? There we are again. It's like playin' a sport that only gives negative points. No incentive to do better than the minimum; only punishment for doin' less. And in your case, it sounds like he can change the definition of minimum at his whims. We really need a better system."

Jake felt dismayed and shook his head. "But how can we know whether some change would actually be better? Solity has worked for over four hundred years."

"Has it really worked all that well? I mean, look at Janus and Bricka. They're overjoyed just to be able to touch hands."

"Of course they are; they've got permission. If people start having uncontrolled sexual contact, we're going to have genetic problems with babies."

"Hmph. That's the party line. The real issue is control—making sure people toe the lines set in front of them. Solity controls everything."

Somewhat confused now, Jake had no answer to that. Conversation lapsed when they arrived at the Tangled Tackle. They had no trouble getting a table, then sat down and kept up the discussion.

Over dinner, he became increasingly interested in her thoughts about Solity. Even more, he found himself fascinated by Zofia herself. She was vibrant and intelligent as well as gorgeous, a stirring combination. It didn't hurt that she sometimes bubbled over into playfulness.

"What did you do over the weekend?" he asked.

"Oh, I played with some friends. We raised a little ruckus together, had some fun. We probably annoyed some people."

He laughed. "Isn't it funny how older people can get irritated when young people have fun?"

Her eyes gleamed with secret amusement. "Yes, it is. Especially when we make fun of their established ways. Old people can be so set in their ways." It seemed to Jake her words had a double meaning, but he let it go.

"What do you do for fun?" he asked.

She seemed surprised by the question, but brightened even further while she talked. "I do some artwork. I work out. Play zero-G racquetball. Talk with friends."

"Zero-G? I play racquetball, too. I'm surprised we haven't met there. What courts do you use?"

"Mostly the ones at the rec center in Mallory. They're clean and easy to get to."

"Ah, that explains it. I never go over there. I use the courts at Hadley. Maybe we can arrange to play sometime. Are you any good?"

She snickered and wiggled her fingers above her head. "Only top of the ladder at Mallory."

He whistled in appreciation, rubbing the mole on his chin. "Then you'll be a challenge for sure. I rise up the ladder, but I also get knocked down." He grinned. "Try not to hurt me too much?"

"I promise. But I won't go easy on you." Her smile was genuinely friendly.

Jake felt himself drawn in more and more, but they eventually had to end the dinner and get some sleep. Evenings during the work week were always too short. Also, they didn't want to stay together too long, or someone might consider it an unauthorized date. This time, though, they made sure to trade imp addresses so they could contact each other again.

While he walked home, he wondered why her aptitude tests hadn't Assigned her to something more than just testing imps. It bothered him, called into question his trust in Solity. He'd seen other people who seemed to be mis-Assigned—some doing menial work despite great capabilities, and others floundering to perform some complex job for which they had not the aptitude. His thoughts spiraled into dark spaces, wondering if her comments about Solity might not be justified after all.

The next afternoon, after a team lunch, the lock on the lab security door issued its loud clack and a young man stepped in. The fellow looked tentative, and his light green coveralls still had creases from the packaging.

The entire team looked up from the workbench where they had shared the lunch delivered from the refectory. Jake was surprised to see the man enter. This was, after all, a Defense project with strict security. No one could enter without authorization. "Can I help you?" he asked, while the rest of the team listened with curiosity.

The fellow took two steps toward them and stopped. He looked uncomfortable. "I guess so. I think I've been temporarily Assigned to work here."

Jake cocked his head, amused. "Work here?"

The man blushed, his fair features crinkling in doubt. "Well, my Assignment gave me this room number and told me to ask for Jacoby Palatin as supervisor. Are you him?"

Jake sat back in his chair, stunned. "I wasn't aware anyone was coming. Why don't you join me in my office?" He turned to the team. "The rest of you, please get back to what you were doing."

He and the young man moved into the semi-privacy of Jake's cubicle while the others went back to their desks and workbenches.

Jake waved a hand at the side chair. "Hold on a minute and let me check."

The fellow sat and waited.

Jake accessed privately the team roster, with the imp results displaying only in his retina. Sure enough, he saw a new addition, listed as "clerical help." His addition had been authorized by Director Denmark yesterday evening.

"Would you be Samuel Entago?"

The man brightened and eased. "Yeah, that's me. Please, call me Sam."

"Okay, Sam. I'm Jake. I have to say I'm a bit surprised. The director said he was going to get help for us, but I don't know why you're here. What do you know about our project?"

"Nothing, Jake. I just finished my secondary exams last week. Haven't even been to graduation yet, so I'm surprised they gave me light greens to wear instead of my student greys."

"What can you do? This is a highly technical project, and secondary education isn't likely to give you enough knowledge to take part."

Sam scratched his head. "I'm not sure. I was expecting an Assignment to become a shopkeeper. Then, this morning, I got this. What I've been told is you can use help in organizing things. Perhaps I can find things and make them available for you. I don't know how long they mean by 'temporary,' either."

Jake nodded. "Okay. I think I understand. I had a conversation with our director yesterday, and he's pushing hard for us to make faster progress. I guess he had you Assigned to unburden us from non-technical work."

"I could do that, as long as it doesn't get too confusing."

Over the next hour, Jake explained what they were trying to do. He gave a tour of the lab. Sam was astonished and alarmed at the idea of an antimatter bomb, even though he really didn't know what antimatter was. He looked at the glowing dot in the chamber and shuddered. Then Jake settled down with Sam to figure out what he might do to help the team. Jake came up with several useful things, and accepted the reality that another person was indeed helpful to progress, even if he weren't an engineer. Jake thought silent thanks to the director for the assistance.

30

Over the afternoon, Jake watched Sam fit in quickly. He couldn't deal with the engineering, but he could arrange and fetch and carry. Shortly after Sam came in, a ring at the door presaged a moving team bringing in another desk unit with InfoNet and holo. Sam was definitely organized, and he swiftly started shaping the project information into storage categories that helped the team.

❧ ✳ ☙

When they left work three hours later, Jake invited the team to join him at the easygo for some social time. They arrived to an empty place that filled quickly when others also left work for pleasure. Jake used his team allotment to order snacks and drinks.

Afonso was curious about Sam. "How long have you been out of school?"

Sam blushed. "Actually, I'm not even graduated yet. I finished exams at the University of Oriens last week; graduation is in another week and a half."

"And you're not an engineer, are you?"

"No." Sam shook his head. "I'm hoping to keep a shop. Inventory, ordering, arranging goods. I can run a general distribution shop, with whatever goods are available."

Minya smiled her bright smile. "Yeah, you've been helpful today. Very organized." She wasn't quite flirting.

Indy was more interested in Sam's idea of a shop. "I've always been curious about those places. I go in, and they seem to have lots of different things. Not like the usual distribution lines, where people are called in to get their allotment. How does that work?"

Sam said, "For the major items, Capital arranges distribution lines. They create the production for specific needs, and they know who has the need. For the smaller items, production is more generalized and statistical. They make toothpaste and hairbrushes and snack bags in estimated quantities, then make them available in the small shops where people can get them out of their general allotment. In my last year of secondary, I interned in several shops."

To Jake's surprise, Zofia materialized out of the growing crowd, drink already in hand. She flipped her long black hair over her shoulder while she looked at Jake. "Is this a private party, or can anyone join?"

Jake stood up with a big smile. "This is my work team, but we're just enjoying ourselves. Grab a chair."

She laughed and stayed standing. "No, I'll let you all do your thing. I'm here with some others." She pointed to a table in the corner. "But I saw you and wanted to say hi." She smiled to the other four. "I'm Zofia."

Jake went around the table with introductions. "Zofia's an implant technician. I met her here last week. It turns out we both play zero-G." He turned to her. "When are we going to play? I want to see how good you really are."

She laughed. "Oh, I'm good. Count on it. Tomorrow's Wentday. My schedule's pretty light in the afternoon."

Jake winced. "No, not during the workday. Our director's pushing me pretty hard."

Indy laughed from his seat. "That might be an understatement." He raised his glass in tribute to Jake's ability to take the pressure.

"But perhaps in the evening," Jake continued. "Where do you want to play?"

"Let's do your usual courts at Hadley. I'll see if I can get a court after work. You stop work at 11-00 hours, right? I'll let you know." With a wave to everyone, she rejoined her other group.

Jake watched her go, enjoying the movement of her hips. When he turned back to the table, everyone else was watching him. Raised eyebrows and grins greeted him. He gave a self-deprecating smile. "Hey, she's interesting."

Minya laughed the loudest in response. "What, and I'm not?" That brought another laugh from everyone.

Indy waggled his eyebrows. "So that's that girl that had you distracted yesterday? I can see why."

Sam had a puzzled look on his face. "There's something...I'm not sure."

"What?" asked Jake.

"I think I've seen her before...but I don't know where."

CHAPTER 6

Find the right people, train them in the right way, connect them rightly, and watch rightness happen.

—*Collected Sayings of Yitzak Goren* by Ellen Thranadil, Tileus Press 439 A.T.

Jake left work on time to get to the Hadley courts. Seeing Zofia again excited him much more than working on the antimatter bomb. He had no idea where their relationship might be going, but he liked it so far. She was gorgeous, exciting to be with, and her intelligence about things that mattered challenged him to think. He didn't really know how good she was at zero-G racquetball, but it didn't matter whether he won or lost. He would get closer to her either way.

On this beautiful evening, cloud banks in the west were edged with brilliant blues and greens by the setting sun. It had rained earlier, and the air smelled clean and fresh.

When he entered Hadley Park, he saw her warming up on an outdoor stair-stepper machine. She wore tight shorts, a halter top, and large-soled zero-G shoes. *Man, oh man, but she looks good.* Her body definition in the tight gear was superb, and he noticed a couple of other men ogling her, too. It made him feel good to know he was meeting her and they weren't.

She stepped off the machine and started doing lunges. He stopped to absorb the image of her legs tightening with each rep, and he loved the way her ponytail bobbed. She hadn't seen him yet, so he ran in place for a minute to get his blood flowing. Then he stepped next to her, dropped his equipment bag, and joined her in the lunges, matching her pace with each repetition.

He watched her eyes light up when she saw him beside her.

She picked up the pace, so he chuckled inside and matched her. Her light scent wafted around him while they moved together.

She finished her set and stood up, so he did, too. Picking up her towel, she raised her arms to wipe the back of her neck, which also thrust her breasts forward. *Do women do that on purpose?* he thought, *and is she doing it for me?* He felt special to think she was attracted to him, also.

"The court's still in use. Our reservation isn't until 11-30," she said between breaths. "We can sit and talk while we wait."

"Sounds good to me."

ಎ ✳ ೕ

Seeing him in gym gear turned Zofia on. That wasn't supposed to happen, but she smiled inside at her own reaction. *Live with it, girl. Might as well enjoy it.*

She sat beside him on a park bench facing the courts. While talking, she pushed herself to effervesce, to be as attractive as she could be.

"I want to know more about you," Jake asked. "Where do you come from? What do you do?"

She laughed and shook her head. "Shoot, not askin' a lot, are you? Should I put my whole life into two sentences?"

"No," he laughed with her. "You can just tell me the interesting parts."

Zofia thought about what she could tell him. There would be more later, but for now, she could open up about some of her background.

"Well, I came from the Warrens."

He looked surprised. "No. And you're working technology?"

"You bet. For whatever reason, my aptitudes came up higher than most. So I went to secondary school for software programmin'. Never had to go back to the Warrens. It's been interestin' stuff."

"Like what?"

"Well, you're an engineer. You probably know we do most programmin' through artificial intelligence. I learned to talk to the AI like talkin' to an idiot savant. It's a knack, and I got good at it." She winked her eyebrows at him. "The knack works with people, too."

"What, talking to them like idiots?"

"Maybe. Not quite idiots, but bein' careful how I say things so people understand."

Let's steer this to the politics again. Maybe I can tell him more about Tileus and how it's different. How can I do that? Oh, yah, I remember...

She continued without a break. "And I get to talk to people all over Prime. I once fixed an implant for some woman high up in the Department of State—dark green coveralls and all. She talked to me just like anyone."

"Very nice."

"Yah, she told me I'd probably go far—maybe even travel to other countries."

Jake sat up straight. "That's unusual."

"Well, the amazin' thing was she was right. I did get to travel to Tileus. Twice. For technical training on implants." *Okay, it's only a little white lie.*

"Wow. What was it like? I don't know anyone who's been out of Prime."

"Very different than here. School tells us Tileus is a democracy—a pure democracy—but they really don't tell us much about it. It's pretty wild, like chaos. They vote on everythin', the whole country. Several times a day, everyone stops what they're doin' to vote on things through their imps. Sometimes big things, sometimes small. Apparently, the laws change in response to every vote. I have no idea how they keep track of it all.

"They argue a lot, too, about issues comin' up for vote. People walk the streets wavin' signs for and against, shoutin' across the street at each other. A lot of people wear guns, but you know, they rarely shoot each other."

"That's amazing," Jake said. "How do they get anything done?"

"Well, it's also an excitin' place. People have more freedom than here. That part was kind of thrillin'. There are no Assignments. People choose their own work, and they can change any time they want. If they like someone, they can be together and their friends rejoice for them. They choose their own livin' quarters and life style. They decide for themselves how to spend their time. They seem happier than here."

Jake cocked his head, a puzzled look on his face. "I don't understand how all that can work. If they decide their own work, how do they make sure there's enough people doing what's needed...preparing food, for instance? Or making clothing?"

Zofia shrugged. *How to explain free enterprise?* "It all works out. Better than you can imagine, bucko. Mostly it happens around what they call 'money.'"

"I've heard the term. Isn't that the credit they use to get things they want?"

"You bet, but it's much more, see? It's sort of a medium of exchange. People don't just work to do what society needs, they work to get money. Work isn't all equal. More useful work gets better payment; more trivial work gets only a little. Money buys food, goods, services, everythin'. You make your choices for housing, lifestyle, and enjoyment based on how much money you have. If someone wants more, they get it by workin' longer or by changin' to a better-paying job. If someone wants to be lazy, they can—they just have a lower standard of living."

Jake still looked puzzled. "But doesn't that mean some people get lots more, while other people don't have so much? That's what Solity tries to even out for us."

She laughed. "Yeah, and how well does it work? Bangit, just look at the difference between the Warrens and where one of our Solity directors lives. Things aren't so evened out here in Prime, either. And the ones who have are the ones who get it through power rather than ability."

He shook his head. "It sounds like a very different life than here. Some of it sounds too good to be true, but the chaos sounds almost scary."

"You bet. It is scary at times, but I found it very attractive. That's part of why I talk about the problems of Solity. I think we can do better."

Jake smiled. "I like to hear what you think." His smile made her tummy flutter. "But before we get into the court, I need to use the facilities. Be right back."

"See you."

When he walked away, she thought back on what she'd said. *Good grounding. Good start. Gotta get him thinkin' about differences.*

Then her mind went back on why she was here.

✦ ✳ ✦

Zofia had been a Lazarite for five years, since shortly after completing secondary school at age twenty-one. That same implant client at State had introduced her to an older man named Yitzak Goren, who turned out to be leader of a Lazarite cell.

Yitzak was a highly intelligent visionary who stretched her mind with his thoughts. He wasn't much to look at. Rather short, with scraggly grey hair that couldn't seem to stay in place, bright eyes, and an impressively large nose.

"What do you think about clouds?" he asked in the middle of their first greeting.

Zofia was taken aback by the question. "Clouds? They're in the sky. They move."

"What about ideas? How do they move from person to person?"

In that first meeting, Yitzak had seemed scatter-brained, almost fragmented, with his conversation bouncing from subject to subject. Before long, she came to realize he actually connected those disparate thoughts, using an integrative faculty possessed by few. He truly understood how the complexity of clouds in the sky gave insight to the movement of ideas in Solity, or how the movement of an autocar was similar to the distribution of goods from a factory. When he jumped from subject to subject, he was helping others to see the world as he saw it—fully interconnected with every part affecting all other parts.

He nodded when she began to grasp the connections he was making. "I think you'll do well in our group. Come join us."

She grinned, feeling honored. In doing so, she took the first steps toward becoming a revolutionary.

As part of a cell, she learned how to resist Solity. She printed and distributed anti-Solity materials. Discussion groups were the mostly-benign entry point to the Lazarite network, where people talked of Solity problems while unaware they were being vetted for more. Attending two discussion groups, one of her jobs was looking for candidates for further advancement. The Lazarite members taught her how to get past the Sentinel Shield system. They also showed her how to shield her implant from connection to the InfoNet when she needed privacy.

Under Yitzak's mentorship, Zofia did well in the Lazarites. As an implant technician, she went into lots of places—which meant she was often a courier for information that needed to bypass surveillance.

Her trips to Tileus had not been for technical training; they'd been clandestine work for the Lazarites. Zofia had to set aside some guilt about her little white lie to Jake.

Yitzak kicked it off two years ago. "I have something important for you to do, Zofia."

She was immediately interested. "What is it? I'm ready."

"I want you to carry a message to Tileus and bring back an important reply. The message is pivotal to getting advanced weapons from Tileus. It can't be entrusted to electronic means."

She was astonished. "That sounds excitin'. Shoot, I'll actually go to Tileus?"

"Yes. But you should know if you are exposed in either country, you might be convicted of espionage."

Astonishment turned to shock. "Espionage? You're askin' me to be a spy?" She found herself whispering, even though no one was around. She also found the idea incredibly exciting. Adventure.

He chuckled softly. "Only in a small way. And being a spy is no less dangerous than many of the Lazarite things you've already done."

"How can I possibly get to Tileus? I'd have to have a travel permit."

Still grinning, he said, "No. We have ways. There's a secret path out of Oriens. You'll travel on your own to the city of Timpi on the coast. Shield your implant. Borrow rides and meals. Don't use distribution centers or your rationchip. That would identify you to the Sentinel Shield system. In Timpi, we have people to help you get across the Vissensee Channel to Freetown. You'll use the same path to return. The trip each way should take you about a week. You'll be gone half a month."

"I can't be gone that long. What about my Assignment? Someone will notice." Her head was reeling, even while she was thrilled at the prospect.

"We'll log your record as being on temporary Assignment. The work order will be genuine. Your work leaders will be satisfied. You'll have as much time as you need to make the trip."

Yitzak spent more time with her, going over the details until she had them memorized. He also had her memorize the message until word-perfect. She would offer a contract from the Lazarites to the Governor of Outside Affairs in Tileus to exchange manufactured goods for advanced weapons. The role made her feel incredibly important.

"You'll also need to take care. First, the tunnel out of Oriens is one of our best-kept secrets. It's important to us, and you should do anything you can to protect the secret."

She nodded in understanding.

"Second, you'll find people in the country to be different than what you've known. They're more friendly, open, and giving. Don't let their ease lull you into revealing something you shouldn't. They are still subject to scrutiny by the Solity Guard."

The trip became a pivotal moment in her life, a chance to meet people from outside Oriens and then—in Freetown—people from outside Verdant Prime.

Through a series of contacts, she delivered her message to a woman who worked for the Governor of Outside Affairs. They recorded her message, and she memorized their response, a non-committal message saying they would seriously consider the offer to provide weapons.

In a second trip a year later, the contract was completed. She became a courier, carrying goods to Tileus and advanced weapons back to Prime.

The risk of the trips was exhilarating, though both had gone smoothly. At no point did she face any imminent danger.

When she returned to Oriens, she saw Verdant Prime through completely new eyes.

She saw clearly for the first time the overwhelming controls Solity forced on its citizens in the interest of balancing production with needs, something they could never do successfully anyway. She saw how little freedom they had. People were not free to move, neither to different housing nor to different jobs. Every aspect of their lives was controlled. Everything was "equal," but she saw how Solity leadership had benefits and perquisites unavailable to ordinary people. The contrast with what she had seen in a few short days in Tileus was palpable.

Before the trips to Tileus, Zofia worked to change Solity. After the trips, she became passionate about implementing change.

☙ ❋ ❧

TWO WEEKS BEFORE PRESENT: TWODAY, 2 QUARTEMBER, 416 A.T.

Zofia's mind came back to her directions from Yitzak two weeks ago. This is why she was here with Jake.

"I have a new task for you, Zofia. I think it's one you'll enjoy." His cheeks nearly glowed with his grin.

She cocked her head, interested. "What might that be?"

"We need to slow down Solity's development of new weapons. These Tileus products give us some advantage, but General Defense here is working fast."

"How can I do that? Yah, I go into Defense sometimes to fix imps, but I'm not part of Defense."

He grinned even broader. "There's a way. I want you to subvert a key person to do Lazarite work." He looked down and up her body, a blatant acknowledgment of sex. "You'll be good at it."

38

She blushed slightly. Yitzak was enough older she had never thought of him as having sexual desires.

"You see, Zofia, I have a new technology."

Her interest rose; Yitzak had never spoken of his Defense work before.

"It may be as important to humanity as fire, or the printing press, or the repellor beam. It can change humankind itself, by helping us to understand each other. I call it the 'transpath.'"

"What does it do?"

Yitzak gathered his thoughts. He didn't have his usual quick but oblique answer. She realized this transpath must be very important.

"The transpath lets us feel each other's emotions. Under its influence," his quiet, gravelly voice paused for emphasis, "it is impossible to lie."

Zofia trusted Yitzak completely. If he said the technology was this important, then it was. It sounded strange, wonderful, and hardly believable to her. But he was asking her to help.

"What can I do?" she asked.

"I need a very special individual to carry the technology to Tileus and build it there. I can't take such a trip, but there's a younger man working in Defense who can both take the trip and understand the technology. Unfortunately, he still believes in Solity. I want you to interest him in the Lazarites."

She smiled. This new task would be an interesting challenge.

CHAPTER 7

Prior to the new humanity, any meeting with an unknown group was fraught with uncertainty. One never knew what to expect, and often the conflicting individual goals resulted in personal danger—so one approached the meeting with caution and secrecy.

—*The Making of a New Humanity* by Ellen Thranadil, Tileus Press 448 A.T.

Wentday, 21 Quartember, 416 A.T.

When Jake came out of the bathroom, he saw Zofia just standing up. She did some stretches to loosen up again after sitting.

"It should be open in a minute," she said. "I was just warmin' up." Her grey eyes did that twinkle thing he liked.

"Of course," he chuckled. "You'll need it."

"Oh, it's goin' to be like that, is it? Smack talk?"

"Only if you can take it."

Zofia laughed out loud. "I've been takin' it for years. I take some, and others take me. There's always someone better." She twinkled again. "You think you're that one?"

When the court opened, they were ready. Zofia and Jake got racquets and balls out of their bags. She ducked to enter the enclosed court. Jake followed and slammed the heavy door shut behind them.

He watched Zofia inspect the six-by-eleven-meter white box. She said, "I've not used these Hadley courts before. They're not as clean as the ones at Mallory."

Her words were another kind of smack talk, and suddenly he felt uncomfortable, looking at his home court with new eyes. Dirt smirked in the corners where no one ever landed, and the walls were smeared with ball marks.

"Maybe it's because we play harder at Hadley." He relented on the gibes. "I don't know about the Mallory courts. I'd never noticed the dirt, because I just come to play. But it's dirty, you're right." Then he grinned. "I can give you points if you think it'll affect your game."

"Ha!" she responded. "You give me points, you'll just increase my lead."

Dirty or not, he knew the court met zero-G standards. The front wall had a thirty-centimeter red metal strip on its edges, where the ball always sounded a dead clank. The side walls had a 1.5-meter red area adjacent to the front. You lost a volley if you hit red. You also lost if the ball hit any wall more than once. Whenever the ball hit the front wall, it became the opponent's ball.

Jake loved this game with its feeling of freedom, like a bird in flight. The wide-soled shoes gave him additional traction. He liked being able to use all six walls, shoving off in any direction. The computer-controlled beams counteracted gravity for every object in the court. With the system active, "up" and "down" were completely relative. Most of all, he loved the challenge of the game against a skilled opponent.

He uncovered the power panel and gave the standard warning. "Ready for Zero?"

She responded, "Yep. Ready for Zero."

He pushed the power button and closed the panel. With an almost imperceptible hum, the repellor beams in the floor smoothly reduced his apparent weight to zero. Staying where he was, he was ready to launch from either the floor or the back wall. Zofia chose to be active. She quickly shoved off the floor and spun to catch the ceiling with her feet. She rebounded from the overhead and quickly whacked a ball toward the front wall.

Seeing Zofia's shot, he shoved off the floor toward the left-hand wall. Meeting the ball there, he hit it hard toward the upper left corner of the front wall. In a smooth motion, he pushed off to the right to clear the ball area for her. As planned, his ball just missed the metal strip, which put it in a difficult path close to the ceiling.

Zofia anticipated his shot. She rebounded off the back wall to meet the ball after it grazed the ceiling. Her shot zinged to the lower-left corner of the front wall, again just missing the out-of-bounds strip.

Jake was caught off-guard. He was still moving right. By the time he reached her fast-moving shot, he barely got a racquet on it. The ball hit the out-of-bounds band with a clank. Even more, he was off-balance and rebounded off Zofia. Bruises were definitely a hazard of the game, but this time he enjoyed the brief contact. Stopping his motion head down against the upper back wall, he laughed at himself.

"Okay, you caught me with that one. I'm going to have to work harder, I see."

She scooped up the ball and paused on the floor, head upwards. "Let's do a few more volleys to warm up...and learn each other's moves."

He agreed. "I'll teach you everything you need to know."

She grinned and served again.

An hour later, they finished the match dead even. In fierce competition, she won the first game, and he won the second. Along the way, they had made physical contact many times. Violent or not, every bump felt good to Jake. He couldn't help being aroused. When they ran out of time in the court, they had each won two games.

He turned off the antigrav and gradually settled to the floor. The two of them left through the low door, laughing and drenched in sweat.

"I can't believe you nailed that last serve right on the edge of the wall," Jake said. He was energized by the rivalry. "That was over the top, after taking five points in a row."

She winked at him and cocked her hip in a sexy pose. "I had to do somethin'. You were ahead and about to win. I couldn't let you take the last game."

"Of course not."

"Well, it looks like the competition here at Hadley must be tougher than at Mallory. Your level of play would put you at the top of the ladder over there."

"Perhaps so. All I know is what I play here."

Jake stopped walking to wrap his towel around his neck and dry off. The evening was balmy with the sun down. A light breeze cooled him off. He smiled at Zofia and saw her smile in return. Talking with her was easier each time they met. He was beginning to think about applying for fraternization to date, and he wondered if she'd like that, too.

Then she surprised him.

"There's some people I'd like you to meet," she said. "I think you'll enjoy them."

THRUDAY, 23 QUARTEMBER, 416 A.T.

Two days later, Jake met Zofia's friends at lunch. Before he left, Jake met with Indy next to the new magnet enclosure Indy was working on.

"The enclosure looks like it's coming along."

Indy pointed into the interior of the tangle of metal and wires on his workbench. "Yup. This is the aperture. If we get it all cold enough, this small device will hold enough antimatter."

"Good. Have you seen what Sam's doing to help the team?"

Indy stood up and nodded. "He's been a lot more help than I expected from a storekeeper. Not only has he organized our records, he's also straightened up the lab benchtops. We're not losing things in the clutter anymore."

From the next bench, Minya spoke up. "Yeah, he gave me a fright yesterday because he put away the wire coil I was winding. But he was able to lay his hands on it right away when I freaked out." She smiled. "He's doing good for us all."

"Indy, I'm leaving a few minutes early. Please take charge during lunch. I've got a meeting. I should be back an hour after noon, perhaps 9-00 or 9-30."

Indy nodded. "Okay, boss. We'll do fine."

Zofia had directed him to a small factory near the Warrens. The street was clean, like most of Oriens, but shabbiness was creeping in like piproaches. The autocar dropped him off at the front door. A faint odor of decay floated in the air. The area was empty, because everyone was working. Whirring and clanking machine noises sounded from a building across the street. Jake rubbed the back of his neck while he looked around. He felt terribly exposed. When he glanced around, however, he didn't see any of the usual surveillance cameras. The factory had a wide-open truck entrance to his left and a series of dirty windows to his right. He wasn't sure whether to go in the wide opening or the front door, but he chose the door.

Inside, a small office with two desks filled what might have been a reception area in other circumstances. A couple of shelf units held odd composite shapes like a wizard smith's secret cabinet. A faint, tangy odor like hot metal made his nose wrinkle. Jake realized he had no idea what this factory made.

"Can I help you?" said a frumpy young woman at the first desk. Her voice was tired, almost bored. The worn-out woman at the other desk didn't even look up.

"I'm looking for Zofia Dobrunik," he answered. "I'm supposed to meet her here."

"Oh, yeah," the woman said. She gestured with a thumb. "Go through the door. They're in the meeting room, second door on the right." She turned back to the work on her desk, dismissing his presence.

Jake was having second thoughts about this meeting. Zofia had said he'd enjoy meeting these people. They were the discussion group she'd talked about, who had enlightened her to the fascinating topics she'd shared with him. He'd taken time off work to come. So far, he wasn't very comfortable with it. But he was here, after all, so he went through the door and turned right. The hallway was as shabby as the entire building, with peeling paint and dust balls on the floor. Two doors down, he found an open door with voices emerging. He heard one older voice answering questions from several others.

He stepped in and saw half a dozen people standing around a table talking, smiling, laughing. He felt the warmth of togetherness and an intensity unusual in Solity. The contrast with the hallway was like a bright morning after dirty fog. Someone had brought sandwiches and drinks, setting them on a side table. There were stacks of wooden boxes against the far wall. Instead of the usual gathering of people within a single department, Jake saw five different coverall colors.

When he entered, conversation stopped for a moment. Then Zofia peeled off from the other side of the table with a big smile.

"Jake! Glad you made it," she enthused when she came to him. She put a hand on his shoulder and turned to the group. "Hey, everyone. This is Jake Palatin, the man I told you about. Let's make him welcome."

Jake wondered what she'd told them.

They all waved and said, "Hi," but he was distracted by the warmth of her hand on his shoulder. It reminded him of their physical contact in the zero-G court.

An older man ushered everyone to seats at the table. His rather short frame was stuffed into Defense light green. "We don't have much time, folks, so let's sit down and get started." He took the seat at the head of the table. "I'm Yitzak Goren, Jake, and I usually lead this motley group." Yitzak's voice was quiet and gravelly. He had a surprising appearance with unruly grey hair and a huge nose. His eyes watched Jake intently, as if trying to see into his soul.

The next man wore the dark green of State. He had narrow eyes and a flat nose. "I'm Chao Hin, Jake. Good to meet you. I'm an admin working on Tileus relations."

"Abdu Nenge, Jake," said the third, his nearly black skin and wide features complemented by Capital dark blue. "I'm a mathematician."

The last two, both in Labor light blue, were Camila Lopez and Léo Moulin. Camila had curly brown hair and a muscular figure with a light of interest in her eyes. Léo was hefty, well-muscled. Camila did factory work on cabinets, while Léo was a truck loader for transportation.

Zofia was still standing, holding an implant interface unit. She winked at Jake. "Of course, you know me already. Why don't you tell everyone a bit about yourself?" She gestured for him to start talking, while she put the interface on the side of Abdu's neck, next to his implant, and concentrated on the device.

Jake hadn't expected to have to introduce himself, but he could do so without compromising security. "I'm Jacoby Palatin—Jake for short—and I work in General Defense." He plucked at his light green coveralls. "But I guess that's obvious." He added, "I'm an engineer working on research."

"Good," said Yitzak. "As you can see, I'm in Defense, too. Maybe we'll meet there someday." Then he turned to the group. "Does everyone have lunch? Let's get started. I believe today is Abdu's turn."

Abdu spoke next. "The topic from last week was how production quotas get met by Labor. Today, I'm going to talk about how the quotas are set."

He launched into a description of the commissars across Solity gathering information from their assigned groups, then percolating that information upward in layers to central Capital, where Abdu worked. The topic could have been deadly dry, but he filled his presentation with anecdotes about problems that made it incredibly interesting. Jake ate while Abdu talked.

Zofia moved around the room while listening. She laid her imp interface against each member's neck, then took the readings to a processing unit at the other end of the room. No one objected. Jake wondered what she was doing, and if she did this every meeting. After working with the processor, she returned to each member to interface their imp again. By the time Abdu had finished, twenty minutes later, Zofia had done everyone but Jake. He caught her eye and cocked his head toward her in query. She smiled at him and shrugged, then finally sat down to join the group.

"Thank you, Abdu," said Yitzak. "Thanks also, Zofia, for your extra work. We'll try out your changes later. So, the floor is now open for questions and discussion. Anyone want to know something more from Abdu?"

Léo said, "Yeah. When I load a truck, a manifest arrives in my imp telling where each pallet is supposed to go. How does that happen?"

Abdu explained how the commissar requests are tracked through the production quota system, so each production lot is specifically tagged for a target group.

Zofia asked, "How long does it take for the requests to create production quotas? How much time before the actual items reach the commissars for distribution?"

Abdu scratched his head and chuckled. "Well, that's the real problem, isn't it? Sometimes, there may be surplus goods awaiting distribution. Then the request can be filled in a day. But surplus sitting around represents wasted labor, so we try not to have back inventory. Usually, even with automated processing, the upward propagation takes at least two weeks through the multiple layers. The delay between request and distribution can be anywhere from a month to a year. Often, the needs change faster than the system can respond. We try to calculate the quotas in advance so products can be available, but then we often have wasted inventory surplus or shortages."

Zofia added, "Yeah, I've seen both of those many times. That's what got me involved in the...discussion group in the first place." The pause was slight, as if she had changed what she was about to say. Quick caution flashed in Yitzak's eyes at her slip.

Jake felt prompted to ask, "So, I'm new to this. Zofia invited me to come. She's told me a lot about things I'd never considered in Solity. Is this what you do each week? Talk about political issues?"

The others looked to Yitzak, who answered for the group. "That's about it, Jake. We talk together to learn what we can about Solity and its ways. If we're better informed, we can be better citizens. We can help Solity do better." Everyone nodded enthusiastically.

Jake continued, "On this topic of the supply chain, I'd never thought about how it all works until I met Zofia. But last week, some friends discovered a distribution center with a surplus. One of my friends was even a distribution manager. He was as surprised as any. He said they had a party in the streets, just because the center was passing out extra winter jackets. How can that happen?"

Abdu turned serious. "Probably, the calculations for those jackets were done six months earlier. It takes that long for the factory to tool up and start making them." Jake saw Camila nod in agreement, probably based on her knowledge of factory work. "By the time the jackets arrived, people had already received sweaters or blankets or something else, so not as many people needed the jackets."

Jake added, "At that incident last week, a bunch of Warrens people descended on the distribution line to seize the surplus."

Abdu nodded. "Yup. The commissars in the Warrens have a particularly tough job because so few people there have imps. The surveys and calculations are all flawed there."

An alarm went off in Jake's imp. He checked the time and realized he needed to leave to get back to his lab on time.

"This has been fascinating, folks. I'd like to come back if I can."

Yitzak responded, "Of course. We'd enjoy having you. Zofia can let you know when and where."

Everyone stood up to say goodbye. Zofia came around the table to lay a hand on his arm. "Thanks for comin', Jake. I think you'll fit right in."

"I think you're right. When will I see you again?"

"I'll let you know. Maybe a return match at zero-G in a few days?"

Jake turned to leave, feeling good about the meeting and the group. He anticipated some enjoyable learning here, despite the shoddy surroundings. While he walked down the hall, though, he heard the chairs scrape when everyone sat down again. Yitzak's quiet voice penetrated the hall just enough for Jake to hear.

"Okay. Let's get down to business."

CHAPTER 8

One of the most amazing consequences of the new technology has been its impact on mental illness, because psychological problems nearly always stem from a lack of empathy.

—*The Making of a New Humanity* by Ellen Thranadil, Tileus Press 448 A.T.

FRIDAY, 24 QUARTEMBER, 416 A.T.

The late afternoon explosion destroyed an entire city block in northeast Oriens. Shelton Overlock saw it happen, though he was unable to prevent it. While doing dirty work for Director Denmark, he had gotten a tip about a catastrophe. The tip was vague but real enough to explore, though he didn't know what to expect.

He arrived at quitting time to see workers leave the building normally and the crowds disperse. He moved his position every few minutes, gradually circling the single large building that filled the block. Most people had left, and a few stragglers were still departing.

Should I call for help? Search teams? Evacuate the building? But the tip was vague.

By chance, Overlock had just stepped into a side street to watch from behind a protecting wall. The first thing he saw was the building...diminished. No other word described it. Both east and west porticos slumped downward, as if the materials were becoming plastic in a hot sun. He straightened his head in surprise. He'd never seen such an effect. Then came the explosion. With a deafening roar, the building expanded. The noise was overwhelming. The walls spread outward. The roof lifted. Blocks in the walls separated from each other and flew toward him. Gobbets of slumped material splashed. Smoke and flame forced their way through the expanding cracks.

Suddenly, the air was full of broken building pieces flying at gunshot speed. As fast as he was, Overlock had no time to react. Projectiles bulleted past him down the street. The walls of surrounding buildings sprouted pockmarks like a heavy rain hitting a dusty surface. Glass shattered, adding to the dangerous debris. Overlock moved further behind his protecting wall, but his movement felt as slow as sludge.

Dust and dirt followed the projectiles. A wall of dust billowed rapidly past him, filling the street and coating the flying debris even before it landed. The stench of explosives and dirt was acrid. It stung in his nose. He covered his face with a sleeve. Witnesses later said materials flew two blocks from ground center, and the dust went further.

Light shone from above through the thick dust, and Overlock's attention went to the rising fireball above the site. It carried more dust roiling upward, gradually cooling and spreading into a mushroom shape a thousand meters above his head. The cloud showered a rain of more dust and debris on the area, hard objects tinkling as they landed.

Overlock prized his knack for being in the wrong place at the right time. Unfortunately, this time he had randomly been on the wrong side of the building when it happened. The perpetrators must have done their work from the other side. Now, while the dust settled, he stood and fumed on the remains of the street next to what had been a building.

The block had held a General Defense project lab. That was all most people knew, but Overlock had the clearance to know the lab had been working on advanced repellor-beam weapons needed for the upcoming war with Tileus. He clenched his jaw, one of the subtle signs he was exceedingly angry. People who knew him backed off when they saw this, because they knew the un-subtle signs of his rage could explode without warning. When they did, someone often died.

The dust was still thick. Overlock held his sleeve across his face to breathe clearer air. Then he saw a civilian running toward the building, probably to help.

"Back off, fool!" he shouted. "There's nothing you can do in there but die." His own voice sounded muffled in his ringing ears.

The man stopped.

"Get back, get back. There might be more."

He heard sirens approaching from a distance. People were lying on the pavement around the building, some screaming in pain. Others were starting to gather in the surrounding streets.

Overlock looked with a critical eye at the damage. This had been more than an explosion. He saw blocks of debris, yes. That was consistent with a large explosion. The shape of the cloud was consistent with other explosions, any time the detonation was large enough. But beyond the normal signs, he also saw melted materials and pooled sludge that had once been composite materials. No explosion would have caused those. Worse, he didn't know what kind of weapon could melt composite.

Something like this had never happened before in Oriens.

He scanned the surrounding area. With the building collapsed and the dust scattering, he saw the entries to the surrounding streets all around the block. The buildings were all damaged from flying fragments, and all the facing windows were shattered. Curious people were starting to gather at each street entrance, some to help, others in horror. *Amazing how people will flock to look at misfortune.* Overlock saw a steady progression of the curious moving toward the disaster.

In the next street to Overlock's right, he saw a large man in light blue. Unlike the assembling gawkers, his shirt was bloody. He looked unsteady on his feet, but he was also looking around suspiciously. Overlock's eyes narrowed. The man's demeanor was just strange enough to attract his attention. Then a woman two streets over shouted and pointed at the man.

"He was there! I saw him running from the loading dock when it happened."

Overlock averted his eyes to not alert the man to his notice, then he stepped back from the disaster into the street behind him. A cold anger filled him when he thought about the man, the type of anger he often used to formidable effect.

After sliding out of sight, Overlock turned and ran around the block to intercept the man. He always kept himself in impeccable shape, his wiry frame made both for running and for mayhem. He rounded the corner to the left at the next street. When he reached the adjacent street, he stopped to look carefully around the corner to where the man had been standing. The heavyweight was now staggering unsteadily up the street toward where Overlock waited. He was leaving a trail of dripping blood behind him. Overlock was satisfied he had the right man. The curious were still arriving; no one but the guilty would be leaving this scene.

When the man reeled into the intersection, Overlock stepped up behind him and threw an arm around his neck with a sharp knife blade at his neck.

"You're under arrest," he hissed.

The man hardly reacted beyond a futile wave of his arms. His breath was ragged and heavy. He muttered senseless words.

Quickly, Overlock threw tangle-cuffs on one wrist, then pulled his arms back to capture the other as well. He pushed the man through the intersection.

჻ ✳ ჻

Zofia was now five blocks away from the explosion. She was still in awe of the unexpected power the new weapons had delivered. By some miracle, the fragments had missed her. She'd left immediately, taking a pre-planned path away from the event, a path that avoided streets with Sentinel Shield cameras. Her imp programming of the other day worked as planned, so she still had the reporting aspects of her imp illicitly turned off.

She patted the bottom of her heavy backpack, almost fondling the incredible firearm hidden in it. This beam device had actually melted the composite materials holding the building together. She'd thought nothing would melt composites. Then, when the explosives they'd planted were triggered, the violence was beyond comprehension. She was still in awe of what the team had done. They had struck a strong blow for freedom this morning.

Store fronts along the next block had recessed openings. She met with Yitzak as planned in the third opening for a brief check-in. The whine of several Guard aircars sounded above, homing in on the explosion. The sirens of emergency vehicles flowed past them, inbound to the disaster.

"I made it here without incident," she said, "and it sounds like the Solity Guards are only now arriving."

"Good," he said. "I've already met with Adbu, Camila, and Chao, too. Abdu still had his beam weapon. The other two had successfully planted their explosives."

"Those devices did everythin' the Tileus people said they would. I've never seen anything like it."

"Yes. When coupled with regular explosives, they're amazing. And your mod to our implants worked as smoothly as flowing water. We are hidden. I can't locate any of us through the InfoNet. That's a problem for our coordination, but it also keeps the ticks from tracking us."

"Remember, our imps are still accessible if the authorities target one of us. I can't turn them off completely."

He nodded. "Don't forget to re-activate your imp reporting at your safe place."

Then Yitzak paused and looked around, obviously worried. "Have you seen Léo?"

"I know he planted the explosives. I saw him exit the building through the loading dock. He was clear of the building and across the street when we fired the beams."

"I'm worried. He was supposed to meet me at the last block, and he didn't."

Zofia's breath caught. She looked around quickly, both for Léo and to check the area for ticks. She heard more aircars arriving. The ticks would expand their perimeter quickly.

She said, "I saw a lot more flying shrapnel than we expected, movin' as fast as bullets. He might have been hit. Should I go back for him?" She hoped he wouldn't say "yes." Going back would be exceedingly dangerous.

Yitzak thought for a long time, tapping his foot nervously. "No, we can't. There are too many ticks now. We'll have to hope he got away and check on him later."

The two separated again. Zofia followed a wandering path, avoiding cameras, until she reached the safe street corner where she had originally turned her imp reporting off. She subvocalized the proper coded sequence of words to re-start it. Her success at the programming made her smile, but she was still filled with awe at what they'd done.

ⁿ※ⁿ

Overlock conscripted the help of two Solity Guards and their aircar to get the captured heavyweight back to the basement of the main General Defense building. The man wasn't in good shape. He'd been struck by at least three projectiles, one in the leg and two in the chest. By the time they had him tangle-cuffed into an interrogation chair, his breathing was ragged and his head lolled. He was muttering incoherent memories like fractured phrases. Blood was still flowing from his wounds.

The man was clearly dying. Overlock would do everything he could to get information from him before he was gone. Not only was Overlock skilled at this kind of wet work, he enjoyed it. Immensely.

"Leave us," Overlock said to the two guardsmen. They closed the door behind them.

The room was equipped for extended interrogation, including a deep sink in one corner and various drugs and chemicals in a wall-mounted cabinet. Overlock chose a nootropic coupled with adrenaline and injected it in the man's thigh.

Surprisingly, when Overlock used his imp to check the man's identity, the interrogation room responded that only one person was present in the room. Overlock told the room to probe further, confirming there were two people. The room suddenly responded with the man's information, as if he had been invisible before.

Léo Moulin, Labor, Truck loader, Factory block 134 dash five.
No criminal record.

Overlock set aside the mystery of the hidden imp until later. This man wouldn't last long, so he had to use quick and effective measures. He slapped the man's cheek, snapping his wobbling head back to vertical.

"Who are you, Léo Moulin? Why were you at the explosion?"

Léo's eyes focused briefly. "Explosion. Flying stuff." Then his eyes glazed again.

Overlock struck him again, across both cheeks, slamming Léo's head to right and left.

"Pay attention, Léo. Answer the questions. Why were you there?"

The man straightened in alarm. The drugs had taken effect. He looked at Overlock with recognition and looked around the bare interrogation room. He pulled at the cuffs on his hands with no effect. His response was breathless but determined. "No comment."

Overlock walked around the chair. Léo's head and eyes followed him partway, but then he let out a heavy breath and slumped in the chair. From behind, Overlock grabbed his dark hair and yanked his head back, but Léo's eyes were closed. Even the drugs couldn't keep him alert. His chest wounds were still seeping blood, staining the floor under the chair.

Overlock snorted. "Damn." He dropped the man's head onto his chest again.

Overlock got a small bucket from the deep sink and filled it with water. He walked in front of the chair.

He was about to splash the water into the man's face when the door opened.

"What have you gotten from him?" demanded Director Berndt Denmark, slamming the door behind him.

"Nothing yet. He's nearly gone, and not responding well. His imp reports his name as Léo Moulin. He's a truck loader."

Denmark stood in front of Léo, his mouth set in a line as hard as granite. "This was the worst incident we've ever had in Oriens. Tell me again why you were there?"

"I got a tip, Director. Anonymous and vague. Something about a catastrophe this afternoon, but no details. I arrived there at closing time and circled the building, looking for anything suspicious. I was about to call for support teams when the explosion happened."

"Damn. An entire city block is gone, containing one of our most advanced weapons labs. We don't even know the death toll yet. Dozens of people are at the hospitals. The Guards have cordoned off nine blocks, but they've caught no one. All we have is this one you found."

"I'm not even certain he was part of the incident. He was hit by flying debris, so he was there when the explosion happened. I brought him in because another woman fingered him." Overlock paused. "But his implant did a strange thing. When I first queried it, it acted as if it weren't there. Only on a stronger query from the room did it respond."

Denmark turned quickly to look at Overlock. "So. Someone tampered with his implant. This is the second incident with imp problems. I don't believe in coincidences. Was this the Lazarites again? Or...Tileus makes the imps. Is this Tileus acting directly?"

Overlock's irritation rose at the questions. Denmark delayed him from getting to the interrogation, and this man wouldn't last long.

"Perhaps it's both, sir. The Lazarites working with Tileus? In any case, someone has learned how to defeat our tracking."

"The initial investigators tell me this explosion included some weapons effects we've never seen. Something actually melted composite materials in the building structure, making the explosion more effective. We don't have anything to do that, do we?"

"No, sir. It's some sort of new weapon. Where did it come from?"

"Only one place. Tileus" Denmark growled. "We've been trying to stay ahead of them, but they must have something we don't. If this man knows anything, we've got to get it out of him."

"Stand back, Director, and let me get to it. We don't have time for this conversation. I have to keep him awake to answer before he dies." With that, Overlock flung the bucket of water into Léo's face. He followed it up with a fist to the solar plexus. "Wake up, fool."

Overlock aimed the fist to land just below the two chest wounds, and it probably felt like a sledge hammer. Overlock didn't get to play with extreme wet work often enough, and he enjoyed every moment.

Léo snapped awake with a shout.

"Wake up. Where did you get the new weapons?" Overlock slapped his head again, harder than before.

Léo might have been awake, but he was muzzy again, clearly not in control of himself. He muttered, "Weapons. Traded weapons for goods."

"Traded with who? Speak up."

"Tileus. Good weapons. Helped Lazarites." His eyes widened, still glazed but apparently remembering the sight. "Melted stuff like goo." Then he started to droop again.

"Don't you dare fade out on me. How'd you get them from Tileus? Who did this?" Overlock hit him again, this time choosing to land the punch right on the chest wounds. Blood splattered everywhere.

Léo stiffened and cried out again. "Aahh." He shook his head and clenched his teeth.

Overlock kicked the chair over backwards. Bound to the chair, Léo went with it. His head slammed back against the hard floor. Overlock was instantly on his knees beside him, grasping his face with fingers that dug into his cheeks. He had to stimulate the man with extreme pain so he would stay alive long enough to get more answers.

"Who brought the weapons, Léo? How'd they get here?"

Léo's breathing was shallow and rapid, his eyes unfocused. Overlock used his grip to slam the man's head against the floor twice more.

"Tell me, Léo. Who did this?" His voice hissed like a snake.

Léo's lips moved, but Overlock couldn't hear. He put his ear close to the man's mouth.

"Timpi." The consonants spit blood at Overlock's ear.

Then Léo's entire body collapsed. He was gone.

Overlock slammed the man's head against the floor once more in frustration, hearing the crack of broken bone, then wiped his bloodied hands on Léo's shirt sleeve. He got up slowly, controlling his breathing. He hated not getting what he wanted from someone. Overlock walked quietly over to the sink and washed his hands and the side of his face.

Denmark spit on the dead man. "Dirty bastard."

Overlock took a deep breath, then spoke over his shoulder while he washed. "At least we know I got the right man. He wasn't some bystander."

"True."

"And we got some information. Not much, but some."

Denmark spoke harshly. "Damn little."

Overlock refused to accept the rebuke. "I think it's more than a little, Director. We know now Tileus has at least one weapon we don't have, something that melted composites like plastic goop. We also know they made a deal with these Lazarite people, providing those weapons for use in this attack."

"All the more reason to accelerate our time table. We need to move rapidly on Tileus, before they can be ready for us. But I hate to have lost the work going on in that lab."

"We know something else, sir. Someone on the coast at Timpi is a conduit."

"Not very actionable yet."

"Director, I beg to differ. I think we have a chance now. Let's set a trap for the Lazarites in Timpi. They don't know yet what we know. We have an advantage here. I can find a way to use it." Overlock's eyes were as cold as ever, but the session with Léo had sparked a fire of hateful desire in them. "It'll probably take me a couple of weeks."

"Do it. Sooner if possible. I want these people."

CHAPTER 9

The transpath was the brainchild of the polymath Yitzak Goren, one of the more colorful figures in Verdant's history. His international reputation as a scientist and creative thinker allowed him to transgress the rigid bounds Denmark tried to impose.

—*The Making of a New Humanity* by Ellen Thranadil, Tileus Press 448 A.T.

FRIDAY, 24 QUARTEMBER, 416 A.T.

Yitzak Goren worried about Léo while he walked through the main General Defense building. Léo was the biggest and strongest in their cell, but he was also the least intelligent. He followed directions well, and he believed in the cause.

Yitzak knew what they were doing was right. They needed to change Solity. They needed to slow down the war effort. But what might have happened to his friend? How many more had been hurt? The explosion had been much bigger than expected. They had wanted to shut down the weapons lab, not destroy the entire block and hurt people.

Guard aircars had been everywhere, apparently scanning the streets for anything suspicious. He'd watched one aircar go directly from the explosion area to the General Defense building.

Yitzak desperately hoped they weren't compromised by Léo's absence, but as always, Yitzak's agile mind also connected the unrelated facts. The explosion was surprisingly large. Léo might have been hurt. He might have been captured. Léo knew to follow directions. But he hadn't shown up for their check-in after the explosion. No one else had seen him afterwards. That aircar headed to General Defense might have carried a captive. Putting together this kind of correlation was second nature to Yitzak. In this case, he didn't much like the answers.

He barely noticed his surroundings or the other light green coveralls while he walked down the main hallway to the lift tube and his lab. He feared Léo was captured, and the Solity Guards would get enough information to target their group. He had avoided any exposure of his Lazarite work for ten years. Was he now compromised?

He identified himself to the lab door with both imp and a DNA scan, pressing his finger to the scanner. The security lock clacked open.

His lab office was small and crowded with equipment. Yitzak had earned the trust of Solity through fifty years of successful research, so he worked alone. A cluttered desk held a box of holochips, a few papers, and his holohaptic computer interface. The walls were adorned with framed art, his own work. Separate from his engineering work, Yitzak had invented a new style of art combining music and visual arts into fluid forms. The pictures changed each time music was played in their vicinity, taking in the essence of the music to modify the impressionistic images. The change was embedded into the atomic structure of the materials.

His *pièce de resistance*, however, was in the laboratory proper in the next room. A large cabinet filled with wires, waveguides, and blinking lights stood against one wall. Tall, narrow cones stood two meters high in each corner of the room like ancient Egyptian obelisks to the god Re, who had to defeat the snake god Apopis each day to make the sun rise. Loops of miniscule waveguides connected the cabinet to the towers. He nodded in satisfaction at the device. This was his crowning achievement.

Yitzak had long been recognized as one of the most brilliant minds on the planet, but he didn't feel brilliant. Most of the time, he felt out of step with the parade of people. No one else seemed to see what he saw. A visionary, he was fluent in many disciplines. Of course, he knew he had abilities others didn't. That was clear to him when he graduated from tertiary at age nineteen with simultaneous doctorates in psychology, physics, engineering, and art. He used those abilities, but also saw how they separated him from others.

Over the years, he had come to appreciate he thought in networks while most people thought in linear sequences. He connected things others didn't.

He sat at his desk and contemplated the device in the next room, what he called the "transpath." He'd been watching the political, economic, and societal trends for years, putting together information from disparate sources into a complex network of data and knowledge. The results of his analysis led to a frightening conclusion.

He was certain the conflicts of humanity would destroy the planet within the next thirty years.

In all four countries on two continents and the islands, Yitzak knew people were generally dissatisfied with their lives, and much of that dissatisfaction resulted from an inability to communicate well. The examples were all around, for those few like him who saw the connections. Distribution of goods and services in Prime frequently failed to meet the needs, causing frustrating supply shortages. Economics in Tileus, where people used money, suffered from long-term inflation that defeated peoples' hopes. Rathas used a rule-based religious "faith" to control its people. Political pressures in every country created selfish, destructive policies feeding the malaise. Growing international tension would soon lead to war.

Even worse than the overall situation was the false hope. He watched people and their leaders believe erroneously they could solve the problems. Each short-term "solution" only added to the negative trends, because people just didn't think through the consequences.

Yitzak often felt very alone, a familiar position he had known all his life, because he clearly saw the connections. No one else seemed to understand. The loneliness went back sixty-five years to primary school and the bullying he suffered for being different. Sometimes, he wished he had not been given high intelligence. But such a wish was not useful.

Instead of wishing, he used his gift to change the probable outcome of the planetary situation. Perhaps he could even change the trend of humanity.

Yitzak had worked in academic research for over forty years. He'd made international news combining particle physics and mind wave patterns. Fifteen years ago, after working on it for a decade, Yitzak had shown thinking minds emanated recognizable patterns of sub-atomic particles. He had frightened people with his accuracy in "reading their minds." Some claimed he was telepathic, but his technology did the work.

Two years after that breakthrough, Berndt Denmark had pulled him out of his comfortable academic world. Yitzak had a sudden re-Assignment to Defense, an area where he had no desire to work. Of course, in Solity, no one could refuse an Assignment, not even an international star. Denmark wanted Yitzak to create devices for mind control. The director told him the devices would be used as weapons, but Yitzak knew they would also be used to control the Solity populace. So, Yitzak redirected his progress.

Instead, he created the prototype transpath in the next room. Used properly, Yitzak believed this device could turn the tide for the planet.

Zofia had brought her assigned target to the meeting yesterday. She had done well, even if she was becoming emotionally entangled with him. Jacoby Palatin would be crucial to Yitzak's plans.

PLAYDAY, 25 QUARTEMBER, 416 A.T.

Yitzak knew the truth about Franklin Edobar's dual life, and he was careful not to compromise Franklin's safety. The day after the explosion, they met for a weekend lunch.

He'd selected the Dilly Deli facing the grass and trees of Touchdown Park. The restaurant was unique, with a privacy technology at each table that scrambled both sounds and vision to anyone not at the table. Purple-garbed administrators often held private conversations here, and Yitzak wanted both he and Franklin to be safe. Use of the restaurant was restricted to those with access.

They touched on many topics while they ate. No one could match Yitzak's varied interests, but Franklin came close. Yitzak hop-scotched from the coming summer weather to the growth of blue-leaved trees to the effectiveness of nano-medical devices. As often happened, he saw Franklin left behind a few times when Yitzak changed subjects. To Yitzak, the connections were clear. When they finished eating, the talk turned serious.

"Your team did an incredible job yesterday, Yitzak." Franklin gave a slow, disbelieving shake of his head. "We never expected such a complete destruction."

"The explosion was much bigger than we anticipated. We don't know the full toll yet, but I'm sorry so many innocent people were hurt. And we lost one of our team."

Franklin raised his eyebrows. "I didn't know that."

"He did his part but disappeared afterwards. I haven't heard from him or been able to contact him. I don't know whether he was captured." Yitzak's stomach still curdled when he thought of Léo.

"Should we protect ourselves in case he was?"

"I don't think there's much we can do. The man only knew the members of our cell. I'm probably the one most at risk, and I have precautions in place to protect us both if I am exposed. We've already taken action to move the weapons and supplies to locations he didn't know."

"In any case, your team has certainly put the Lazarites into the Denmark's gunsights. He'll be looking for anything he can do against us."

Yitzak paused for effect. This seemed to be a good opportunity. "I have a new plan, Franklin. It may have an overwhelming effect on the entire situation."

Franklin cocked his head and took a drink. "Tell me about it."

"I've told you about the transpath I've created and what it can do."

"Yes. But you said we have to get it to Tileus, that it can't be built properly here."

"Exactly," said Yitzak, "and I think I've found someone to get it there, while also striking another blow against Denmark's weapons development. Two birds with one stone."

"How can you do that?"

"We have a new player, one with special significance."

In the next few minutes, Yitzak briefed Franklin on his latest idea. Franklin added a few thoughts, and the two agreed it made sense.

SITDAY, 26 QUARTEMBER, 416 A.T.

"Thanks for coming in on the weekend, Director," said Yitzak. "I think you'll be impressed with this demonstration."

"Hmph. I hope so," said Denmark. "I've been funding you for thirteen years now, my man. It's about time. But if your mind control works, it'll be timely."

The two stood in Yitzak's laboratory, surrounded by the clutter of electronics, particle physics, and art. Dominating the room were the four antenna pillars of the transpath.

"There's still work to be done. The results are erratic. They seem to work best on the emotive centers." Yitzak was prevaricating. The transpath worked perfectly, but he'd been putting off a demonstration for months. Not only did he want to hide the perfection from Denmark, he also hoped to mislead the director as to its purpose and capabilities. This demo was one of Franklin's ideas from yesterday.

"How much longer?" Denmark's voice was gruff and demanding.

Yitzak shrugged. "Basic research is like the flow of wind, Director. Sometimes it goes over mountains, but you can't make the air go downhill any faster than the slope of the ground."

Yitzak busied himself with the apparatus. He chose to turn on many devices having nothing to do with the transpath, with blinking lights, annoying beeps, and actively-moving displays. One device—a simple aromatic dispenser—wafted an acrid scent into the room. Yitzak smiled inside, picturing himself as an old Earth thaumaturge impressing the yokels with flim-flam. He waved his hand through the stream of scent, washing it toward the director.

Denmark stood impassively, watching the bustle, a mixture of irritation and expectation on his face.

Finally, Yitzak put a hand on the transpath switch.

"Please remember my warning, Director. It's still a bit erratic, and I don't always know how strong the effect will be. But you should be able to feel something of the mind control effect." Yitzak had trouble not adding a tone of derision to the word "mind control." What a silly idea. Yet that's what the director hoped for, so that's what he would use to tease him.

He calmed his own emotions, because the transpath worked both ways. He would feel the director's emotions, but Denmark would also feel his.

Yitzak turned it on, with the power control at max.

It worked perfectly. With his eyes on Denmark, Yitzak immediately felt every emotion raging through the man: a mild expectation, impatience, contempt, underlaid with a permanent sense of anger. When Denmark felt the effects, Yitzak sensed his emotions change to surprise, then alarm. A huge wave of fear rode along with the new senses.

"Turn it off," Denmark shouted. "Turn it off, now! Damn!"

Yitzak nodded. This was exactly the effect he'd wanted. Director Denmark would never again want to experience the transpath.

Jake had spent the three days of the weekend worrying about the huge explosion. The destroyed Defense lab had held a companion project to his own, developing beam weapons which, among other uses, could trigger his antimatter bomb. If someone knew enough to destroy that lab, might they also know of his work? *What if they bomb my lab? Talk about an explosion! Releasing our bit of antimatter would destroy most of the main General Defense building and some of the surrounding city.* Increasingly, Jake didn't want to be doing what he was doing—but he didn't know how to get out.

He'd never been in such a position before. Things had gone smoothly for him throughout his education and work. Easy advancement at each stage, Selection for the next. He'd gained amazing knowledge about particle physics in school, and he'd hoped to use it for the good of humanity. Even his Assignment into Defense had felt good at the time. He was valued. Then Director Denmark had taken Jake under his wing, and he felt important.

Now, it seemed to be coming apart. Denmark wasn't happy with his lack of progress. Jake was beginning to see the cracks in Solity that had been there all along, and those problems seemed to be accelerating. On top of it all, he'd found Zofia and wanted to be with her more than he wanted to be advancing the antimatter bomb. But this was his Assignment. Despite her discussions about its problems, he still mostly believed in Solity and his duty.

Now, however, it appeared his Assignment included the real danger of possible attack by the Lazarites.

By the first day of the week, he went to work feeling great dismay and uncertainty. Indy greeted him as soon as he stepped in the lab.

"Jake, we've got a problem."

Jake's thoughts were still on his personal problems. He held up a palm. "Not yet, Indy. Give me a moment to get here."

"No, boss, it can't wait. When I got in this morning, the containment chamber had a warning light."

Jake's shoulders sagged and he swallowed hard. "Okay. Which warning?"

"Critical Containment Error. We hadn't lost any antimatter, but it had dispersed three millimeters."

"What? That's like thirty million kilometers in atomic distances."

"Yeah. It scared the hell out of me. I was able to realign the fields and regain containment, but—"

"But we could have lost it all over the weekend, right?"

Indy's voice lowered to a whisper. "Yeah."

Both of them slumped and looked at the glowing pinprick in the chamber. Jake visualized again the incredible damage their antimatter would do if it touched any normal matter. At least none of the other team members were here yet. Jake thought about the explosion at the beam lab. *Is it a coincidence our lab has a problem at the same time?*

"Thanks for fixing it," he acknowledged.

"Yeah." Indy looked as defeated as Jake felt.

"You know about the explosion last Friday evening, right?"

Indy shuddered. "*Know* about it? I *heard* it. I live only four blocks from that lab. The dust swept down my street just when I got home." He scrubbed his hand over his face. "I spent the evening helping the wounded. On Playday, I went over there to see it, but the Solity Guards had the whole place cordoned off."

"Did you know that lab was doing a project like ours?"

"No, but I assumed they were doing something similar."

"So…" Jake looked Indy in the eyes. "Was there anything about our containment error that indicated tampering? We've not had such an error before."

Indy gasped. "I hadn't even considered the possibility." He thought for a long time. Jake almost saw the gears turning while Indy considered everything he'd seen this morning. Finally, Indy shook his head. "No, boss. Nothing. We had the error, but I didn't see anything that looked like tampering."

"You're sure?"

Indy waved it off. "If someone meddled with our equipment, it had to be in an extremely subtle way. I know the chamber like the back of my hand. Nothing was out of place. I think a software glitch in the control routines caused the error. But of course, that makes me worry, too."

Jake nodded in relief. "Okay. I trust you. Let's get back to work today and make progress. But before you do, I'd like you to reprogram the containment chamber to report any errors immediately through the InfoNet to you and me. We thought our automated controls had triplicated safeties. We can't ever have it untended again."

The door lock clacked. Afonso and Minya came in, already chatting with each other. Sam was close behind. After greetings, everyone returned to the work they had been doing on Friday. The new low-temperature containment device was taking shape on the prototype workbench. Their current concept was to have the device tethered to a supercooler while in storage or transit, then to disconnect it for self-operation during delivery. The device was designed to hold internal temperatures low enough for at least a half hour, sufficient time for delivery by missile or aircraft.

The morning went fast, a good thing for Jake's state of mind.

Near lunch, Zofia called on his imp, a bright spot in Jake's day, bringing a warm smile. They hadn't spoken since the meeting last week. He was surprised at the depth of his feelings for Zofia. They reminded him of two prior times in his life. He'd had a brief infatuation with Hama in secondary, and a longer affair with Imani in his twenties. He winced to remember them, because both relationships had ended when Solity refused permission to fraternize based on their DNA tests. He hoped the same wouldn't happen with Zofia.

He moved to the semi-privacy of his cubicle to talk with her through the imp.

"How're you doing today?" Jake's voice was easy and light for the first time in three days.

"I'm doin' great, Jake. Flippin' down the slidewalks with music in my head. My workload is light today, just some minor repairs. People are crazy; you should see the reactions they have to little problems." She sounded carefree.

"How were you affected by the explosion on Friday?"

"Yah, I heard about it." She had paused before answering, and her voice became guarded. "A few of my clients today have had damage from it. I'm meetin' with two who are in the hospital. What happened was terrible. I understand twelve people died."

"You sound like it touched you personally."

"I'm very sorry it happened. It's part of the Solity problems you and I've been talking about." She shifted the topic. "But I'd rather not talk about the explosion. Are you plannin' to come to our group this comin' Thruday? I hope so."

He nodded. "Yes. I was intrigued by the discussion last week, and hope to learn more." Jake looked up to realize Sam Entago was standing outside his cubicle. He nodded to Sam and held up a finger to ask him to wait.

Zofia continued, "Good. See, I also have a special invitation for you."

"Oh?"

"Yitzak was very pleased to see you there. He'd like to meet with you separately, to tell you more about what we do. It would be a good way to get involved quickly."

Jake was surprised. *Get involved? What would that mean?* He hadn't thought he'd made any great impression last week. But he was pleased. "Yes, I'd like to know more. He struck me as a very interesting man."

"Oh, he is. He's one of the most brilliant men on the planet, been recognized in many fields. He also works on Defense research, like you."

"Let's do it, then."

"How about this afternoon at 11-30, just after work?"

They settled a place for the three to meet—a small restaurant on the edge of the Warrens—and said she'd take him there after work. They finished the conversation with casual good-byes. Zofia also ragged on him about zero-G racquetball and asked for a rematch. They settled on Wentday after work.

When the call ended, Jake waved Sam into his cubicle. The young man sat down in the side chair, looking nervous.

"What's going on, Sam? By the way, you've been doing a great job organizing our work. Thanks."

Sam smiled at the praise, but he still acted nervous.

"So, what did you need?" Jake asked.

"Well..." Sam started, then stopped. He seemed reluctant to speak.

"It's okay. Go ahead."

Sam rubbed his hands down his pants leg. "I've got something to tell you that you might not like, Jake. Something personal."

Jake raised his eyebrows, wondering what problem Sam might be in.

Sam pointed toward Jake's imp. "The woman you were just talking to. That was Zofia, wasn't it? The one we met at the easygo?"

"Yeah, it was." Jake was taken aback. "What about her?"

"I'm not sure, but..." Sam's eyes bounced around Jake's desk. "I think I've seen her before, somewhere else."

This was as difficult as walking the wrong way on a slidewalk. Jake waved his hands to continue.

"Do you remember when I told you about the protest at the University? Where a Lazarite group came in and threw rotten fruit at us?"

"Yeah, I remember."

"Well, I think she was there. I recognized her long black hair." Sam sat back in his chair, relieved. He looked like he was done with what he had to say.

Jake furrowed his brows. "There? You mean she was with the students? But she's not a student."

Sam shook his head emphatically. "No, not with the students. She was one of the protesters."

CHAPTER 10

One of the greatest difficulties in any negotiation is getting the other side past their own entrenched beliefs, so they can see the benefits you offer. Often, you must help them work through the conflicts by themselves.

—*A Practical Guide to Negotiation* by Ellen Thranadil, Tileus Press 426 A.T.

Jake stood outside the General Defense building that afternoon in a turmoil. He'd researched Yitzak Goren's accomplishments and was astonished such a prominent man wanted to meet with him. He still feared someone would bomb his own lab; that fear was fed by the news continuing to scream about the Tileus/Lazarite bombing three days earlier.

Now, his mind had also spun for the entire afternoon over Sam's news. *Who is Zofia? What is she? Is she involved in the Lazarites? What are the Lazarites, anyway?* He wanted to be with her. He wanted to test for fraternization with her, overcoming the fears from his two prior failures. Now he thought it might be dangerous even to associate with her.

His stomach was uneasy while he waited. He didn't know what he would say to Zofia. To stop the useless spinning of his mind, he took a deep breath and looked around at the plaza. The four-story buildings along its edge were all familiar. He saw them every work day. People flowed around him on the pavement, the multi-colored coveralls creating a rainbow. He watched slidewalks and autocar tracks organize the chaos. The street was crowded because work had just ended, and the noise of the throng gave him assurance Solity still worked. A breeze in his face freshened his thoughts.

"Hey, there." Zofia surprised him from behind and poked him in the waist.

He turned, caught off-guard, and all he could say was a lame, "Oh, hi."

She was so beautiful he felt torn inside. She stood almost as tall as he; the two of them rose above the heads of the crowd. Her waist-length hair lifted in the slight breeze of the street, and her grey eyes were so focused on him, it took his breath away.

I want to be with this woman. But does she want me? Or is she playing me, reeling me in for some reason?

She tilted her head to one side. "You're quiet, Jake. What's the matter? Did somethin' happen?"

"Nothing." *Just that you've been identified as a protester.* He hated lying to her. "It's just been a long day, and I'm a little nervous about meeting Yitzak."

"There's nothin' to be nervous about," she said, reaching out to touch his elbow. "He just wants to get to know you more. I think it's an honor, myself. He's quite a thinker." She twinkled at him. "And you're a good man to know."

He winced inside at her illegal touch and glanced around to check for Solity Guards. She apparently hadn't noticed his prevarication. He was relieved at the same time he felt guilty for keeping a secret.

"I'd gotten that impression about him even from one meeting. He thinks in ways most of us don't."

They strolled toward the Warrens, changing slidewalks a few times at corners. He felt her touch over and over, on the elbow or the hand or the shoulder, casual touches making his blood sing. It worried him, because contact like this was illegal without fraternization approval. Yet Jake enjoyed every stroke.

The huge unspoken issue of her Lazarite involvement trumped his ability to hold conversation, so he talked about architectural features in the buildings, the people they passed, and the clouds in the sky.

"Oh, smell the bread from that shop," she said. "Butter and flour fresh from the oven. I love fresh bread! Maybe we should get some."

"It would spoil our dinner with Yitzak, I think."

He couldn't help but notice the sinuous way she moved, like flowing waves in the clouds. Despite his inner turmoil, this excitement in his blood was exactly the kind of relationship he wanted with her.

Zofia seemed to accommodate the light natter, adapting to Jake's lead. *Is her reaction natural? Or does she do this as a technique? I no longer know what to think about anything she does or says.*

"There's the restaurant," Zofia said.

Jake saw the sign—the Dinner Winner—and smiled at the play on words. The place was cleaner than most of the Warrens.

"Yah. I see Yitzak, in the booth by the wall." She took his elbow again to guide him there. Though he was still confused about Zofia, he did look forward to a longer conversation with the famous scientist.

The man stood to shake Jake's hand. "I'm glad you came, Jake." His smile went all the way to his bushy eyebrows.

"Good to see you, too, sir. I was intrigued by your meeting last week." The three sat down, and Jake continued, "Though, I can't imagine what you might want with me. I'm a complete freshman when it comes to your level of science."

"No, I think not. I've looked into what you've done so far in your work," said Yitzak, "and I think you have more potential than you know. You've

65

shown yourself to be an outstanding particle physicist. I know of no others as good…," he chuckled lightly, "other than me."

The high praise was startling. Jake was curious how someone so famous knew about him, particularly when his work was under security wraps, but accepted that he did.

Zofia said, "Yitzak has brought me here before, Jake. There are good things on the menu, but if it's okay with you, I'll order for us all so you two can talk."

She's kind, too. I am so confused.

"Please do," he said. Jake looked around and realized no one paid them any attention. Most people couldn't even see into their booth. Just what was needed for a clandestine meeting.

When Jake turned to Yitzak, his breath caught at an expansion of that thought. *Is the "discussion group" more than it appears. Is it part of protest work? What "business" were they "getting down to" after I left?* The thought startled him so much he accidentally knocked over his empty glass.

"Are you okay, Jake?" The scientist's concern sounded everyday normal, but Jake's heart raced while he straightened the glass.

"I'm fine. Just fine." He'd been so focused on his feelings for Zofia and what she might have been doing in that rotten fruit protest, he'd never even considered the larger issue until now.

While Jake's mind spun, Yitzak jumped right into discussion. Jake was reminded of how abrupt the man had seemed in the meeting last week.

"First, you must know what we do is much more important than just discussing Solity."

"I think I'd figured that out." *Was Yitzak admitting they did protests?*

"Have you ever thought about the ocean, Jake?"

The shift in topic caught him by surprise. "Uh…sometimes?"

"The ocean touches every shore on Verdant. Waves happen because of wind and earthquakes and random motion. And those waves caress every shore."

Confused, Jake looked at Zofia. She had finished tapping menu buttons and was listening, enthralled. He turned back to Yitzak. "Yes, that's true."

"When a large fish—say, one of the dangerous five-meter tsiftim of the northern seas—swings its tail to swim, its motion makes a wave that eventually washes up on the white shores of Timpi, right?"

"Yeah, I guess so. But it wouldn't be very large by then."

"Large or not, the point is the ocean is completely interconnected. And so is humanity."

Another shift. Jake struggled to follow the man's quick thoughts. Somehow, though, the struggle was worth it. He put things together in unusual ways, almost like a network of information instead of the usual sequential thought.

"Let me ask you a question," Yitzak continued. "What do you know about Earth?"

Yet another shift in thinking. The question surprised Jake, but he answered simply, "Earth was the source for humanity. They sent out the colony ships, and the people who landed here came from Earth."

"Only partly right." Yitzak paused, just for a moment, but the pause was significant due to the rapidity of his ideas. "Are you aware Earth is no more?"

Jake looked at Zofia. She was as surprised as he. "What? How can that be?"

The scientist slapped gently on the table. "There. You see? Solity's education system fails us yet again. We have suppressed important knowledge."

"Education?" Yet another shift in topic. Jake felt like he was in a video game, dodging the lighted balls bouncing from all directions.

Yitzak waved a finger in the air for attention. "Remember the ocean, Jake. It all ties together. Yes, our education is part of the problem, too. You see, our colonists did not come from Earth; they came from the world One Hope in a second wave of colonies. Earth destroyed itself even before the last colony ships reached their destinations. During colonization, fighting among the Earth nations escalated for a hundred years. Technology became more and more powerful, until they held a nuclear war so devastating it devastated the ecology. The planet Earth has not yet recovered beyond the level of lichens and moss. No one lives there. No one can."

The image of a shattered Earth was a shock that weighed heavily. In the silence, the automated servitor returned with three bowls of stew and flatware. They starting eating while Jake pondered this realignment of history as he knew it.

Then he stopped eating in surprise. "This molfa stew is marvelous!"

Zofia grinned and shrugged. "You bet. I told you."

Conversation lapsed again while they ate, until Zofia broke the silence. "But Yitzak—why don't we know this?"

"That's the education part of the issue. Solity deems this history to be too sensitive for us to know. Central control is important to them, and knowledge of history fosters independent thinking. Solity doesn't want independent thinking.

"History is available in the records for anyone who searches diligently. Ansibles and occasional spaceships keep us in touch with the other worlds, even if travel does take months to years."

He paused and looked down at the table. "But the rest is worse."

"What could be worse?" Jake asked.

"Worse is that One Hope, which launched our colony, is also gone, in an internal war to the death in our year 224. Also gone are twelve other colony planets. Each one destroyed itself within five hundred years of founding."

Jake blurted, "What? Earth, One Hope, and twelve others? Fourteen worlds are ruined?"

Yitzak gave a deep, sad sigh. "The most recent was Branch, where countries flung rockets with biological weapons at each other in our year 403. Just thirteen years ago. People in Tileus and Rathas learn this history. But Solity doesn't tell us.

"It is both simple and terrible. Humanity seems to repeat a devastating cycle. We use our technology to found colonies. They thrive with great hope. When they grow, tensions within each colony cause a split into different countries. A diaspora on each world spreads people into different areas with different ideals. Each country, each society sees the others as 'not like us.'"

"You mean, like the four countries here on Verdant."

"Yes, exactly like our four countries." Yitzak focused his eyes so intently Jake felt like a minor rodent before a predator. The scientist repeated himself. "Exactly like."

The lesson was so clear, Jake's stomach tightened and hardened.

"Eventually, the differences in our societies create conflicts. We grow to hate each other so much we fight wars, concluding in mutual technological termination." He emphasized each of the last three words with a fingertip pounding the table. "For hundreds of years, humanity's creation of new colonies has barely kept pace with the world deaths. Today, there are only three planets left: Verdant, Newland, and Brightness. Of the three, we on Verdant are furthest along the cycle of death, close behind Branch—and our continents are so small, our resources so poor, we have not sent out any colony ships."

He paused to let the lesson sink in, then finished. "Humanity is the ocean. We are connected. We must find a solution to the cycle, or humankind will die."

The silence at the table stretched like cooling taffy, threatening to shatter into pieces.

Jake finally broke it. "What can we do?"

"I'm glad you asked. It shows the way you think, going beyond the limited views you've been taught by Solity."

Then Yitzak shifted the topic again. "Zofia, Jake, do you know of the croombear living in the mountains of Beta continent?"

Jake looked at Zofia, who shrugged with a helpless smile.

Then he answered, "I've heard of it." He was almost getting used to these topic shifts. Each time, they seemed to come together again, so he'd trust this one would, too. The discussion was so fascinating he had set aside—for now—the anxieties he'd had when he arrived.

"It's a huge animal. Stands four meters tall when it's angry. Weighs up to eight hundred kilos. It is the top predator in its domain, eating fish and other animals."

Zofia asked, "I seem to remember...doesn't it have some special ability to find prey?"

He nodded. "Yes, it does. I've studied them. The croombear has a mental sense with which it can find other thinking creatures, even if their thoughts are rudimentary like fish. The creature was one basis for my research linking particle physics and mind waves. I'd heard of strange, unexplained croombear behavior, so I looked into it. Its sense seems to give it a kind of empathy, received over distance through the wave propagation of sub-atomic particles."

Jake blinked. "I didn't know that. I thought they just ate fish."

Yitzak chuckled dryly. "Remind me not to let you wander in the Beta mountains. The croombear sometimes eats people, too. They like the way we think." He smiled. "But the most important thing to know about the croombear is...it never fights another croombear."

"What, never?" Something about this topic, tied with the other topics, made Jake's skin tingle. He rubbed at the mole on his chin. "Not even when mating?"

"Not even then." The scientist shook his heavy head. "They sort out their mating pairs without ever fighting. Somehow, their empathic sense allows them to give and take in a way humans have never learned to do."

"And so,..." Jake was beginning to anticipate him, "how does this relate to humanity's destructive cycle?"

"Again, you ask. Again, you show me your broader thinking. This is good."

Yitzak stopped for a moment to double-check the privacy field on their table. He seemed to come to a decision.

"I am choosing to trust you with a secret, Jake. A big secret that may change humanity. Something you can help.

"Croombears and humans relate, Jake and Zofia...because I have created such an empathy field for humans. I call it the 'transpath,' and no one but me and one other—and now you two—know about it."

Another long silence followed while Jake took in the idea.

"Do you mean," he finally asked, "you have a way for people to understand each other the same way the croombears do?"

Yitzak nodded. After all his quick talking and shifts in topic, his silence was overpowering.

"And do you believe…" Jake caught his breath in the middle of what he was about to say, "this transpath can keep people from fighting? It might stop war?"

"Exactly."

Jake was dumbfounded by the thought. *People understanding each other well enough they didn't have to fight? It's been my dream since school to find a way to stop wars, and I've hated working on a weapon.*

He started to speak, but found he didn't know what more to say.

✿ ❈ ✿

Zofia's knuckles were white where she gripped her glass. She'd been fascinated by Yitzak's explanations—some of which she already knew—but his solution seemed unreal.

"But there is a problem," Yitzak continued. "We cannot build it here in Verdant Prime."

"Why not?" asked Jake "Is there some technology we're missing? Some missing resource?"

Zofia felt like she was at a tennis match, watching the rapid-fire questions and responses. She began to understand why Yitzak had selected Jake; the two were well-matched. Jake seemed to stay right with Yitzak's rapid shifts. Her admiration for Jake grew.

The scientist gave a wry chuckle. "No, the problem is not technical. It's ideological. Solity would never allow the transpath to be built. Director Denmark will never permit it. War and the fear of war is how our leaders control Solity. Without war, they'd lose their control. Even worse, empathic understanding among people would lessen their power.

"So, the transpath must be built elsewhere. The best place would be Tileus. They also have high technology, coupled with a variety of ideas. Such an approach would not be unusual in Tileus."

Zofia agreed. "Yah, it'd fit in there." She'd seen that kind of variety.

Yitzak pressed on. "Once it's built, the best use of the transpath would be for international negotiations. Can you imagine what talks would be like, if Prime and Tileus diplomats could fully understand each other? If they couldn't lie?"

Jake's eyes went wide. "Ouch. Now *that* would be a diplomatic negotiation to watch. I'd like to be a flea on the wall for that."

"And you can be, Jake. If you build it for us."

Zofia tilted her head. "Is this why you've had me learn how to get to and from Tileus?"

"What?" Jake's head whipped around to her. "I thought you were there for technical training?"

Zofia realized she'd been caught in one of her lies. She hunched her shoulders and grinned self-consciously. "Well…maybe not. But I couldn't tell you until now."

She saw Jake's attitude close in on himself. Her surreptitious approach to bring him to the Lazarites was coming unglued. This whole conversation now had him whirling in tight circles of surprise and concern, and she saw it on his face.

Bangit, why did I have to lie? I've put a steel wedge between us, just when I'm really getting to like him.

Jake looked like he was rapidly distancing himself from the two of them like a spaceship receding into the black firmament. Yet Zofia knew what Yitzak proposed to stop war appealed to Jake. Perhaps it would suffice to keep him here.

"And Jake," Yitzak reached across the table and put his hand on top of Jake's, "that's why I wanted to talk with you today. You see, I can't go to Tileus. Too many years have gone by for me to start traipsing around the world. But you can. You have the needed knowledge of particle physics, and great engineering skills. I'd like you to go to Tileus. Both of you. Together."

Jake snatched his hand back. He jumped up from his chair. "What? I can't do that. Good heavens, I'm working in Defense research. And…Tileus!…It's Tileus. They're the target for the weapons we're creating!"

Yitzak waved a calming hand. "Please, Jake, at this point we're just talking about it. Please sit down, just consider it and talk with us."

Zofia saw him torn between curiosity and the need to run. He obviously knew now she'd approached him for this purpose, and he probably couldn't trust anything she said.

She stood up beside him and put a hand on his arm, but he went rigid. She said, "Please, Jake. I trust Yitzak. I can tell you more later about why. But please, just think about it?"

Her heart was in her throat, seeing Jake slipping away.

"I…Zofia, I just…what?…don't know." Jake was yammering. He stopped and tried again. "I'll think about it, dammit. But I…" He stopped again, confused.

"And in the meantime," she urged, "we're meetin' on Wentday to play zero-G, right? I'm giving you a return match—maybe give you a chance to win this time? We can talk more, then."

Jake nodded with a jerk. "Yes, we'll do that." He looked at Yitzak. "It's been…amazing…to meet you, sir. Thank you."

He spun away from the table, walking quickly. He gave no opportunity for her to join him.

Zofia slumped into her chair, tears brimming. "Yitzak…I think I've screwed it all up."

CHAPTER 11

With all their differences, one way in which Verdant Prime,
Tileus, and Rathas were dangerously alike was in their military
build-up. Rathas had its holy order of Khubar f'Elláh, and Tileus
had a citizen army. Of the three, Prime was the most militant.

—*An Annotated History of Verdant* by Ellen Thranadil, Tileus Press 442 A.T.

Wentday, 30 Quartember, 416 A.T.

Berndt Denmark loved and hated Solity Council meetings. On one hand, he
enjoyed the power of being at this level of Solity, of crossing swords in
bloody battle with the top predators. When he won each verbal clash, he felt
the warmth of satisfaction suffuse his entire body. On the other hand, the
tensions and conflicts with the other directors threatened his own progress
and got in his way.

Overlock briefed Denmark before the meeting. "There were two more
protests today, Director, one here and one in Timpi. These people seem to
be popping up like bubbles in a boiling pot. Groups appear, do their damage,
then disappear before we can converge. It seems to be different people each
time. InfoNet disruptions impair our communications. Here in Oriens, they
threw rotten eggs at Defense employees while they arrived to work. In
Timpi, they set fire to a distribution center."

Denmark set his lips in a thin line and clenched his jaw.

Chairman Rodion Lukin entered and tapped gently on the conference
table with the time-honored engraved silver gavel of his office.

"Take your seats. This meeting of the Solity Council is now in order. On
Newday, we talked about the internal issues and the Lazarites. Today, our
topic is the international situation."

Crowned with grey hair and a flowing beard, Lukin wore a crisp and
sparkling white coverall, raiment unique in Solity. Even at age ninety-four,
he had broad shoulders, carried himself erect, and had a powerful,
commanding manner. He held supremacy through his formidable character,
coupled with a willingness to use force when necessary.

Denmark fully intended to challenge Lukin for his position, but not yet.
Perhaps the success of Denmark's plans to re-integrate Tileus into Solity
would trigger that confrontation.

Denmark took his seat, nodding to the chairman and the six other
directors—State, Capital, Labor, Technology, Justice, and Development.
Along with his own Defense, these seven controlled all the people and

assets of Solity. Each wore crisply tailored purple coveralls with a color band on the right shoulder indicating their department.

The highly-polished solta-wood table at which they sat was called The Fundament, where Verdant Prime leaders had made their decisions for over four hundred years. The table had been one of the early luxuries created in Prime. The long-ago craftsman had organized stunning wood grains to swirl in symmetric patterns that focused attention on each director. Some of the dents in the wood testified to occasions when power had changed hands less smoothly than others. The Fundament resided in this glass-walled Council room overlooking central Oriens city, and the table exuded the rich history of the country.

Chairman Lukin's white coveralls were a stark contrast to the sea of purple. He displayed a set of all seven color bands on his shoulder. Behind Lukin stood two members of his private security force, rigid in their off-white coveralls with white needle guns in their holsters. The shade of their attire was just sufficient to accentuate the brilliant white of the Chairman's. The other directors each had one or two auxiliaries seated in chairs against the wall to provide information when needed.

Chairman Lukin didn't hesitate to start the meeting with a salvo. Eyes locked on the Director of State, he growled, "Intelligence tells me Tileus is dragging their heels, not prepared to negotiate with us. I'm not surprised. But I had expected better. They may even be behind these protest events. What's the situation with Tileus, Director Pires? Are we reaching any agreement with them?"

Denmark had little respect for Calie Pires. She was a highly capable diplomat, frustrated by Tileus' reticence. She was also an obstacle to Denmark's own plans for war, because she preferred to negotiate.

Pires answered, "They're still disorganized and not ready for either diplomacy or war, Chairman. They talk with us, but cannot seem to make effective, lasting decisions. Part of it is their decadent culture, but it's also due to their current governors. It's hard to know what factions exists, but you're right—it's nearly certain some of their splinter groups are helping the Lazarites here."

Denmark cut in. "They are certainly a thorn in our side. Every protest in the last two weeks has incorporated InfoNet disruptions using Tileus technology. The Defense lab explosion last Friday was aided by new technology weapons from Tileus."

Pires turned to him and said with derision, "How can you know that, Director?"

"We caught one of the perpetrators at the explosion, and he admitted it before dying." Denmark saw a couple of the directors suck in surprised breaths. "The Lazarites have been trading goods for weapons across the Vissensee Channel."

The chairman raised a forefinger to forestall Pires' response, then tapped his finger on the table while he considered this startling knowledge. Denmark smiled inside to know he'd used the information at just the right time.

He said, "This is good to know, Director Denmark. Thank you for the intel. We'll come back to it, another time. But for now, let's continue with the external situation."

"In addition to the strained relations with us," Pires continued, "Tileus also has recent problems with Rathas. There have been violent incidents in the border mountains between the two countries, with fringe groups in Tileus attacking missionaries. The religious leaders in Rathas are talking Holy War."

The chairman added, "I understand Rathas is doing more than talking. They're expanding their holy army, the Khubar f'Elláh. Have you spoken with them?"

Pires appeared uncomfortable with Lukin's advanced knowledge. "Yes, Chairman. They bear us no ill will at present. Their focus is on Tileus."

"And what about Winter?"

"The northern islands of Winter mostly separate themselves from all this with their tribal lives. But there's a level of irritation there as well, because Tileus sends teachers to proselytize the Tileus brand of chaotic democracy."

"Director Denmark," the Chairman said, turning to face him, "Is there any military threat in Winter?"

"Hmph. They have small units capable of guerilla warfare, but nothing of a threat to us."

"It sounds like we need to be ready for anything," said Technology.

"Such is always the case," expressed Development in ponderous tones. As an academic, his words were often important-sounding but useless aphorisms.

Denmark knew each of the directors like he knew the tools in his kitchen. He might not be ready yet, but he fully intended to be the successor to the white coveralls. Some of the directors were viable threats to that goal, like Miriam Keita of Justice, who had left a trail of dead people during her rise to power. Others were wilted cabbage, like 102-year-old Frederic Pontol of Capital, represented by his deputy, Denmark's old protégé Franklin Edobar.

"So, are we ready to bring Tileus back to Solity?" asked the Chairman. "Director Pires, do we have appropriate diplomatic plans and alternatives?"

"Of course, Chairman. If we can get Tileus to come to the table for serious discussion, we have developed open trade solutions to satisfy most of their issues and keep us from war."

Lukin paused, probing Pires with his eyes. To Denmark, his expression seemed skeptical of Pires' assurances. Then Lukin turned to him again. "And what about war, Director Denmark? If it comes to that, are we ready?"

"Of course, Chairman. I'm still moving toward the goal of integrating the entire planet back under the stabilizing force of Solity. I would hope any diplomacy we use will facilitate that." He raised an eyebrow toward Pires.

She opened her mouth to speak, fire in her eyes, but Denmark cut her off by continuing.

"Until last week, I believed we had an edge on anything Tileus could offer. The loss of our lab was a double blow. Not only did we lose the beam weapon research, but we also discovered Tileus has a new melting beam, and we have no idea how—"

"So our plans for war," Pires couldn't restrain her rejoinder, "are not as certain as they need to be. Diplomacy is still—"

"On our side, however," Denmark rode over her voice, "we are very close to having an antimatter bomb overwhelming in its power. We are ready. We have the military forces. We have the weapons. I believe, given an element of surprise, we could win a war with Tileus in two weeks."

"But we hope not to, right?" asked Pires. "War is the last thing we want to do."

Denmark laid a hand flat on the table for emphasis. "Perhaps. But war is often less destructive than continuing the situation. Tileus is a nexus for problems with every country. If we had them back under the authority of Solity, those other problems would die away."

Pires responded with disdain, "So we're back to our perennial issue. Wouldn't it be preferable to negotiate than to make war?"

Denmark answered simply by inclining his head, letting Pires' weakness hang in the air.

"Chairman," said Miriam Keita of Justice, "I'd like to return to something Director Denmark said earlier, if that's acceptable?"

Lukin waved a hand to proceed.

Keita turned to Denmark. "Am I to understand your minions," she glanced at Overlock behind Denmark, "are in the practice of killing captives during interrogation?"

Denmark leaned forward in his chair. "Director Keita, you have misstated the situation. The man we captured was badly hurt in the explosion he helped to create—"

"And you did not seek immediate medical attention for him?"

"—and he was on death's door when we questioned him."

"So, in violation of our Justice standards, you withheld palliative measures?"

Denmark paused, keeping his face neutral. "Director Keita, we do what we must to protect Verdant Prime. This man had information we knew would save many of our lives."

Keita nodded once with an intent gaze.

Denmark clamped his jaw. Keita's rise had been thoroughly as ruthless as his own, but she had just portrayed Denmark as openly bloody. He looked down at the table while seething internally. He would have to knock her down a few notches in the near future.

Chairman Lukin took over the conversation again. "None of us knows yet what path lies in front of us, whether it will be diplomacy or war. Each of us must ensure our departments—all the branches of Solity—are ready for either. Director Denmark, do we have any advantage over Tileus if it comes to war?"

"Our information networks tell us Prime and Tileus are similar in the technology of our weapons development, though we have a significant ascendancy in training and readiness. They have the advantage of this new beam weapon; we have the advantage of the antimatter bomb—"

"But only if your development succeeds quickly, yes?"

He nodded. "Yes, Chairman."

"Then make sure it does."

Denmark continued his outward attitude of compliance. Inside, he was boiling. This meeting had not gone well for his plans.

Lukin turned to the rest of the table. "This isn't enough. It sounds like we have partial diplomatic solutions and partial military solutions. We don't want partial; we need completion. All of you, examine your departments for weaknesses and remove them. Be ready to move quickly on Tileus with everything we have."

❧ ✳ ☙

When they were clear of the Council building, Denmark loosed his anger on Overlock.

"This is completely unacceptable, Shelton. Damn, that *bitch* painted me as a bloody executioner, when her entire history is riddled with the bodies of her opponents. Department of Justice, indeed! She may be the most unjust woman in Prime."

"What should we do about her, Director?"

"We're not ready to move on Keita yet. I need you to find something more, something real enough to sink her boat."

"I'll see what I can find, sir, but she's careful."

"Careful or not, we need to be prepared to take her down. Down, I say. She's a threat."

Denmark set her aside and returned to the main issue. "Where do you stand on the plans to catch the Lazarites in Timpi?"

"It's still a couple of weeks away. We're laying temptations now. They will come to fruition when the Lazarite people there take the bait. The trap will close on them all at once like steel teeth on fungus." Overlock sounded like he enjoyed the chase.

"Good. Now, we need to make sure our bomb development doesn't go astray. I'm becoming concerned my Palatin fellow is losing impetus. I'll push him harder tomorrow."

CHAPTER 12

Love? Don't tell me about love. Tell me how to work through the problems caused by love.

—*Collected Sayings of Yitzak Goren* by Ellen Thranadil, Tileus Press 439 A.T.

Jake drifted down the slidewalk after work toward the Hadley courts and his zero-G match with Zofia. Had it really been only a week since their previous match? And only two weeks since he'd met her? So much had happened. He felt frozen and burning at the same time. What was it going to take to climb out of this emotional pit?

He'd tossed in his bed covers all night, not getting more than an hour of sleep. At work, he could hardly keep his mind on what they were doing. Indy had noticed, correcting his math a couple of times. When he did get his mind working, his thoughts were as jumbled as the trash piles in the Warrens.

His conflicts skittered around his mind like ants at a picnic. Zofia was the most exciting thing that had happened to him in years. The match last week had been exhilarating. His heart pounded when he was with her. But Sam's suspicion and Yitzak's revelation now had him wondering if Zofia was involved in the Lazarites. Her conversations sounded like Lazarite talk.

Perhaps she was even involved in the explosion last Friday. Yesterday, he'd met with the leader of the beam weapons lab that had been destroyed—Jake knew him, but not well. He'd been shocked at the man's appearance. The fellow looked gaunt, as if he'd aged thirty years. Three of his team members were now dead—and his project might not recover.

Finally, Yitzak's offer blew everything else out of the water. Go to Tileus? Drop everything and build the transpath to stop war? What an exciting challenge, right in line with his dreams. But he would be a traitor to the country he'd always believed in. He might never be able to return. Yitzak had given him the offer of a lifetime, but it meant giving up all he'd ever known.

All his problems revolved around Zofia.

I want to be with her, but now I wonder. Was it all a game on her part?

While wrestling with his thoughts the last two days, his confusion had transformed to anger. *How could I be so naive? Why didn't I know all this?*

By the time he got to the Hadley recreation center, he no longer drifted. His stride had lengthened and anger smacked his feet into the pavement. He needed the exercise. He also needed to have it out with Zofia.

She was waiting for him at the court with the door open. She was in skin-tight shorts and exercise shirt, with her spectacular hair in a ponytail.

Damn it, she's so gorgeous.

"Hey, Jake. Are you okay?" She frowned at his attitude.

"Let's just play." His answer came out harsh even in his own ears.

She let it go. "Sounds good. We can talk afterwards, right?"

He nodded brusquely, dropped his gear bag outside, and brushed past her through the low doorway. She followed and closed the door.

"Ready for Zero?" she asked while she uncovered the power panel. She sounded careful, like dealing with dynamite.

"Right. Ready for Zero. Let's go." He still didn't know how to talk it over with her, but the exercise would help.

As soon as he cleared the floor, he slammed a hard volley into the front corner.

"Whoa," shouted Zofia when she scrambled to return it. "Wasn't ready!"

He didn't answer, just slammed the second shot off a perfect upper corner past her. "One," he said. He didn't look at her, and he served again, an ace she couldn't even touch. "Two."

The competition of the game brought his anger and frustration to the fore. He felt like he'd been overtaken by a racquetball demon with a direct comms channel to evil. He was fast. His positioning was superb, in the right place every time. He knew exactly where she was without looking. Most of his shots were harder than he usually played, brilliant in their placement. Then, he changed it out with several soft drop shots that caught her in the back court. He was so focused on the game his play was zen-like in its single-mindedness.

As good as she was, Zofia was unable to keep up with him. Last week, they'd played nearly even. Today, the score climbed to twelve-to-one in short order. Her shots almost matched his in brilliance. Almost. Yet volley after volley, she fell just a little short, not quite anticipating, in the wrong place at the wrong time.

The demon in him burned higher. He ground his teeth while he slammed shots all over the front wall and repeatedly took advantage of center court position. When she got in his way, he used the momentum of his greater weight off the wall or ceiling to bump her out. They'd both have bruises when this was over. His play was becoming violent, and the combat was feeding the anger he'd built for days now.

He smashed her into a wall while positioning for a shot.

She shouted, "Ow! Take it easy."

"Gotta play the game. Don't get in the way," he grunted, and served again.

The next time he smashed her into a wall, she yelped in pain, then slid behind him. He pounded his shot off the side wall into a spinning cut on the front wall, another winning volley. She wasn't anywhere near position to return it.

Then he sank to the floor, the zero-G power fading.

Zofia was standing by the power switch.

"What are you doing?" he shouted. "Dammit, we're in the middle of a game."

She responded with matching anger. "No, what are *you* doin'? Bangit, this isn't a game. It feels like war. What's *wrong* with you?"

"I'm playing the game as best I can," he barked, "and I'm winning, in case you hadn't noticed."

"No, you're not playin'. You're bein' an ass. I don't know what your problem is, but I'm not goin' to do this."

She opened the door and ducked out into the cool evening.

Jake stood in the center court and shook his head, teeth clenched. He wanted to shout, to scream, to fight. The longer he stood, however, the more sanity came back to him. In his rage, he'd forgotten what this match was all about. Racquet dangling from his hand, he hung his head and looked at the scuff marks on the floor. Then he kicked hard at the side wall in frustration, nearly knocking himself over.

He took a single hard breath, failed to clear his anger, and ducked out through the door.

಄ ✳ ಄

Zofia sat on the exercise equipment, arms crossed, trying to hold in her tears. She rocked in place, her shoulders shaking. Her hip and shoulder hurt, where he'd slammed her into the wall. Her mind flitted among uncomfortable thoughts like a moth at the light.

This is awful. He's still angry, and he's got every right to be. I've used him for our purposes, and now I wish I never had. I've screwed it all up.

Her head was down, sinking into the bleakness she felt. She didn't even see him come out of the court until he stood in front of her with his gear bag. His fists were clenched.

She couldn't hold in the tears any more. Hiding her face in her hands, her whole body shook with the sobs. Zofia wanted to be with him. She wanted to do this adventure, and do it with him. She admired him, was fascinated by the way he could go toe-to-toe with Yitzak.

And he just stood there. Saying nothing. Breathing hard.

She took a deep breath, wiped away her tears and jumped to her feet. She forced herself to look him in the eyes.

"Damn it, Jake. You're angry. I understand that. And I know why. No more hidden agendas."

She knew what she had to say would put them both at risk. Solity monitored the audio from imps. They couldn't monitor everything at once, but their automated Sentinel Shield system would flag it if she said the wrong word.

"Yes," she said. "I'm in the resistance. I can't say the name here in the open, but you know what resistance I mean. So is Yitzak. If you spend time with us, it'll put your future, your whole life at risk."

Jake stepped back in shock.

He hadn't figured that out yet? But Yitzak practically told him they were Lazarites. Or is it my admission that surprises him?

She continued, "We're makin' a difference, see? I wanted to do that with you. I'm sorry."

She'd just confessed a capital crime, put her life in his hands. She saw the revelation—and the trust—floor him.

Yet his fury wasn't appeased. His hands quivered with it.

"Dammit, this isn't right," he said. "I'm angry and I'm frustrated, and I need to know more. It feels like you've been *playing* me all along." He slammed his gear bag into the equipment post, making the metal ring with the impact. "What am I supposed to do with you?"

"Oh, hell," she said. "This is all so messed up. I don't know what to say."

"How about the truth?" he shouted.

"The truth," she yelled back through her tears, "is you are the most interestin' man I've met." Her voice dropped to a whisper. "Ever." She held her hands wide, her wet eyes looking up into his.

He looked stunned. But she still felt all wrong, too.

"But the *truth*," she continued, crossing her arms again, "is I wasn't supposed to have these feelings for you."

"What do you mean, 'supposed to have'?" he responded, skeptical. "Did Yitzak put you up to this? Good heavens, was it all a game for the two of you?"

She gave a quick, high-pitched laugh. "A game? No, there's nothin' about this that's a game. I trust Yitzak. He's so brilliant he scares me, and he knows where we need to go. And yes, you are important to that. You're brilliant, too, almost in his class. Yitzak asked me to get close to you, to bring you in, get your expertise to build the transpath in Tileus."

Her tear-filled eyes pleaded with him for understanding

But she watched her words just feed his ire.

He spun around and slammed his gear bag into the post, harder. The metal rang like a gong this time.

She was so startled and frightened by his violence, she jumped back. But she didn't give up. *I have got to make this right, or I'll lose him.*

81

She kept going. "But the *truth* is also you've become important to me. You. Not the engineer who might advance our plans. You. Damn it, I don't know what to do any more." Her voice trailed off.

She stood quivering. She wanted to lash out, to rage at everybody and everything, and at the same time she wanted to crumple into a tiny ball.

He didn't look any better. He was quivering with emotion while he stood there, fists clenching and unclenching. Through her tears, she saw him fighting inside himself. His jaw muscles looked so tight her own teeth hurt.

Finally, he screamed out a guttural wordless fury.

Jabbing a finger in her face. Words sprang out of him like an explosion of agony.

"You *lied* to me."

Spinning away, he left. He ran, his fists clenched as tightly as the strings of her heart.

She stood in shock and watched him disappear. He turned a corner without once looking back. Then he was gone. She had no idea whether he'd ever come back. She dropped back down onto the exercise equipment, her face in her hands and her heart somewhere south of Hell.

CHAPTER 13

Those who served under Denmark unanimously called him difficult. Most also begrudgingly called him effective. He was appropriate to Solity in that time,

—*An Annotated History of Verdant* by Ellen Thranadil, Tileus Press 442 A.T.

Following yesterday's Council meeting, Franklin Edobar took an hour to assess his position. For some months, he'd been filling in for Frederic Pontol as the current Director of Capital declined in his abilities. He saw his opportunity coming near. Very soon, it would be clear Pontol's age had become irreversible senility. Franklin was the likely candidate to replace him.

His sights were already set higher. Gaining a position as director wasn't enough. He wanted to be Chairman when Lukin faltered. He easily imagined what he could do for Verdant Prime if he ran both the Solity Council and the Lazarites. However, the step to the chair would be difficult, because both Denmark and Keita were already well positioned. If he had sufficient time, he could swing it.

He would need support. Franklin thought about the remaining directors. Shanah of Technology and Kerr of Development, though capable in their fields, had little power in the Council. He could sway them to his side when needed with the right arguments against Denmark, but he needed someone first who had some level of power. Wang of Labor was already tight with Keita.

That left Calie Pires as a possibility. She was a capable diplomat, despite her frustration over Tileus. She carried herself well in meetings, had a good relationship with the chairman, and certainly did not support Denmark and his goals. She seemed to have no aspirations for the chair.

Deciding was acting. He put in a secure call to her.

"Calie, I wanted to thank you for your summation of the international situation yesterday. It helped me to know what's going on."

"Thanks, Franklin. I'm glad to hear it."

"Working in Capital, I don't have much information about what's going on in the other countries. Are they truly as unstable as Berndt Denmark makes them out to be?"

She seemed a bit reticent in her answer. "To some extent, yes, though he magnifies the problems. You know, of course, about his plan to re-integrate the countries by war?"

"Yes. I actually worked for him in State when he devised it. I disagreed with him, and we parted ways."

"I didn't know that," she said, surprise in her voice.

Franklin used her reaction to advance his relationship with Pires. "He's been working toward it since then. I've been working toward alternate ways to make things better."

"Alternate ways are good."

"Which brings up another reason I called you. I'd like the opportunity to do more. Very soon, Chairman Lukin will need to appoint a new Director for Capital. I'd like to be that, and I'd appreciate your support."

Jake suffered another sleepless night and walked the eight blocks to work, ignoring the slidewalks. His mind was fuzzy and confused.

Blowing up at Zofia yesterday hadn't helped. He'd made things worse, and now he'd have to apologize. During the night, he'd realized his anger was based on fear. He feared her connection to the Lazarites would put him at risk with the Solity Guards. He feared failing in his work and the director's condemnation. He feared losing Zofia.

Loud shouting and commotion sounded behind him. At the same time, his implant filled with a flood of unwanted news stories, clouding his thoughts. Though he tried, he couldn't silence his imp. What was going on?

A dozen people in light blue and yellow ran toward him, hopping on and off the slidewalk, ducking around the crowds on the street. They were shouting slogans.

We want meat!

No more Guards!

and most of all,

Freedom!

Shaking aside the news voices yammering in his head, he realized the boisterous group was connected to the InfoNet problem. Another protest. His heart began to race when he saw scarves hiding their faces. They seemed to fill the street, weaving back and forth, men and women. Normal people around them drew back, yet they still managed to bump aside passersby, creating a swirl of agitation.

They held glass bottles with rags hanging from them.

He sucked in a breath when he saw a bright flame flash among the agitators. They lit the gas-soaked rags stuffed into each bottle. Only twenty meters from him, they threw their flaming bottles at the windows of a small distribution shop—the kind Sam wanted to run. The bottles shattered the glass. Flames roared through the shop. Jake heard screams from inside. The door flew open, and two people ran out through the flames. One of them frantically waved his arm, engulfed in fire.

The protesters dodged around the screaming bystanders and pushed past Jake, yelling in triumph. Someone in yellow bumped him hard, sending Jake sprawling onto the edge of the moving slidewalk. He thrust out his hands to catch his fall, pain shooting up from his right wrist when he landed. His head hit the ground hard. The slidewalk dragged him along, half on and half off. His forearm scraped on the moving pavement, screaming at him with pain.

Jake looked up at the retreating protesters, his vision dazed. His head was still filled with yapping news feeds. He hadn't seen any faces, but Zofia wasn't in this protest, and none of them looked like any of the people in her group. The protesters disappeared into several streets like piproaches into the dark.

As suddenly as it started, the babble in his head cut off to a great, ringing silence. The external noise of the recovering crowd grew around him: shouts of alarm at the fire, cries of pain from others. Slowly and carefully, he shook his head and got to his feet. His right wrist throbbed, and his left forearm was stinging. Blood seeped out of the scrapes. Befuddled, he didn't know which arm to hold with which hand.

Another passerby had helped the shopkeeper smother the fire on his arm. The flames in the store heated Jake's face. Fire consumed a large sign on the storefront saying "No Meat Available." It seemed a trivial reason for setting fire to the shop.

A sign of the times, though. If it's not meat, it's always something.

Still dazed, Jake stumbled back onto the slidewalk toward work, two blocks away.

☙ ✻ ❧

"Great gods, what happened to you?" Indy cried when Jake entered the lab.

Sam turned and sucked in a breath. Minya and Afonso hadn't arrived yet.

Jake cradled his left forearm in his right hand despite his painful wrist. His forearm was smeared with blood, and he'd gotten some on his sleeve. His injured wrist was starting to swell. He wondered if his wrist were broken or only sprained

But Indy was looking at Jake's head. The man took a clean cloth from the workbench and wet it, then started dabbing at Jake's forehead. The cloth came away bloody.

"I got knocked down on the way to work. Another protest." Jake still didn't feel steady. Things looked blurry. Dizzy, he sat down.

Sam opened the first aid kit from the wall and took out some gauze and bandages. "Let's get you cleaned up, boss."

Sitting helped. While the two tended to him, Jake's mind started to clear. His wrist throbbed, and the scrapes now stung like fire when they applied antiseptic. Wrapping the wrist helped. Jake felt helpless and weak. He was supposed to be in charge here.

"Where did it happen?" Sam asked. "Was it like the rotten fruit protest I saw?"

"No, much worse. They fire-bombed a shop two blocks from here. One of the shopkeepers got burned. All because the shop was out of meat, I guess."

Indy stepped back from bandaging his head. "That'll heal." Then he stooped to peer into Jake's eyes. "How do you feel, boss? Your eyes look okay, not dilated."

"I feel rotten, Indy, but I'll be fine. I've got a headache and both wrists hurt. Any painkillers in the kit?"

Sam found an injector and held it to his neck. Jake felt the momentary stab. "Maybe you should go to the clinic."

"I will if I keep feeling bad. Let's give it some time. Meanwhile, we have work to do." With the injection, Jake's vision was clearing.

"This stuff is getting worse," said Indy, closing the first aid kit. "There are so many angry people these days, and they seem to be organized."

"Yeah," said Sam. "First rotten fruit, then explosions and fire. Say, boss, did the InfoNet screw up again?"

"Yes, it did," Jake said. "While the protest was going on, my head was filled with news stories. I couldn't think. Whoever is doing this is using our own implants against us."

The door clacked open. Director Denmark strode in, followed by Afonso and Minya.

"I found these two out in the hallway, Palatin," he growled. "Can't you even get your team to arrive on time for work?"

Jake jumped to his feet, then almost fell over when dizziness washed over him. Before he could answer, Denmark stepped near him and looked closely.

"Good grief, man, what happened to you?"

"Protesters, sir," Jake replied. "I got knocked down on the way to work. They set fire to a store down the street."

Denmark straightened, his lips compressed, and looked him up and down. "You look battered. Can you still work?"

"Yes, sir, I can."

"Good. I came down here to see a demonstration of what you've got. Show me."

Jake looked to Indy for help, so his assistant stepped in. "We've got the prototype almost built, Director." Indy guided Denmark and Jake to the workbench while the others went to their workstations.

Pointing into the tangle of tubing and electronics on the bench, Indy explained, "You can see here the incoming ports for supercooling while the device is in storage. Here is the cooler that maintains temperature for up to a half hour when disconnected in transit. These cylinders are laser ports that activate the containment. The antimatter goes here." Indy pointed to a small globe in the center. "That space will be evacuated so the antimatter doesn't interact until the vessel is broken."

Denmark scowled. "Doesn't look like it holds much material."

Jake held up a hand to take over from Indy. "It doesn't need to, sir," Jake said. "A few grams of antimatter will generate kilotons of explosion."

"Does it work yet?"

"Not yet, Director," Jake said. "We hope to have it operating within a day or two. Then we'll be able to run tests to determine how well it works."

"How well it works?" Denmark asked. "You mean you're not even certain it *will* work?"

"No, sir. I have the theory, but reality almost always brings surprises."

Denmark turned directly to Jake and glared. "Damn it, we don't want surprises, Palatin. We want success." Then he turned to the entire team. "The Solity Council itself is watching what you're doing. We need this device working within the next six weeks so we can move into production. If you people can't make that happen, there will be serious consequences."

Denmark strode out, slamming the door behind him.

Jake's head throbbed. He turned to the team and spoke quietly. "Get busy, everyone, will you? You heard what the director said."

彩

By mid-morning, his headache had subsided and Jake was able to direct the work. He was helping Minya with a calculation for test planning when his implant buzzed.

An official voice sounded in his inner ear. "Jacoby Palatin, report to the Assignment Office."

He sighed. Another interruption. Despite Zofia's ideas, he believed in Solity. Sometimes, though, he wished they'd ask instead of command. Giving instructions to his team, he hurried out. It didn't do to delay.

Slidewalks took him through the huge five-story General Defense building. The Assignment Office was two floors down at the other end, an austere room with a few hard chairs and a clerk behind a battered desk. A sour smell infused the lobby. He looked around but could not identify the source.

The desk clerk pointed at a numbered door, so Jake went in. Inside was a tiny interview booth with doors at both ends. A built-in glass wall divided the room in half, clinically separating the administrator from the client. The lower part of the glass wall merged with a two-sided desk with a small opening. The plastic chair on his side faced a larger, more comfortable chair on the other side. Jake thought the booth looked like an aquarium, but he wasn't sure whether he was inside or outside the glass.

He sat in the hard plastic chair, his fears from this morning rising again. Why was he called? A summons was rarely good.

After a few long minutes, the opposite door opened. The older woman who entered looked so haggard Jake winced. Like the clerk, she wore the purple coveralls required for Administration jobs, but it made her skin look sallow. She had pinched eyes and pointed ears, with her mouth set in a permanent scowl. Her hair hung in uneven, bedraggled curls. She bustled into the leather chair on the other side of the glass. He saw her glance at his bandages, but she ignored them otherwise. His wrist still throbbed.

"Jacoby Palatin." Her voice was flat and nasal.

"Jake," he responded with what he hoped was a friendly smile.

She stared at him for a long moment of petty power, then repeated, "Jacoby Palatin. You are an engineering leader for General Defense."

His irritation morphed into dark humor. "Yes, that's me." He pointed to his name on the coveralls.

She ignored his gesture. "Jacoby Palatin, Solity has determined your skill is providing less value than in the past. Balancing the value with the benefit is essential to Solity. 'From each according to his ability...'"

Jake joined her saying the ages-old mantra in the approved fashion. "'...to each according to his need.'" This interview was going bad places, and he didn't like it.

"Therefore, Solity has decided your reduced value should be matched with appropriate compensation. Your allotments are now reduced by twelve-point-two percent for the common good, and you are being reassigned to a smaller apartment. You have five days to move your things. Your engineering duties at work will remain the same. Here are your new parameters." She slid a holochip across the desk, stamped with "Solity Approved." While she touched the chip, the holo of his information appeared in the air above it.

Jake stiffened. His ears were ringing. Do the same work, yet receive less compensation. He'd heard of this happening to others, but he thought Denmark had earmarked him for advancement instead of demotion. This had to be the director's doing, in punishment for not creating results faster. He felt betrayed and wanted to lash out at Denmark. Anger filled him, and his headache came back, but he didn't know what he could do. Would Denmark find someone else to replace him? Perhaps. A few had equivalent knowledge. But worse, he realized, Denmark was also in charge of the Solity Guard.

He knew this petty martinet couldn't change the situation, but he spoke anyway.

"Is there any avenue for appeal?"

She looked directly at him, her lip curling in disgust. "Of course not. This is the decision of Solity. It is your responsibility to support it."

She stood up, signaling an end. Then she turned and left without another word.

Jake sat alone in the sterile booth, his jaw clenched. He knew Denmark wanted more from him, but this made him want to do less. Everything in his life this week conspired against him, and now the last thing he had working for him wasn't. He hated the idea of returning to his lab. Zofia. Protests. Explosions. His failure at the bomb. Zofia.

Yitzak's offer was looking more and more like the solution to them all.

CHAPTER 14

In the midst of the events, Jacoby Palatin was young, uncertain, and hesitant. It must be remembered what happened after was driven by the events of his life.

—*The Making of a New Humanity* by Ellen Thranadil, Tileus Press 448 A.T.

MIDDAY, 31 QUARTEMBER, 416 A.T.

One large box, three mediums, and six smalls. That evening, Jake slammed down the stack of boxes he'd requisitioned for his move.

I've got so little to move. Six years of "success" working for Denmark, and this is all I have to show for it?

He unfolded the first medium box.

I can't believe Denmark demoted me. Is this supposed to motivate me to work harder, by taking away what few privileges I have? What else might he do to me?

When he'd emptied his clothes drawers of underwear and socks and sweaters, the box was still only two-thirds full. His jackets and athletic gear from the closet took up the rest. He picked up the small trophy he'd gotten three years ago in zero-G and started to stuff it into the soft clothes.

Then rage took over. He threw the trophy at the wall, as hard as he could. The motion made his bandaged forearm sting. The cheap plastic shattered, pieces flying around the room from the impact dent in the wall. One piece came back and slapped into the dressing on his forehead, re-awakening his headache.

Damn it! This is a load of crap! The last thing I need to do right now is move, for crying out loud. Another distraction—another time-waster—isn't going to help me make progress on Denmark's damned bomb. Do I really want to be killing people?

What do I want, anyway?

An image of Zofia swam into his consciousness. It startled him, that his mind made that association.

Man, oh man, why did I have to get so angry with her yesterday? I want to be with her, not chase her away. I left the courts so fast last night. Is she really interested in me, or just in what I can do for the Lazarites?

He looked again at the one filled box, and didn't even close the flaps on it. Throwing his hands in the air, he grabbed a book holochip and stalked out of the apartment. Maybe a bar-food dinner at the easygo would help.

Maybe he'd find friends there who could take his mind off his problems. Or maybe he'd just read.

Walking down the street, his thoughts kept skittering to every aspect of his problems. He'd learned so much in the last two weeks about Solity, and he was no longer the firm patriot he had been. There were real problems in Verdant Prime. Unequal power, supply shortages, too much control over personal lives. He'd like to solve those instead of contribute to war.

Hoping for someone to distract his thoughts, he slumped when he saw the easygo nearly empty. Two people he didn't know sat by the front window.

Ah, well. I'm here. I might as well eat. Someone might come along.

He sat by himself in an enclosed booth and ordered nachos with barbequed brolmeat. The waitress brought him a brew. They were always watered down, but he drank them anyway. *Yet another thing wrong with Solity. Why can't we get good brews?* This one tasted particularly bitter and the bar music seemed more raucous than usual.

He lost himself in a holobook, an escapist story of Utopian life where all the controls of Solity made everyone happy. He remembered Zofia's comment about Sentinel Shield, and he wondered if Solity monitored his choice of reading. But this book was from the approved library. *Could they do that with every single citizen?* What else had they been controlling without his knowledge? His thoughts were entirely too dark this evening.

A shadow fell across his holo while he nibbled at the nachos.

"Got room for another in that booth?"

His breath caught when he recognized her voice. Looking up, Zofia stood there with one hip cocked, her arms crossed under her breasts. Her hair flowed over one shoulder and down past her elbow. Despite their conflicts, seeing her again somehow eased his pain. His mind flashed to his last vision of her, standing destroyed at the zero-G courts.

He let loose a heavy breath and looked down at the table. "I don't know. Are you sure you want to sit with me? I wasn't very kind to you yesterday."

"Maybe you had good reason to be angry with me." Her voice was calm.

Her almost-apology released a dam inside him. "How'd you find me?"

When she sat down, her hand brushed his. It felt like an electric shock. He looked down at his hand, half expecting to see burn marks, but it didn't look any different.

"This is where we first met, remember? Right over there at the bar," she said, pointing. "And...uh...I spent some time investigatin' you before I arranged that meeting."

There. The core of the problem. After starting with such a huge lie, how could he trust anything about her?

"Right. Nothing with you is simple, because the whole situation was...arranged."

"No, not all of it." Pain hushed her voice. "I didn't arrange to like you so much."

"Even so, I'm sorry about being angry yesterday. I could have handled it better. I wanted to." He paused and realized he'd been ambiguous. "Handle it better, that is."

"It hurt, Jake. But what hurt most was you were right. I came on to you with false pretenses."

He kept his eyes on the table. The mention of false pretenses set his jaw again, but he didn't want to be angry with her. He clamped his eyes shut for a moment.

"What I said yesterday is still true," she continued. "I didn't even know it until I said it, but you are the most interestin' man I've ever met. You're smart and athletic. I like the way you think. I like the way you move. I like *you*." She shrugged and gave him a hot little smile, "And…you turn me on like a hot stove."

He had looked up at her just in time to catch the heat. He felt the color rise in his face. "Yeah. Me too."

"I wish with all my heart," she said, leaning toward him, "I'd met you for something other than…our goals."

He gave a wry chuckle. "I really wish you had, too. I don't know what I can trust about you." Taking another breath, he said, "But here we are. What do we do about it now?"

"Do about which?" She lowered her voice. "Us…or the offer?"

"Both, I guess." His heart softened and he laughed helplessly. *Damn it, I do like her. I don't know what to do.*

࿐ ✳ ࿐

Zofia had to breach this gap. Her heart raced. She reached out to touch his hand, one of those Solity-disapproved gestures. It made him nervous enough he glanced around the mostly-empty room. She kept her voice quiet enough not to go beyond the confines of their booth.

"That's the crux of it all, isn't it? I like you. A lot. But I couldn't live with myself if I didn't also do everythin' I can to change Solity and to stop this comin' war. I can't give up what I'm doin'. So, what happens with us is really up to you."

Jake matched her quiet voice. "Your work with the…" He waved a hand instead of saying the name. "…is scary. I've always believed in Solity, been the dutiful patriot. How can I give up all I've accomplished, to fight for something as ephemeral as improvement?"

Then he slumped in his chair.

Her breath slumped with him. *Oh, no. He must have something else.*

"But today has added to my problems," he said. "It's been a bad day. I'm glad you found me, because I need to talk."

"Yeah, I hadn't said anythin' yet, but you look like a walkin' disaster area. What's with the bandages?"

His warm scent drifted across the table when he reached for a nacho, and a tingle of desire shivered through her, warring with her need to think this through.

"I got caught up in a protest this morning, a fire-bombing of a store. One of the resistance things." He held up his forearm. "They knocked me down onto the slidewalk."

"Oh, I'm so sorry." She touched the bandage gently. "I didn't know of a protest today. It must have been another cell."

His brow furrowed. "What do you mean, 'cell'?"

"Oh. That's what we call each small group. They're all kept separate like jail cells. Most of us don't know what the others are doin', or even who they are. You met my cell at that discussion group."

"Ah. Okay." He paused. "But the physical injuries weren't the worst of it today."

"There's more?"

"Later in the day, I was called to the Assignment Office." He looked away and rubbed his eyebrow. He had difficulty admitting the rest. "Solity has reduced my benefits. I'm getting fewer allotments, and I have to move to a smaller apartment. But I still have to do the same work."

"What? You've gotta be kiddin' me." She sat up straight, eyes wide. "I thought you were doin' well in your work. Shoot, you're bein' mentored by one of the Council Directors."

"Yeah. I figure it's got to be the director's doing. He's displeased with my lack of fast progress."

"So, this is goin' to make you work faster, to demote you?"

Jake clenched his jaw. "Interesting, that's what I've been thinking, too."

She reached out to hold his hand in both of hers.

"I'm so sorry, Jake. I've heard of this happenin'. It's horrible."

"I'm as angry with Denmark as I was with you yesterday. I thought the man had my best interests at heart. I thought he was my mentor. But it seems all he wants is results."

She nodded. "One of the deepest problems with Solity is the way it's segmented into castes. At the top, like Denmark, those with power get all the goodies, and they do everythin' they can to advance their power. At the bottom are the people of the Warrens, who just exist from day to day. Those of us in the middle get the worst of it from both ends. We're too intelligent to just get by, but we never get the benefits that come with power."

Jake's mouth fell open. He relaxed his shoulders and looked into her eyes. "Do you know...one of the things I admire most about you is your ability to get to the root of our problems."

She felt like purring at his praise, but the bleakness of yesterday was still with her. "Which problems? Us, or Solity? So far, I don't think I'm doin' such a good job on the 'us' part."

He laughed gently. "I think you're doing a great job on the 'us' part, but this time I was talking about Solity." Then he thought a moment, eyes still locked on hers. "Perhaps, in our case, the two are pretty intertwined."

She cocked her head, questioning.

"I mean," he continued, "my being with you is tangled up with Denmark's power. You want to soften Solity's control. He wants to make it stronger."

"What about you? Are you ready to make any decision yet?" she asked.

"About us, or about Solity?" he chuckled, firing her own question back to her.

She shrugged helplessly, still holding his hands. "About both, I think."

He looked down at the table, apparently thinking hard. She kept silent and watched him.

What's he weighing? This has got to be hard for him. He has always believed in Solity, but he's forced to build some war weapon. I know he'd rather stop war, and we could do it together. But I've got to rebuild his trust.

"Great stars, I don't know, yet. You're asking us to risk our lives for a dream. This is all rather...intimidating." He looked up quickly. "Oh. It's not you, Zofia. I've got no doubts about wanting to be with you."

His words relieved her so much, she let loose her husky laugh. "That's good to know. I've always wanted someone to tag along with me."

Then she went serious and looked at him intently. "Do you know that's the first time you've said somethin' like that? I've wondered if you wanted to be with me."

"Of course I do." He sat up straight, sucking in a quick breath. "Haven't I said that already?"

"No, you haven't." She spread her hands. "It's good to hear."

He gave a wry chuckle. "Well, that's one on me. I guess I haven't been as open as I thought." He stopped to collect his words. "But I don't know what Yitzak wants us to do. His business is very risky. We might die. I don't know what we can accomplish, or what's the probability of success."

Her heart skipped. *He said "we."*

"Oh, sure," she laughed again. "Talk about death like an engineer. 'Probability.' Sheesh."

He laughed with her. "I *am* an engineer. Can't help that."

She softened her voice. "I spoke with Yitzak today. I had to. I was so devastated by our fight yesterday I needed someone to talk to."

"I'm sorry."

She waved it away. "It happened. We're movin' past it...aren't we?"

Jake nodded and gave a small smile. She saw he was beginning to trust her. The touch of their hands helped, too.

"Yitzak had an offer for you," she said. "Instead of the discussion group tomorrow, he'd like you to come Friday night to his lab for a demo of his prototype transpath."

CHAPTER 15

The best way to convince someone is to show them.

—*Collected Sayings of Yitzak Goren* by Ellen Thranadil, Tileus Press 439 A.T.

FRIDAY, 33 QUARTEMBER, 416 A.T.

The rest of the team had departed for the day, leaving Jake private time to ponder a dangerous glitch he'd discovered in the test data. When the supercooled laser temperatures rose through nine degrees Kelvin, the lasers momentarily lost focus. That would be disastrous, releasing the antimatter prematurely. He still had to figure out what to do about it.

The alarm he'd set went off. Time to go to Yitzak's lab. Zofia had given him the room number, two floors up at the other end of the same building. He shut down the antimatter lab, leaving the glowing dot in the care of the monitors Indy had set up.

Up two lift tubes, he went to an interior area he'd never seen. The hallway smelled stale. Every door had a security lock, most of them labelled only with a room number. He knocked at door number 5218. The door was different than the rest, a heavy door with the copper fingers of a Faraday cage on the door edges.

Yitzak opened the door, his blue eyes twinkling while he ushered him in. "Hello, hello. I'm glad to see you. Zofia's already here."

☙ ✳ ❧

She'd been waiting with anxious anticipation. Their last meeting had gone well, for both her Lazarite and personal goals. She was relieved Jake had followed through on coming. She was also eager to experience what Yitzak had for them.

"I'm particularly glad to see you again, Jake," Yitzak said, shaking hands with him. "I was afraid we'd frightened you off."

Jake took a deep breath. "I can't say I'm completely comfortable with what you're asking yet. But I'm willing to learn more—and to keep your secrets."

Zofia raised a shoulder. "Secrets. Yah, we do keep secrets. I'm so sorry we've had to."

"Doubts are normal," said Yitzak. "Fears can also be normal. I gave you the basic idea at the restaurant. In this lab, I can prove the reality." He led them into the space and added, "This room is shielded. Your imps will not report what we say."

Jake stopped in surprise. "Do our imps report everything we say?"

Yitzak stopped also and turned to face him. "Of course, my boy. Didn't you know that? If they wish, Solity can use your imp to listen to everything you say. That's a large part of what Sentinel Shield does."

Jake looked at Zofia. "Have we been careful enough in our conversations?"

She hesitated. "Mostly. It's always possible."

"But we were talking about the Lazarites and your part in it. Isn't that dangerous?"

"Yes, it can be," she said, "but they can't monitor everyone everywhere. Their system looks for key words and phrases; if we avoid saying 'Lazarite' or 'bomb' or 'protest'—or other words like that—they probably won't catch it. Mostly, we avoid any serious talk unless we're in a safe place away from the InfoNet. Sometimes, we have to take the risk. When it's very important, we have ways to block them—but see, blocks are also dangerous because they can raise red flags."

She caught herself and stopped. She was still so nervous, she tended to explain too much.

Jake put his hand to his forehead. "For star's sake, I'd never thought of it. That's another level of risk. With the sensitivity of my work, they probably watch me more closely than most. We need to be more careful."

Good. He's thinkin' again, instead of just being angry. Maybe we can get through this together.

"If you join us," said Yitzak, "we can give you more power over your imp. But you're right; we need caution. In this room, in any case, what we say is safe. I convinced Director Denmark my experiments needed the shielding."

Yitzak shifted topics. "And that's the point. I'm happy to see you here, Jake, because you are unique. You can strike a blow for us all no one else can. I believe you...were chosen."

Zofia was surprised at Yitzak's choice of words.

Jake staggered back a step. "Chosen? Who would choose me? And why?"

As always, Yitzak's rapid delivery startled Zofia. She knew Jake was a highly intelligent man, but Yitzak operated on a completely different level.

"Before I can answer that, I need to show you what we have for you." Yitzak led them into the next room.

Zofia had been in Yitzak's office a few times, but never into his lab. She saw a large cabinet against one wall, complete with tangles of wire, waveguides in several sizes, and rapidly blinking computer lights. At all four corners of the room stood cone-shaped towers two meters tall, connected to the cabinet by metal structures lining the wall. When she peered closer, she realized the structures supported wires so tiny they looked like strands of hair.

"Amazing, Yitzak," said Jake. "What frequencies are you sending through those waveguides? They must be extremely high."

Then Zofia realized they weren't wires but waveguides.

"Not frequencies, my boy. I'm using them to transmit sub-atomic particles. Or particle waves, if you prefer. Remember, I told you my transpath relies on particle waves perceived by the brain. Now, imagine what life would be like if you were a croombear."

Without further explanation, Yitzak touched a small pad on the cabinet. The computer lights flickered, and a tiny blue circle on its front illuminated.

When the device came on, Zofia felt a strange intrusion. Gradually, it seemed new feelings and ideas became part of her mind. Startled, her eyes opened wide and she stepped back from the equipment, but it made no change to the invasion. Before she could react further, though, Yitzak touched the pad again and the feeling faded.

"What...was that?" she stammered.

"This is what I brought you two here to experience." Yitzak paused. "Surprising it may be, but the transpath is not harmful in any way. Notice we can turn it off as easily as turning it on."

Jake shook his head to clear it. "What was I feeling?"

Zofia was also shaken. "I was feelin' it, too."

"In that short time, you two felt the beginning of a deep empathic connection with anyone else in the field—in this case, all three of us. Imagine what it would be like if you were deaf and suddenly given hearing. Like that, this device gives you a new sense that allows us to feel each other's emotions."

Zofia shook her head in amazement. She looked again at the miniscule waveguides and cone antennas. Even her limited technical knowledge gave her a sense of awe at what Yitzak had accomplished.

"I'll turn it on again now and explain to you what we expect from it." While he spoke, Yitzak again touched the pad and the light came on.

This time, Jake wasn't as surprised by the feelings. While he listened to the scientist explain further, he sensed Yitzak's honesty, integrity, and zeal for his goals. He felt Zofia's intensity for change. He also sensed her surprise and caution at these new feelings, just like his own. The feelings came into Jake in the same way as hearing and smell, an additional self-evident sense.

"The transpath is not what Solity tasked me to produce," Yitzak explained, "but I've done it anyway. Director Denmark has experienced this same effect you are feeling, though without a proper explanation. He thinks I'm supporting the war effort by creating a device to control the minds of our soldiers. Often, soldiers' personal doubts weaken their resolve to fight. Even in long-ago history, studies showed most soldiers purposely miss their targets during war. They have difficulty bringing themselves to fire directly at the enemy."

Through the transpath, Jake felt much more from Yitzak than his words. Distaste for weaponry and war was paramount. Resentment at the director factored in, as well as personal fortitude to do the right thing regardless of Denmark's power. Jake realized Yitzak was trapped, as was he, into doing distasteful work. Jake's trust in the man took a leap forward.

Yitzak continued, "I've been unable to make a true mind control device, because motivations, words, and other complex thoughts seem to be beyond our current technology to create." He looked down for a moment and shook his head. "I also admit to great reluctance to create such a technology, because I'm sure Solity would use it to manipulate all of us, not just the soldiers."

Zofia nodded emphatically. "You bet they would."

While she spoke Jake also sensed certainty of the controlling nature of Solity coming from both of them. He was astonished at the clarity of understanding he gained when her simple words were augmented by the emotional connection of the transpath.

When Yitzak continued, his words echoed in Jake's mind with the sense of conviction that underlaid all the man conveyed. "Indeed. I wish to change Solity. This empathic communications device can do so. Within the transpath field, it is impossible to deceive because everyone senses the emotions you feel. The field enforces honesty and understanding to a level diplomacy has never managed to achieve. National diplomats could actually work toward agreements without hidden secrets."

Jake felt the energy behind Yitzak's words. He also sensed Zofia's emotional reactions, and he knew both of them perceived his own emotions. With the depth of understanding he got through the transpath, Jake wanted to help Yitzak achieve his goals. The man's conviction was captivating enough to convince.

"The device seems amazing, Yitzak," he said. "Okay. I want to help."

While he spoke, Jake felt Zofia's reaction to his words, a maturing of faith and trust in him, coupled with the personal attraction she'd shown him recently.

Yitzak answered, "I'm glad you do, because we are going to ask a great deal from you, Jake. But first, I need to give you another reason to trust." He reached to the cabinet and turned the transpath off. "Now, please probe your own memories and motivations without the connection active. Do you believe we have in any way manipulated you?"

When the light turned off, Jake was suddenly thrust into an isolation chamber. His normal senses were still active—sight, hearing, smell, touch, taste—but he felt crippled when he looked into Yitzak's and Zofia's eyes. His understanding of each of them was limited to what he could infer from facial expression, body language, and words. The historical human communications now seemed wholly inadequate.

At the same time, he remembered clearly the emotions he had received from both. His fingers pinched a fold of his coveralls, and he looked down at them. He didn't question the truth of his eyes in seeing shapes and colors, nor of his touch in discerning the fabric. The transpath gave him a new sense like those. The emotions he'd felt through the transpath were as real as the coveralls under his own fingers. Just like the cloth, he did not doubt the truth of Yitzak's integrity or Zofia's deep caring for him.

As an after-effect, his body felt alive with adrenaline, as if he'd just finished an intense zero-G match. This new sense amazed him.

He shook his head, answering Yitzak's question. "No. Everything you've shown me—everything I've felt through the transpath from both of you—is true. I still have the same fears and desires I've had before. You've only opened a door to a new sense I never knew we could have."

"Good. The last thing I wish is for you to doubt what you've experienced or to think we have controlled your mind, especially after you leave here. Now, let's turn it back on for our discussion."

The blue light came back on, and Jake's head was suddenly connected again. The connection was like turning the light on after a room had been plunged into darkness, or the sound of an orchestra after sudden silence. Jake locked eyes with Zofia. Her desire for him nearly overwhelmed him, yet he also sensed her doubts about how being with him might change her. They spoke nothing, sharing only the emotions. In addition to her feelings for him, he also perceived her reaction to the feelings she got from him. Her doubts eased when she felt his desire for her. Everything he felt from her filled him with joy—with the exception of her zeal for change in Solity, which raised his fears about risk.

He reached out to hold both her hands, the first time he'd done so.

"Is this really possible?" he asked. "Can we reconcile how much we care for each other with the differences in our lives?"

"I don't know," she said in wonder. "But the more I feel from you through the transpath, the more I want to be with you."

He felt her blossoming joy, and it filled his own heart with hope.

Yitzak cleared his throat, interrupting them. He seemed amused at their personal connection. "Yes, yes, of course. Young love and all that. Is this going to be a problem?"

His merriment embarrassed Jake, who dropped Zofia's hands and turned back to this charismatic leader.

"We still need to make plans, you two." Yitzak was chuckling while he spoke. "You will have a lifetime to get to know each other."

Jake felt Yitzak's emotions turn serious. "Jake, I said you were chosen. I made that choice, but I felt guided. Unlike most in Prime, I have faith in

Elláh and His hand in our lives. You appeared with the right skills and availability at the right time, and I don't believe in coincidence. Very few have sufficient knowledge of particle physics to rebuild the transpath. And if you go to Tileus, it strikes a double blow for the Lazarites because it takes you away from building your bomb."

Jake felt a sudden shock through the transpath, coming from Zofia.

"A bomb?" she asked. Her transmitted emotions were practically flailing. "Bucko, you're building a bomb? What kind of bomb?"

Jake let out a heavy breath and looked up at the ceiling. "Dammit, Yitzak. That's classified information." He knew his emotions were radiating dismay and fear.

Yitzak only chuckled, amusement filling his demeanor. "My boy, I know much of what Denmark is doing, whether or not it's classified." He turned to Zofia. "He's been working on an antimatter bomb more powerful than anything Tileus has. But he's right. That's classified information you shouldn't share—or even know."

Zofia's alarm radiated into Jake. "Why would you be workin' on something so destructive? You told us the other day you wanted to stop wars."

Jake shrugged, feeling more than a little helpless. "It's what I've been tasked to do. It's been my Assignment for six years." Confusion tangled his thoughts. "Until I met you, I trusted Solity. I did what they told me to do. But...I didn't like it. I wanted to do something positive."

He felt her alarm transformed into caring for him. His own confusion and dismay seemed to trigger an even deeper compassion in her. Impulsively, she wrapped her arms around him.

"Jake, I'm so sorry. Shoot, you've been doing somethin' you hate all this time."

Her scent, the warmth of her body against his, her deep empathy for his confusion, combined to awaken a surprisingly sexual response. His blood rushed to his head and his breath quickened. He tightened his arms around her, pressing her body against his. His pulse raced. The transpath magnified each response, his emotions transmitted to her and her emotions feeding his. Sudden arousal warred inside them both against their long-ingrained obedience to Solity rules. The intensity of it caused them to spring apart again. Jake sucked in a sharp breath, and couldn't seem to take his eyes off hers. He was panting like a brol in heat.

Yitzak clapped his hands sharply twice. "Enough, you two. I can see the transpath might have other uses than I envisioned." He chortled. "Rather powerful ones, I suspect."

Jake felt himself blushing. He forcibly turned back to Yitzak, his blood singing.

"For now, my boy, you need to think about how much you are actually willing to give. Your allegiance? Your resources? Your livelihood?" He paused and added, "Your life?"

"My life?" Jake asked.

Yitzak nodded. "Possibly." He waved a hand at the roomful of equipment. "This prototype will never suffice the way it is. We must rebuild it, much smaller, so it can be transported, used in different places, replicated. My vision is the transpath can become the fulcrum on which humanity finally learns to understand itself."

Then he shrugged. "At least for now, we must build a version to help the leaders of Tileus and Prime understand each other. And that means you and Zofia will have to risk yourselves to escape from Prime and get it to Tileus"

Jake shook off the powerful feelings of lingering desire. He avoided looking at Zofia beside him, completely aware she could sense his feelings just as much as he did hers. He focused on the task and asked, "You said at the restaurant it cannot be built here, right?"

Yitzak nodded. "True. More research and experimentation are necessary to reduce its size. Research into particle physics, psychology, and physiology. Jake, your knowledge and experience are the best I have found. Are you willing to go to Tileus and do it?" His earnestness, his concern, his fears, all came through the transpath to fill his words with a depth that gave Jake a fluttery euphoria in his belly.

Jake stood, open-mouthed, considering the question. This was the moment to decide. While he weighed the balance, he knew the emotions he felt were transparent to them through the marvelous agency of the transpath.

Pros and cons. He thought about his demotion and the impersonal disdain of the Assignment clerk. The many times Denmark had burst into his lab to push harder on the team. The depth of emotional connection he'd found with Zofia. Denmark's large office upstairs, and all the director's wonderful possessions—compared with the meager belongings Jake had still to move to a reduced apartment. More time with Zofia in Tileus. The resentment flaring up in the streets of Oriens and Timpi. Getting out of the constant repression he now saw in Prime. The trust he felt for Yitzak. But most of all, he could set aside all the problems of injustice and explore a life with Zofia.

After the previous two weeks of turmoil, he made his decision.

"Yes. I've got to do this, whatever it takes. I'm in."

CHAPTER 16

Before: Fear justified avoiding the hard choices.

After: Fear is exposed for what it is: the truth-destroyer.

—*Before and After* by Ellen Thranadil, Tileus Press 446 A.T.

"We can't do this very often, Yitzak," said Franklin Edobar. "The tables here at the Dilly Deli are secure, but the monitors know we met." Franklin always had to be careful of his Lazarite meetings to avoid the Sentinel Shield system and its artificial intelligence.

"My work and reputation are in many fields, Franklin. Last year, I published a monograph on algorithms for capital distribution. We could be discussing that. I'm fairly certain our meetings will not raise concern." Yitzak paused for a moment. "But I do agree with you. There is no sense tempting Lachesis to insert new threads into our spun lives."

Franklin's mind bounced from the reference. "What? Your allusions sometimes astound me, Yitzak. Who is Lachesis?"

Yitzak smiled. "Mythology from old Earth. She is the one of the three Fates who weaves events. Clotho tends the beginnings, and Atropos seals the endings. But I have good news for you today, which is why I asked to meet. Palatin has agreed to our plan."

"That is good news indeed. He's willing to go to Tileus?"

"Yes. Yesterday, I gave him and Zofia a demonstration of the transpath. The final sand of his personal hourglass dropped through. Zofia did an excellent job of interesting him—in more than one way—but Denmark also helped." Yitzak had a twinkle in his eye when he said the last.

Franklin couldn't help but bite. "Denmark? How did he help?"

"He did his usual heavy-handed 'management,' trying to motivate Palatin by reducing his benefits for slow performance. As you might expect, the young man is rather upset about it."

"I understand. I worked for Denmark for many years. His methods often sicken me."

"So, I am meeting with Palatin this afternoon to give him technical knowledge. We must now find a way to spring Palatin free to make the trip. He won't be coming back, but he will need an excuse to be gone for a few days to get out of Prime."

Franklin nodded. This would require some political manipulation, which was his bailiwick. "I'll work on it."

For the first time in six years, Jake gave himself permission to be late to work. Riding the slidewalk through empty streets felt awkward, but he was still floating on the excitement of his commitment. He'd spent the weekend with Zofia and Yitzak to further the plans, feeling freer than he'd felt in several years.

Cheers and laughter greeted him when he entered the lab, but they weren't directed toward him. The entire team was gathered around a workbench strewn with party goods.

"Boss! You finally got here," said Afonso. "Sam's got great news."

Jake stepped in and closed the door. Good news? He liked the idea. "What's the good news? And how did you get cake and ice cream in the morning?"

Everyone turned to him. Indy laughed and said, "Oh, Minya's got connections at the bakery—"

Sam cut him off. "I'm going to run a distribution shop!"

Jake did a double-take. "What? You're leaving us? You've done such good things here, I hate to see you go. But that's great news for you. That's your dream, isn't it?"

"Yeah, I just got the new Assignment last night. Working with you was temporary. I've organized your stuff about as much as I can, and I can't really help you with the engineering."

Jake shook Sam's hand with enthusiasm. "I'm glad for you, Sam. You're getting to do just what you wanted. You are one of the lucky ones."

The excited chatter went on around him while he stood and grinned. Sam's news added to the good feelings from his weekend.

Zofia had helped him move his apartment. Doing the unpleasant chore with her made it a delight. Afterwards, he spent most of two days in Yitzak's lab getting an infodump on the transpath design. They went over every part of it, and Yitzak gave him two identical holochips with the data—one for him and one for Zofia as backup. Yitzak was also working on a way to get him off work for a few days so he could make his escape.

Zofia had modified his imp yesterday, touching his neck with her soft hands, something he'd enjoyed. He'd seen her give the same mod to her cellmates when he'd first met them, but had not understood then what was happening. He could now turn off the automatic imp reporting with a subvocalized command.

"When you turn reportin' off," she'd said, "you can still use the InfoNet, but your imp won't report its location unless it's given a specific override by someone in authority."

Then she'd added, "But be very careful where and when you turn it on and off. You must be in an InfoNet hole, or the sudden stop or start of reporting might trigger Solity monitors. Your signal strength should be zero or one."

This morning in the Defense building, the new imp feature felt to Jake like a boil on his nose. He knew in his head no one would know, but carrying such a capability made him feel as if it marked him visibly, somehow, as Lazarite. Would Solity be able to detect the change in his imp? Zofia said no, but was she sure?

He returned his thoughts to the celebration. Minya was serving up the ice cream and cake. He got a share big enough to make his sweet tooth smile. "When do you leave, Sam?"

"Today, boss. I hope that's okay."

"Of course. If that's what Solity wants, that's what we get." The common words felt bitter to him, and he laughed to cover his true feelings. "We'll muddle along without you."

Indy joined in the humor. "But we'll get all disorganized again."

Behind Jake, the security lock clacked, and two older men entered. One was tall and crisp, with touches of grey in his hair and eyes that took in everything. The other was shorter, somewhat unkempt, looking academic but competent. They stopped in surprise upon seeing the party.

"Hello?" said the tall man in a dry voice. "Are we in the right place? We're looking for Jacoby Palatin and an antimatter lab."

Jake stepped forward with a smile and held out his hand. "We're just finishing up a little celebration. I'm Jake Palatin."

"I'm Rodrick Griffin and this is Suma Tanaka. We've been Assigned to help you." While he shook hands, he looked at the party materials with disdain. "It looks like the director was right; you could use some help with team focus."

All Jake's light-heartedness fell through the floor. His stomach tied into a knot. "This is team building eent, a worthwhile bit of festivity," he said. He waved a hand to Indy, and the team started cleaning up. "So, were you sent to be critical, or are you going to help? What can you do?"

"I'm a team leader with eighteen successful projects behind me. I've been Assigned to show you how to be successful, too. Suma is a respected particle physicist who will review your results."

Jake looked at Suma and his heart fell further. The man had sparse hair and gimlet eyes; he was already scanning the lab equipment. Jake recognized him. He'd seen the man's picture in professional publications associated with the advanced work in particle physics for ansible communications.

"Welcome, Dr. Tanaka," Jake said. "I've heard of you. It will be an honor to work with you." While he said the words, Jake's mind was back-pedaling as fast as it would go. *Now I don't want this bomb to succeed, but Suma Tanaka could make that happen. This is just what I didn't need, for Denmark to throw a couple of outside experts into my project.* Then he interrupted his own thought. *But it won't be my project much longer.*

"Good to meet you also, Jake," said the scientist. "I've been briefed on your work, and it is quite advanced." His praise seemed sincere, but he spoke with the arrogance of an established expert. "Perhaps I can help you solve whatever problems are holding back your final success."

"Perhaps you could. We'll have to go over the science with you." *This is a disaster. I can't have them succeed. What can I do?* Things were moving too quickly. *I need time to think. First, I've got to divert these two.*

He made a quick decision what to do with them for now. "This party was a celebration for a team member who's moving on to another Assignment. We can fit you two into his cubicle."

Jake led the men to Sam's desk. "Sam, it's been great having you here. You've done excellent work for us, and I'm glad you're getting what you want. But now I need space for these two. Do you mind if I install them here?"

Sam shrugged, his joy bubbling through everything he did. "Not at all, boss. I've already got my things together. I can leave. You'll be able to find me at the distribution store on Wently Street."

"Thanks, Sam. Good luck to you." Turning to Rodrick and Suma, Jake said, "We'll get another holo station in here today. In the meantime, it might be best if I give you access to our project plans and designs through this station. You can familiarize yourselves with what we're doing."

Rodrick looked around the lab, apparently seeking any empty spaces. There were none, but Jake watched his eyes linger on Jake's own slightly-larger leader cubicle. Rodrick responded, "This paired cubicle can do for now. The director wants us all to move as fast as possible, so we'll start immediately."

Indy pulled a spare chair out of his own cubicle. "You can have this extra chair."

Suma nodded. "Thanks." He and Rodrick sat down and opened the holo station.

Jake filled them in on the basic project goals and status, then guided them to the core files about the project science and design. "I'll organize some of the more recent data for you. I should have it ready by the time you've been through the core files." He expected that would give him a couple of hours to figure out what to do about this new development.

While he stepped across the aisle to his desk, the lock clacked yet again. Director Denmark strode in.

"Good," he said with a hearty smile. "I see Rodrick and Suma are already here. Jake, join us. I've got some direction for you."

Damn. No time to think yet. "Yes, sir."

106

"I've already spoken to all three of you. This bomb needs to be ready now. War with Tileus could happen practically any day. Without it, our military forces are equal with theirs. With it, we can win a war easily." He turned directly to Jake. "Palatin. Show me your progress."

Jake felt a flash of angry resentment; his demotion still burned and the addition of these two outside experts embarrassed him.

He suddenly noticed Denmark's purple coverall. Better tailored than others, made from smooth material, it looked much more comfortable. He had never noticed this before.

Flustered by his realization, he hoped Denmark hadn't noticed his pause. "Yes, Director. We're still assembling the supercooled lasers. But on Friday, we got some new data from another test. It's good news. It shows we can increase the containment field ten percent by also lowering the temperature of the fixed magnets—"

"Good grief, ten percent isn't nearly enough, Palatin. You know that, don't you?"

"Yes, Director, I do. It's only an incremental improvement, but it shows—"

"We need you to be working smarter, Palatin. We need breakthroughs, not 'incremental improvements.' Right?"

"Yes, Director." Jake glanced at Rodrick, whose smirk revealed a superior attitude. Suma focused on the holo-projected design data, though he had perked up at Jake's mention of the containment field.

Denmark continued, "If we don't have your bomb working in time, Verdant Prime will waste a lot of lives in this coming war. Lives, my boy. Those deaths would be your fault, Palatin, the real effect of your...incremental progress."

"Yes, Director." Jake felt his face burning.

"I would think, after your correction last week, you'd be spending every possible moment in the lab. Your new apartment can't be very comfortable. So, what were your working hours this past week? Did your team work during the weekend?"

Jake knew Denmark likely knew every minute of their work hours. He blushed deeper. This was even worse because Rodrick and Suma—and Jake's entire team—were witnessing Denmark's verbal lashing. "We've been...uh...making progress."

"Progress." Denmark spat out. He glared at Jake, who became more nervous in the lie. "Right." Denmark looked to Rodrick, who nodded agreement. Another long pause left Jake's hands shaking. "We are watching your progress closely. Or lack of it. Overtime is expected, much overtime. This work is critical to the war effort; you must not be doing anything else."

Jake could only nod as his throat closed up.

The director strode to the door, then paused again with his hand on the knob. He turned back and nailed Jake with his burning gaze. "Wasting time with a useless Technology wench is not helpful." He pulled the door open and left.

Jake sucked in a fiery breath that seared his soul. *They know.* They must be watching him, even away from work. Yitzak had told him imp reporting made everything visible to them. Without knowing that, Jake had been foolish in what he'd said and done in the open. But the more he thought about it, the more his fear turned to anger, to determination to do something new and different.

Rodrick filled the silence with his sneering voice. "Perhaps you should prepare that data for us, Jake."

"I'll do that." He moved to his own cubicle, his mind racing.

He realized Denmark was setting up to replace him, while ensuring the success of the project under Rodrick's leadership. Six years of work, on something he never wanted to do, and this was all the trust he'd earned?

He'd had a marvelous weekend making plans to build the transpath. With Yitzak's solid science, Jake could see the path forward. It would be challenging but feasible to make the device portable, much easier than his technical problems with the bomb. He finished yesterday's session unable to sit still. He'd moved around Yitzak's lab like a flitting bird, looking into every detail of the prototype.

In contrast, this morning came crashing down like an avalanche into a happy valley. The reality of his commitment came home to him. He wanted to leave. He intended to go to Tileus as soon as possible. But Denmark was increasing his hooks into Jake. He couldn't let this happen. In particular, he couldn't leave this bomb behind. Prime would use it to take over Tileus before he could ever get the transpath into action.

Jake's jaw was clamped tight, and his blood boiled. Every time he looked over the cubicle wall at Rodrick and Suma, poring over his project data, he resented Denmark all over again. He needed a way to ensure the bomb would never work, even after he left. The solution suddenly came to him.

I'll sabotage my own project.

The plan popped into his head fully formed. Last week, he'd noticed a dangerous anomaly on the supercooled lasers at nine degrees Kelvin. No one else knew about it yet. The glitch was only momentary, but at sub-atomic speeds, the fleeting loss in focus would be like a year-long holiday for the antimatter. The latest device design used external power to keep the temperature safely at four degrees during storage. When they put the bomb into delivery mode by aircraft or missile, it switched to weaker internal power. The design allowed for the temperature to rise as much as thirty degrees during delivery while still maintaining the lasers. Now, however, he knew when the temperature passed through nine degrees, it would trigger this newly-discovered malfunction. It would be devastating; the antimatter would release somewhere between launch and target. Premature explosion, every time.

From his own station, Jake quickly brought up the recent test files. His heart pounded, and he glanced up at the two intruders in his lab. Knowing what he did was illegal, even treasonous, he modified the data in the test files to hide the anomaly. The files now showed successful tests.

He buried the falsified test data into the mass of other recent tests, as a package for Suma Tanaka. It would take the scientist days to go through the data, and he would still never see the now-hidden flaw.

CHAPTER 17

During his reign, Denmark weaponized the Solity Guards under his authority, using them to advance his personal goals. It is likely he believed his goals to be in the interests of Solity, but they were nonetheless his own.

—*An Annotated History of Verdant* by Ellen Thranadil, Tileus Press 442 A.T.

TWODAY, 38 QUARTEMBER, 416 A.T.

Shelton Overlock took vicious delight in the director's office, the position of power. He looked around at all Denmark's possessions, prizes of a successful career. Overlock's own "possessions" were of a more psychological nature. His position with the director gave him the wherewithal to indulge his own cravings. Some might call him psychopathic, but he didn't see much difference between his thirsts and those of others.

Today, their plans were coming smoothly to fruition. Overlock had worked with the Solity Guards leader in Timpi, who was now carrying through the plans.

"When do you spring your trap, Lieutenant?" growled Denmark into the air. His imp connection was echoed to the room so Overlock could take part.

Kai Ariki's voice answered from Timpi. "Any day now, Director. We've got round-the-clock surveillance on the boat captain and his mate, everywhere except at sea. They've attended our false discussion group twice, staying quiet in the back of the room. But we're listening to their conversations through the imps, and we know what they're planning. They're going to invite us to join their Lazarites at the next meeting."

"Excellent progress. Let us know before you close the jaws. I want Overlock there." Denmark's eyes sparkled with dark delight, and Overlock felt the excitement of impending action course through him.

Overlock added his voice to the air. "I'll be there, Ariki. You can count on it."

"Is there anything else, Director?" Ariki sounded smooth and efficient.

"Only for you to make sure it happens as planned. We want these people, and we want their entire network. Keep them alive. I want to know who's directing them from Oriens."

Denmark closed the call and turned to Overlock. "Now, what about our errant engineer? What are you doing with him?"

"We've had Palatin under close surveillance for most of the last week, Director, ever since you demoted him. He's doing things in his off-time he shouldn't."

"Like what?"

"He's still meeting with that Technology girl. Together, they've visited several places unusual for him. Their conversations verge on unauthorized fraternization—and on sedition."

"Damn. We can't allow that, Shelton. Keep the pressure on. I confronted him yesterday about the girlfriend. Have you found out anything more about her?"

"She's dangerous, Director, and a bit of an enigma. On the surface, she's just a maintenance person fixing people's implants. That means she goes all over the city and has contact with lots of people. Every once in a while, though, we get indications she's something more. She and Palatin have talked about the Lazarites. She took him to a discussion group, though nothing happened. It's not clear exactly what she's doing with him, but it looks like grooming to me."

"We're going to have to tighten the screws even more on Palatin, then. We need to keep him in line. Should we pick her up?"

"That would certainly make him take notice, but I'm thinking she might have even more use to us. She can lead us to others. For instance, she made mention to him of Yitzak Goren, and she took Palatin to Goren's lab."

"Goren?" The director seemed stunned. "What would his work have to do with Palatin?"

"I certainly don't know, sir. You've never let me know what Goren's doing."

Denmark sharpened his eyes on Overlock. "Hmph. That's a technology I'm keeping to myself until it's time." Then his demeanor softened. "You'll be in on it when it comes up, I assure you. I don't do much without you."

Overlock dipped his head. "Thank you, Director. About Palatin, though, I'd love to bring him in for questioning. We could probably get some excellent data from him now." His breath quickened, thinking of the bloody delight he could have with another victim.

Denmark's response was suddenly violent. "No, you can't do that yet. Take control of your urges, man. We've got Palatin where we want him, with pressure from all directions. If he weren't so important to us, I'd have let you wring him dry long ago. As it is, we'll keep him under close surveillance until I get what I want from him. Maybe even have the Guards go around to intimidate him. That ought to keep him in line until we can splatter Tileus with this weapon."

≈ ❈ ≈

Rodrick kept everyone in the lab until 13-00, two hours into the evening. By the time Jake got to his apartment, he hardly had time to eat and sleep before he'd need to arrive again in the morning.

He still had to maintain the appearance of compliance while Yitzak arranged his departure. The tension of Rodrick and Suma probing deeper into the project plans put him on constant edge. On one hand, he was certain no one would discover his sabotage. The data he'd given them showed successful tests of the supercooled lasers. He'd made sure no record remained of the original failed test data, and no record of his changing the file. On the other hand, he worried he might have missed something. More than likely, no one would discover it until they tested the bomb—another concern for Jake, because he had no idea where it would prematurely explode. Who and what might be hurt?

He looked around his new, smaller apartment. A couch and a chair in a living area, a kitchenette in a corner of the room with a small table and two stiff chairs, a bedroom barely big enough for his bed. *It's convenient I don't have much stuff since there isn't any place to put it.* His jaw felt stiff from the tension, and he listened to the noises from the adjacent apartment. Shaking his head, he punched the dispenser for a brew.

A hard knock at the door made him jump.

When he opened the door, two Solity Guards were in the hall. Jake had never before realized how menacing the "ticks" looked from this close. Both wore slick black head to toe, with gold identification and badges. Their faces were hidden behind helmets with bulging dark face shields. Each had a utility belt filled with arcane devices Jake didn't want to know about. He recognized the needle guns in their holsters, which loomed large in his mind.

"Jacoby Palatin, we've had a disturbing report about your associations. Where were you at lunch on Endday?" The two remained standing in the public hallway where anyone could hear. One dropped an artifact from his belt onto the floor. The object scurried to the door and blocked it open.

Jake fought rising panic. *They know.* His blood pounded in his face. He had never before had any interaction with the Guards. He knew Solity could track his position at all times through his implant. He now knew they could also monitor his conversations. So, why would they be asking where he'd been? They should already know. Lies to the authorities were punished severely—but in this case, complete honesty would mean admitting to sedition. He decided a half-truth was best.

"Uh…I went with someone to a café in the Monument district."

The guardsman paused, perhaps checking records. "You were with Zofia Dobrunik, not just 'someone.' Correct?"

"Yes, that's true. We were eating lunch."

"You and Dobrunik have been together frequently. Do you have authorization to fraternize?"

"No, sir. We're just friends." He felt sweat popping out on his forehead.

"Your 'friendship' is pushing the boundaries, Palatin. You're seeing too much of each other to be 'just friends.' You need to apply for fraternization if you wish to continue."

"Yes, sir."

"Has Dobrunik asked you about your General Defense work?"

"No, sir." Jake's heart continued to race. He'd heard Solity Guards could monitor your biometrics just by looking at you, and he was sure his bio functions were going crazy. The sweat was starting to drip on his temple. His hands shook. They would know he was telling half-truths.

"You're sure of that? Has she asked anything that might relate to your work?"

"No, sir, she hasn't."

"Are you aware Dobrunik is under suspicion?"

His heart rate spiked. *Under suspicion for what? I thought she was in the clear.* "I had no idea. We were just talking."

"Has she introduced you to others? People who might have anti-Solity goals?"

Jake saw in his mind a vivid picture of the discussion group he'd met. That might be public record, so he had to acknowledge it. And possibly admitting to that would shield Yitzak. "She took me once to a group that talked about how Solity worked. They seemed to be concerned citizens, not anti-Solity."

"Did they talk about their purposes?"

"I was only there once, sir. It seemed more like a learning group about Solity. They talked about how distribution worked." He forced himself not to rub his sweaty hands.

The two Guards stood perfectly still for a long time, staring at him. For all he knew, they might have been conferring through implants with each other and with others in authority. He remained in place, frozen in fear.

"Jacoby Palatin, be careful. She is a dangerous person. Do not fall into the trap of becoming a risk to Solity. This is your one and only warning." They abruptly turned away and marched down the hall. The device blocking the door followed them, jumping itself up to re-attach to the guardsman's belt.

Jake closed his door and slumped against the wall in a fit of shaking. *Great stars, that was close...too close. What can I do now?*

His hands quivered while he opened the brew he'd ordered and moved to the couch to think. Solity no longer felt like the protective umbrella he'd known all his life. It felt more like a sharp lance aimed at his heart.

He was supposed to meet Zofia for breakfast tomorrow. He'd not yet told her about Denmark's threat yesterday. He'd expected to tell her at breakfast. As much as he wanted to see her again, the Guards had frightened him badly. Could they meet as planned?

She had knowledge of the implants through her work. She knew of areas in Oriens where the signal strength was too weak. She had suggested one of those areas—the Warrens—for breakfast.

But how could he meet her at all, no matter how secure the place? She was under suspicion, and now he knew Solity was watching him, too. He needed to warn her. The thoughts raced in his mind like tight little whirlpools in a stream, going nowhere while the world rushed past. He drew similar circles with his finger in the condensation on the side table, trying to make sense of his conflicting desires. Being with her made him feel excited and whole—but she was dangerous. She wanted him to change Solity, and he'd committed to do it. Now the consequences were coming fast.

That night, he kept waking from terrible dreams. He lay awake with his decisions as tousled as his sweat-soaked bedding.

ॐ ❀ ॐ

WENTDAY, 39 QUARTEMBER, 416 A.T.

The light of morning through his window brought clarity. Meeting Zofia was dangerous, but he was committed to this new path. And to being with her.

I need to be ready. If he were going to be Lazarite, he'd better protect himself in new ways. With no idea what today would bring, he should prepare for anything, including doing a runner. *I'll need some supplies with me.* He filled his normal backpack with some toiletries, basic first-aid materials, a change of clothes, a few food bars and a water bottle. He pulled his pocket knife out of the dresser drawer. *They don't like us to carry even a small knife.* He dropped it into the pack as a small act of defiance against Solity.

He still didn't know when he would depart for Tileus, but he'd meet with Zofia this morning and see what happened.

The slidewalks ended at the edge of the Warrens. His imp gave him a map to the breakfast place Zofia had chosen, but his live connection to the InfoNet faded while he followed the map. Taking the opportunity, he commanded his imp to cease reporting. A block later, his imp showed another brief connection with the InfoNet. The imp might otherwise have betrayed his position in that moment; he was glad he'd turned that function off.

The Quik 'N Easy was small but clean, filled with people in light blue coveralls getting food before work. His entry interrupted the rough conversation and he saw people look up at his light green for a moment before returning to their private talk. Choosing an empty booth near the back, he ordered coffee and put his backpack on the seat beside him. The place had a live waitress instead of service bots, a brusque, faded woman who seemed harried.

Had he come to the right place? His stomach was queasy. Avoiding contact with the other patrons, he kept his eyes on the table.

The waitress set coffee in front of him, sloshing a little over the edge onto the napkin. "Ready to order?" she demanded.

"Not yet. I have someone joining me." He looked up and was relieved to see Zofia enter. "And here she comes. Bring her a coffee, too, please."

The waitress rolled her eyes and walked away without responding.

Jake stood to greet Zofia. She slipped into the booth.

"You're lookin' too nervous, Jake," she said quietly. "I saw that from the door. Stop lookin' around so much."

He gave a brittle laugh and nodded. "You're right." Sitting back down, he held her hand. "Is it okay to talk here?"

"Did you turn off your imp reportin'?" She seemed preoccupied.

"Of course, as soon as I came into the Warrens." He kept his voice down, also.

Zofia said, "Yah, remember it's only the automated position reporting you've turned off. If you're in range of the InfoNet, they can still listen to everythin' you say and hear, including your commands to the imp. They can also turn the reportin' back on by override if you're connected and they know where you are."

"Okay. It still feels like I'm standing out in a crowd when I do it. Doesn't Solity monitor for the unusual?"

"They do," she said. "They're very good at it, with sophisticated algorithms to pick up anything' out of the ordinary. We can rely to some extent on the sheer volume of information to hide what we do, but you..." she paused for emphasis. "You can't hide easily. Because of your work, they probably watch you.

"You asked if it's okay to talk here. My reportin' is turned off, too, and there's no InfoNet connection here. But we have to watch out for people. Most people in the Warrens don't care—but some will turn you in for trifles."

All the time she spoke, Jake saw she was thinking about something else. She seemed nervous, not her usual cheerful self. He decided to ask.

"What's wrong?"

"Solity Guards threatened me last night," she said.

He looked up with shock, meeting her eyes. "Me, too. They came to my apartment." Then he slumped. "It must have been coordinated. I didn't like being helpless. Even more, I realized I have that feeling in small ways all the time."

She shrugged. "Yah, me too."

"I want to live without fear."

Her laugh was prickly. "I'm not sure that's ever possible. There's always fear of somethin'. What did you tell them?"

"Nothing they didn't already know." He looked around the place to see if anyone was listening, and he lowered his voice. "They asked about you, and whether we were fraternizing. I told them we had lunch, just as friends. The Guards acted like they didn't know where we'd been, and they didn't say anything about Yitzak. But they obviously knew more than they let on. I don't know how much they know and didn't say."

She let out a breath, obviously relieved, and squeezed Jake's hand. "Good. That's essentially what I said, too. They were probably checkin' our stories against each other."

"Uh-huh. But there's more. They told me you were under suspicion."

She sucked in a breath. "That's bad."

"Well, we've been pretty free in talking about the Lazarites. They've probably had me under surveillance all along due to my sensitive work. I wish I'd known."

"I couldn't warn you until you committed."

"Yeah, I understand." He took a breath. "I have new problems at work, too. Denmark knows about us."

"Us? Ouch. That's bad news. What'd he say?"

Jake chuckled and waggled his eyebrows. "He called you a 'Technology wench,' and told me time with you wasn't useful."

Zofia snorted out loud, almost spilling her coffee. "'Wench'? Did he really say that?"

"Yeah, he did. It'd be funny if it weren't so serious." Jake raised a hand for the waitress. "He wants us to work overtime until the project's complete."

The waitress came by. Each of them ordered a simple breakfast.

When she was gone, Jake continued, "Denmark's push will make it almost impossible for Yitzak to spring me free." He shook his head. "We have more oversight, too. Denmark added two experts to help the team."

Jake filled her in on the new development and his anger about it, but he couldn't bring himself to tell her about falsifying the test data. *Knowing about it would implicate her. Better to keep that secret to myself.*

"We're goin' to have to be ready to move fast," she said.

"I was thinking the same thing." He showed her his pack. "This morning, I stuffed some essentials into my bag. I'm going to carry it around wherever I go while I wait for Yitzak's action. I want to be ready to move at a moment's notice."

"That's a good idea."

Jake had been thinking about this during the long, wakeful night. "If we have to escape suddenly, we need a signal between us and a place to meet."

"I know a place here in the Warrens, another restaurant even further in. It'll do for a meetin' place if we need it." She sent him the address imp-to-imp. "I also know how to get out of Oriens secretly, from my prior trips to Tileus."

"Good. For a signal, we need something innocuous we can say through our imps we wouldn't say accidentally. A codeword. I thought of the phrase 'grassy tree.' It's ordinary but doesn't make a lot of sense. If either of us even mentions that in an imp message, it's time to drop everything and go."

"That's good. 'Grassy tree.' I like it."

"Now, tell me what you can remember about how to get out of Oriens safely."

Zofia told him about her last trip. A tunnel under the Mueller Memorial, hitch-hiking rides to Timpi, a fishing boat to smuggle her across the Vissensee channel to Tileus, the spy network in Freetown. Jake took it all in, amazed he would consider such a clandestine trip—yet excited to look forward to it.

They finished breakfast while she briefed him. At the end, she added, "Don't forget to turn your imp reporting back on when you leave here."

Jake suddenly grabbed her wrist, alarm coursing through his body. A single Guard had just stepped in the door, dressed all in black just like the two last night. Zofia spun her head to see what he was looking at and took in a sharp hiss of breath before turning back.

Jake felt like a mousel with a hookbird circling overhead. "I thought this place was safe," he hissed.

The tick looked around the café, pausing on Jake's light green in the midst of blue and yellow. Then he strode to the bar and lifted his visor to talk with the surly waitress. Jake couldn't hear what they said, but at one point, the waitress answered a question by lifting her chin toward Jake.

CHAPTER 18

Stress makes the heart grow fonder. Absence makes the heart grow fonder. In fact, anything but fulfillment makes the heart grow fonder.

—*Collected Sayings of Yitzak Goren* by Ellen Thranadil, Tileus Press 439 A.T.

Thruday, 41 Quartember, 416 A.T.

Another day and a half of constant pressure was too much for Jake. Suma was buried in the technical test data. The false data would stand up to any scrutiny, but the scientist's penetrating analysis still had Jake on edge. The pressure was even greater today, because he'd gotten another message from Zofia.

She and Yitzak are waiting for me at lunch with more information. He may be ready for me to go to Tileus today. I've got to get out of here.

He headed for the door.

"Dammit, I can't think straight anymore," he said. "We've been at this for three long days now. I've got to get away for a bit to get my head straight."

"Where're you going?" Rodrick's question was edged with threat. "We've still got a lot to do."

"I'm going out to lunch. Alone." Defying Rodrick was increasingly dangerous as each day went by. *I've got to get away from him. I'm committed to the Lazarites now. I really don't care about making progress on this bomb.*

Rodrick responded with a set jaw and disdainful eyes. "This is part of why you've been failing, Palatin. You've got to learn to push through every obstacle, even inside yourself."

"Great stars, Rodrick, I'll make mistakes pushing this hard, and we can't afford mistakes."

Jake looked up to see Indy, Afonso, and Minya bent over their work with a concentration they'd never given to him. *Maybe he's right. Maybe I am a lousy leader.* What Rodrick had achieved irritated him, because they'd had a team that worked together and enjoyed each other. All that was gone. Now, work was everything.

Not allowing any further discussion, he simply turned and left.

"Don't do this, Palatin. I'll have to report you."

Jake ignored him. While he strode down the hallway, he was able to breathe more freely.

≈ ✳ ≈

"He just left? Out the door? Even when you told him he shouldn't?" Denmark's growl was deeper than usual when he spoke by imp with Rodrick. "Did he give any reason?"

"He said he'd make mistakes if we kept pushing. But I think he was going to meet someone."

"Thanks. I'll handle it from here."

Denmark disconnected the call. He sat for a moment at his desk, tapping a finger while he thought. Palatin was getting too independent. He put in a call to Overlock.

"Shelton, what do you have on Palatin's location?"

"Hold on a second, Director." Overlock paused, apparently to check his tracking. "We've got him, sir. He just entered the Warrens, and we'll lose him there."

"What about his girlfriend?"

"She entered the Warrens also, twenty minutes ago. Don't have her location anymore."

Denmark ground his teeth. Was he done with Palatin? The man still had unique knowledge, but he was becoming unreliable. Denmark couldn't let this go on.

"Bring him in, Shelton. Bring them both in. Send a Guard team into the Warrens to find them. They'll be at lunch someplace."

❧ ✳ ❦

The café Zofia had chosen hovered in a tiny back road like a squirrel among rats. *How does she find these places? But no matter how hidden, they're not safe. Day before yesterday, I thought we were finished when that tick came in. But he didn't do anything.*

This was a different place, the Pligged Plug. Jake would never have entered such a dive on his own. With his newly heightened awareness, however, he noticed this alley had no surveillance cameras; probably why she chose it. Inside, the feeble lighting hardly penetrated the secretive booths along the wall. He nodded to the watchful bartender, a large man with a bald head whose sharp eyes quickly flicked to the fourth booth. When Jake slid in beside Zofia, he dropped his backpack on the floor beside him. He was surprised to find Yitzak also waiting for him.

"Welcome, Jake." Yitzak's gravelly voice was as subdued as the dark surroundings.

Jake nodded. "Thanks. It's good to see you both...I think. I had difficulty making it. This new leader Denmark has brought in is more than pushy."

"Hi, Jake," said Zofia quietly, touching his hand. "Good to see you, too. Did you silence your imp today?"

"As soon as I entered a dead area—"

The bartender stepped up to their table. His voice scraped like rocks on a washboard. "You three want something to eat? We got some stew working."

They looked at each other and shrugged. "Sure," Yitzak said. "We'll have three."

The bartender nodded and walked away.

Yitzak pursed his lips in thought. "Zofia told me about your visits from the Guards, and about your changes at work. We're not safe anymore. We need to move now."

"I realized that the other day. I've been carrying some travel essentials in this backpack ever since."

"Good," Yitzak said. "As for your absence, I'm having some difficulty. I'd thought we could log you sick for a few days, but Denmark's watching you too closely. He's very sensitive to changes in your schedule."

"Yeah, it's getting harder to take," Jake said. "The pressure is intense this week. I'm ready to go anytime." He patted the backpack.

"Let's talk about your trip to Tileus. Zofia's done it before. She tells me she briefed you on how to get out of Oriens. You'll go through Timpi, and you'll be met by a ship captain named Han Yenstil. He'll smuggle you—"

They were interrupted again by the bartender, who stepped around the bar to their booth without any food. He leaned down close, looming over Jake, his eyes intense. He pointed at Jake and Zofia and spoke, his hoarse voice quiet.

"The ticks is coming up the street, asking about you two."

Yitzak looked up in alarm. The bartender cocked his head to a man who had just come in, who nodded once and then quickly left the café. The bartender returned his attention to them. His face was impassive and nearly inscrutable. He looked like he'd done this before for others.

Jake and Zofia looked at each other in alarm and spoke simultaneously.

"Grassy tree."

Jake took charge, asking the bartender, "Do you have a way out the back?" *I'm becoming a different man. Greater responsibilities, rising to the role.*

The bartender pointed to a door at the end of the bar. "Yah. It goes to the next street. Turn left outside, you go farther into the Warrens."

Jake's muscles were taut, as if he were ready to volley a lightning fast zero-G serve.

"Let's go," he said.

Yitzak said, "I'll be alright here if I'm alone. But you two must go...now."

Jake turned back to the bartender. "Thanks. We owe you, maybe for our lives."

The bartender returned to his station. Several dark figures loomed in the window of the café, moving purposefully toward the door. Jake hardly thought about what to do; his body already knew. He slid swiftly out of the booth, grabbed his backpack, and ran to the back door. Zofia followed on his heels. They sprinted through the door, Jake bashing his shoulder on the door jamb. Behind was a storage room. The door closed behind them on a stern command voice back in the bar.

"Solity Guard. Everyone stay where you are. We're looking for two criminals."

Jake hurried through the jumbled piles of liquor and snack boxes, stored glasses and napkins, and found another door. It opened into a street even narrower and filthier than the one in front of the café. Turning left, Jake led Zofia deeper into dark risk.

Zofia pointed directions at each turning. They ran streets that twisted around each building like rats in a trash pile. Dead-end alleys were more common than through streets. She knew her way through the Warrens and how to avoid the few surveillance cameras. Each time, she pointed the camera out to Jake for them to bypass.

Jake thought ahead about what to do next. *How do we get to Touchdown Park?* Then he stepped on a patch of broken glass, feeling the crunch under his sole. The alley smelled of waste. Filth covered every surface. He couldn't think properly while moving.

"We need a place to catch our breath and think," he said. "We've got to figure out what to do next."

❧ ✳ ☙

Several streets later, the two sat side-by-side in an empty lot strewn with trash and debris. Jake found a battered green couch with torn upholstery, sprung supports, and mildewed cushions, only slightly better than sitting on the ground. The empty lot stank of urine and garbage.

He'd heard no sound of pursuit since the café. The ticks must not have discovered they'd been there. They were likely still searching cafés.

"Okay," Jake said. "We have to assume the Solity Guards know we're together somewhere here in the Warrens. By now, Rodrick has reported to Denmark that I didn't return from lunch."

"We're committed now, aren't we?"

"Yeah," he said with conviction. "Denmark will have them search until they find us. You said there were informers in the Warrens. Overlock probably already has a network watching for us. We need to avoid contact with anyone."

"This empty lot's a good place, then."

Jake looked around. "We're out of sight, even from the alley we took to get here. Soon, though, the director will have them turning the city upside down. We've got to go."

She nodded, her eyes wide. As competent as Zofia had always seemed, she suddenly looked frightened.

Two rats emerged from a downspout, noses quivering in the air. They moved forward boldly, as if exploring whether these humans might have food for them.

"Uck!" said Zofia. She grabbed a bottle from the ground and threw it at the rats. "Ugly, stinkin' vermin."

The creatures ran back and hid again. Jake noticed one had a missing hind leg. Its gait was strange, but it didn't seem to slow the rat.

He shuddered and continued. "We have no choice now but to move forward. Can we get to the tunnel from here?"

Zofia was talking fast, unevenly, nervous. "Yah. But I've never done this with the ticks chasing me. It worked well without someone chasin' us. But now...I don't know. We're in new territory here."

A discarded washing machine caught his eye, its automatic loading arms hanging crooked and useless. A battered, mildewed doll hung halfway out of the machine as if trying to escape.

Jake needed to calm her. "What's it like outside of Oriens? I've never left the city."

"People are easier, less rigid," she answered. "They're still part of Solity, but they're less likely to follow every rule. I got rides easily, just by standin' on the side of the road."

He nodded, encouraging her to talk. "What about in Timpi? What are they like?"

"It's a city," she said, wincing, "like Oriens. It has the same kind of surveillance, and the same rigid people. Not like the country."

"Our implants no longer report to Solity, right?"

"True, unless they can find out where we are. Then they can override and start the reportin' again. And if they find them, they can listen to us. There aren't many cameras in the Warrens that would finger us. But to get to Touchdown Park, we have to go through areas with full surveillance." She looked sideways at him, as if she were still withholding an awkward secret.

"How do we do that? One camera sees us, and they'll have our imps reporting again."

She paused and looked at the ground, avoiding his eyes.

Jake saw something was wrong. Her reticence made him nervous. "Well? We have to do something."

After a long pause, she finally answered. "There's only one thing we can do, see? We need to get rid of our implants."

What she proposed was serious. Tampering with an implant was a major criminal offense with severe punishment. Everyone knew that. But of course, so was treason.

"Well, you're the implant tech. How do we do that?"

She shrugged with fear in her eyes. "We can't disable them with anything we have. We have to cut them out. I'll take out yours, and you take out mine."

Jake sat up straight in surprise. This whole business seemed to slide from bad to worse. Still, he saw no other way out. Going back to his old life meant squaring what he was doing with the Solity Guards and with Berndt Denmark—as impossible as flying from here to Tileus. And he didn't want to go back.

"Cut them out? Good heavens. You mean, like cutting into our own necks? I thought removing the implant was life-threatening."

"No, no. That's an intimidatin' fiction from Solity. We can cut it out easily. It hurts, but it doesn't even bleed. Well, not much."

Jake shook his head, amazed he'd even consider such an action. Yet what choice did they have? Changing Solity was more important, more imperative than building an antimatter bomb. And now he knew what he did affected more than Verdant Prime. The whole world was at risk of destroying itself as others had done. His new responsibility even included those in other countries. With each step they took, he gained more clarity. Despite the risk they faced—of capture, of torture, of death—he felt at peace sitting with Zofia, even in this trashy lot. In his own well-equipped lab, he'd felt defeated whichever way he went.

Zofia nervously pulled a folding knife out of her sidepack. "I never know when I'm goin' to need this. Solity doesn't like us to carry knives; they consider them weapons. I've always thought of a knife like a useful tool. I keep it as sharp as I can, because a dull tool is worse than no tool." She was almost babbling.

He looked at the knife in her hand and remembered his own in his backpack—just as suspect, just as useful. In a sudden epiphany, he realized how alike they thought. Both of them had chosen to bring a knife. He remembered the overwhelming attraction they'd felt for each other under the transpath. They were meant to be together.

He made his decision. *Let the devil take fraternization.*

Jake looked into her eyes and leaned over to kiss her lips. Her breath hitched, and she leaned into him. He had never kissed anyone before.

He discovered kissing was nicer than he had ever imagined.

The sensations took him back to his first infatuation, with Hama in secondary school twelve years ago. Fraternization had been denied them for incompatible DNA, so they had never kissed. He remembered being with her and how it had made his teenage blood pound. He'd imagined kissing then, felt his own sexual response. He'd spent evenings—when he wasn't studying and advancing—daydreaming about Hama.

And here was the reality, with Zofia. Even in the middle of his fears, the kiss aroused him like the youth he'd been. His body couldn't get close enough to her no matter how hard he pulled her to him. Boldly, her hand caressed his belly, causing him to hiss in a hot breath. Then she broke from the kiss and laid her head on his shoulder.

He held her tight, his heart pounding and blood singing. With glazed eyes, he looked at the squalid surroundings of broken furniture, cast-off appliances, and strewn trash. *What a place to fall in love.* For a long time, he just sat and enjoyed the feeling of her body next to his.

Eventually, his mind returned to their dilemma. Time to do some unlicensed surgery and get out of Oriens.

CHAPTER 19

Implant technology was first developed on One Hope, after centuries of imagining it. What made it so difficult was the connection to the sensory nerves. Yet implants were a crude precursor to the transpath, connecting people as never before. On Verdant, the center of implant technology was in Tileus.

—*The Making of a New Humanity* by Ellen Thranadil, Tileus Press 448 A.T.

FRIDAY, 42 QUARTEMBER, 416 A.T.

Jake untangled himself from Zofia and stood up. She looked up at him, questioning in her eyes. He glanced at the sky and noted the afternoon wearing on.

"Okay, let's do it," he said. "We have to cut out the implants before we leave the Warrens, and we need to go today. The Guards won't stop looking."

Jake watched her stand, marveling at the grace of her body. In the midst of the squalor around them, her face glowed. He leaned down, and she lifted her lips for another kiss. They lingered in it, pressing their bodies against each other. It finally trailed off into several tiny pecks with a life of their own. Neither of them wanted to stop. Jake's whole body shivered in a frisson of visceral sexual energy, but their situation couldn't allow lingering.

"This place is as good as any," said Zofia. "It's private. We're not goin' to find a doctor's office for our surgery." She gave him a nervous smile and pulled out her knife. Jake reached out to test the blade with his thumb. Her knife was sharper than his, with a finer point.

He was still uneasy. "Do you know how to do this? Have you ever done it before?"

"No. My work always involved modifyin' the software in place. But I know where it is, and I know how it's connected. I'm familiar with the medical diagrams."

He took a deep breath. "Okay. Let's get it over with. You do mine first." Jake held himself still, exposing his neck. Some of his rigidity might have been fear.

She pointed her knife to the muscle at the right side of his neck.

"The implant's buried in the upper trapezius muscle. You can feel it with your fingers if you pinch. Got to open one vertical slit to expose it..."

While she spoke, he felt the knife slice into his neck. He gritted his teeth and clenched his fists against the sharp pain.

"...then cut across just below and just above it to sever its connections."

When she cut across the top, his mind exploded with a flash of visual brilliance, a loud bang, an explosion of acrid scent, and a tingling along every nerve in his body. His mouth filled with acid. The reaction lasted only a split second but left him shaking and breathless.

"Wow." He exhaled the word; it was all he could say.

"Yah. I'm told cuttin' the sensor paths is pretty intense." Her eyes were locked on his with deep concern while he shook it off.

"That might be understating it."

She had a handkerchief in her hand and pressed on the cut to stop the minor bleeding. She held up a lozenge the length of his thumbnail. Shiny silver with his blood smeared on it, the implant looked like a large vitamin pill. Square-edged traces made designs on the metallic surface, and one end had a bundle of cut fibers.

"This is it. You are now disconnected from the net."

He inspected the implant and touched it with his fingertip. "That's amazing."

Jake probed his mind for the presence of the implant and found a disconcerting emptiness there. He couldn't contact the InfoNet. He couldn't think a message to Zofia, even though she was right beside him. He felt more alone than he'd felt since he'd gotten the implant fifteen years ago.

I'm free. This is astounding.

He put his fingers on top of the handkerchief, pressing against his wound. The pressure eased the pain and staunched the blood.

Zofia brought him back to reality. She pulled a first aid kit out of her pack and gently moved his hand and the handkerchief out of the way. She put a heal-pat onto the wound to seal it and hold the edges together.

"The one thing to avoid," she said, "is the carotid artery. It's right here." She put her finger further forward, under his jaw. "If you hit the carotid, I bleed to death quickly. So, make sure you make a vertical cut on top of the implant.

"Okay. My turn," she said.

Jake's stomach lurched. The only surgery he'd ever performed was removing a splinter. He didn't know whether he could do this.

"Okay."

He dabbed again at his own neck, removing some new drops of blood escaping the heal-pat. She handed him the knife. He wiped it on the handkerchief.

"I wish we had a way to sterilize it," he said.

"That's okay. The heal-pat afterwards provides enough."

When she held back her flowing hair to bare her neck, he thought about how precious she was to him. What if he slipped? An unbidden image of copious blood made him shudder.

126

He took a deep, shaky breath before starting.

With his left hand, he probed at the junction of her neck and shoulder. Her skin was smooth and soft to his touch. He was suddenly aware of her soft, flowery scent. His own pulse pounded in his wound, and with his finger he felt her pulse accelerate in time with his. His fingers still buzzed with the sensory shock of his lost implant. He shook his hand to clear the feeling.

The hard lump of her implant bulged between his fingers, leaving a vertical space in which to cut.

"Am I pressing too hard?" he asked.

"Don't stop, Jake. You've got to do this." Her voice quivered. "It's the only way to be free."

"I know, I know," he breathed. "But I've never done anything like this before."

"Neither had I."

He didn't pause to think; doing so might have stopped him. The sharp knife went smoothly into her skin and muscle between his fingers. The cut was clean at first, then blood oozed out onto his fingers.

"Ack. I didn't cut deep enough." He hissed in through his teeth. "I'm going to have to cut again." She just nodded, holding herself as still as she could.

He cut a second time until he felt the knife hit the implant. He cut easily below it, but when he cut above it, she suddenly jumped under his hand.

"Aaaah" She cried out, then froze in place.

She had only moved half a centimeter, but it made the cut ragged and started a greater flow of blood.

"Oh, no. You're bleeding more. Hold still. I have to finish this."

He pressed the handkerchief against the flow. It seemed manageable, so he took the cloth off again and used the tip of the knife to cut behind the implant and pry it out into his palm. He pressed the handkerchief to the cut again, then followed it with the heal-pat. *Our blood is mingled.*

"Done. I've got it out. Are you okay?"

"Yeah, I think so...You're right. 'Intense' is understating it."

He handed the second implant to her. She held them side-by-side in her outstretched palm. Jake marveled at the technology hidden in those two capsules.

"We can't take them with us," she said, and threw them into the piles of trash. It felt like throwing away their identity, their very selves.

Bolder than he'd ever been, he leaned down and kissed her again. She melted toward him, but he only hugged her quickly.

"We need to move."

They stayed in the alley for a few more minutes, putting a heal-pat on her wound, cleaning up and letting their jangled nerves settle.

⤳ ❋ ⤳

A half hour later, they stood at an intersection. Jake's neck still throbbed with each beat of his pulse. Soon, they'd have to leave the anonymity of the Warrens. His breathing was shallow.

Zofia pointed halfway down the block at a bakery, then moved her finger to the surveillance camera just above it.

"Do we need to get some food for tonight?" she asked. "Every food place will have a camera like that above it. They'll identify us."

"I think that might be too much risk. We'd have to use a rationchip to get the food. I have a few food bars."

Their decision was suddenly made for them.

"Hey, stop there," they heard from the other direction. Jake whirled around to see two black-garbed Guards at the end of the street, pointing at them. The rest of what the ticks may have said was lost when he ran.

Together, they ducked back into the alley. At the next intersection, they dashed left into the small streets. Behind them, they heard the deep whine of an arriving heavy aircar. Organized shouting filled the streets. The sound made him sprint. Seconds later, heavy boots sounded in the alleys and they heard the aircar lift off.

"We can't stay in the streets," Zofia shouted while she tried doors on both sides. When one of them sprang open, she hurtled inside and he followed, just when the aircar roared to life where they had been. A loudspeaker in the car overrode the noise of the engines.

"Jacoby Palatin, Zofia Dobrunik, move to the center of the street."

They didn't wait to hear anything else, but ran through the empty dwelling. The rooms were carpeted with trash; dust covered the counters in the kitchen. They found a back door onto a different alley.

While they looked out, Jake shook his head in dismay. "Dammit, I know that voice from the aircar. It's the director's hitman, Shelton Overlock."

She looked at him in surprise. "I know of him. He's psychotic. Is he chasing you?"

"Apparently so, but it sounds like he's chasing both of us."

Jake put his head out the door, looking both ways, almost oriented again.

"Touchdown Park," he said, "to the left?"

"Yah. It's not far."

This alley was empty, so they dashed through the door, turned left, and ran again. They heard the loudspeaker over the buildings. By the sound of it, the aircar was moving around. To remain hidden, they brushed the walls on one side of the alley under second-story overhangs. Jake's engineering sense read the streets like a blueprint, and he guided them through three, then four turns before coming to the edge of the Warrens.

"I know where we are now," Zofia said. "See? The park's only two blocks down that way."

Jake nodded, and they ran again. Shortly, they burst out into the open area of the park like rabbits from a lair. Zofia pointed at the Mueller Memorial in the center of the park. They raced across grass and paved walks, their goal in sight. On this Friday evening, a few people were in the park relaxing after work. Jake aimed straight for the Memorial, running through the gaps in the people.

They reached the Memorial grounds, but Jake heard shouts behind them from back in the streets. "There they are. Call the aircar."

Needle flechettes zipped past them. People screamed in sudden panic and rushed away from the active chase. Jake dove over a low stone wall connected to the Memorial, and Zofia joined him. They glued themselves to the ground in a narrow space between the wall and trees. Hot flechettes pinged on the stones over their heads. They had only moments before they'd be pinned by the aircar.

Zofia pushed him to the right toward the Memorial. "Go that way," she said. "The escape hatch is there." She pushed him again.

Jake nodded and moved to the right, crawling as fast as he could. Zofia followed, urging him faster. The ticks continued shooting where they had dived for cover; they left the smell of the hot metal and the smack of darts behind. Forty meters of crawling got them to the Memorial, where they stood up hidden behind the shrubbery.

The wound in Jake's neck throbbed with the exercise. He pressed his fingers to it. They came away bloody. He wiped his fingers on his leg.

At their feet, some grey city utility boxes hid behind the landscaping shrubbery. Zofia lifted a metal hatch cover and scrambled down the ladder inside. Jake checked the area before following her. No one in sight. He closed the hatch above him, quieting the sounds of the chase. The aircar's loudspeaker sounded muffled but suddenly closer. When Jake cut off the daylight, the dim lighting of the vertical manhole seemed nearly black.

His hands and feet scrambled to find the ladder rungs. He reached the bottom by feel, and the loudspeaker in the aircar above amplified Overlock's voice.

"Jacoby Palatin, Zofia Dobrunik, stand clear with your hands up!"

Jake's eyes adjusted to the dim lighting, a pale light panel every ten meters. The passage had smooth walls with utility pipes and wires stretched on each side.

Zofia scurried down the tunnel. At a three-way intersection a short way in, she turned right, Jake on her heels. Twenty meters in, she suddenly stopped at another vertical ladder up to a hatch.

"Damn. Wrong way," she shouted in frustration.

Jake rapidly led the way back to the intersection. They raced through it, taking the left-hand path. With a loud clang, sudden light shone behind them. The hatch was open. Voices shouted down the tunnel. They heard the whine of the aircar above.

Overlock's voice rang clear. "Check everything. They're here somewhere."

More voices sounded in the tunnel behind them. "Follow the tunnel. Down there."

"There's an intersection here. Got three choices."

Jake raced down the shaft away from the voices, but came to a sudden stop around a bend thirty meters away.

The tunnel was blocked. The ceiling had caved in. The path was gone, and he felt sudden panic. Jake saw the dead end of his life.

"What do we do now?" he whispered.

Breathing hard, Zofia pulled at one of the huge rocks blocking the tunnel. Surprisingly, it moved easily, creating an opening in the rubble large enough for them to crawl through. She motioned Jake inside, followed him, then closed the hinged rock behind them.

"The Lazarites set this up years ago," she whispered. "The authorities haven't found it."

The darkness was so deep, Jake couldn't see his own hand. For an agonizing minute, they sat quietly and listened. Nothing. He groped for Zofia's hand. Finding it, he wove his fingers between hers and squeezed tightly.

Boots sounded in the tunnel on the other side of the cave-in. Jake held his breath. More voices, the searchers shouting to each other.

"Follow this tunnel. This way."

"It doesn't go far. It's blocked. They're not here."

"Look for openings."

They heard scrambling on the other side of the cave-in. Jake and Zofia both reached out to hold the hinged rock in place, but nothing moved it.

"There aren't any. Nothing but a cave-in."

"Then let's get back out there and find them. They must not have come down here. Try the other tunnels. Maybe they're in the woods."

The voices receded. Jake still heard the aircar and the loudspeaker, but the sounds in the tunnel moved off. His entire body was on fire. One heavy release of breath eased the tension.

Zofia activated a tiny penlight. Her face was ashen. "That was too close."

"We haven't seen the last of them. Overlock never gives up. We've got to keep moving." He got up and led her down the tunnel, further into darkness.

CHAPTER 20

Smuggling was a constant fact of life; the societal differences of the four countries guaranteed it. Individuals in Prime, Rathas, and Winter frequently could not obtain goods they wanted, due to regulatory constraints, religious objections, or simple lack of supply. The free economy of Tileus came to the rescue.

—*An Annotated History of Verdant* by Ellen Thranadil, Tileus Press 442 A.T.

Friday, 42 Quartember, 416 A.T.

Renfo Yenstil daydreamed at the rail of the twenty-meter trawler *Solo Solar* while it rolled through the waves of the Vissensee Channel. Or was he brooding? He wasn't sure. He'd been working for his so-called father, Captain Han Yenstil, on this boat for four years, but still resented being here. He'd wanted the life of a shopkeeper in Timpi, not a fisherman. However, this was his Assignment, and Solity made it impossible to change an Assignment unless you "knew somebody."

A wave splashed up from the bow, sprinkling him with a light spray of salt water. The sun sparkled on the water on this balmy day.

He didn't mind hard work. But he had different dreams for his life while in school, and his interfering father Han had waylaid those dreams. "Father." What a useless term. No one in Solity knew their parents—except him, the different one. He hated being special. The whole situation was stupid.

His mind wandered to the beautiful, exotic Zofia he'd met a handful of times when she passed through Timpi. *Now, there's a girl I'd really like to know. She could snuggle up to me any old time.* He wondered when she'd come again, and if he'd have a chance to talk with her. She came from Oriens. Maybe she had connections with someone who could change his Assignment. He wasn't sure which he wanted more, the girl or different work. Maybe they could get together in fraternization. He'd been approved twice with other girls, enjoyed the tease each time, but neither had wanted marriage with him. It frustrated him. He'd like to know what sex was like.

Zofia. She and Han were both part of the Lazarites. He knew her because this boat had smuggled her across the channel to Tileus and back. Twice. Smuggling scared him. Actually, the Solity Guards scared him, but smuggling could bring them down on the whole crew.

Just like today's trip. A small boat had brought two men and several oblong boxes over to *Solo Solar* from a Tileus trawler. They were hidden under the hold. *This is so dangerous, and so foolish. We've been searched several times already, and I'm more afraid each time.*

He looked around the deck. Wang and Gonga, the other two crew members, were sitting on the main hatch cover and talking. Han, the captain, was forward in the pilot house, steering. They were all members of the Lazarite cell Han led. They had weekly meetings of a discussion group including another dozen people, talking about Solity. Han, this crew, and two others stayed after each discussion group meeting to plan Lazarite actions. Han required Renfo to be part of it because he was part of the boat's crew, but Renfo hated it.

The raised booms creaked with the waves while they dragged the purse seine through the ocean. The nets splashed into every wave. He liked the peaceful time while they closed the seine. They worked hard to deploy the net and even harder to bring in a load of fish. Between those times, they relaxed while the boat made a large circle, spreading the net wide then closing it again. *Twice a day, every work day.* He shrugged and spat into the ocean.

One good thing about this job was the sea air. His hand brushed the flopping dark hair out of his eyes, and he took a deep breath of the salt breeze. The sea air was rich and clean, unlike the stink of the harbor. The motion of the boat was relaxing.

"Stand by, crew," Han's easy, friendly voice called out from the pilot house. "Closing the seine in another few minutes." Everyone else liked Han. Even Renfo had to admire his manner.

"Aye-aye, Captain," said Wang, the oldest of the crew. He and Gonga got up from the hatch. Gonga moved to the net rigging. Wang motored the hatch cover up out of the way.

Renfo, the youngest, made his way past the pilot house to the bow and the heavy boat hook with which he'd snag the buoy marking the start of the net. Once brought on board, the boat would have both ends of the net under control, and they could start to haul in the catch. He picked up the hook. The wood was weathered smooth as glass from the daily grip of his hands.

He saw the marker buoy ahead. It would be another few minutes. The bow rose and fell into the waves while he was braced on the rail, a gentle motion that felt easy and calm.

He thought again about his situation. What could he do? His thoughts kept chasing in the same circles. The resentment bubbled like the tar kettle they used to seal seams. Maybe Zofia was his solution.

Han had started the problem long ago. Renfo had gone to primary school at age four like everyone else. Most kids never saw their parents again, and that was fine. While Renfo was in primary, Han kept track of him. The man visited him monthly, awkward times that confused Renfo and his friends. The visits set Renfo apart. He felt coddled and different. Other kids laughed at him and made fun of his "family." Renfo pleaded for Han to stop. He even asked the teachers to stop him, but somehow Han's easygoing manner got past the rules.

The dreadfulness coalesced when Renfo finished primary at age fifteen and got his life-long Assignment from Solity. He'd done well in math. He was organized and careful about details. He talked with his friends about becoming a shopkeeper, fairly distributing the small goods of Solity to others. That seemed like a worthwhile job. All his aptitude tests before graduation aligned with it. Then, out of the blue, he was Assigned to learn the trade of fishing as a crewmember on Han's boat.

Han was ecstatic during his next visit, sharing how he had influenced the Labor department to get Renfo this Assignment. That visit was the first of many blow-ups between the two.

The buoy was getting close. Renfo had done this job for four years, making it routine. He rested the boathook on the rail in preparation. When the marker slid by, he made a smooth and easy motion to snag it and lift its dripping weight over the rail.

"Marker on board," he hollered. He carried it back and fastened it to the net rigging to start the haul-in. Time to work.

Renfo, Gonga, and Wang set up the haul. Han idled the engines with the boat headed into the gentle waves. Then he slid below into the pilot house deck hatch.

"I'm checking on our guests," he said to the three while he disappeared. "You start hauling when you're ready. I'll be right back up."

Gonga and Wang rolled their eyes at each other and grinned.

"Guests," said Wang. "They won't feel much like guests after the rest of this trip."

Gonga agreed. "Dem bilges aren't much of a place to enjoy dah ride. Dey stink of dah fish. And dey'll be lying down in de oily bilge-water all day, cramped with dem boxes dey brought. But dey'll live. And we'll let dem out late tonight."

"I've never understood why Han does this," Renfo said. "He puts us all at risk with his smuggling." But he immediately regretted the words. They'd had this conversation before, and bringing it up again only separated him from the rest of the crew.

Wang answered with a sharp tone. "Your father does great things for us all, Renfo. Solity doesn't work, and it hasn't for a long time. Verdant Prime needs something different, and that's what *we* are doing." He pounded a fist into his chest, making clear both he and Gonga were part of Han's smuggling.

"Whatever." Renfo couldn't help expressing his resentment. "What do you think is in those boxes under the hold this time?"

133

"Don' know," said Gonga, "but I guess dey's weapons for de Lazarites again."

The next hour was filled with hard work and the reek of fish. When they reeled in each segment of the seine, all four of them sorted the haul, throwing overboard anything but the koifa fish they wanted. When the net segment was sorted, the rigging hauled it over to slide the fish into the hold in a slimy waterfall of fluttering, glistening silver. Their gloves and rubber aprons glopped with fish, one of the truly disgusting parts of this job.

Renfo imagined the two Tileus spies in the tiny space under the hold with their boxes, hearing all those fish fall above them. The hold just above their heads would fill with water to keep the fish alive. They'd stay dry, but it would be a close, scary place. He sneered at the thought of someone enduring it for something as useless as principles.

꙳ ❋ ꙳

That afternoon, with nets furled, the *Solar* motored back to Timpi complete with spies and fish. They'd had a good haul today. Han and Wang chatted, sitting on the closed hatch. Gonga had the helm. But Renfo, as the youngest, still worked at coiling and storing lines and washing the deck. He thought it completely unfair he had to keep working while everyone else relaxed.

Yet he had to admit this time wasn't too bad. Some days, the rough seas would splash over the deck at every plunge. Today, the ocean was still gentle and the ride was easy; motoring home gave them a cooling wind in their faces.

Wang sat up straight and pointed ahead. "We've got company, Captain."

Renfo turned to see another craft between them and harbor, speeding toward them with wide-splashing bow waves. It had a flashing blue light. Solity Guard. His heart raced when adrenaline suddenly spiked. *Not again. This gets worse every time, and this time we've actually got people and contraband aboard.*

Han stood up. "Hold your course, Gonga. We've done this before. Be easy."

Renfo watched the fast Guard boat close the distance quickly. One black-helmeted tick manned a post-mounted gun on the foredeck. Two others were on the aft deck and a fourth at the helm. All four wore the flat black of the Solity Guard with mirrored, high-tech helmets and utility belts with needle guns. Renfo always thought they looked like ominous insect aliens. When they approached closer, he heard the roar of their powerful engine. He shuddered.

The tick on the aft deck lifted a loudhailer. "Heave to, *Solo Solar*. We're coming aboard for inspection."

Han spoke to Gonga. "Turn us into the waves and go to idle." Gonga was already complying.

The speedboat came alongside with thick rubber fenders between the two craft, bobbing against each other in the waves. A tick on the aft deck heaved a grapple over the rail and hauled them in tight, cleating the line on the deck, though the Guard boat deck was half a meter below the *Solar's* deck.

The tick on the foredeck swiveled the gun toward them, and Renfo winced. The two from the aft deck leapt up, landing heavy when a wave heaved the deck of the *Solar*. Han stepped toward them.

The taller one in charge regained his balance and spoke. "Captain Yenstil, our tracking showed you approached a foreign vessel this morning while fishing."

Han shrugged with a warm smile. "Of course. They were also fishing. The Channel has boats from both Timpi and Freetown. We can't avoid them."

"Right. 'We can't avoid them.'" The man's voice was sarcastic. "But Han, you hardly try. Freetown is across the Channel in Tileus. You know the danger in contact."

"We go where the fish are, Kai Ariki. The boats from Tileus do, too. We can't help but be close to them sometimes."

Renfo tried to hide his fear. Han knew the leader by name and rank— the lead lieutenant for the Guards in Timpi—but that didn't make him the tick less dangerous. Standing behind Gonga and Wang, Renfo's legs shook. He hoped he wouldn't have to speak. What he really wanted was to run away. Even with Han's sociability and affability, the Solity Guards were bad news. People disappeared around the ticks.

"You know we still must search your boat, Han. Any possible contact with Tileus requires it." The man was firm and factual.

Han smiled and waved them forward. "But of course, Kai. As always, go ahead. Wang, Renfo, please help them. Open whatever they wish."

Lieutenant Ariki and the other tick moved forward of the pilot house. Renfo followed Wang, staying as quiet as he could. The next twenty minutes were a flurry of orders. The boat had no people spaces below decks, so the entire search focused on spaces they could reach from the main deck. Under the Guard direction, Renfo opened everything. He moved around the foredeck, opening each storage hatch to look at lines, anchors, and spare equipment. Wang pulled gear out onto the deck when directed, grumbling about the disorder. In the pilot house, they opened each cabinet and drawer, while Gonga moved from side to side to hold the helm steady and stay out of their way. Renfo opened the pilot house deck hatch into the below-decks storage area. They bypassed the main hold and went aft to the engine compartment. Wang opened the engine hatches while Renfo stood aside clamping his jaw tight. The ticks shone their beamlights around every cranny of the repellor-beam engine and storage batteries.

Finally, they turned to the main hold.

"Open it up, Han. Let's see your catch today," ordered the lieutenant.

Han motioned to Wang, who motorized up the hatch cover. They all looked down into the hold, filled to within a half meter of the top with fish swimming in just enough water to cover them.

"Looks like a good catch," said the lieutenant.

Renfo's anxiety increased. This was where it could get dicey. The smuggled people and contraband were right down there, under the rubberized tank.

"Is it all fish, Han? You're friendly, but you're a tricky man. What else might be in there? How can we search it?"

Renfo yelped and immediately stifled it. Lieutenant Ariki and the other tick both turned their mirrored helmets to look at him. The sun sparkled on their visors, so he saw nothing of their faces. He felt his face flush and clamped his teeth to keep from quivering.

"What's with you, Renfo Yenstil?" Ariki's voice was official, formal, and threatening. 'Perhaps *you* should show us what's in there."

He didn't even know the Guards knew his name. Renfo felt frozen in place. He tried to make himself smaller when everyone looked at him. His heart raced, and he darted his eyes to Han for help.

Han laughed. "He's just a nervous type, Kai. You people scare him. Renfo, get the boat hook and we'll probe the entire catch for them."

Renfo barely got out the response, "Aye-aye, Captain." He practically ran away, going to the bow for the hook.

When he returned, Han snatched the hook from his hands, giving him a momentary glare out of sight of the Guards. Renfo resumed his place behind Gonga. He knew the hidden bilge space was underneath the hold, and probing with a hook wouldn't disturb it. The contraband was closer to discovery when they looked into the pilot house deck hatch. But he till quivered with terror.

Han thrust the pointed hook into the hold, probing every area and waving it around through the mass of fish. At each probe, the fish churned, some of them jumping and splashing the hatch cover and deck. A few managed to clear the hatch and flop on the deck. Wang picked each one up and threw it back into the hold. The ticks watched everything without comment.

Finally, Kai spoke. "Enough. Put it away. We're done."

Renfo felt the lieutenant's intent gaze on him while he took the hook back to the bow.

Then Ariki turned again to Han, pointing a finger in his face. "I don't know what's going on here, but we are watching you. Keep yourselves clean."

"But of course," said Han with his usual unruffled composure. "We always do."

❧ ✳ ❦

The Guard boat departed and sped back to the harbor, while Gonga returned to the pilot house. Renfo stood at the rail watching the foredeck tick secure the deck gun while they moved away. He covered his mouth with his hand and shuddered.

Without warning, a hard hand slapped him on the back of the head. He lost his balance and almost fell overboard, but caught himself on the rail.

"You're getting worse, you fool," Wang shouted. "Can't you keep your fears in check? You nearly gave us all away."

Han curled his lip and looked at Renfo with cold, dead eyes.

"That was the worst behavior I've seen." Han sounded disgusted. "I've tried and tried to build you up, and you still can't control yourself. What kind of son are you?"

Renfo's fears flashed into anger. "Don't call me son! You humiliate me. We're grown men here, not some stupid 'family.' If you wouldn't do this crazy smuggling, we'd not be in danger at all."

Wang and Han traded a look of disgust before Han spoke again. "We do this to make Prime better. Can't you understand that? Don't you see how demeaning it is to be searched like this? We want it to stop. We want to live our lives freely. And we're willing to risk ourselves to make it better for everyone. Get a grip on yourself and learn some courage!

"Now, go clean up from the inspection. Close the hatches and stow the gear. While you do, think about the extra work *you're* having to do because the ticks did this to us. Do you want them always to have power over you?"

Renfo spit over the rail while he went forward. "I don't want to get arrested, that's what I want."

He vented his frustration by flinging gear back into the hatches and slamming them shut. He calmed down and thought what he could do. Maybe he should go to the ticks. If he turned in Han and the crew, perhaps he could get a new Assignment.

Or, he thought again, perhaps the ticks would just arrest him with the rest.

Maybe he really should approach Zofia next time she came. She'd help him, if he approached her right.

CHAPTER 21

Humanity is connected to nature. To find creativity, commune
with a tree.

—*Collected Sayings of Yitzak Goren* by Ellen Thranadil, Tileus Press 439 A.T.

Early dawn tinted the still-dark clouds with luminescent shades of olive and
sage. Zofia stood in the mouth of a cave watching the growing light define
the forest shapes in front of her. The threatening sounds of the night were
giving way to early birds calling out their joy of life.

The wound in her neck throbbed. She had cleaned the dressing. It would
heal.

She turned back to watch Jake asleep on the hard tunnel floor, his head
resting on his backpack. Her chest swelled, and she shook her head with a
silly grin. She'd never felt this way before, never known any man whom she
admired and loved so much.

After their desperate run through the city, followed by an hours-long
trek through a dark burrow, they'd been exhausted and hungry when they
reached the end. The tunnel opened into pitch black swallowing the tiny
glow of her penlight. She'd assured him no one frequented the forest ahead.
They'd eaten the food bars out of her pack while staring into the darkness.
Jake had decided they needed to sleep here in the tunnel, and she agreed.

Zofia turned back to the mounting light in front of her. The dawn got her
thinking about the dawning change in the two of them. She had started this
relationship in charge. Yitzak had given her a task, to groom this key
engineer into the Lazarites. She'd done well. Too well. *I guess it wasn't part
of the task to fall in love with him.* The thought made her fingers tingle, and
she laughed gently at herself.

This week had changed her. Zofia was no longer in charge. And she felt
good about it. She'd spent most of her life managing things for herself. Now
she'd found someone on whom she could lean. She didn't have to do it all.

It started with that visit from the ticks. Her years of Lazarite work had
all been clandestine. She'd thought herself brave, doing her part in spite of
risk. She'd even made this trip to Tileus twice. But the risk had never before
materialized. She'd heard bravery was doing what needed to be done even
in the midst of fear. When faced with immediate danger, though, she
discovered she wasn't all that brave. Her stomach clenched and her mind
stopped working. Yesterday, she found herself more frightened than she'd

ever been before. She couldn't seem to make her mind work when peril loomed.

She needed someone to rely on. Yitzak had filled that role for five years, but he was now far behind them. She caught her breath. *Is Yitzak safe? We left him in that restaurant. Oh, damn. What if they forced him to reveal our plans?*

But there was nothing she could do about that.

This week had changed Jake, too.

She'd watched him grow. While she discovered her fears, this wonderful man rose to the challenge. Four nights ago, he'd apparently handled the visit from the ticks as if he'd faced danger all his life. When she next saw him, he'd transformed. The confrontation seemed to be a springboard for him to jump into readiness. She, on the other hand, had been terrified when they visited her. Again yesterday, with the ticks outside the café door, she froze. She'd been unable to think. Jake took charge. He hurried them out the back door and through the Warrens. Though she knew where to go, his leadership kept her going.

Zofia wouldn't stop using her knowledge and drive. She'd give everything she could for their success. Yet she was very glad to be able to trust and follow Jake.

"Is it time to move on?" His voice warmed her neck while he put his arms around her from behind.

His surprise touch made her jump in sudden fear, but then she immediately felt safe, protected. She turned in his arms. He was smiling down at her, seemingly at peace. Her own stomach fluttered like the birds in the forest with her marvelous feelings for him. She reached up to kiss him gently, then pulled free.

"We should eat before startin' out," she suggested, and reached into his backpack for a couple of food bars.

~✹m

"How could he be gone?" Denmark stormed, his voice loud and harsh. He stood at his desk with Shelton Overlock and Rodrick Griffin standing across from him. Rodrick looked frightened. Overlock's lips were compressed into a tight line of frustrated anger.

Overlock stepped forward and dropped two tiny objects onto the director's desk. They clinked when they landed. "We tracked them in the trash of the Warrens," he said, "only to find their discarded implants. They cut them out."

"You had three squads of Solity Guards, an aircar, and two drones all active in that chase, and they just...got away? Brolshit. How could you let them escape?" Denmark glanced at Griffin's fear-filled face. The man stood nervously waiting his turn. Denmark hadn't addressed him yet.

Overlock answered. "We've been searching all night, Director. We had them in sight in Touchdown Park. Scampering like mousels, with the Guards right behind." He shook his head, irritation on his face. "The damn fool Guards were shooting at them, even though we'd told them we needed Palatin alive. Your Solity Guard is undisciplined, Director."

"Damn!" shouted Denmark. He shook his fist. "I'm surrounded by incompetents."

"The two dove behind a wall next to the arboretum, and that's where we lost them. We don't know whether they slipped through the woods, down into a utility tunnel, or back into the Warrens. The aircar's heat sensor was inoperative. Another Guard failure. By the time they got one working, nothing was there."

"What about a bounding perimeter?"

"The Guards had one, sir. Or thought they did. The fugitives never crossed it."

"So, you're telling me they're gone into thin air."

Overlock closed his eyes, "Yes, sir. It seems so."

Denmark turned and looked out the window toward the Warrens. "Keep searching, Shelton. Turn the place upside down." His voice turned to a low growl. "Find them."

The command was a dismissal. Overlock turned and left, his back rigid.

The director sat in his chair, hands and eyes on his desktop. He kept Griffin waiting. Denmark hated having to change his plans. Palatin was brilliant and useful, but somehow the situation had completely turned to maggots. Taking a deep breath, he looked up.

"And you, Rodrick," he said, "what do you have to say for yourself? You were supposed to keep his damned ass at work until we got the bomb."

"I think he was already lost, Director, by the time I arrived on Newday."

"What do you mean, 'lost'?"

"I've watched him closely all week, sir. His mind has not been on advancing his work. It's been somewhere outside the lab. I got the other three working hard, but Palatin—"

Denmark slapped his hand on his desk. The crack rebounded from all four office walls. "Damn it! That's what I put you there for. I already told you he was drifting."

"Yes, sir."

"And then, you still let him go dancing out to lunch?" He filled his voice with derision, flipping his hands in the air like jumping acrobats. "How could you do that?"

Griffin straightened and answered Denmark with his own fire. "Director, I let him go to lunch because he was a hindrance. They were holding a damned party when I arrived there! All week, Palatin's attitude was holding back the team. The others kept looking to him for guidance, and he was moping in his cubicle."

"You should have reported that to me. I would have motivated him."

"I reported to you every day this week, sir. You had the Guards visit him and his girlfriend. What more could we have done?"

Denmark ground his teeth. "Something. Anything." He shook his head in disgust and paused to think.

Griffin let the pause last for a few moments, then resumed with a more helpful tone. "But, Director," he said, "I also have very good news for you."

The director looked up and cocked his head in interest. "Tell me. I can use some good news."

"This week has been productive, even without Palatin. We've got a prototype warhead, and we're ready to test. We can do it in two days."

Jake walked from the hillside cave down into the forest, occasionally pressing against the bandage on his neck to soothe it. He looked every direction at once, or tried to. New marvels were everywhere. The sun dappled through forest foliage to reveal a barely-visible trail winding through the tree boles. The scent of the forest filled his head with rich loam. A riot of leaves shouted at him in vibrant colors of dark blue, green, and russet. Birds chirped. Hidden animals rustled. The ground was uneven, and he slipped on damp leaves before catching himself.

He'd never been outside the city. The closest he'd been to a forest was the arboretum in Touchdown Park. He had no idea a real forest was so rich in look and sound and smell.

"This is...remarkable," he whispered.

Zofia had stopped beside him when he'd been stunned into stillness. "Yah. It's good, isn't it?"

Beautiful, yes, but he also had the sense the forest was dangerous. Everywhere he looked was brawling life, competing in a slow-motion affray for sunlight and food. Every branch pushed aside its neighbors for sunlight. Vines hung from trees, strangling trunks in their coiled embrace. Flowers from pinpoints to a half-meter size made brilliant spots of brightness. He watched one small bird touch a vivid red-and-yellow growth that snapped its petals closed to trap the creature.

"Great stars! Did you see? That flower just ate a bird."

"It's a jungle. Most of Prime is still like this. Particularly in the mountains farther south, closer to the equator. Defense mostly controls the mountains and uses them for test and training ranges. But we're headin' northwest toward Timpi on the coast. And Tileus is farther north, in the temperate zone. It's cooler and not so..." she paused for the right word, "...aggressive."

"Except for the croombears, apparently," he laughed. Then, more seriously, "Are we safe? I don't want a flower snapping me up." A part of him was on edge. Yesterday had been intense.

"We're safe on the path, bucko," Zofia said with a laugh. "I've been this way twice before. We have several days ahead of us before reaching the coast. Then we'll make contact with Han."

"Is it that easy?"

She snorted. "No. The coast is watched closely by Solity Guards to 'prevent subversive intrusions.'" Her voice held scorn. Then her tone softened when a touch of fear entered. "And they're chasin' us. We're not out of danger at all—but we are on the way."

She looked up at Jake. "You know Overlock better than I. How long do you think it'll be before he starts searchin' outside Oriens?"

"Today, probably. He's not a man to give up. When Overlock doesn't find us in the Warrens, he'll ransack the country." The thought got his feet moving. "So, let's get on with it. We've got to get out of Prime as quickly as we can."

Zofia took his hand and they walked on. Jake smiled, buoyed by the physical connection.

༄ ❈ ༄

They came out of the forest onto a quiet road alongside farm fields. A stream passed under the road, where they were able to refill their water bottles and wash their wounds. Jake had seen pictures of scenes like this, but he had no idea about the rich scents and sounds surrounding them. He stepped into a field of corn, risen as high as his chest, just to feel the leaves and smell the dry taste of the plants. Farther on, another field had been recently fertilized. The acrid scent made his nose itch.

"We'd better cover our necks," he reminded Zofia. "Wouldn't want someone to wonder about our bandages."

They rarely walked far before someone offered a ride.

"We're visiting friends in Timpi," he said, over and over. It always worked. He couldn't imagine such a simple lie standing its ground in the city.

"Oh, who are your friends?" was the frequent reply.

Zofia always answered, "It's the Umbolts." Jake laughed to himself at her creativity. Of course, none of their drivers ever knew the fictional Umbolts, though they tried to find a connection.

The drivers often shared food with them, so they didn't have to dig into their packs for their meager supply of bars. They also had friendly conversations with each one, easy and relaxed.

The first night, evening came while they were walking. They moved into a light wood before dark, watching carefully for anything that looked dangerous before they slept under the trees.

142

The second and third night, their drivers offered dinner and beds for the night.

The first time someone offered such hospitality, Jake whispered to Zofia, "Is this okay?"

"Sure," she whispered back. "Country people are friendly."

He nodded and turned back to the driver. "We'd be honored, sir." *It sounds like Solity hasn't intruded on their lives much. This could be a better life.*

At dinner, he learned something about farming. This was a big house with many bedrooms, holding the leaders and a team of workers. They had the equipment to plow, plant, till, and harvest a square kilometer of land. He also learned Solity was indeed firmly in control here. Each year, the Capital department told them what was needed and provided the seed. They returned the produce to Capital at harvest and prepared the fields for the next crop. Here in the semi-tropics, they got three harvests in a year—and it all went back to Solity.

The farm leaders were an older couple who'd been Assigned to it for over forty years. Another married couple kept the house, fixed meals, and raised two pre-school children. They talked cheerfully about giving the children up to the school system at age four, a reminder to Jake that Solity still controlled their lives.

⁂

ENDDAY, 45 QUARTEMBER, 416 A.T.

Two days later, the second farmer they'd stayed with gave them a ride to the edge of his fields.

"Timpi's only another ten kilometers down the road. You'll start seeing outskirts shortly."

"Thanks very much, sir," Jake answered. "You've been kind."

"It's what we do, young man. We take care of each other. That's always the highest goal of Solity, isn't it?"

Jake nodded, they shook hands, and he and Zofia were on their feet again. The farmer waved a hand and took his autotruck back to the farm.

"This life is very different than any I've known," he said to Zofia. He turned toward Timpi.

"It is, isn't it? But we're comin' back into a city shortly. There'll be surveillance again, and people will be more cautious."

"What do we do about the surveillance? We don't want face recognition to find us, and we don't want them to realize we don't have imps."

She seemed dismayed. "I don't know. On my prior trips, no one was chasin' me and I was just anonymous."

Jake stopped walking to think. "We need to create a reason for surveillance not to notice our missing imps, even when a camera sees us."

143

"Some clothing can block the imp signals. We used that in Lazarite events."

"Then we'll start with that. If we wear scarves, that will give a 'reason' for our imps not to be reporting." Jake was doing what he'd always done as an engineer. Give him a problem, and he could find a way to solve it. He pulled the spare shirt out of his backpack and tore it into pieces that could serve as scarves.

Satisfied with one part of the solution, he thought out loud. "Now we need to change our facial features to defeat the recognition algorithms."

He saw a muddy patch by the side of the road. "Here's our solution. Make-up."

"Make-up? What do you mean?"

"We'll use some dirt to change the key lines of our faces."

Zofia immediately took up the idea. "We don't want to just smear it on and look dirty. We want to create shadows to modify the contours of our visual features." She stepped over to the mud and knelt down. "Like this. When I put a shadin' of dirt under my cheekbone, it makes my cheeks look sharper and higher. Not enough for people to notice the dirt, just enough to change how I look."

The two of them laughed at each other while they played in the mud. Each one checked the other's face for the effect. Underneath Jake's laughter, however, he felt his stomach tightening again with fear. As confident as he sounded, he wasn't at all sure it would work. Was this enough? Or did they need to do something about facial symmetry and feature placement? He just didn't know.

They'd done what they could, so they started forward again. The farms around them were ending, with the last few farm structures off the road to their left. They saw buildings along the road ahead, the beginning of the city.

Suddenly, the buildings ahead were lit by an incredibly bright light. Jake spun to his left to see a brilliant ball of fire over the farms, trees and fields to the south. He guessed the ball was thirty or more kilometers away, but it looked like the rising of a new sun.

He recognized it.

"Get down, Zofia! Now!" He grabbed her arm and dragged her down beside the road, lying flat in the ditch on the side away from the light. He laid partially on top to protect her.

"What?" she said, struggling to rise.

"No. Don't get up. Don't look at it." But he couldn't help himself. He had to peek at what he had created. The scene was frighteningly awesome, like a touch of primal creation. A white ball of fire slowly rose in the sky, bathing everything in silent violence. A mushroom-shaped cloud climbed faster, the water vapor swirling and whirling like dancing demons while it ascended.

Below the cloud was a hastily expanding sphere, a demarcation between normalcy and inhumanity.

He dropped his face to the ground. "The fools. The damned fools. They tested it."

"Tested what? Your bomb?" She raised her head to look at him.

"No, stay down! The shock wave will be here in about a minute, and I don't know how big it'll be." He kept his head down, waiting for the shock wave. Their faces were only centimeters apart.

"I sabotaged my project before I left, Zofia. It'll never work properly the way they have it. It'll always go off prematurely. They must have launched a missile toward the test ranges to the south, and it went off in transit."

"You sabotaged your project?" Her eyes were alive with fear and admiration. "I never thought you'd do somethin' like that."

"I had to. I couldn't let Prime have the antimatter bomb. It would change the balance with Tileus." He saw in her eyes an even greater trust in him.

Jake took a quick peek above the road. The expanding shock wave was speeding across the fields toward them. He quickly plastered his head onto the dirt again.

A powerful blast of hot wind erupted upon them, tearing at their clothes and threatening to lift them out of the ditch. The air filled with dust driven at tremendous speeds. Trees behind their heads whirled and thrashed and cracked as branches broke. Plants and debris flew over them, crashing into the forest. Glancing sideways, Jake saw outdoor chairs flying through the air. A flower pot, strangely intact, fluttered like a demon while it pinwheeled past only a meter over them. Thousands of glass shards glinted in the sun. The air smelled burnt. The two hunkered together behind the small protection of the road berm, holding each other in desperate fear while the world went crazy.

CHAPTER 22

It remains argued to this day whether the first antimatter explosion was planned or an accident. Some historians point to Berndt Denmark's funded development of the bomb; they believe the explosion was a planned test. Others point to Jacoby Palatin's defection and believe the explosion was never intended to happen. Supporting the second opinion is the fact of significant damage to the farming communities south of Timpi.

—*An Annotated History of Verdant* by Ellen Thranadil, Tileus Press 442 A.T.

Denmark watched the antimatter team in the test control building launch the missile. They seemed to be handling the test with competence under Rodrick's leadership. Denmark stood behind them, anticipating his success. His attention was on the wall-sized display screen showing two parallel videos, one sent from the chase plane and the other from a ground tracking site. A third screen documented the technical telemetry streaming in from the missile in flight. The steady sequence of computer coded information documented the missile launch from west of Oriens and its low-altitude, terrain-hugging track over the foothills to the target range southwest of Timpi.

Then the telemetry suddenly froze. The videos showed a blindingly white explosion. The female chase pilot screamed over the audio link and pulled hard to the right, but the sphere of the explosion overtook her and the video from the aircraft showed momentary interference snow before going dead black.

Denmark's heart stopped with the video. He shuffled back a step, eyes wide.

The tracking site video showed the rising fireball, expanding shock wave, and climbing mushroom cloud. The violence looked like an exploding nova. In another thirty seconds, the shock wave overtook the ground site and the site video also went black.

Shocked silence filled the test control room. Indy, Afonso, and Minya sat without moving. Denmark's scientist Suma shook his head in dismay. Rodrick punched keys repeatedly, muttering something about active video.

Denmark ground his teeth and clamped his eyes shut. This weapon was essential to his plans to bring Tileus to heel—and for his personal advancement in the Council.

Something in him exploded. He shouted inarticulate rage at Rodrick. The others turned at his bellow, backing away from him. He rushed forward to where Rodrick had stopped pushing buttons. Denmark, still shouting incoherently, spun him around in his chair and slammed his fist into the man's face. Rodrick fell to the floor like a boulder from a cliff, landing with a heavy thump.

"Incompetents!" screamed Denmark. "You're all going to die for this!" Then he pointed a heavy finger at his scientist. "You! Tanaka, what just happened?" Denmark's fist hovered in the air, ready to strike again.

Suma spoke shakily from his seat. "It should have worked, Director. I reviewed everything. All the tests were 'go.' Palatin must have done something."

Denmark lowered his clenched fist and opened an imp call to Overlock. He shouted, not bothering to sub-vocalize.

"Palatin!" he thundered. "I want him, Shelton. I want him more than anything else in the world. Find him. Find them both, and bring them to me. Alive. Kill them slowly while I watch."

CHAPTER 23

The role of the Lazarite network in Verdant Prime has often been underappreciated. Palatin found help in the most unlikely places.

—*The Making of a New Humanity* by Ellen Thranadil, Tileus Press 448 A.T.

Endday, 45 Quartember, 416 A.T.

Han asked Renfo Yenstil into the living room to talk. Renfo hated the room. He hated living here in Han's house. It made him feel like a pre-school child. He'd been forced to live with these biological parents for the last five years, ever since age fourteen and the unusual Assignment to the fishing boat. Han had done that to him, and his mother Ilsa did nothing to stop it. The other crew members lived separately. Only Renfo was under Han's thumb all the time, apparently part of what Captain Han meant by "being father."

"Two years ago," Han said, "you and I had a huge blow-up when you tried to get your Assignment changed."

Renfo just nodded, wishing the man would get to his point. Han had blocked him then and continued to block him. He still seethed inside at the unfairness of it.

"I've been watching you closely since then, Renfo. I'm sadly coming to realize this isn't working out."

Renfo cocked his head in surprise. These were the words he'd had been waiting to hear. But what was Han planning? "Of course, it isn't working out. I'm not a fisherman. I never was. My aptitudes—"

Han held up his hands as if to stop the onslaught. "Yes, I know about your aptitudes." His jaw was set with disappointment. "Shopkeeper." He paused. "And that's what you're going to be."

"What? Really?"

"Yes. You're dangerous to us on the *Solo Solar*. You're competent at your work, but you do it sullenly." Han spoke firmly but with kindness, stating truths without a blaming tone. "You're so bitter you're careless, so you break equipment unnecessarily. Your resentment puts the rest of us at risk, particularly in our Lazarite work." He paused, took a breath, and shook his head. "Maybe if you're doing what you want, you'll fit in better. I'm going to get your Assignment changed."

"Can you do that?" Renfo felt the hair rise on the nape of his neck. *Was this possible?*

"Yes, I can. I know the right people in Labor." He reached out and grasped Renfo's shoulders tightly, his eyes boring into Renfo's. "But, my son—"

"Don't call me that!"

Han ignored his response except to shake him once, hard. "—*listen* to me. You know too much about the Lazarites. Our lives depend on your silence."

His voice was intense. "Others say we should kill you, so you won't talk."

"Kill me?" Renfo squirmed under Han's hard hands.

"I've convinced them not to do so, but we will be watching you. Always." Han shook him again. "You can go have the life you seem to want, but you *must...not...talk* about anything you've seen."

∽ ✻ ∝

Renfo rushed out of the house. He was going to the *Solar* to remove his stuff, dodging occasional groups of people enjoying Endday. A part of him bubbled with wonder, excitement about a new future. Another part fumed at the way Han had treated him physically, gripping him and shaking him like a child. He set that part aside. With a new Assignment, he could expect new living quarters. He'd finally get out from under his father.

A bright light suddenly filled the street. Renfo looked up at the sky, but he couldn't see the source. The light was like a huge lightning flash shining on the roofs, except it kept on shining. He stopped walking and turned in a circle, looking upward but seeing nothing to account for it. Others had also stopped what they were doing to look up. *Probably some stupid technology test.*

When he got to the wharf two blocks later, he looked down a southerly street. He couldn't see anything other than one distant cloud over the rooftops, climbing and spreading. *Wait. What's coming up the street? That looks like a rushing wall of—*

Before he could finish the thought, a focused blast of wind hit him. It threw him to the ground, landing on his side. He instantly realized he'd been very fortunate, because a sheet of composite plyboard whumped rhythmically while it spun through where he'd been standing. The air was full of detritus—clothing, street chairs, coils of rope, shards of glass. He smelled heat.

Renfo rolled over, covered his head and waited in miserable fear for it to pass. Every muscle in his body shook.

Debris crashed and tinkled to the ground all around him. He lifted his head cautiously, then got shakily to his feet. He was bruised and aching from his fall.

The street was transformed. Wreckage littered everywhere, covering the street, sidewalks, stoops. Windows gaped empty of their glass, except for shards hanging here and there. Signs, cameras, and lights were knocked loose from their mountings, disappeared as if by magic. He realized the jumble around him was made up of all those objects blown down from blocks away. The debris also included many large objects like that sheet of plyboard. *Any of those things might have hit me. I could have been killed.*

"An atomic bomb. That was an atomic bomb." He muttered the words angrily to himself while he walked again, picking his way through the debris. Then more dangerous thoughts occurred to him. *Have I been radiated? Are we at war?*

He checked the InfoNet through his imp, but no news flashes jumped out at him. He shook off his fear and walked through the mess to the boat.

The *Solo Solar* seemed okay. They always left things secure as a precaution against storms, so nothing had blown overboard. Debris from the sudden wind covered the deck and floated in the harbor. He went below to get his things. *Never again do I have to ride this stupid boat.*

But his earlier thought about radiation came back. *Am I even going to have a future? Am I just a dead man walking? When do I start to have symptoms?*

☙ ❋ ❧

By the time Renfo dawdled back to Han's house, two people were standing on the front stoop. They wore back packs, and they were dirty, as if they'd been rolling in the mud. *More trouble.*

Then he recognized the girl, and his heart leaped out of his morose worries.

"Zofia!" he shouted, and ran the last few steps. "You're here again."

She turned to him and smiled. "Yes, I am. I left Oriens for good this time. Didn't you know to expect us?"

"Maybe Han knows. He doesn't tell me everything." Renfo felt almost giddy in her presence. Maybe his entire life would turn around with his new Assignment. She'd left Oriens. Having her here in Timpi would give him a chance—

"This is Jake. He's with us."

"Hi, Renfo. I've heard about you," said the man with Zofia. Under the mud and disorder, Renfo realized Jake was older than him, closer to Zofia's age. He was also fit and handsome.

"Uh...hi, Jake." Renfo's soaring heart fell. The two were traveling together. They'd left Oriens together. *Damn it. They're a couple.*

He felt his jaw clench. "Okay."

He looked around at the busy people in the street and remembered the process from her prior trips. "Let's get you two inside and off the street."

☙ ❋ ❧

The next few days held a flurry of activity for Jake. He and Zofia had little time alone. Jake had recognized Renfo's infatuation for Zofia from the outset. Since then, the young man had shown resentment toward Jake, acting sullen and angry at any contact.

Thankfully, Captain Han and his wife Ilsa welcomed them. Han had gotten a call from Yitzak and expected them. He gave them a couple of cots in the basement as a place to sleep. They didn't have enough privacy for the intimacy he wanted with Zofia, but they still managed to find quiet times in the night. They moved the two cots together—not enough to sleep together, but enough to touch each other and talk in the night.

Because of the damage from the blast, windows were broken all over the city. Some buildings had structural damage. Everyone was cleaning up, working together. Repair materials were in short supply, so people made do with what they could find. The fishing boats didn't go out for two days while they cleared the harbor and decks.

Most important to Jake was that the Sentinel Shield surveillance system for the city was mostly destroyed. With moderate care, they could move more freely than before.

Jake worked on the boat each day with Han and his crew, finding satisfaction in the physical labor. When they went into the city for supplies, he and Zofia watched closely for surveillance cameras; most of them had been destroyed by debris. They sometimes had to bypass a particular street where the cameras were intact. He suggested to her to keep their scarves on to hide the healing wounds on their necks.

Solity put news on the InfoNet about a large explosion at an unnamed factory. The news attributed it to a group of workers who did not follow proper safety rules, using it as an occasion to enjoin everyone to do their work properly. The news also implied the workers had been subverted by Tileus spies.

Most people did not believe the disinformation campaign. Rumors about radiation poisoning were rampant. Fearful people expected to lose their hair and see their skin fall off. Jake privately reassured their hosts the blast was not nuclear, that there would be no radiation and no fallout, but he couldn't tell them all he knew. He also told them not to share it with others because it would reveal classified knowledge. Han and his crew thanked them for the information.

On the fishing boat the first day, Han pulled Jake and Zofia aside. "Come below with me, please." Han looked around at the adjacent pier.

Jake followed his eyes and confirmed no one paying attention to them. "Yes, sir."

They went down a hatch in the pilot room deck into a small storage space. Han said, "This is the framework for the fish hold." He opened a hidden hatch at floor level. "The rubber you see through here is the lining for the hold. Before we get underway, you two will crawl into this space under the hold. That's where you'll be when we transit the channel."

Jake saw Zofia wasn't as surprised as he was. He said to her, "You've done this before?"

"Yes. It's small and cramped, but there's enough air for us to breathe. We'll be okay."

Han closed the hatch again. It blended in so well with the wall of the hold Jake couldn't see the hatch at all.

"Yitzak also asked me to give you some training—"

"How is Yitzak?" interrupted Zofia. "Have you spoken with him since we left Oriens?"

"Yes, he's fine. He told me you'd gotten away and he was under no suspicion. He wanted me to provide you with some personal weapons and training to use them. We'll do that tomorrow."

Jake stiffened. "Weapons? Good heavens. Won't that get us in trouble in Tileus?"

Zofia laughed. "Hardly, Jake. A third of the Tileans walk around with guns on their hip. It's normal there. Not like us."

Jake chuckled wryly, shaking his head. "Now, *that's* a different kind of country!"

☞ ✳ ☜

WENTDAY, 3 QUINTEMBER, 416 A.T.

Two days later, the fishing boat was cleaned up and had gone out. Han intended to signal his Tileus counterpart to arrange the trip for Jake and Zofia the next day. Apparently, the coordination always required an extra day.

Jake and Zofia were free for the day, so long as they practiced suitable caution about surveillance. They could take a day to breathe and be together.

Yesterday had been interesting, learning to fire a needle gun. They'd done their practice in the basement after work hours, firing at a target five meters away. Jake discovered he was quite good at it, hitting high scores after only a few rounds of practice. He imagined what it would have been like to fight back, there in Touchdown Park. Silly thought. There'd been way too many ticks chasing them.

Today, Ilsa gave them her rationchip to appropriate some necessities for her. It gave them purpose for a day of quiet enjoyment. The surveillance cameras were still mostly broken and, of course, Jake and Zofia had no implants to be tracked. The situation gave Jake a light-hearted feeling of freedom tempered by caution.

As much as he would have liked to be alone with Zofia, Renfo was with them as a guide.

152

"I hope to get my new Assignment in a day or two," Renfo enthused, "so I'm free today. I can show you around."

Jake said. "We don't really need a guide, Renfo—"

"No trouble, man. I'm glad to do it. I know where to avoid."

Zofia laughed. "Sounds like a dance. 'Go left—avoid right—skip it up and step it light.'" She hopped around on the street while she chanted.

Jake saw clearly Renfo still had a crush on Zofia, even in the face of the obvious pairing she had with Jake. Jake had little idea what was going on in the young man's head. Renfo had a constant attitude of resentment and an occasional offensive outburst. Mostly, though, his issues were personal rather than political. He could be cheerful and enthusiastic when something interested him.

The city was still recovering from the blast. The glass was gone from many windows, while others were covered with sheets of composite. Trash removal crews were slowly working their way through the city to remove the piles in each street. Mostly, people were getting on with life and had returned to their Assignments.

While they walked around, though, Jake often had to turn away from the worst of the damage. He was all too aware his bomb design had caused all this. He'd sabotaged the fuze timing so the bomb wouldn't work properly, but it had still exploded. He'd known all along the danger existed. You could "fail-safe" a nuclear explosion because all the parts had to work for it to go off, but an antimatter bomb was always "fail-fail." It took all the parts working to keep the antimatter safe. Any failure in any part, and the antimatter would contact matter and explode. *Why did Prime want to build it? It's crazy.*

They passed a hospital and he bit his lip. He whispered, mostly to himself, "Dammit. All the people I've hurt…"

Zofia gripped his arm tighter and leaned into him. He smiled sadly, appreciating her gesture of comfort.

"I'd like to walk by the shops," Renfo said. He was so eager, he looked like a puppy wagging its tail.

Jake chuckled at the combination of Renfo's sour attitude with this sudden enthusiasm. *I wonder how well the boy will do in a store. He's got to settle down and learn to take life with responsibility. Otherwise, how will he handle the boredom of empty hours in a shop? Or difficult customers?*

"Okay. So long as we're careful."

Jake kept a close eye out for cameras that might be functioning. Most of the camera mounts were empty, the devices having been ripped off the walls by the blast.

He reached out to hold Zofia's hand.

Renfo led them to a street of shops and stopped across from the first one, telling them about his new work. Jake stood with him, listening to his rushing words. Zofia bored quickly and wandered away to the next few shops, seeing what was available.

"This is it, Jake," he said excitedly, almost friendly. "Soon, I'm going to be working in a place like this. It's what I've wanted since I was in school. My aptitudes were all for shopkeeping, but Han twisted my Assignment to keep me on his boat."

"What do they distribute here?" Jake asked, mostly to keep up his end of the conversation. His mind was really on watching Zofia with a smile. She appeared to be having a good time window-shopping.

"Clothing," Renfo said. "All sorts of clothing, in all sizes. The way it works, they get the stock from Capital when it's produced, in accordance with the stated needs of the area. Then citizens come in to get their clothing, recording it against their rationchips." The boy was babbling.

Jake only partially listened to Renfo. It reminded him of Sam's enthusiasm for shopkeeping. Mostly, he was still watching Zofia enjoy herself. He saw her step into one of the shops.

"I'll get to organize the stock, make it attractive, keep track of it, record the distribution—"

"Oh, Earthfire," Jake suddenly whispered. His heart was pounding.

He watched Zofia back out of the shop she'd just entered, followed by two Solity Guards in their dreaded black. They looked like two huge insects with bulbous eyes. One of them had her arm caught in his hand. She glanced in Jake's direction and surreptitiously pushed her hand toward him. *Get away!*

Jake couldn't think what to do. His mind raced in circles. Should he run up and grab her away from the guardsmen? Should he turn and run? Stand where he was like an innocent bystander? He couldn't hear what they were saying to her, nor what she answered, but the tick had not released her arm.

Renfo hadn't noticed what was happening. He was still watching the action around the first shop and babbling about shopkeeping. Jake tapped his arm to get his attention. Renfo just kept talking and hardly noticed. Jake couldn't risk any sudden movement that might draw the attention of the Guards.

Instead, Jake backed away to the street corner and stepped out of sight, then peered around the corner from relative safety.

"Hsst. Renfo!" he hissed, trying to get the young man's attention. Renfo finally stopped talking to the air. He looked around for Jake, then looked down the street and saw what was happening.

The discussion between Zofia and the ticks suddenly became more heated. She tried to pull away, and the guardsman spun her around to grab both wrists behind her back. The second tick slapped a tanglecuff to her wrists. She struggled, and the first tick whacked her on the side of the head with his gloved hand. Citizens on the street backed away from the incident,

154

everyone watching. The second guardsman scanned the crowd and the street.

Eyes wide, Renfo jumped for the corner, exactly the wrong thing to do because his sudden movement caught the eye of the tick. Jake saw the guardsman turn to face them. Zofia looked their way, her hands captured painfully behind her back, abject fear in her grey eyes. Jake had to pull himself away from watching the disaster as Renfo rounded the corner.

"Run, Renfo," Jake urged. "Run now! They'll be on us in moments."

CHAPTER 24

Power protects power.

—*Collected Sayings of Yitzak Goren* by Ellen Thranadil, Tileus Press 439 A.T.

Lieutenant Kai Ariki paced in the darkened room behind the one-way mirror. The Guard detective with him stood and watched. This unknown woman without an imp sat in the bright interrogation room on the other side of the glass, hands chained to the seat of the chair between her legs. Her long black hair hung around her lowered face. She kept her eyes on the table in front of her, obviously frightened and cowed by her situation.

"She's a beautiful woman," Kai said to the detective.

"Yes sir. That's what caught the eye of the patrol officer in the first place. He might never have noticed her missing imp if he hadn't wanted to know who she was."

"Are we certain she had one in the first place? Some people in Prime never get tagged."

The detective shook his head. "She's got a wound on her neck, not even healed. She was wearing a scarf to hide it. But we still don't know who she is. She's said nothing since her arrest."

"We'll find out. Do we have the results from the DNA test yet?"

The detective held up a finger. *Wait.* His eyes glazed when he received something in his imp. Kai waited, watching the woman.

"We have it, sir," said the detective, while his eyebrows shot up, "and it's hot. Her name is Zofia Dobrunik."

"What? She's one of the two wanted in Oriens?"

"Yes, sir. Apparently so."

Kai knew what he had to do, and the gears slammed into action. "Let's move, then. Send a message to the Guard in Oriens we've found one of the two. Then expand their APB to include Timpi. Notify all the duty officers her companion is likely here. What's his name?"

The detective paused, checking his information. "Jacoby Palatin."

"Put out his information, pictures, and description to the patrols on the street. Warn them the man has no implant."

"Yes, sir." The detective left.

Kai paused to look through the glass again. *The detective's right. This one is hot. But it's a shame to have to act so quickly.* He watched her for another minute. She hardly moved in the glare of the interrogation lights. She and her boyfriend had brought a world of doom upon themselves.

He took a deep breath. Time to make a scary call. He directed his imp to make the connection.

"Overlock here, Ariki. What do you need?"

"We've got one of your fugitives."

⌘

"You and your shop!" Jake screamed at Renfo. They had escaped the ticks by running through a tangled sequence of streets. "If we hadn't gone to that street, Zofia wouldn't be caught! What are we going to do?"

"Hey, not my fault," Renfo shouted back. "I didn't send her down the street. And I don't want her caught, either. I love her!"

Renfo's claim stopped Jake in his tracks. "What?" He glanced around to make sure there weren't any functioning cameras on this street. "Love her? You hardly *know* her."

"She's so beautiful," Renfo nearly whined, "I've been her contact for both of her trips to Tileus and back."

"Then if you care for her, help us! I've watched your resentment about the Lazarite work for the last couple of days. You're so filled with it you're dangerous. Did you set this up? Did you take us to the shops so we'd be arrested?"

"No!" Renfo screamed. His face was smeared with shock. "I'd never do something like that. Specially to Zofia."

Jake checked the street again. He feared the ticks coming around the corner at any instant. They still had to get to safety. Yet he needed all the help he could. He would need Renfo. He grabbed Renfo's arm and dragged him to a doorway where they could be more hidden.

"Dammit, you could be helping to change Prime," he said, "like Han and the rest of the crew, so things like this don't happen to people we love. You could stand up for what's right instead of complaining all the time."

"But Han's been breaking the law and putting us in danger."

"Of course, he has. That's what it takes to change. Grow up. Do you really not understand the power the Guards have?" Jake asked, puzzled. "Haven't you watched how Solity works?"

Even while he asked the questions, though, Jake realized he wasn't all that different. He remembered his own naivete of a few weeks ago, how he trusted Solity and wanted to do whatever they asked.

Renfo shook his head. He was standing up straight with a light of determination in his eyes Jake hadn't seen before. "I'd never seen it first hand, except when they boarded our boat. We were smuggling then and deserved it, but today...Zofia wasn't doing anything at all. She was just shopping."

Jake considered telling him about their missing implants, but he wasn't ready to trust Renfo with any new knowledge. He went back to the immediate problem.

"What can we do, Renfo? How can we rescue her? For star's sake, the Guards *arrested* her! We've got powerful people after us, and she's in their hands now."

"I don't know. I'm not good at this stuff. Han tells me I put them in danger every time we face the Guards. We need to tell Han. He'll know what to do."

Jake agreed. *We need to get hidden again. It was foolish, coming out like this.* "But he's still out at sea. When will they return?"

"Not until sunset."

"Then let's get to his place and see if Ilsa can help. We've got to get Zofia out of there. It won't take them long to connect her with our troubles in Oriens. Damn, they'll send Shelton Overlock out here to interrogate her."

❧ ✳ ☙

"We have a problem, Franklin." The secure call was from the Guard informant in Timpi. The man only knew Franklin by first name, but he knew how to report information upward.

"What's the problem?" Franklin was not at all sure he wanted to know. He'd never expected Palatin to sabotage his bomb project, and the repercussions were significant on both Capital and the Lazarites. He didn't need more trouble.

"The Guards in Timpi have captured Zofia Dobrunik."

Franklin dropped his face into his hand in momentary despair.

"Did you hear me?" the informant asked after a silence.

"Yes, I heard you. Did they also capture Palatin?"

"No, sir. Only the girl."

Franklin thought quickly. "Is there any way we can create a rescue? Have them slip up and release her again?"

The man gave a short, hard laugh. "Working on it, but unlikely. Overlock is on his way to Timpi now."

"Okay. It is what it is. Anything else?"

"That ought to be enough."

Franklin sighed. "Thanks for letting me know."

They ended the call, leaving Franklin's thoughts in further disarray. He'd hoped Palatin and Dobrunik would be of Prime by now, but the explosion must have delayed their departure. Everything was interconnected, just like one of Yitzak's bad scenarios.

He could think of nothing to help Palatin at this time, so he turned back to the Capital problems. The explosion had destroyed both crops and stored reserves. He needed to come up with answers, then call Chairman Lukin to report. He hoped to be appointed director at the next Council meeting in two days, and it would be essential to handle this crisis well.

CHAPTER 25

When things turn to worms, remember worms create the soil to encourage growth.

—*Collected Sayings of Yitzak Goren* by Ellen Thranadil, Tileus Press 439 A.T.

Jake paced the floor in Han's living room like a caged vulf while he talked with Renfo and Han's wife Ilsa. "We've got to do something."

"I don't know," Ilsa said. "Han does this dangerous business, not me."

"Is there any way we can contact him now?"

"Not when he's on the water. You'll have to wait until he returns." She was clearly agitated and didn't know how to help. "I'll fix some tea while we wait."

Jake wanted much more than tea, but it seemed tea was all that was available now. Ilsa left them alone. The next two hours passed interminably while he waited for Han. Renfo kept offering ideas, but none of them sounded realistic.

"Maybe you could go to the Guard station to ask about a missing person," Renfo suggested. "Then, when you're there—"

"No, no, no," Jake said with irritation. "I can't have any direct contact with the ticks. They'll arrest me just as quickly as they did Zofia."

"Why, Jake?" Renfo asked. "Why did they arrest her? She didn't do anything but step into the shop." His attitude was supportive instead of resentful, and Jake was grateful.

Jake closed his eyes and huffed out a heavy breath. He had noticed a difference in Renfo this afternoon. The boy might still be a loose quark, but his crush on Zofia had him really trying to help.

"Okay, Renfo. I'll tell you, just so you know what might help. No, I'll show you." He unwound his scarf. "See the scar on my neck? Zofia and I cut out our implants so we could get out of Oriens. *That's* why she was arrested. The tick looked at her and couldn't get anything from her imp."

Renfo's eyes were wide. "You cut out your implants? And it didn't kill you?"

"No, that's something Solity tells us to scare us. It hurt, but we can live without implants."

"Wow." Renfo's eyes were wide. "That's a serious crime."

"Of course, it is! She's in deep trouble." Jake paced to the door yet again. "I can't wait here any longer. I'm going to the harbor to meet Han when he comes in. We need his help."

"I'm going with you."

❧ ✳ ❧

The *Solo Solar* was docking when they arrived. Jake walked across the wharf, checking for Guards. and bounded onto the deck as soon as the boat came alongside, even before Wang and Gonga had secured the lines. The two crewmembers joined with the dockworkers to unload their fish, lowering a huge vacuum hose into the hold to transfer the contents into the processing plant. Jake ducked into the pilot house where he could talk privately with Han.

"Han, we've got trouble," Jake said.

"Trouble? What trouble?"

Jake was so relieved to see Han, he suddenly felt weak. "Zofia was arrested today."

Han closed his eyes and growled deep in his throat. "Arrested. Aye. That's deep trouble for all of us. What happened?"

While he recounted the incident, Jake listened to himself and realized again how foolish they'd been. Having escaped from Oriens, and with the surveillance network damaged, he and Zofia had felt free to do what they wanted. But they weren't free, and wouldn't be until they got out of the country. Now, he had no idea how that would happen. *Am I going to have to go to Tileus without her? Leave her behind, to get the transpath built? How could I do that? I love her.*

Han stood as rigid as a tree when Jake was finished. Renfo said nothing. Jake waited. He needed Han's help.

"Well?" Jake finally asked. "How do we save her?"

Han shook his head. "I know the Guard lieutenant here in Timpi. Kai Ariki. For something like this, he'll barge in immediately. And he's good. Very good. He'll keep Zofia under guard."

"There's got to be some way we can break her out." Jake said. He felt a primal scream building inside him and held it back by sheer will.

"No. And it's worse. Ariki will probably contact Oriens when they know who she is. I know from informants he's been having conversations with Shelton Overlock."

"Dammit. Overlock is the one chasing us."

"May Elláh help her, then, and all of us. Overlock will get out of her all she knows."

Renfo's eyes had bounced between them like at a tennis match. He finally spoke. "Then we've got to do something. We can't let this Overlock guy get his hands on her."

Han shook his head again. "I doubt there's anything we can do to get her out." He called his first mate into the pilot house. "Wang, Zofia's been arrested. Go find our Guard contact. Now. See what's going on."

"Aye-aye, Captain."

Han turned back to Jake and Renfo. "We are swept with the current here. We can't get her out of a Guard station. They'll have to make a mistake."

⌒ ✳ ⌒

Jake and Renfo stayed in the *Solar*'s pilot house with Han into the evening, waiting for Wang to return.

"What will Wang be able to find out?" Jake asked.

"Not much," said Han. "He may be able to discover where they're holding her. Perhaps he might get some of their plans."

Jake shook his head, dismayed at the situation. He felt helpless. He wanted desperately to do something, to take action—but what could he do?

Renfo asked, "Should we go ahead with Jake's transit tomorrow?"

Jake hadn't yet gotten that far. He looked up, alarmed at what Han might say. Either "yes" or "no" carried its weight of danger.

"Yes," Han answered. "Getting him across is more important than Zofia."

Jake's heart nearly stopped. "No! No, no, no. Dammit, I can't go without Zofia."

Han looked him in the eyes. "You have to, you know. Currents flow where they will. We might not be able to cast her free, and you're in more danger the longer we wait."

"Yes, I know all that. The risk is high and getting higher. But she's important to me." Jake was facing Han, half a meter apart, glaring at the man.

"More important than saving the world?" Han asked.

Han's question put Jake squarely on the knife edge of a dilemma. He knew both sides of the challenge. His knowledge, coupled with Yitzak's holochip, would build the transpath and might stop the looming war. He'd had a dream all his life to use his technology to stop war, and now he had the chance. Billions of lives were at stake.

But Zofia. He'd never in his life known someone like her. Intelligent, beautiful, saucy. He'd given his heart to her. What kind of man would he be if he left her behind in danger? And what incredible danger! The rumors about Overlock were all bad, filled with evil incarnate.

Jake still stood face-to-face with Han, their opposing options mirrored in their body language.

"There's got to be a way," Jake said. Desperation made his throat sore. "Another day can give us the chance to get her back before Overlock gets here. And then we can both go to Tileus."

"No. That's not realistic. You're blowing against the wind, Jake. All that happens in another day is you get caught also. Then all our plans are sunk."

"Wait a minute," Renfo said. "I don't understand. Saving the world? What's so important about getting Jake to Tileus? More important than Zofia's life?"

Jake and Han's eyes were still locked together. Now they traded a look of dismay. Jake didn't trust Renfo with the knowledge, and he saw Han didn't, either.

Han answered "It's important, Renfo. That's all you need to know."

The boat rocked when Wang jumped back on board. He stepped into the pilot house. "I got a little, Captain."

"Go ahead," Han said while stepping back from Jake.

"She's at the Solity Guard station here in Timpi. Lieutenant Ariki is controlling her situation." He glanced at Jake. "He's put out an APB on our friend here."

"Ouch," said Han. "Jake, you see the signs of the storm. You can't stay here in Timpi, not even another day. We have to go tomorrow morning. I already set it up today with my Tileus contact."

"There's more," Wang said. "The rumor is somebody big from Oriens is coming in tonight."

Jake felt his heart freeze. "Tonight? Do we know who?" *It's got to be Overlock.*

"No, my contact didn't say."

Renfo had been looking outside at the gloomy docks. He said, "We can't get her before he arrives."

Han tilted his head toward Renfo. He seemed surprised his son would come up with a useful thought.

Jake said, "Renfo's right." His shoulders slumped. He dropped his face and let out a deep breath. "There's nothing we can do to stop Overlock from getting to her."

Everyone stood silent, waiting.

Jake lifted his face again. He felt tears on his cheeks. "So that's it. We need to go to Tileus tomorrow. Where do I stay tonight?"

He felt helpless and needed guidance. Jake was devastated, as if one of his bombs had scrambled his insides.

"Here on the boat is best," Han answered. "Lights out so as not to attract attention. Minimal movement. Stay inside if possible. We'll leave normally and bring some food back to you later."

"I'd like to stay with him." Renfo's offer was surprising.

Jake looked at the young man and saw a kindness he hadn't seen before, perhaps a desire to atone for their huge mistake today.

"That'd be good. I'd like the company."

The crew secured the boat and shut down the lights while Jake stayed seated in the pilot house. He was bleak. The necessity to go was real, but he had no idea how he could live with himself later. A short time later, Renfo joined him.

Han leaned into the pilot house. "We're off now, Jake. Gonga will be back later with some food."

"Thank you, Han," Jake said. "For everything. Let me know what I can do."

CHAPTER 26

An essential foundation of Solity was to keep its citizens feeling helpless without pushing them into despair. Letting them exercise their own agency would remove power from the leaders of Solity. Letting them despair would remove their utility to those same leaders.

—*An Annotated History of Verdant* by Ellen Thranadil, Tileus Press 442 A.T.

WENTDAY, 3 QUINTEMBER, 416 A.T.

Still here, still awake. *How long has it been?* Zofia didn't know. The bright lights hurt her eyes. The room was so warm sweat trickled down her forehead, armpits, between her breasts. Her wrists were chained to the chair between her legs, an embarrassing position. The chair was hard metal. Bolted to the floor. Unmovable, part of the building.

Zofia tried to sleep. She put her head down on the table in front of her. Every time she slipped into slumber, a strident alarm startled her back to sitting straight. Now, her head lolled onto her chest, dazed, but she couldn't sleep. Sometimes, the room filled with raucous music. Loud, painful. Couldn't block her ears.

How long? No windows, no clocks, no change. Just bright light. *Hours? Days?*

Damn, she was tired. Couldn't think straight.

She only moved from this chair once. A large tick, intimidating black with his helmet on, burst in and released her chain from the chair. Her hands stayed cuffed. Hard, gripping hand on her arm yanked her up to stand. Dragged her down a featureless hall...to the toilet. He unzipped her yellow coverall. She tried to stop him, do it herself, saying, "I know how to do this, damn it." He clouted her across the face. He pulled down the fabric over her shoulders, letting it dangle from her hands and behind her legs. He yanked her panties down. Bare from the thighs up except for her bra. His gloved hands caressed her from thighs to shoulders, then shoved her down onto the seat. No clean-up. Stood her up and dragged up the panties and coveralls. Didn't bother to zip them up. Brought her back here and chained her to the chair again.

Brightness and heat again. No relief.

He came in once with a hunk of bread and a bottle of water. Was it the same "he"? She couldn't tell. Didn't unchain her, didn't speak to her. Just shoved the bread into her mouth. She chewed to keep from gagging. Squirted water into her mouth; nearly drowned her.

Tired, so tired. Couldn't sit straight. Painful music again. She screwed up her face, trying somehow to shut her ears.

All the time, the mirrored wall glared at her. Reflected her own helplessness. They were watching her, she knew. Waiting. For what?

Oh, damn. Get on with it, buckos, whatever it is.

The Lazarites had seemed exciting and worthwhile, like a game against the authorities. She'd loved watching the establishment squirm. Do this and strike a blow for freedom. Do that, see the heavy-handed reaction. Talk about change. Spread the word through discussion groups. Cheer when the Lazarites succeeded. What she did mattered, could make a difference, she'd thought.

It didn't seem like a game anymore, and she didn't know how to face this. *I don't want to be tortured. Am I going to die?*

Jake. Surely, he'd rescue her. She was counting on him. But how could he?

Her fatigued mind slipped into memory. The wonderful trip with Jake to get to Timpi. Quiet times with him at night in Han's basement. Her horror when she stepped into the shop and saw the ticks. All those years of doing risky things had been exciting. The reality of being caught froze her in place. Her heart stopped, just like when they'd come to her apartment. The ticks in the store turned to her, ogling. She started to back out of the shop, full of fear. One of them stepped forward and grabbed her arm. *What is it with grabbin' my arm?*

"Who are you?" he demanded.

She was too terrified to speak. By the time she tried to pull away, they were in the street. He'd *hit* her.

They'd brought her here. *How long had she been here?*

Her bladder cried for relief again.

❧ ❈ ❧

The door blasted open, slamming against the wall with a crash.

Zofia jumped, eyes wide. It felt like she broke the skin of her wrists on the cuffs. She thought she'd urinated in her pants, but she was so sweaty, she couldn't tell.

Two huge, black-garbed insect-men strode in. One in the front corner of the room. One behind her, where she couldn't see him. They'd done that in her apartment, too.

The door was still open. The empty wall of the hallway loomed. What more was coming? Who?

So silent in the room, she heard the two ticks breathing. No one spoke, least of all her. She'd said nothing since they'd cuffed her in the street.

166

Hard bootsteps in the hall. Two sets of feet. She couldn't help but watch the door, her heart pounding.

Director Denmark stomped in. She recognized him from videos. Rich purple coveralls, sharp creases. His face an angry scowl.

Behind him—*oh, damn*—she'd never seen this man, but he was unmistakable from rumor. Ice blue eyes in a dangerous face, full of eager anticipation for what he was about to do. It had to be Overlock. His reputation filled her with dread. He carried an ominous clinking black bag. His terrifying eyes never left hers, and she couldn't look away from him. She felt like a mousel watching the sharp-beaked coastal harrier about to tear her apart. Very aware of her trapped hands and unzipped coveralls.

Denmark strode to the table and slammed his palm down. The *crack* reverberated in the room. She jumped a second time, tearing more skin on her wrists. The existential danger of Overlock was surpassed by the immediacy of Denmark.

"Just *who* do you think you are, you *prole-breed*?" he shouted.

She said nothing, just watched him. Heart pounding, breathing fast. Needing to pee. Aware of her helplessness. Her disheveled appearance.

Denmark leaned on the table. "Damn it, you think *you*, a tiny little part of Solity, can *change* us? You're a flea on the dog, raising minuscule itchy welts. A flea. You are nothing. *Nothing*,"

A spark of fire flashed in Zofia. "If I'm nothin', why are you and your trained vulf here..." She spat out his title, "Director."

He slammed his palm across her face. It felt like a sledgehammer blow. Her jaw dislocated for a moment, leaving a deep residual ache.

Overlock stayed near the door, watching. His voice was low, sibilant, and dangerous. "You will tell us all we want to know, Zofia Dobrunik. You will."

Denmark stood up again. "Yes. You can start by telling us where we find your *boyfriend*, Palatin." The derision with which he said "boyfriend" cut to her heart.

She lowered her face and shook her head. "I don't know where he is. They've probably moved him by now."

The director slammed his palm on the table again. Despite herself, she jumped once more. "No delays. No mercy." He stepped back and turned to his assistant. "Do it, Overlock. Enjoy yourself. Find out what she knows." Then he paused and looked into her eyes. "For now, keep her alive. Make it last." He strode out.

"Yes, Director," Overlock said to Denmark's departing figure. Then he stepped forward quietly to clank his bag on the table. He unzipped it, leaned down, and spoke.

"I will find out, young woman."

He pulled things out of the bag and set them on the table. Shiny things. Sharp things. Knives and clamps. Drug vials. Needles. A propane burner. Other things stayed hidden for now. She felt her eyes locked on each item he exposed. *What else does he have in there? What will he do with them?*

He quietly stepped back to close the door. The click sounded like the ending of a life.

His pale eyes locked on hers. Zofia quivered with fear.

"And yes," he hissed, "I will enjoy myself."

❧ ✳ ❦

Terrible hours passed.

She hurt. Head groggy. Bright lights. Wrists bleeding, blood on her hands. Mind fuzzy with drugs. She couldn't focus. Needles. How many times? Wet all over. Sweat? Blood? Sticky. She thought she remembered a bucket of water thrown at her. Or was it something else? She stank. Drug sweat, urine, vomit. Her ears rang. Coveralls pulled back, binding her elbows to her body. As if she could use her arms anyway. Exposed from the waist up. Knife cuts in her skin, stinging unmercifully and unendingly from whatever terrible, lingering ointment Overlock had added. Bleeding still? Above all else, she hurt.

Her ankles cuffed to the back legs of the chair. When did that happen? Legs awkwardly spread. Muscles in her groin stretched, cramping. Couldn't move them to ease the spasms.

Voices faded in and out. Some were here. Some were memory. She couldn't tell what was real.

Jake shouting, "You lied to me!"

"Algorithm failed." The programming AI from school. Failure from her past intermingled with now.

Yitzak soothing, "This will work."

Overlock. "And then what? Where did you go?"

An image of Léo Moulin, staggering away from the explosion. Blood dripped from his head and hands.

The Guard in the Warrens, shouting for them to stop.

Blistering burns on her thighs. Her coverall legs slit and pulled away. Confusion. The room whirling. How many people were here? Four? Eight? They moved too fast.

Jake. "The tunnel's blocked!"

"Jake!" she cried, and Overlock slapped her.

She shook her head, trying to clear it. The room spun. "Please, yes. End this." Was it her voice?

Another punch to her diaphragm. Another period of gasping for air her body couldn't find. Head swimming, spots in eyes. Finally, her diaphragm worked again. She sucked in miniscule gasps until it eased. Air. Blessed air.

She was in Tileus. Running through the streets. Guns firing, darts splashing on the rocks. No, that's not here. Never happened in Tileus. Or did it?

Closed into the darkness under the hold. Damp. No, that's not here, either.

What's real? What's not?

Running in the streets of the Warrens. Picking pockets and running. Chased by the ticks. Was that childhood? Jake was with her—or was he?

"Léo's gone, Zofia." She shook her head. No, that was Yitzak's voice, and he's not here.

Voices in the room. Whose voices?

"Han Yenstil, yes." She didn't know this voice. It sounded firm, in control. "He's the one we told you about."

"And who else, Ariki?" Overlock, and she winced at the terrible hissing voice. "What about Yenstil's first mate? She didn't know."

"Yes, his mate was part of it, too. Wang Quong. And five others, different boats, different Assignments." The firm voice. Ariki?

"And what did you get about Oriens?" Deep gravelly voice. Oh, right. Denmark.

Oh, damn. How much have I said? Mind still spinning, now filled with shame. And hurt. Too much hurt. Zofia wanted to shut down. The pain wouldn't let her.

"Yitzak Goren." Overlock.

And Denmark again, furious. *"Goren!* Damn them all to hell! I've fostered the man for thirteen damned years. What's his role?"

"He's the leader, Director. Or at least *one* leader. He's the one who gives orders to the Timpi crowd. And to this pathetic creature and her crew."

"And what about Palatin?"

"She doesn't know. They stayed at Yenstil's house this week, but she doesn't know where he might be now."

Long pause. Zofia's pulse pounded in her neck. She tasted blood.

Could she get her head straight to think? No, it wouldn't do any good, anyway. *Oh, damn, just let me sleep. Let me go.*

She barely heard the next words.

Denmark. "Okay, do it. Hold your raids here in Timpi and bring them all in. Question them if you can. Kill them if you must."

"Yes, sir." Ariki's voice?

Overlock spoke again, "What do we do with her, Director?"

Zofia cringed at the voice. She'd learned to cringe in these awful hours.

A pause. Long pause. Her mind wandered again. Were they talking about her? The girls in school talked about her sometimes. Jake talked to her. Darkness intruded.

"Take her back to Oriens, Shelton. Tomorrow. We'll expose her as bait to bring Palatin back."

Bait? I'm bait?

Oh, Elláh, all these voices swam in her head like huge tsiftim teeth raking in the feedfish. *I've given them so much. I don't even know how much. I just want to die.*

"And Shelton," Denmark paused. "Get rid of Goren. That mind control of his never did work, and it's not worth it to me. See what you can find out from him, then kill him. But make him suffer on the way."

Finally, Zofia faded out. Obscurity was bliss.

CHAPTER 27

The primary power of any government resides in its ability to impose its will on the people.
—*Collected Sayings of Yitzak Goren* by Ellen Thranadil, Tileus Press 439 A.T.

WENTDAY, 3 QUINTEMBER, 416 A.T.

Jake sat with Renfo. At first, they hardly talked, but company was better in his misery. Every sound reminded him of how helpless he was. The stink of the harbor illuminated his life.

The more he thought, the angrier he was at himself for not acting when Zofia'd been caught. On the other hand, he couldn't think what else he could have done. The ticks had weapons. He kept telling himself to calm down; he knew he'd be less effective in this agitated state. He wanted to go out, to do something to save Zofia. He also knew being out on the street was as dangerous as traipsing into the Guard station with "Here I am. Arrest me!" emblazoned on his coveralls. Instead, he stayed where he was.

Renfo got up to stand at the pilot house door, darting glances at the darkness in every direction. Anyone watching him would realize something shady was going on.

"Get back in here, Renfo, and stop looking around so much. Be more careful. You'll attract attention just by being so jumpy."

"Thanks, Jake. You're right. I've got to learn to do better."

"Do you? I thought you were going on a new Assignment to a shop, to get away from all this." Renfo might not be the best person to talk to, but talking was better than brooding.

"No, I haven't gotten my new Assignment yet. I don't think Han has set it up yet," said Renfo when he sat on the edge of the bench. He was bouncing his knee with nervous energy. "But I've been thinking about that. What happened to Zofia isn't right."

"Of course, it isn't." Jake sat beside him, listening.

"I never wanted to be part of the Lazarites. Han forced me into it. We've been smuggling across the Channel, and I wanted no part of it. I never saw it as doing much good, and it just put us all in danger."

Jake cocked his head in interest. Renfo seemed to be growing up.

"I'm beginning to realize there are more important things at stake." Renfo rubbed his eyebrow. "Any of us could be dragged away, just like Zofia. The Solity Guard can do that.

171

'I don't think I want to go to a shop after all. I want to be part of fixing this."

Jake raised his eyebrows. "That's a good thing to want." He paused a second, thinking. "But Han says you haven't exactly shown a positive attitude for the Lazarite work so far."

Renfo shook his head. "No, I haven't. I've been lazy about..." he gave a dry laugh at the play on words "...the Lazarites. I've been afraid."

Then he looked up to Jake with young, earnest desire. "But I can learn."

Jake snorted. "Well, it can start with what you just did at the door. You looked so worried and tense, glancing all around, anyone passing by would wonder what you were up to."

"Okay. Be calmer, more in control. I can do that."

Jake was skeptical, but right now Renfo was all he had.

After midnight, Gonga Onai returned. Jake and Renfo had been hungry for a while.

"Ah got some food," Gonga said, "but ya can't stay here. Come wit' me."

"What?" Jake jumped to his feet.

"We gots to go. Mebbe a raid tomorrow mornin', and de boat might be a target. Ah tell ya more as we goes."

The three of them checked the quiet of the harbor area, then quickly left the boat. Gonga led them through a few small streets near the harbor. He stopped at some steps down to a dirty, unused-looking basement door.

"Dis be a safe house. Only a couple people know 'bout it." He unlocked the door and handed Jake the key. "We stays here 'til morning, then get back to de boat if it's safe to go out."

Jake entered the apartment seeing a couch, a small table, a kitchenette, and a couple of chairs. Another door probably led to a bedroom. Several crates were set against the back wall.

Gonga gave them some sandwiches and water. They sat to eat.

"So what's happened?" Jake asked.

"We heard again from our Guard contact. De ticks got new information, mebbe from Zofia, and dey gonna make raids in de morning. Don' know who or where."

"Is Han at risk?" Renfo chimed in.

"We all at risk. If dey gots de information from Zofia, we all in danger."

"Dammit. How are we going to get across the channel?"

"De boats still go out tomorrow. Han say we gonna try. He and Wang will set up de boat. We suppos' to slip on board just afore dey leave."

This late at night, hungry for a while, food tasted good. But Jake had a more urgent question.

"Did you hear anything about Zofia?"

Gonga nodded. "Yah. Overlock been here already, and he gone again. De ticks gonna take her to Oriens tomorrow an hour before noon. Probably by aircar."

So that was that. There didn't seem to be much Jake could do, and he'd be leaving first thing in the morning. *Will I ever see her again?*

Jake got up and poked into the supplies. As bare as it seemed at first, Han had actually provided well in this stash house. He'd provided plenty of food. The electricity and water were running. The bedroom closet held coveralls in several colors and sizes. Jake changed into the light blue of Labor, knowing his own Defense green stood out in Timpi. He'd worn green all his adult life. It felt like a betrayal to change color, yet he knew it would be an effective camouflage. *I wish I'd thought of that earlier. Both of us could have been better disguised.*

He still beat himself up about Zofia's capture. *Can I ever forgive myself?*

The apartment also had a weapons cache with several needle pistols and enough ammunition for a small war. The cache included a shoulder-fired weapon Jake didn't recognize. He envisioned pointing it and pulling the trigger, but he had no idea what it would do. He decided to use some time cleaning one of the pistols.

His mind kept going all the time. He didn't lie down, because he feared what his mind would do while trying to sleep. Was there anything they could do? What about Zofia's transfer tomorrow? Could they rescue her while the ticks were moving her? He envisioned coming in with guns blazing, taking down a few Guards, and whisking her away. Then he shook his head. *Silly thought.*

However, the more he thought about it, the more flesh went on the bones of the idea. With the right preparation, it might actually be possible. Han said they had no chance to rescue her while she was in the Guard station—but a transfer might give them a chance. He'd need a team. Maybe Gonga and Renfo. *Would it be possible? We've only tomorrow morning to make it happen. Or is this foolish thinking?*

"Gonga. Renfo. Join me for a minute. I've got an idea."

The two stopped what little they were doing and sat with him.

"Gonga. Are you willing to help in a rescue? It'll be dangerous, but it may be our only chance."

The deckhand nodded emphatically. "Yah bet I am. These ticks do too much around here. It's time we did something back."

"Can you shoot?"

"Yah. Han taught me, using pistols just like dat one." He pointed at Jake's gun.

"Good." Jake was thinking fast. "Renfo. We'll need you, too."

"I'm listening. But isn't it *too* dangerous, Jake? And aren't you supposed to leave in the morning?"

"Yes, it's dangerous. I might not get to Tileus, and that would destroy the whole plan. We'll plan it out tonight, though, and talk it over with Han in the morning. I don't know whether he'll agree."

Renfo nodded. "Okay."

"Gonga," Jake said, "Zofia might not be able to walk. Can you find something we can use to carry her through the streets? Something ordinary to hide her?"

"Sure, boss. Ah know where there's a cart we can push."

"Get it now. We'll load guns into it in the morning if we decide to do this."

Gonga left, and Jake went to the gun cache to look again at the strange shoulder-fired beam weapon he'd seen before. He remembered what had been said about the building explosion in Oriens three weeks earlier. Some strange weapon had melted the composite materials of the building.

"Renfo, let's test this thing on a piece of furniture. Put a chair in the middle of the room, then stand back."

Jake did it cautiously. Aiming the weapon at the chair, he quickly blipped the trigger. A momentary buzz sounded, but nothing else. He triggered it for half a second, and the buzz became an unnerving sizzle. The chair slumped and melted onto the floor, leaving a dirty cloud, a pool of composite, and a stench of ozone.

Renfo shouted, "Whoa!"

Jake smiled. This would do.

☙ ✳ ❧

MIDDAY, 4 QUINTEMBER, 416 A.T.

Before dawn, after a short sleep, the three of them prepared for the day. The boat would be ready to leave at first light.

Jake still wouldn't know which way today would go until he spoke with Han. *I still don't even know which way I want it to go.* He wanted to rescue Zofia, but the risk was too large. He wanted to get to Tileus and stop the war, but he'd have to leave Zofia behind. He didn't like either option. But he could talk it over with Han.

"Let's load the guns onto your cart, Gonga. If Han decides our plan is worth doing, we'll be ready."

"Okay, Jake. Ah'll take de cart to de harbor and put it in a safe place."

"Be careful. Remember the Guards are doing some sort of raids this morning. Keep everything covered, and act normal."

It took only moments to load. Gonga left first, pushing the cart. Jake gave him a few minutes to get clear, during which he put two loaded needle guns into his backpack.

"Let's go, Renfo." Jake opened the door and checked the street. All quiet.

"And for star's sake, remember what I told you. Walk normally. Talk with me while we walk. Keep an eye out for cameras and trouble, but don't

174

be obvious about it. We'll go directly from here to the harbor. That's been mostly safe for us."

Still no Guards around. Pre-dawn tinged the sky with pale color. The new day smelled fresh. Jake led Renfo out onto the street. *I can't believe I'm doing this. How is it I understand what we need to do? A week ago, I knew less about clandestine work than a scaly hooliphant in a crowd.* The image of a huge beast tearing up a throng made him chuckle in the midst of the trouble.

❧ ❋ ❦

Renfo followed Jake up into the street. He still wasn't comfortable with his decision to dedicate himself to the Lazarites. He saw the unfairness of what happened to Zofia, but he didn't really know whether he could do this.

The street had a smattering of pedestrians headed to work. Renfo watched Jake and the way he moved. By looking and acting normal, they got zero attention from other people.

So Renfo took to heart the advice Jake had given him. He walked with Jake as if they were friends or co-workers, two light blue coveralls among many others transiting the streets. He was nervous, no doubt. His heart beat faster than normal, yet he took care not to let it show in his actions. Without moving his head, he scanned for danger: cameras, people watching them, Guards.

Three blocks later, the water of the harbor glinted in the darkness ahead of them. Some streets had been cleared, but near the harbor, piles of debris from the blast wave were still stacked in the street. Even this early in the morning, residents picked through the piles looking for useful items.

Then Renfo heard the whine of a powerful aircar overhead. He looked up and saw a Guard car flash by.

Jake had seen it also. "Quick, into this doorway."

Renfo followed Jake into a recessed apartment entrance. The door was set back into an alcove a meter deep, giving them cover from above.

"The ticks are everywhere." Renfo said.

"Yeah, stay hidden."

Suddenly, a group of five men wearing light blue sprinted into the far end of the street from the dock area. The men dashed partway up the block before a half-dozen Solity Guards in black rushed into the street behind them. Renfo caught his breath and plastered himself against the door behind him. He tried the handle, but the door was locked.

The air was abruptly full of flechettes. The ticks advanced into the street, firing on the fleeing men. The fugitives ducked behind piles of trash and fired back, forcing the ticks to seek cover. People in the street screamed and ran for the doorways. Needles pinged off the walls and splatted into the piles. Renfo peered out from the corner of the entryway, fascinated and petrified by the exchange. Then his breath caught.

"That's Han!" he whispered to Jake, "and Wang with him. The other three are from different boats."

Jake joined him at the corner of the entry, watching the action a mere hundred meters away. He pulled one of the needle guns out of his backpack.

"Give me one, too," said Renfo. "We can open fire from here."

Jake stood with the gun ready, but didn't fire. He shook his head. "No, dammit. We can't. We've got to stay hidden. I have to get to Tileus, even if people die."

Renfo glanced at Jake in surprise. *What could be so important about getting to Tileus? More important than Han's and Wang's lives? How will we get to Tileus without Han?*

"What about Zofia, Jake? You're willing to risk your plans to save her."

He saw Jake slump. "I don't know, Renfo. It may be just stupidity. Getting to Tileus is vital. But whether we try for Zofia or not, we can't expose ourselves to the Guards by shooting at them."

The Guards were using the trash piles and doorways as shields, firing at the Lazarite men from several angles. Renfo's heart pounded while he watched, helpless. Han and Wang both leaned out to fire from opposites sides of a pile, then took off running back to the next pile. Renfo had heard the phrase "fire and retreat" in entertainment; now he saw it for real. The other three fugitives were doing the same.

Retreating wasn't working well. Every time the Lazarite people dropped back, the ticks advanced. The rebels weren't getting any farther from the ticks, and they were working their way back toward where he and Jake hid.

When the Guards did their next advance, Han was ready. When one tick exposed himself to run forward, Han caught him in the neck. Renfo saw blood splatter, and the guardsman staggered to a wall before dropping to his knees, then onto his face.

On the same advance, another tick reached a doorway with a better angle on the other three Lazarite men. He fired as soon as he was in position, and one fugitive fell against the trash pile he'd been using for cover. Han and Wang returned rapid fire to the newly-positioned officer. Flechettes hit the doorframe, then his shoulder. The tick spun away, and more flechettes hit his chest. He dropped.

The odds were even, four against four. Could they get away?

The aircar whine grew loud above them, and Renfo drew back into the entry. The car swooped overhead into a hover. He heard the rapid spit of fully automatic needle guns over the aircar noise. Flechettes blanketed the area where the fugitives hid.

With the withering fire from above, the remaining two rebels in the forward position broke from cover and scurried toward Renfo. They scrambled only a few steps before the fusillade of darts took them down.

Both fell to the street, their guns skittering across the pavement like water on a hot, oily griddle.

Han fired at the aircar, but the flechette guns wouldn't hurt the machine. He and Wang also fled their protection and ran toward a doorway across the street from Renfo. The door would give them cover from above.

The aircar shifted its fire and the stream of metal death raked across Wang. He jerked repeatedly in his stride and fell.

Han kept running while the fatal river swept toward him. Two steps from the doorway, his blue coveralls were torn by the darts. He dropped to his knees and continued crawling. On the doorstep, the flechette flow riddled his body. He fell into the doorway he'd been trying to reach. Unmoving.

"Han! Father!" shouted Renfo, moving forward, his shout muffled by the noise on the street. Jake yanked him back into the entry.

"No, Renfo," Jake urged. "We can't show ourselves." The two huddled against the door behind them.

CHAPTER 28

No person was ever bold who was not also fearful.

—*Collected Sayings of Yitzak Goren* by Ellen Thranadil, Tileus Press 439 A.T.

Renfo shuddered in Jake's grasp, filled with remorse. "Damn. He really was my father." He couldn't believe it had come to this.

A click sounded behind them, and the door opened. A woman's voice spoke quietly. "Come in, you two."

Renfo stumbled through the door into a hallway with stairs and numbered doors. He collapsed on the floor in tears, his heart aching.

"He wanted to do right by me, Jake. I always fought him. Oh, damn, what have I done?"

"We've got no time for that now, Renfo," said Jake, then he turned to the woman. "Thank you. We owe you our lives."

"There's a back entrance at the end of the hall." She ducked into the first door on the left and closed it. Renfo hardly saw her, but he heard the lock click, sounding like the final gate before Hell.

Renfo sobbed while he sat. He'd wasted his entire life in selfish desire, not seeing the reality of what was around him. He'd resented Han for his overbearing manner, for controlling Renfo's life, for forcing him into the Lazarites. Now, watching Han die so suddenly, Renfo realized he had only resented Han so much because the man was indeed his father. Han had tried with everything he had to give Renfo a life that mattered. For five years, Han had taught him despite Renfo's own defiance. He'd become a competent fisherman and crewmember. He knew how to run the boat. Han had protected him from the controls of Solity and had sought to give him purpose.

Through his tears, he said to Jake, "He didn't give up on me until this week. And even in giving up, he was going to help me get what I wanted."

Jake knelt down and put a hand on his shoulder.

Renfo kept on, "Solity doesn't let people be fathers, but Han did the best he could to be one. And I shoved him away every chance I got."

He looked up at Jake. He couldn't hardly see him through the blur of his tears.

"I hate Solity."

Jake nodded. "Good choice." He sounded nervous. "But we need to be gone, too."

Jake looked out through the window in the door. "They'll be checking the street. The aircar might have sensed our presence in the doorway. Grief is real, but we need to live."

Renfo looked up at him and nodded. He wiped the tears off his face. "Where can we go?"

"I think the safest place is still the boat. We can meet with Gonga there. But I don't know."

Renfo nodded and got to his feet. This was purpose. "Then let's do it." He led the way to the back door.

Renfo eased open the door. The alley was empty. When he and Jake stepped out, the heavy whine of the aircar sounded above them. It was still watching.

The back streets of Timpi took them toward the harbor. They avoided anywhere the cameras looked intact. The aircar continuously circled overhead, so the two never got far from cover.

Jake guided their actions with his heart in his throat. Not only was Zofia still in danger, but also now the Lazarites themselves. Han had been the Timpi leader. Now he and his first mate Wang were dead. He overhead chatter on the streets that others had been killed or captured. Jake was particularly concerned about interrogation of arrested members. Information gained by the ticks could lead to danger for the few, like Renfo, who had escaped Guard purview.

When they got to the harbor, Jake scoped it out as carefully as he could. Things were quiet. There were no Guards around. The sun was now up. Most of the fishing boats were underway, heading out, leaving the *Solo Solar* and another three still at the wharf. The men they'd seen in the firefight probably belonged to those boats. Or maybe a couple of boats were still damaged from the blast.

Gonga was on board the *Solar*. They watched the older man while he moved around the deck, cleaning and straightening gear. Nothing seemed amiss, so he and Renfo stepped aboard. Gonga started in surprise when the boat rocked, then he quickly urged them into the pilot house.

"Yah, de ticks was here," Gonga told them. "Dey came into de harbor with nets wide for big fish. I saw Captain Han and Wang, dey jumped ship and ran, shooting at the ticks. Ah don't know what happened to dem. All of dem went up that street over there, shooting and shooting."

Jake shook his head sadly. "We saw the end of it, Gonga. Han and Wang were gunned down in the streets by an aircar."

"Oh, man." Gonga hung his head. "Dat's bad. Very bad. Dey was good men."

"The ticks didn't come back for you?" Renfo asked.

"No, man. I guess dey don't know ah've been working the Lazarites, too."

Jake thought about their predicament.

"Now I don't know what to do," he said.

Yitzak nodded when he got an early morning secure call from their Guard informant. From his correlation of events and people's reactions, he'd expected this call for a week.

"You're in trouble," the mole said.

Yitzak smiled to himself. "I've always been in trouble of one sort or another, my friend."

"Listen, you should know you were exposed last night in interrogations here in Timpi."

"Everything is connected. Trouble in Timpi breeds trouble in Oriens."

"You can't philosophize your way out of this, Yitzak. You'll need to protect yourself. They'll be after you today."

"I know, I know. I have plans in place. Good plans. I'll activate them."

Then Yitzak felt a pang of fear for his long-term plans for the transpath. *Who's been captured?* "Was it Jake or was it Zofia?"

"Palatin was never caught, but Overlock worked over Dobrunik."

Yitzak winced. He knew Zofia better than she knew herself; despite her front of boldness, she was always a very frightened woman. "Did she survive?"

"Physically. Don't know whether she'll recover emotionally."

"How much did she reveal?"

"Overlock knows you're her cell leader in Oriens. She also gave up the names of the other people in your cell, and what they'd done."

Yitzak closed his eyes, the pain almost more than he could bear. So many people in danger. So much hurt.

"Are you still there, Yitzak?"

"Yes. Did she reveal our plans for Jake?

"No. Overlock never thought to ask."

Relief mixed with his fears. *At least the transpath is still safe.* "Is there more?"

"I'm trying to arrange for her rescue," the informant said, "but it will depend on Palatin to succeed. In the meantime, protect yourself."

They ended the connection on that bleak note.

Yitzak got a cup of coffee from the autocater and took it onto his balcony. With years of successful research, he'd earned a level-4 apartment overlooking Touchdown Park. The vivid green grass below led to the Mueller Memorial and the varicolored trees beyond. He'd enjoyed this view he would now have to give up.

The informant's call fit another piece into the puzzle Yitzak always assembled. He followed everything he could find and saw, as few did, how it all came together. Tileus had a problem with the insistent missionaries sent by its neighbor Rathas; they were almost at war over the intrusions. Prime aimed to bring both Tileus and Rathas back into subjugation. Even the isolated tribal islands of Winter were disgruntled, withholding their shipments of fish. The ocean waves washed the shores of all four countries, binding them together.

He and Franklin Edobar had accelerated their Lazarite plans to increase pressure on Solity. Valuable lives were now lost or at risk. They'd hoped the internal problems—protests, fire bombings, explosions—would delay Denmark's movement toward war with Tileus. Jake's antimatter explosion had been a nice touch, not part of their Lazarite plans but fitting well. Yitzak smiled. Damage to Timpi, a fishing city, added to the pressure from the islands of Winter. Everything was connected, like strands of a godly spider web stretched across the entire world.

Who knew his long life would have reached a point where he was in personal danger? Yet the question answered itself, for Yitzak himself had foreseen this risk the day Denmark changed his Assignment from academic research to defense. He'd sensed the disaster creep closer year by year, like the erosion of cliffs under a waterfall. His personal disaster presaged the larger disaster of humankind on Verdant, or of humanity throughout its few remaining planets.

He was too old for this. Where could he run to find safety? No place on Verdant offered security. He had completed his part. So now he had the opportunity to end it with—*What was the phrase? Ah, yes*—with extreme prejudice.

Maybe—just maybe—his transpath would have a positive effect.

Today, he would protect the transpath. He finished his coffee and went to his lab. With deep sadness in his heart, he used the morning to check and activate explosive devices and remote detonators.

As for himself...he also had good plans to surprise Denmark.

An hour before noon, Jake, Renfo and Gonga walked up the street beside the Guard station as casually as they could. City crews had been repairing surveillance cameras, so Jake had disguised the lines of his face with angular make-up, as he'd done coming into Timpi. He wore a light jacket with a hood covering his head. Gonga pushed the large hand cart piled high with fishing equipment. The handguns and beam weapon were hidden under a tarp.

Jake had made the decision. Without Han, he didn't know how to get to Tileus. So, he had time for plan B: rescue Zofia.

Even so, this had to be the most harebrained scheme Jake had ever created. *I'm an engineer, for Earth's sake. I design things and try to anticipate the consequences, but I have no idea what's going to happen.* He could feel his heart pounding in his neck.

They stopped around the corner from the front of the station. With lunchtime approaching, the street was far from empty. Good. They didn't want to stand out.

Now, they had to wait until the transfer. To justify their wait, Jake stopped the hand cart and had Gonga fiddle with the wheels and axle as if they needed repair. Jake leaned against the wall where he could see the street in front of the station, as if waiting for Gonga to finish.

"Just remember, you two. Watch where you aim. Don't hit Zofia!" he whispered to Renfo and Gonga.

"Yah bet, boss. We'll charge in close first, so we can hit what we want." Gonga was cool and ready. His calm helped Jake compose himself.

"I'm not that good a shot," Renfo said in a worried tone. "This is crazy. I can't believe we're about to attack the ticks. We're probably going to die."

"Surprise is the key. Just do your part, friend," said Jake. "Get to the other side of the street and attract their attention. Don't shoot until we do, and wait until you can get close enough. Let's just hope there aren't more than four or five of them. If they have more than that, we'll call it off."

Renfo stayed nervous, but Jake saw him smile at being called "friend." Renfo walked to the far side of the street across from the station entrance, his gun now hidden in his coveralls. Jake was satisfied at his act of nonchalance.

The whine of an approaching aircar echoed in the confines of the street. Jake saw a Guard aircar approaching above the roofs. It settled onto the street in front of the station. People immediately gave it a wide berth.

Almost time to act. Jake took a shuddering breath and watched the station door.

Two black-helmeted ticks stepped out of the aircar, scanned the street, then stood, guarding the car.

The station door opened. Three more ticks came out. Two of them nearly carried a weak figure in yellow coveralls. Zofia's long, black hair hung like seaweed. She was hardly walking, her feet dragging in shuffling steps, her hands cuffed in front. Blood and grime splattered the coveralls, and the torn leggings flapped behind her, exposing her thighs with every painful stagger. Jake heard a collective gasp from the passers-by.

The third guardsman had a needle gun out, scanning the crowd. He seemed to take in everything. When he looked toward their position, Jake lowered his face to focus on Gonga and the 'broken' wheel and axle. The tick looked past to others.

Seeing Zofia, Jake was at first too shocked to act. The caravan of three ticks had already dragged her halfway to the aircar where the two aircrew waited.

"Best move now, boss," whispered Gonga.

Jake set his jaw. Stepping to the cart, he pulled out the beam weapon and aimed it at the back of the aircar.

When he pulled the trigger, the weapon sizzled like resin in a fire. The invisible beam hit the car, instantly leaving it melting onto the street like slow lava. Smoke and stench drifted upward. Jake quickly played the beam forward on the car, watching the side and door liquify.

The two aircar ticks jumped away at the noise and stink of their car disintegrating. Shocked, facing the car, both of them drew their pistols. The two dragging Zofia stopped in their tracks. The third Guard stood stunned, looking at the aircar, before frantically scanning the street.

Renfo started shouting on the far side of the street. He pointed at the aircar. "Look at that! Oh, damn, that aircar's melting!" He ran from his place toward the car, gathering all the attention of the ticks. Everyone else on the street was backing away.

Jake dropped the beam weapon on the cart and grabbed his needle gun. He and Gonga charged the distracted ticks from the side. Jake sprinted, quickly pulling ahead of the older man. As soon as he was close enough, he started firing.

He aimed at the Guard behind Zofia. His first shot missed. The Guard shouted, "Take her back inside!" He turned to face Jake while the other two dragged Zofia toward the door.

Jake aimed again and hit the Guard, who dropped.

The two aircrew fired at them. Gonga, right behind him, was shooting at the aircrew. Now Renfo also sprayed flechettes toward the aircrew.

"Fast, you two, fast!" shouted Jake. "Before any others come out."

Jake couldn't shoot at the two holding Zofia; he might hit her instead.

He used one of his zero-G moves, putting his shoulder into the nearest of the two. He was moving fast enough both officers and Zofia were thrown off their feet. Jake fired point-blank at both of them. The faceless creatures were black bug vermin to him in that moment; he filled with wicked glee at the chance to get back. Neither one rose from the ground, and he kicked their weapons away.

He knelt beside Zofia.

"Jake?" Her voice was weak and confused, her eyes unfocused, her body limp.

"I'm here," he said, "No time to talk."

Jake gave his gun to Gonga, then lifted Zofia off the ground and ran to the corner of the building. Gonga and Renfo had taken out the aircrew and joined him, acting as guard against the surge of ticks they expected from the station.

Around the corner, the push cart was waiting to receive her. Renfo pulled aside the canvas and ropes covering a hollow in the load of fishing gear. Jake laid Zofia inside.

"Stay still. We're going to cover you up and push you out of here. Don't make a sound."

She looked up at him, but her eyes didn't focus. Her response was a small whimper.

Renfo reached to cover her with the canvas when a deep, threatening voice spoke from behind them in the side street.

"Jacoby Palatin, don't move."

Jake whirled around to see a Guard. The man's needle gun was already aimed at Jake, ready to spit death. The man's face shield zipped upward, showing his angular features, intense brown eyes, and an unyielding set to his mouth. *Oh, Hell and Earthfire! We're all caught now.*

Renfo named him with a quavering voice. "Lieutenant Kai Ariki."

CHAPTER 29

Governor Welton Moller made every effort he could to counteract the belligerence of Prime. While responding effectively in both negotiations and personal contact, he also initiated many efforts within Tileus aimed at defusing the antagonism caused by simple cultural differences.

—*An Annotated History of Verdant* by Ellen Thranadil, Tileus Press 442 A.T.

Two days earlier, in Tileus: Twoday, 2 Quintember, 416 A.T.

"Must be nice, being related to one of the five national Governors of Tileus." Manny was always so cheerful.

Soren Moller shrugged, scowling. "No, it's more trouble than good. The connection compromises me, makes me vulnerable in ways a police detective shouldn't be."

He and his partner, Manny Hong, climbed the steps of Freedom Aerie, the central government building, on their way to see Welton Moller, Soren's uncle. Soren stopped on the steps and turned to look down at the trees and grass of the city park behind them. Some parts of Thad City were worth looking at.

Soren thought for a moment how fortunate he was to be in the country of Tileus. People scurried through and around the park, each on their own pursuits. The vast majority of citizens were responsible and contributed to their democratic civilization. They did their part, for their own benefit, but all the parts worked together to make the country work. Most of the time, anyway. He admitted to himself conflict did happen. Groups with different ideas sometimes fought it out—in rhetoric and politics mostly, but sometimes physically. Tileus could be a mess at times. The decisions were always made as a whole, though, through the nationwide vote. Everyone had a voice on every law.

Of course, some citizens had other ideas and decided to take instead of give. They were leeches, not contributing to the whole. That's where laws came in. And where Soren and Manny did their work.

"Are we going in," said his partner, "or are you just going to let the breeze blow through your hair?"

Soren snorted and turned toward the doors of Freedom Aerie. The portico imposed above them, carved with figures from Tileus history. Every time he came here, it felt like a massive weight ready to fall on him.

He frowned up at the huge Manny walking beside him. "This little visit is an example," he said, "of the problem with having a powerful relative. Who knows what my uncle wants?"

"Whatever it is, he'll pave the way to make it easy for you," said Manny.

Soren shook his head. "No, that's not the way it works. He calls me in for the most difficult work, the things that aren't easy at all. And this time, he wants both of us. You're going to be right in the thick of it."

He and Manny climbed the rest of the steps and went in. They'd been partners for six years. He'd trusted Manny with his life many times. The man sometimes got on Soren's nerves with his cheerful attitude, but all in all, Manny was a great partner. He had the speed, brawn, and street smarts when they were needed, and he came up with ideas Soren might never have thought.

The private secretary ushered them into Welton Moller's office with no delay. That was a surprise; Soren usually had to wait. As Governor of Outside Affairs, his uncle's time was filled to the minute with national issues related to the other countries on the planet. Soren curled his lip at the spacious chamber with its rich wood furniture. Uncle or not, he'd rather not deal with those in power. He preferred having the power, like he did with the criminals he caught.

Welton stood up with a bright smile and came out from behind his oversized carved desk. "Soren, my boy, how are you?" He extended his hand for a firm handshake. "Glad you could come by." His uncle's voice had a warm country feel he'd fostered for years as a way to disarm political opponents.

Soren gave a wry smile. "As if I have any choice, Uncle Welt, when I'm summoned by a Governor."

His uncle laughed, joining him in the joke. "But you always have a choice. You could ignore me, and I'd just destroy your career." His tone of voice said the threat wasn't real. "And this must be your partner. Manny, welcome."

The two shook hands, and Welton guided them to the sofa and chairs in a corner of the expansive room.

"Sit down, boys. I wanted to thank you both for nailing that trafficking pervert recently. You did some really creative work there, using our constantly-changing laws against him. I understand the charges held up in court, and he's put away now."

Soren noticed his partner sit up straight, almost preening.

"I'm surprised you know about our work, sir," Manny said.

Soren rolled his eyes. He was used to this. His uncle would have had someone research them before the meeting.

"I work for the highest levels of the country, Manny, but I still like to know about the people who come into my office."

Manny shrugged. "Well, Soren did most of that one, anyway. He's the one who saw the connections when the voters changed the law."

"But you two are partners, right?"

"We are," said Soren. "We work well together."

"And that's why I asked you both here. I've got something new for you to do. Something big. Needed for the country."

Soren traded a glance with Manny. "The country? We're just city detectives. We solve crime."

"Don't sell yourselves short. You're the best detectives in Tileus. You've got a higher rate of convictions than any other team in the country."

Soren shrugged. Focused as he usually was on his work, he enjoyed getting recognition, too. "Thanks. We've been lucky."

"Not just lucky. Good. Smart. You do the research to find the connections, then you put the facts together clearly."

Soren glanced at Manny and his huge grin. He was eating it up. Soren waited for the punch line.

And it came when Welton continued, "So, I'm having you two re-assigned to a special mission."

Soren stopped smiling. "Re-assign us?" *But I like what we do.*

"Let me give you some background. This is all top secret, but you need to know. Last month, a minor protest materialized in Verdant Prime, with protestors throwing rotten fruit."

"Sounds rather mild for a protest. We have worse here in Thad City. But Prime? What do a couple of city detectives have to do with them?" Soren's eyebrows furrowed while he tried to understand.

"Bear with me. After the protest, I got a secure call from their Director of Defense, a man named Berndt Denmark. He was rather offensive on the call, blaming Tileus for inserting spies and agitators into their country."

"Do we do that?" Manny asked.

"That's not important." Welton chuckled. "And if we did, it wouldn't have been rotten fruit. What's important is the open accusation. In the last four weeks, they've had additional protests, becoming more violent. Street obstruction, fire bombings, even exploding a city block—"

"How can that happen?" asked Manny. "I thought Prime had all its citizens locked down with surveillance."

Welton shrugged. "Obviously not. However, along with the events, I've had three more calls from Denmark. He's been increasingly hostile, even threatening war—"

"That's not good," said Soren.

"—and they've been ramping up their military forces, too. I'm concerned Denmark is the kettle calling the pot black. I think he's probably got a network of spies here in Tileus, giving them information about our defense capabilities in preparation for a war he's planning."

Soren nodded. "Manny found some puzzling stuff about Prime just last week."

"Yeah," his partner added. "I picked up some papers at a perp's house about smuggling people across the channel."

Welton paused and thought, his gaze far away. "Smuggling across the channel. Yes. That's the likely way to bring them back and forth." He focused again on the two in front of him. "I've got other people working on diplomacy to prevent Denmark's war, but you two have a different job. You're the best detectives we've got. Find the spy network and shut it down. And the smuggling, too."

Soren nodded. "Uh-huh. We can't do the politics, but we can do this. Espionage is a crime." He looked at Manny, who was also nodding.

"There's more. You need to know how important this is. This past weekend, an explosion occurred in the mountains of Prime."

"We heard about it." Manny said. "What does it have to do with a spy network?"

"The explosion was big," said Welton. "Really big. It damaged buildings fifty kilometers away." Soren sat up straight, alert in surprise, while his uncle continued, "Our analysts don't yet understand it, but Prime seems to be developing a doomsday weapon to use against us. We have to stop them."

❧ ✳ ☙

Back at their office, Soren and Manny told their lieutenant they'd been detached for separate work. The lieutenant wasn't happy.

"Yeah, I heard it from the captain, too. Do what you need and get back to us. We're way too short-handed to lose you."

"Right, boss. We'll keep you posted."

They worked on research first, using the holo projector over their shared desk. Soren was good at the research, while Manny often had the best ideas.

Manny started. "We've got a good network of informers. Which of them might know about spies?"

"Follow the money," Soren answered. He put his hands into the haptic field. With a combination of imp commands and moving fingers, he brought information into the holo display. "Here's our list of informers. I can link this to their financial records. Let's see who's come into new money in the last two months."

"I love the way you do this stuff. It's like magic. You've already narrowed it down to twelve."

"Yeah, few enough we could just go question them. But let's get some more goodies first. Which of these lowlifes would stoop to treason?"

Manny laughed. "All of them, if it meant money."

Soren smiled with him. "Right. But which ones would be *most* likely?"

Manny pointed into the holo and highlighted four of the names. "These guys do the dirtiest stuff."

"I also like these other two," Soren said when he highlighted another couple.

Manny nodded. "I'd buy it. Those two are pond scum living high on the hog."

"We can get more. Let's explore the money trail." Soren always enjoyed this part of their work. He was a wizard with technology, putting together searches most detectives never considered. His fingers flew while he subvocalized commands. He was hardly aware of Manny watching him.

"Here we go," Soren muttered. He brought up another display, a dense network of lines and dots, then pointed into the display. "The dots are people and institutions. The lines show money transfers. Still too much, though. I'll narrow the criteria to related transfers."

Soren expanded a section. "Okay, this is good. See? One transfer moved from an institution to a king boss. Another five handovers went from the boss to group leaders. Some of the money went to two of our six."

The patterns were still complex, but Soren kept working. Gradually, he clarified them.

Manny asked, "Do we know what the money was for?"

Soren grunted. "Good question." He added in a search for invoices. Money transfers weren't always tied to them, but could sometimes be linked.

"Whoa. Does that say 'paperwork'?" said Manny. "What kind of paperwork would they be paying for?"

Soren glanced up. "Only one kind. Identities. Implants. The kind of thing a spy would need when they arrive. Yep. It's getting dirtier as we go in."

Finally, he sat back. Now, the emerging patterns linked five of the six names through a network of known money launderers back to...Prime.

"Now, we're talking," Soren said with satisfaction. "Identities for money here in Tileus, bartered for goods from Prime. This can also be a black market for weapons to stockpile here." Thinking hard, he turned to his partner. "How did we miss this, Manny? This web didn't happen overnight. They've been at this a while. And what did Uncle Welt say? They just tested a doomsday bomb?"

"Yeah, they did."

"They would have to know beforehand we'd hear about the test."

"Probably."

"Don't you get it?" Soren asked. "They don't care if we know they have the weapon. Why not? I'm thinking they might be just about ready to make their move against us. We don't have much time to shut this network down."

☙ ✳ ❧

Soren and Manny had been lucky. They'd located a weapons cache in Thad City by following one of their five suspects who'd had a recent transaction. So here they were in front of a single building in a row of walk-up apartments on a dirty back street. The windows were blacked out, so they couldn't see inside. They'd watched their suspect and a driver unload two long, narrow boxes from an autotruck and carry them inside.

"Guns, Soren," said Manny from their stakeout.

Soren grunted in response. The driver took the truck away. Their suspect went inside.

"Should we call in a team?" Manny asked.

"So far as we know," Soren said, "our guy is the only one in there. We followed him and the weapons, so 'hot pursuit' applies. If we wait, we'll have to get a warrant. Let's do it now. You want the back or the front?"

Manny chuckled. "I like the back. They always run out the back."

"He might not run at all, with his weapons here."

The two split up. Soren gave his partner time to position himself at the back door, then walked up the steps and pounded on the front door.

"Police," he shouted. "Open up."

Without waiting for a reply, he thumbed the handle and hit the door with his shoulder. It opened easily. Soren jumped through and slid to the left, away from the darkened window, crouching with his gun aimed forward.

A line of flechettes pinged into the doorframe beside him. They'd come from a stack of six or eight boxes in the otherwise empty room. Someone had ducked behind them. Soren put a couple of rounds in that direction. An interior door led to a back room.

He suddenly realized the perp wasn't alone. Two more men showed up in the interior doorway. Both had guns out and were firing at him.

"Police!" he shouted. "Drop your weapons!" Not that he expected them to, but the announcement was necessary. And habit.

Soren rolled to his left toward the dimness of the wall. He thanked the perps for having blacked out all the windows. The light from the front door probably blinded them. He fired again, this time at the two in the doorway. One of them cried out, but they both kept firing.

He couldn't see any cover he could use. The room had no furniture, no other boxes. Soren was badly exposed, with three active shooters aiming at him. He kept moving, rolling left, then right. He alternated shots at the three each time he paused.

A crash sounded from the back room, of Manny forcing the back door. He heard Manny yell, "Police!"

One of the two in the doorway suddenly yelled in pain, dropped his gun, and fell to the floor. The other started to spin toward the back room, but only got partway before he dropped. Manny had nailed them both from behind.

Soren concentrated his fire on the stack of boxes. The perp there vaulted out and scrambled across the floor toward the front door, shooting wildly in Soren's direction. Soren took the time to aim and hit the man in the thigh. He tumbled toward the door, and his head hit the door jamb with a sickening crunch.

Sudden silence except for Soren's panting. He smelled the hot metal of the flechettes.

Manny jumped in from the back room over the two bodies, gun aimed and at the ready. No one remained at whom to shoot.

Soren slumped to let the adrenaline fade, then stood up to brush himself off.

"Damn it all," he said. "I hate it when they do that."

Manny checked the two perps in the doorway for pulse, shaking his head "Yeah. I don't like the sudden danger part, either."

"I'm not talking about that." He huffed out a breath. "We just killed all our active leads. Now we've got to go back to the research."

"Ah," said Manny. "Yeah. And we might have exposed our case, too. Someone owns these guns, and they'll know we've busted their ring."

Soren stood, thinking. "Okay. Then maybe we should approach this from another direction. Goods are smuggled out, and the spies are smuggled in. Let's go down to the port at Freetown and see what we can find out about smuggling."

CHAPTER 30

Before: Fear came from not knowing.

After: Fear comes from knowing.

—Before and After by Ellen Thranadil, Tileus Press 446 A.T.

Jake froze in place, his heart pounding hard in his cheeks. His eyes flicked back and forth between the dark aperture of the needle gun's muzzle and the lieutenant's equally threatening eyes. Gonga whirled toward the man, raised his gun partway, but stopped when he saw the gun aimed at Jake.

For a moment, all was still. Jake heard shouts from the main street in front of the station. His mind was as immobilized as his body.

Lieutenant Ariki broke the tableau. He looked at Renfo, eyes cold and face stern, his gun not wavering a millimeter from Jake's chest. "Renfo Yenstil. Still shaking in fear? I thought you'd be over that by now." Then he glanced at the third. "And Gonga Osai, becoming more active now, I see."

Jake was as still as a snake-entranced songbird. The slightest press on the trigger, and he'd be dead. *Caught. What can we do?* He glanced at Renfo. "You know this man?"

"Yes. He searched our boat...several times."

Ariki chuckled. "Of course, I never looked in that hidden space under the hold."

Jake heard Gonga suck in a breath.

Jake broke into a sweat. "What are you going to do with us?"

Ariki shook his head in mild disgust. "Isn't it obvious? I'm helping you get away. But you need to move. Now." The last word barked, and Jake jumped.

The lieutenant stayed in charge, his voice commanding the next actions while he lowered his weapon. "Renfo, cover her up. Gonga, hide the weapons. Palatin, get your disguise back in place."

Gonga and Renfo quickly put the weapons away and covered Zofia. She moaned.

"Renfo, split up," said Ariki. "They'll be searching for three men. You go separately to the boat. Palatin and Gonga, you're just simple fishermen moving your equipment."

Jake stood there, confused.

"*Move,*" barked Ariki.

All three jumped at his tone. Jake took the handles of the cart and started pushing it away from the station. Gonga steadied the load. Renfo walked quickly to the next corner, looked back at them, then disappeared.

The lieutenant holstered his gun and walked beside them. He put a hand on the cart rail.

A shout sounded behind them. "You, there! Halt!"

It had to be the Guards. Jake avoided looking around, but stopped pushing the cart. Darkness seemed to loom into the street. Gonga halted, too.

Ariki turned and called back, his voice steeped in urgent command. "I've got this, Officer. This street is clear, and I'm checking this cart. They must have escaped in a different direction. Find them! Run."

"Yes, sir," said the voice in haste.

"Keep moving, Palatin," instructed Ariki. "You don't need to worry about the cameras in this street. I disabled them earlier when I saw you arriving." He snorted. "Technical problems. I've been watching for you; that's why I set up this transfer."

"Why are you doing this?" said Jake, moving the cart again. "We appreciate it, but it's sort of…"

"Astonishing?"

"Uh…yeah. That's the word. Why?"

Ariki turned to look at Jake. "I wanted to meet you, Palatin. Yitzak speaks very highly of you, and I wanted to see for myself."

"Yitzak?" Jake was shocked, yet he didn't want to reveal anything. "Yitzak who?" He kept pushing the cart.

Ariki laughed at him. "You are so transparent. I've been a guardsman for a long time; I know when people are lying." He shook his head. "Of course, Yitzak. Your Lazarite friend, the scientist."

Jake met his eyes with a touch of shame for dissembling. "You know Yitzak Goren?"

"Yes, for many years. Han Yenstil, may his soul rest, was only one of Yitzak's contacts here in Timpi. Han never knew how much I protected him." He shook his head sadly. "But then he got stupid. He fell for a trap I'd set, and I had to identify him to Overlock."

Gonga had been quiet, but this spurred him to speak. "And yah, all dos times you searched our boat?"

"All for show, Gonga, all for show. I searched many boats."

"Ya never let on, Lieutenant, not once. I was most afraid of you."

"As you should be, still." Ariki's words fell flat, leaving Jake worried what might happen next.

Ariki spoke again while they turned the cart around the corner of the next block. "I wanted to look in your eyes, Palatin, to see if you could truly do what the Lazarites need you to do."

Jake was still uncertain. This man was a powerful leader in the Solity Guard. "What is it you think the Lazarites need me to do?"

"Go to Tileus, for starters. Then build your device." Ariki stopped short, glancing at Gonga. "But perhaps you need to keep it more secret."

"So, you wanted to see me. What do you see, Lieutenant?"

Ariki nodded. "I see a man who has grown a lot from what I first heard. I agree with Yitzak. I think you'll do."

Jake felt his heart rise in his chest at the affirmation. He knew he was not the same man he'd been four weeks ago, but hearing it from this competent guardsman filled him with satisfaction. It renewed his purpose.

"Thank you." The cart stuck on a pothole in the pavement. Gonga and Jake pushed hard to free it, to keep it moving. "So, what do we do now?"

"You take Dobrunik to the boat. I'll keep the Guard search away from the harbor for an hour. Get underway now to make your connection to the Tileus fleet. You three take the *Solo Solar* out and get across the Channel."

Jake was so relieved he felt his hands shaking on the push bar. "Okay, Lieutenant. But I have one more question."

"I have to get back and guide the search."

"Just a quick one, sir. How did Zofia do under interrogation?"

It looked as if all the firmness dropped out of Ariki's posture. He shook his head sadly. "No one does well under Overlock's hand. She held off as long as she could, but with that man's methods, everyone gives in. She told him about Han and Wang. She told all the names of her cell in Oriens, including Yitzak. He's in great danger, and I've already warned him. But Overlock did not think to ask about your purpose in Tileus."

Ariki had said nothing about Zofia's holochip copy of the transpath plans. *Did they find it? Did she have it with her?* He decided not to ask. He had his own chip.

Jake nodded, a huge lump in his throat. "What did she say about me?"

"Nothing but good, Palatin. That woman thinks the world of you."

"Thanks. We'll take care of her." He thought again. "I'll take care of her."

"Good." Ariki spun on his heels and ran back up the street to the station, shouting orders ahead of him.

Gonga turned his head to watch Ariki leave. "Ah don't trust him, Jake. He's up to something."

❧ ✳ ❦

A half-hour later, Jake and Gonga pushed the cart onto the wharf beside the *Solo Solar*. Renfo was already on board. People were wandering the harbor area, but no one paid any attention. Gonga stood guard while Jake wrapped Zofia in the canvas. She was as limp as a pile of wet clothes, completely unresponsive. Jake picked her up in his arms and carried her on board and into the pilot house, where he laid her on the bench.

Renfo and Gonga followed with the weapons, also wrapped in covers, all three needle guns and the beam rifle. They quickly stashed the weapons into the hidden space under the hold. Then Gonga went back to push the cart back where he'd gotten it.

"Ah don't want someone to find this here and remember seeing it at the station," he said.

Jake sat beside Zofia on the bench. She looked a disaster. Her hair was tangled with sweat and blood, her coveralls were more grime than yellow. She had been bandaged around her neck and bare thighs, though fluids were seeping through some of the bandages. Her face was bruised purple and ruddy. Burn marks pocked her arms and legs, and one round burn mark marred the center of her forehead.

"Renfo, after we get moving, do we have some clean clothes," asked Jake, "and some fresh bandages?"

"You bet. We've got some on board. Labor blues."

Zofia's breath was heavy and regular. Her sleep was troubled, occasionally crying out and thrashing an arm. When she moved, she immediately winced and whimpered with pain.

Jake laid his palm on her cheek as gently as possible, seeing the damage on her face. He leaned down to kiss her lips.

"Zofia," he said. "You're safe now."

She moaned.

"We'll take you across the Channel now and get out of Prime."

Her eyes fluttered open. They were vacant, unfocused, unseeing, like empty lanterns helplessly trying to illuminate the night. She flung her head around, looking at the surroundings. Her eyes rested on Jake with no recognition.

"Léo?" she asked.

Jake's heart stopped for a moment.

"I'm not Léo. He's gone, weeks ago. I'm Jake."

Puzzlement filled her eyes, then sudden fright. "Overlock!"

"Not here, my love. That's done with."

She shook her head in denial and clamped her eyes shut. "Oh, damn. Not done. Never done. Never done, never done." Her repetition faded away and she fell again into a deeply disturbed asleep.

Jake covered her with a blanket.

"Renfo," he called out. "You and Gonga get us underway. We need to get out of the harbor right away."

"We can do that."

"Is there still time to meet with Han's contact from Tileus?"

"Yes. It's about an hour to the fishing grounds where both countries work."

Jake nodded, then sat beside Zofia in bleak despair.

CHAPTER 31

If you're being forced out, go out well. History has no use for feebleness.

—*Collected Sayings of Yitzak Goren* by Ellen Thranadil, Tileus Press 439 A.T.

After setting up his lab and office, Yitzak returned to his apartment. He assembled the records and equipment there and set explosive devices similar to those at the lab. He wouldn't have much time.

Running away would solve nothing, but he could certainly damage Denmark and his plans. Yitzak would take great satisfaction in finally thwarting the bully who'd restricted and cheapened his life for the last thirteen years. If this worked well, Denmark would have yet another failure to report to the Solity Council.

He fought with himself over what he was doing. He didn't want to destroy the transpath or its records, but he also didn't want Denmark to have control of it. He gave the transpath to Tileus instead of Prime because it offered the possibility to save humanity from its destructive cycle. Solity would hide it and use it only for their own benefit.

On a deeper level, he had much more he wanted to accomplish in life. He saw no way, however, to continue his life in any good way. Not with Overlock on his trail. *All of humankind versus my one life. A true bind, but one with a clear answer.*

By noon, everything was in place. He paused to order a lunch from the autocater, perhaps his last. It couldn't be long now. He sat again on the balcony to enjoy the sunlight and warmth of the day.

A call pinged in his imp when he finished lunch. A secure call, this time from Franklin.

"Hello, Franklin. What can I do for you on this beautiful day?"

"You can get out. Now. I believe Denmark has someone coming for you. We cannot risk you being captured."

"I know, my friend, I know. We cannot expose you."

"I'm working on how to get you out of Oriens. I'll call you back shortly with plans. I only hope we have enough time."

"Ah, Franklin, that isn't necessary at all. I heard this morning from our Guard agent, so I've been making my own plans. I'm ready to go."

Franklin paused before answering, "All right. I've trusted you for ten years now. I'll trust you this time also."

When the call ended, Yitzak remembered discovering Franklin. The man had been a rising political star. Yitzak had used his correlative acumen to discover Franklin's secret leadership of the then-nascent Lazarites. When Yitzak contacted him to offer help, Franklin had been shocked and frightened, worried someone else might make the same connections—but Franklin had actually done his work well. No one but Yitzak could possibly have put it together. He smiled at the memory and the friendship they'd built.

The sky today was spectacular, a good day to end things. He left the balcony for a moment, returning with a glass of wine.

Yitzak sipped his wine and reminisced about key events in his life, putting them to bed.

One such event was the sweet Daiyu when he was twenty-four. She had loved him, and he'd loved her as only a young man can. He'd used his cleverness to transgress Solity's restrictions on sex.

Another defining event was the earthquake twenty years ago. It had destroyed the academic research lab he'd spent thirty years assembling. His work on mind waves and particle physics had already gained international recognition. Rebuilding the lab had shifted his focus into the empathic dimension. He'd discovered the principles of the transpath during the upgrade.

❧ ✳ ❧

Overlock left Prime Courthouse in good spirits. Director Denmark's plans were weakening, closing a door for Overlock; yet he was already pursuing new opportunities without Denmark.

First, he needed to complete the previous chapter. He had clear instructions from Denmark concerning Yitzak Goren. There had always been something suspicious there, more than just research into mind waves, but Denmark had so far protected the scientist. Overlock had not yet managed to pry into that particular secret box. This afternoon, he looked forward to shredding it open.

Where would Goren be today? Overlock frequently monitored the man's whereabouts, seeking to understand what he was doing. He could find Goren nearly always by using the government implant tracking. At times, though, Goren disappeared from the InfoNet into his shielded lab. Overlock had objected to the shielding, but Denmark assured him the shields were necessary to Goren's work.

Today, the Net said Goren was at home. *A posh apartment above the Park. Why should scientific work yield such a comfortable life?*

Overlock was about to remove that comfort.

He made an imp call to the local Guards. "Please have two Guards meet me for an arrest. I'm sending the location."

He strode down the slidewalks toward the Park, shoving past slower pedestrians. The targets of his aggression sometimes started to object, until they saw the look in his eyes or the gun on his hip. It tickled him to see them choke on their objections and shrivel inside themselves.

His dark heart lifted while he strode past the Mueller Memorial. Captain Mueller was an inspiration to him. Overlock particularly relished one egregious shipboard instance of protest against the captain's policy; the perpetrators had been physically flayed before putting them in an airlock for agonizingly slow decompression to the oblivion of space. Perhaps he could use something similar with Goren.

❧ ✳ ❧

Yitzak knew who was coming for him. Denmark would send his right-hand man, his psychopathic agent of evil. Perhaps Yitzak's explosions would solve that problem, too.

He smiled, remembering the bully Gamast nearly seventy years ago, a childhood version of Overlock. Yitzak had been six and Gamast eight. The boy had tormented him for three months. It had been the first major stress in his life, demanding he use his intelligence to find a viable solution. Fighting back had been impossible, just as with Overlock. Disgracing Gamast would only have made him more dangerous. Instead, Yitzak had created a vicious deadfall trap that broke the boy's arm, in such a way Gamast clearly knew Yitzak had done it. Gamast had recovered. That unexpected, extreme solution won the boy's respect, and they became unlikely friends throughout school and after.

He couldn't imagine finding common ground with Shelton Overlock. A psychopath cares for nothing but his own obsession and feels completely justified in everything he does. But Yitzak was using the same solution today.

Over the railing, Yitzak saw Overlock approaching. Tall and wiry, dressed in Administrative purple, striding as if in charge of the world. Other people automatically moved aside to give him room. Yitzak closed his eyes in peaceful sorrow. *No time left.*

He took a last drink of the wine, adjusted his explosive vest, and moved inside.

❧ ✳ ❧

Overlock found the entrance to Goren's apartment building. Two Guards waited for him. He was walking fast in his anticipation. Setting aside his delightful thoughts of what he would do with Goren, he gave his imp a thought command to activate the government override on the building door lock. The three quickly ascended the lift tube to the top floor.

"Change your guns to stun charges," he commanded. He wanted this man alive to agonize through all the pleasures he had in store for him.

Overlock's smile would put dread into a serpent.

He stepped from the lift to the apartment door. The two Guards flanked him. *Time for action. No waiting.* He drew his gun, then took a heavy breath. With sudden violence, he drove his foot through the door lock with all the considerable strength of his body. The lock shattered and the door sprang inward.

The old man sat in a wooden straight chair two meters from the door. He smiled at Overlock and pressed a button in his hand.

The explosion slammed Overlock in the chest. It flung him and the two Guards backward across the hallway, without time to think or react. The opposite wall smashed him in the back like a runaway truck. His head rang with the impact, and his ears shut down to silence. Clouds of acrid black smoke billowed into the hallway. Through the clouds, he saw the flashes of five more explosions.

Overlock plummeted to his knees, panting for breath. He couldn't hear his own breathing. He wasn't sure whether anything was broken, because his entire nervous system was in overload.

Leaving the two Guards behind, he rushed into the room, hunched below the layer of smoke. Nothing moved but the smoke, swirled into the hallway by a breeze from the balcony. The small explosions had blackened the walls. Devices and records were destroyed, the shards of a scientific life scattered around the room.

The first and largest explosion had been in the center of the room, where the remainder of Yitzak Goren's body lay on the floor, divided in two and shredded by the blast. Blood splattered the walls, ceiling, floor and furniture—as well as Overlock's own face.

"Damn!" shouted Overlock into his own silence. All the enjoyment he'd anticipated was ripped away. And he'd have to face Denmark with failure.

Overlock's mind went as black as his soul. Fury filled him. He did what he always did with emotions and converted it to action. He holstered his gun and picked up the fallen chair. Methodically, he beat Goren's wasted body until the chair legs were as bloody as a slaughterhouse floor. His overloaded ears could hear nothing of the impacts, nor of his own cursing. He turned the broken chair legs onto the other explosion sites, uncontrolled violence taking over. Pounding and pounding flowed out of him, using ferocity to regain his normal dispassionate composure. He hardly saw what he was destroying. His hearing recovered. His ears started to ring and the sound of his blows returned to him, but he never heard or saw the neighbors gaping at the door to this bloodbath.

"Sir? Overlock?" came a muffled voice from behind him. He turned to see the two Solity Guards at the door, needle guns out, caution in their posture engendered by his Administrative purple.

He set down the remains of the chair. Instantly calm and in control, he ignored the guardsmen and walked out the door. He enjoyed the shock from passersby who saw the gore on his clothes.

☞ ✳ ☜

At the same moment, in the shielded lab behind room 5218 of the General Defense building, similar explosions destroyed every trace and scientific record of the transpath.

Except, that is, for the holochip carried by Jacoby Palatin and its twin left by Zofia in Han Yenstil's basement, now encased in an evidence bag at the Timpi Guard station.

CHAPTER 32

Even though the border was an ocean channel, border conflicts between Tileus and Prime were frequent. Their boats shared international fishing grounds, with relentless accusations about unfair fishing practices. Both countries patrolled the waters with armed ships, adding to the conflicts.

—*An Annotated History of Verdant* by Ellen Thranadil, Tileus Press 442 A.T.

MIDDAY, 4 QUINTEMBER, 416 A.T.

Gonga took in the lines and the *Solo Solar* motored out of the harbor mid-afternoon. Under any other circumstances, Jake would have enjoyed himself. He'd never ridden any boat larger than a canoe in the park. He marveled at the beautiful day showing itself through the pilot house windows. The air smelled fresh and clean when they left the harbor stink behind, with a gentle breeze blowing toward the rising sun.

After the *Solar* passed through the breakwater, Renfo advanced the throttle. Their own motion added to the breeze. Outside the jetties, the boat hit the first ocean waves. Even at twenty meters long, it surprised Jake how much the *Solar* moved on the waves. Up and down, rolling side to side. The ocean didn't look rough, but the boat seemed to find every wave. He felt queasy and learned to keep a hand on a rail to stabilize himself.

When one large wave rolled the boat, he was alarmed to see Zofia slide toward the edge of the bench. He jumped quickly to hold her safe, then found a cargo strap and fastened her in place, smoothing her hair again.

She suddenly thrashed against the restraint and her eyes shot open. "Jake?" Her voice was thready and filled with fear.

"Yes, love. I'm here. We're safe."

"Jake?" she asked again, as if he hadn't spoken.

"We're on our way to Tileus, Zofia."

The fear in her eyes subsided, and she nodded before falling asleep again.

Jake cradled her cheeks and leaned down to kiss her forehead, careful to avoid the wounds. He exhaled a deep sigh. After a moment, he stood again to look out the windows.

"Renfo, I'm worried about Zofia. She hasn't said anything coherent since we rescued her. We can tend her wounds, but I don't know what to do about her mind."

"You're asking me?" Renfo looked dismayed and helpless. "The guy who can't do anything right?"

Jake stood up from the bench where Zofia lay. When he did, the boat hit a wave and he had to reach out to steady himself on a wall. He pressed a hand on Renfo's shoulder. "Don't sell yourself short. You did right today. We couldn't have rescued her without you."

"Yeah, but Ariki dismissed me afterwards. He chased me off."

"No, he didn't." Jake smiled and looked in Renfo's eyes. "He trusted you to get back to the boat safely by yourself, so we wouldn't look like the group they were chasing."

Renfo's eyes dawned with understanding. "Oh." A gradual smile came on his face, and he looked proud of what he'd done.

"And now, you're getting us to Tileus. I don't know fiddly about boats. We're trusting you and Gonga.

Gonga chuckled. "Yah, dat's right." He glanced at Renfo. "De boy do know. Maybe he'll also do right."

Renfo ducked his head in embarrassment.

Jake smiled. "Now, where is a first aid kit, please? I need to change her bandages."

Zofia's wounds had been dressed at the Guard station, but the bandages were stained with fluids oozing from the wounds. Jake used the first aid kit to spray healant on the wounds and change the dressings. What little she said was still jumbled. She didn't recognize Jake, which cut to his heart. Sometimes when he touched her, she cried out and swept her arm to push him away. He ached inside for the woman he'd come to love. He even wished he were religious, so he could pray to some god for help.

After dressing her wounds, he got a clean set of light blue coveralls and changed her clothes, too. He tried to avert his eyes from her body.

Jake had another thought. "How many men does it take to run this boat, Gonga? It has to appear normal when we get to the fishing grounds."

"Most times we has four." He stopped, and Jake saw the stricken look in his eyes, likely for Han and Wang. "We can maybe get de nets out and back in with two, but we not gonna handle much fish."

"That'll do. Remember, we're not really going out to fish. We can best honor Han by getting Zofia and me over to Tileus."

With time on their hands, Jake stepped out of the pilot house to look around. "This is truly beautiful, Renfo. The sky, the smells, the motion. I've never done anything like it. You get to do this every day, right?"

The young man looked around from where he stood at the helm, as if seeing it all for the first time. "Uh, yeah? We get used to it, I guess. It's hard work later." He paused. "And it's not always this pretty. It's dangerous and scary when storms come."

"How much farther do we have to go?"

"About a half hour. We'll be able to see the coast of Tileus by then, and we'll also see their boats, out from Freetown."

The time passed quickly. Jake became more stable on his feet as he got used to the motion. For a while, he stood at the bow, yearning to push the boat faster. The sooner he got to Tileus, the sooner he could be done with the danger.

Presently, they joined the rest of the fleet—and the Tileus fleet. Jake watched the coast of Tileus. *Another country, how strange.*

"It's time to fish," Renfo said, "or we'll look suspicious. That's what Han always did when we smuggled." Gonga agreed, so Renfo slowed the boat, and he and Gonga worked together to lay out the nets.

"What can I do?" Jake offered.

"Ya can help for sure," said Gonga. "Hold dis line and let it out bit by bit while we move."

Jake began to get an idea what they were doing, trailing the nets until they formed a large circle, then pulling in the fish. He quickly found, though, theory and practice were different things. He had no idea what any given rope actually did, so he just followed directions. At least he was helping. When he could, he checked on Zofia. *Sleep is probably the best thing for her.*

They flowed the nets outward over the left side of the boat—Renfo and Gonga called it the "port" side. The work became easier. Renfo steered the boat in a wide, slow circle. Once they were established in the phase, he used binoculars to check all the boats in sight.

"I don't see any danger," he said, "but I do see our Tileus contact over there, not too far away. I'm going to make the signal." Renfo pointed at a boat closer to the Tileus shore.

Jake watched him uncleat a line to the mast and raise a long yellow pennant to stream in the wind. A minute later, Jake saw the other boat raise a similar flag. Then both boats quickly lowered the flags.

"We don't leave the signal pennant aloft any longer than we have to," Renfo said. "They'll come closer, then send over a boat for the transfer."

Can it possibly go this smoothly? Jake's stomach tied in a knot, and he looked all around at the ocean and other boats. A few minutes later, he saw a smaller boat motoring its way through the swells toward them.

Renfo glanced at Jake. "Get Zofia ready to transfer. We'll take the small boat alongside our starboard rail. We'll have to lower both of you with ropes."

"How gentle can we be with her?" Jake asked.

"Both boats will be pitching and rolling. We'll just have to do the best we can." Renfo went back to the pilot house to steer.

Jake watched the small boat drive up beside the *Solar* with two men on board. One threw a bow line up. Gonga tied it to the rail. Both boats kept their engines running, so they drove through the waves together. The small boat rode a couple of meters below their deck, but the waves kept tossing it up and down against their side. The relative motion confused Jake's balance, and he found it hard to stand straight. His queasiness returned.

Fighting his own body's senses, he carefully carried Zofia to the deck and laid her on the hatch cover. Her eyes opened and she startled with what seemed to be abject fear. Jake soothed her. She calmed somewhat but never spoke.

"Dis's a harness for her," Gonga said. He handed Jake a padded life jacket with a rope trailing up to a boom above them.

Jake got her arms into the vest and fastened it tightly.

"Tie up de leg straps, too," Gonga said. "Dat's what holds her up."

With everything ready, Gonga ran a motorized winch to lift her off the deck. Her arms and legs dangled awkwardly. She kept jerking; the strange motion had to be triggering her fears. Jake held her as steady as possible, then they both pushed her out over the rail. Gonga ran the winch down to lower her into the boat. The men there steadied her against the wild contradictory motions.

Suddenly, Renfo shouted from the pilot house. "We've got trouble!" His voice filled with fear. He sounded like he did when Jake first met him.

Trusting the two to unfasten Zofia in their boat, Jake whirled to see where Renfo was looking. A large speedboat with a flashing blue light was racing toward them, water splashing violently outward from its bows. Jake saw three figures in black. One was turning a large gun mounted on the foredeck. Aiming at them.

"Solity Guard!" shouted Renfo. "Jake, get off the boat, now! We can't have you on board."

Jake's heart raced. Gonga had retrieved the empty harness, but no time remained for him to put it on. He'd have to jump.

"Go, Jake, now!" Gonga hollered.

Jake put one leg over the rail and settled his foot on the narrow ledge outside. Hanging on for dear life, he sat on the rail and brought his other foot over.

The men below were shouting reassurance, waving hands for him to jump.

He glanced back at the Guard boat, approaching fast. He caught a momentary image of the foredeck guardsman hauling on a lever to load the deck gun. He turned back to the small boat. The motion was sickening to watch, up and down and sideways. He couldn't work out the timing. When the boat reached the top of a wave, only a meter down, he took a breath and jumped.

The boat dropped away from him and slid outward while he fell, a terrible feeling of disorientation.

Oh, no, I've missed!

His feet hit the boat's rail. But then it lurched, and he fell backwards. He tumbled off the rail into the salty water between the two boats. Flailing, he caught the boat's rail with one hand. Someone grabbed his wrist just when the boat lurched into the *Solar*'s side. The boats crushed him, and he felt sharp pain in his ribs. He thrashed to keep his head above water.

"Get away! Get away!" hollered Renfo to those in the small boat.

Gonga untied the bow line and threw it into the boat. The men in the boat grabbed both of Jake's wrists and heaved hard. Jake cried out in pain when the haul stretched his ribs. They dumped him into the boat, soaking wet. One of them pushed the throttle forward, spinning the wheel away from the fishing craft.

The Guard boat was on the other side of the *Solar*, so they were hidden from each other for now.

The small boat leaped forward, rocking wildly in the wild waves. The breeze splattered water all over them.

Ignoring his new pains—breathing hurt—Jake reached to hold Zofia steady. She was still unresponsive, eyes open but dazed.

Neither of the men said anything, both intent on getting away.

They pulled out from the *Solo Solar*.

Jake saw Renfo and Gonga throw the guns overboard, wrapped in Zofia's bloody yellow clothes.

When the small boat cleared the *Solar*'s bow, he saw the Guard craft imminently close. A loudhailer on board blared orders at Renfo, but Jake couldn't understand it over the noise of their own boat.

Suddenly, the foredeck guardsman pointed at their small boat. The Guard boat revved its engine and swerved away from the *Solar* toward them.

"Damn," said the man at the helm. "We're doing all we can."

Jake looked ahead. He saw the name on the Tileus fishing boat, the *FreelyGo*, but they weren't going to have time to get aboard. The Guard boat was too fast.

"What do we do?" he shouted to the helmsman, wincing at the pain in his side.

"We get close to the *FreelyGo*. We're in Tileus waters. Those Verdant Prime scum don't have any authority over us, but who knows what they'll do?" He kept the small boat running full bore.

They were close now. The *FreelyGo* was bigger than the *Solo Solar*. A rope ladder dangled down one side, with three crewmen on deck at its top.

"She can't climb that ladder," he hollered over the noise, holding his side against the pain.

"Yeah, I know," came the response. "I've already told them by imp. They'll have to rig a hoist, and that'll take more time."

Jake was astonished. *Their implants work out here?* He set the thought aside and watched the closing of the craft. Their little boat wasn't going to make it.

The Guard boat loudhailer spoke to them. "Heave to, small craft, and deliver your contraband, or we'll open fire."

"The hell with that," said the helmsman. He kept going.

Jake saw a vicious puff of smoke from the deck gun. He heard the report of the gun at about the same time an explosion raised an enormous spout of water in front of them. The small boat drove right through the geyser. Everyone on board was drenched, and Jake tasted the bitterness of explosives.

Unexpectedly, a larger fountain burst from the ocean directly in front of the Guard boat. A moment later, Jake heard the wet explosion, followed by a heavy boom from behind him, beyond the *FreelyGo*.

He spun to look. A sleek grey military hovership, larger than any of the other boats, sped over the waves toward them. Water sprayed outwards from all sides. It had white numbers near the bow with the slanted band of Tileus green-and-red on the side. The ship bristled with guns aimed at the Guard boat. A cloud of smoke trailed behind the forward gun, evidence of the delayed boom he'd heard. While he watched, a second gun belched flame and another cloud. This time, Jake heard a brief whistle overheard before the shell exploded next to the Guard boat. Again, he didn't hear the boom of the gun until after the projectile landed.

The Guards swerved to avoid the second shot, but turned directly into a third shell.

With a tremendous explosion, the Prime boat shattered. Pieces flew upward in a massive column of smoky water. Jake saw the deck-gun guardsman launched upward and outward, arms windmilling, to land in the water.

The men on his boat cheered. "Got 'em! That'll teach those jellyfish to attack us in our own waters!"

The Tileus hovership immediately slowed, settling into the water between the *FreelyGo* and their small boat. He saw the ship's captain in a white uniform on the bridge holding a microphone, his voice issuing from a loudhailer.

"*Solo Solar*, we have no jurisdiction over you. You're free to go."

Jake felt tremendous relief. Renfo and Gonga would get safely home with no one the wiser what they'd done.

The captain continued. "Small craft, bring those fugitives aboard here. Then rescue the guardsmen, if you can, and bring them to me as well."

Fugitives? What's going to happen next?

The unrelenting commands persisted, "*FreelyGo*, return to port immediately. Report to the harbormaster. You are under arrest for smuggling."

CHAPTER 33

The first task in any negotiation is to get the other side to talk with you. Until you have communications, there can be no negotiation.

—*A Practical Guide to Negotiation* by Ellen Thranadil, Tileus Press 426 A.T.

Midday, 4 Quintember, 416 A.T.

Jake was soaked and cold when he stood on the deck of the Tileus hovership. The sea air had seemed so fresh, and now just smelled salty. The sun was lowering toward the western horizon. His ribs stabbed at him with each breath, so he held them in place with his elbows. He had climbed up painfully from the small boat on a set of stairs attached to the side of the ship; now, two white-uniformed sailors carried a stretcher up the same stairs with Zofia. His heart hurt almost as much as his side.

A door opened and the sailors saluted when the ship's captain strode out onto the deck. He was a striking figure in white with colorful ribbons above his shirt pocket and black shoulder boards with three gold bars. His face was stern.

The captain spoke. "So, here we are. Two Verdant Prime agents. Light blue coveralls mean Labor, right?"

Jake realized the captain was talking to him. "Yes, sir, usually."

He looked closer at Zofia, and his eyebrows rose. "What happened to her?"

"Torture, sir." Jake was starting to shiver, as much from the wind on his wet clothes as from shock.

"So, you think you can simply slip into our country and continue your unwelcome activities, bringing a victim along with you? Not going to happen, mister."

Jake was so surprised he stopped shivering. "No, sir, that's not it at all—"

The captain turned to a crewman. "Secure them both, Chief. Get them medical treatment and dry clothes." He glanced at Jake. "Some proper clothes, not those ridiculous Prime coveralls. We'll take them to the police and let them sort it out."

"Wait, sir," Jake said. "We need your—"

The captain ignored him and spoke to another crewmember. "Make sure the boat picks up whatever's left of those Prime guardsmen, too. Hold them separate from these two." When the crewmember acknowledged, the captain turned and left.

The two crewmen holding Zofia proceeded to another door. When they jostled Zofia getting through the doorway, she wailed and thrashed her arms. Jake tried to reach out to her, but the chief grabbed Jake by the arm. "You stay with me, boy. Let's get you to sick bay."

Jake had thought they were being rescued from the Solity Guards, but it seemed they were thrown into a new fire.

They separated him from Zofia. He caught a glimpse of the room where they took her, a medical facility with a surgery table and cabinets on the walls. The chief dragged him to another compartment.

"Get out of those wet clothes. The medic's going to look you over."

"Okay." He was shivering constantly now. Dry would be good.

The chief turned to a cabinet to get clothes for him. While he was turned, Jake palmed the holochip with the transpath plans. His heart pounded, wondering whether they would take it away from him. He did his best to keep his motions natural while holding the chip.

A medic gave him a quick clinical examination, then focused on his ribs. Every breath still hurt; the medic probed his ribs and confirmed one was cracked. The man wound bandages tightly around Jake's torso.

"That's going to hurt for a while until it heals, but there's not much else we can do. Avoid any strenuous exercise."

Jake snorted. "You mean, like running from the Guards and jumping into boats?"

The medic gave no answer.

Jake picked up the clothes the chief gave him. They were strange to him. He had never in his life worn trousers and a shirt, nothing but the standard Verdant Prime coveralls. He made the mistake of fastening the trousers first, then had to open them again to tuck in the shirt. When he was fully dressed, he slipped the holochip into his new pocket.

The chief took Jake to a steep ladder down to the next deck. Climbing down was painful and slow. Each pull on his arms brought a stabbing pain. He quickly learned, though, not to gasp—because that brought agony. By the time he got to bottom of the ladder, he was gritting his teeth and stood, shaking, until his body recovered.

A short way down a narrow metal passageway, the chief put Jake into a small room with nothing but a chair and table.

"You'll stay here until we make harbor. Then the captain will decide what to do with you."

"What about Zofia? The girl?"

"We're taking care of her. That's all you need to know."

Jake was desperate. "She's been brutalized, and her mind isn't right. Can't I stay with her? Please?"

"No. You'll stay here. Captain's orders." The chief closed the door behind him, and Jake heard the lock click.

He felt the ship's engines increase, and the room lurched around him. Not expecting the motion, he stumbled into a wall. When it stabilized again, he sat in the chair to keep from being tossed painfully to the floor.

Alone, he was suddenly overwhelmed by despair and put his face into his hands. *I can't believe this. I thought we'd be safe when we got to Tileus. Was everything a lie? Is there no safe place on the entire planet? How am I going to convince them to help? And how can I help Zofia, if they won't even let me be with her?*

Then he realized despair wasn't appropriate yet. *At least we've escaped from Denmark and Overlock. And we're both still alive.*

The most important thing was the precious holochip, the object for which they had almost lost their lives. *I've still got it.* He grasped the chip in his fist and pressed it against his forehead, almost praying. Then he held it in front of him and squeezed its activator button. The opening holopage appeared in the air above his hand, confirming the chip was still working.

All the risks they had taken, the danger they faced, the hope in their hearts; this piece of glass was the crux of it.

Detectives Soren Moller and Manny Hong had eaten some bitter pills after their bungled weapons raid. They'd gone into that walk-up apartment in Thad City confident, thinking they were facing a single guy. Instead, they'd gotten involved in a shoot-out with three perps. They'd escaped with their own lives, but had killed all three culprits and, along with them, any further leads.

A day later, they were in Freetown, attacking the problem from the smuggling end—and failing here, too. They'd started this morning with the local police forces. Though the locals knew contraband was coming in and out, they had no handle on how or who. The locals were cooperating, though, and had taken Soren and Manny to a series of informers, each with tidbits of information. The process was slow.

"Manny, we need a breakthrough." Soren said, frustrated.

"We're not known here," said Manny. "Maybe one of us could go undercover."

Soren snorted. "Yeah...well, that wouldn't be me. I scream 'police' with every action I make and every word I say."

Manny gave a deep laugh. "That's for sure. You look like every cop anyone's ever known. But I've done it before. I'm big enough and mean enough to look like a criminal enforcer."

Soren cocked his head. "Might work. We'd need some help from the locals to make you look real. They could chase you into some place where you make contact. And we'd have to reprogram your imp."

His own implant warbled in his head with a call from the local office chief. He held up a hand to Manny while he answered. "Yes, sir, go ahead."

"Moller, I think we may have a lead for you—"

"Hold on, sir. Let me patch in my partner." Soren subvocalized the command, and he saw Manny nod as he joined the call. "Okay, sir. Go ahead."

"We just got a call from the Tileus Coastal Patrol. One of their hoverships just broke up a smuggling op from a Prime fishing boat to a Tileus ship, the *FreelyGo*. They captured two fugitives and a couple of Solity Guards who overextended their jurisdiction." The voice paused while he checked something. "Apparently, they killed a third guardsman in the fracas. The cutter is bringing in the captives, and the *FreelyGo* was ordered into harbor under arrest. They're all on their way in. This might be just the break you've been looking for."

"Fantastic," said Soren. "We'll want to interrogate all of them. Where will they be held?"

"The Patrol will bring the fugitives and the Prime guardsmen to us. The *FreelyGo* and its crew will report to the harbormaster in about an hour."

Soren traded a look of satisfaction with Manny. "Okay. Please hold onto the fugitives for us. Put them in separate cells. We'll also want to talk with the guardsmen."

Manny cut in, "Chief, this is Manny Hong. What about the boat crew from the *FreelyGo*?"

"They're complicit in this," said the chief, "but they're locals we know. We'll probably bring them in for booking, then let them go on bail."

Soren nodded and spoke, "We'll go down to the harbor to meet them when they come in. I'd like to get their information first hand."

"Sounds like a good idea. I'll have a couple of men there, too."

They ended the call. As usual, Soren took charge.

"Let's go, Manny. Call us an autocar."

The chief was right. Soren had a solid feeling this might be the break they'd needed. He rarely smiled, but this one had him smiling inside.

An hour in the small compartment had Jake's stomach clenched. He'd gone over everything the captain and the chief had said, and it all sounded like trouble. *How am I going to get someone to listen to me about the transpath? The whole point of this is to build it, here in Tileus, before the next international negotiations. I'll need help.*

The noise of the ship had gone quiet. He still felt movement, now smooth and slow. *Must be coming into port.* Jake thought about gathering his things to be ready to go, then shook his head. The only things he had were himself and the holochip. He doubted his rationchip worked in Tileus—or at all, if Solity had cancelled it.

The engines revved up for a moment and then quieted again. He no longer felt movement. After a few minutes, things got so quiet he heard the air moving in the ducts above him. A strange two-tone whistle sounded in loudspeakers outside his room.

As ready as he was, nothing happened. No one came to the door. The longer he sat, the more nervous he felt. *I'm at their mercy, in their time.*

Another hour passed.

He was dozing when the door unlocked. Startled, he jumped to his feet.

Two people in dark blue stepped into his room. The chief stood in the passageway outside. Though the two didn't wear the all-black coveralls and bulbous helmets of Solity Guards, Jake recognized them. Their uniforms had official insignia and decorations; they wore flat hats with dark blue bands; and their belts held pouches and weapons similar to what he'd seen on Solity Guards. These two must be Tileus police.

The shorter one, a woman, stepped forward and spoke to him.

"What's your name?"

Jake welcomed the opportunity to answer. "Jacoby Palatin, ma'am. I've come from Verdant Prime to—"

"Mr. Palatin, you're under arrest for illegal entry to our country. We're also considering charges of espionage. We're here to take you in."

The taller policeman stepped around Jake and took hold of his hands, drawing them behind his back. "Keep your hands behind your back, sir."

Jake's knees buckled and he cried out in pain. "Ack, no! Broken rib!"

The man released his hands again, and Jake hugged his ribs where the motion had awakened the pain.

The woman cocked her head for a moment, then shrugged. "Okay. No cuffs for now. But if you try anything…"

Jake felt his heart skip. "No, I'm not going to try anything. We're not spies, we're here for political asylum. I've got something to—"

She cut him off again. "You can tell your stories later, Palatin. There'll be plenty of time." She reached out a hand and touched the side of his neck. "What happened to your imp?"

"We cut them out."

She nodded with a humph. "That fits with espionage, hiding your identity."

"No. We did it to get away from Prime, not to hide here."

"Regardless." Her tone was dismissive. "Right now, you need to come with us."

Jake protested when the man grabbed his arm and pushed him forward. "What about my companion? Where is she?"

"We have her in custody, too. You'll be separated for now, but we'll take care of her."

They led him through the passageway back to the ladder. Climbing was even more difficult than coming down had been. The two hours of enforced idleness had allowed his body to calm down. Now, each motion of his ribs screamed at him.

They emerged onto the deck of the hovership with Jake panting. While he recovered, he studied his surroundings. The ship was tied alongside a concrete pier near a row of uninspiring, official-looking buildings. The deck was largely empty, except for two sailors in sharp uniforms gathered around a gangway. A formal carpet and podium had been set up at the head of the gangway, with a canvas awning over them. Some sort of Navy tradition, he guessed. He glanced up at the bridge. No one was there.

"Where are you taking me?" he asked.

"To jail, of course," said the policewoman. "We'll hold you while we gather evidence, then our people will want to talk with you."

"Earthfire, isn't there any way for me to speak to someone in authority? I've got something important to tell."

She looked at him with disdain. "We'll do our investigation first. You'll have a chance later." She nodded to one of the sailors—probably an officer—and led the way down the gangplank. A police autocar waited on the dock.

CHAPTER 34

For over four hundred years, the Solity Council of Verdant Prime
was a place of danger. Those who aspired to its power also put
themselves at risk of destruction. Some stability had been
achieved in the early fifth century through the personal force of
the chairman Rodion Lukin.

—*An Annotated History of Verdant* by Ellen Thranadil, Tileus Press 442 A.T.

Franklin Edobar marched triumphantly down the hallway of Prime
Courthouse toward the Solity Council meeting chamber. He was riding high
on success. From this day, he would be Director of Capital while also
secretly leading the Lazarites. *Talk about diametrically opposed roles!* As
Capital, he would be the manager of every asset of Solity—in which
individuals possessed nothing and Solity owned it all. As Lazarite, he
controlled the network of revolution. The unprecedented opportunity filled
him with excitement and apprehension. *Now I can use Solity's resources to
actually change Solity. But the risk of exposure...well, that's a risk I'm willing
to take.*

The Chairman had finally declared Franklin's predecessor *non compos
mentis.* Franklin was sorry for the man. He'd followed Pontol's lead for five
years and had become close to him. The man's mental problems, however,
had grown to the point where Franklin was effectively doing all the work.

Franklin looked good today, having changed his purple Administrative
coveralls from ordinary fabric to the finest quality, with the dark blue band
of Capital on his shoulder. He was certain his smile echoed the
determination and anticipation he felt inside.

Franklin's assistant strode behind him, reminding him *sotto voce* of the
Capital issues that might apply to this meeting. "Resources are low in Timpi,
sir, after the explosion. We'll be sending the fishing fleet out on the
weekend to make up for losses. The farming areas south of Timpi are worse,
with crops destroyed in a thirty-kilometer radius. We have reserves, but
we'll have to deplete the grain over the next few months until we can get a
new crop. It'll take two years to recover. Cotton supplies are undamaged—"

The voice went on, though Franklin hardly listened. His mind was on
the upcoming meeting. *Why had the Chairman called a special meeting? He
could have announced my promotion next week There must be something
else.*

Franklin entered the Council chamber and his heart lifted in pride. The glass wall across from him presented a spectacular panorama of Oriens city and mountains beyond. Those far slopes drank the sunlight into dark blue and russet leaves and contrasted with the cloudless blue sky. He walked calmly around the Fundament, the spectacular wood table, and stood at what was now his place. He glanced down at the iconic table, giving a wry smile at the many scars in the wood testifying to less sanguine transitions of power.

Franklin nodded cordially to the other six directors present. He took care to greet Berndt Denmark of Defense and Miriam Keita of Justice, the most powerful directors. An assistant stood with each director while waiting for the chairman to arrive.

Chairman Lukin strode in wearing his crisp white coverall. His commanding presence filled the room, eclipsing the other directors. While Franklin knew Denmark and Keita were ascending, Lukin was still a charismatic power all his own. The chairman took his seat and tapped his silver gavel.

"Take your seats, and let's begin." He allowed the shuffle of chairs to cease. "These are unusual circumstances. We have three items on our agenda. First is to formally welcome the newest member of the Council, Director Franklin Edobar for Capital."

Franklin nodded, feeling pride rise in his chest. "Thank you, Chairman."

"You all know Director Edobar," Lukin continued, "because he seconded Frederic Pontol for some months. Sadly, Pontol has reached an age at which his mental faculties are no longer adequate for the position. I've been satisfied with Director Edobar's acumen during his internship, so I've made his appointment permanent."

Polite applause filled the room. Several of the directors voiced congratulations to Franklin. He gave a cordial nod in thanks.

"Second on our agenda," continued Lukin, "is a less savory issue. I have received a formal motion of censure on one of our members. I've spoken with Director Yang to attempt resolution, but others also support it. Director Yang, please present your motion."

"Thank you, Chairman." Wei Yang of Labor rarely spoke in the Council meetings. What he said, though, was always important—and was usually the result of extensive manipulation behind the scenes.

"In this last week," Yang told the group, "a defense test went badly awry, resulting in a massive explosion in the foothills forty kilometers south of Timpi. What was planned to be a keystone of our campaign against Tileus became instead a significant setback to Solity. We lost nearly a hundred members of our agricultural Labor force. The city of Timpi was severely damaged, losing three days of productivity while people were diverted to clean-up efforts. We lost crops from the area, which will deplete our Capital resources for at least a year.

"This disaster follows closely on the increase in Lazarite actions throughout Verdant Prime, one of which was a block-long building explosion with unknown weapons three weeks ago here in Oriens.

"For these reasons, I move we formally censure Director Denmark for his department's mishandling of both its weapons development and its control over dissident elements." He finished his speech with his cold eyes fixed on Denmark.

"I second the motion," said Director Pires, not waiting for the Chairman to ask.

Denmark pounded his fist on the table and jumped to his feet, his swarthy face red. "I object, Chairman. General Defense keeps this country safe from problems both external and internal—"

"You are out of order, Director Denmark. Sit down!" Lukin's strident voice cut through Denmark's ire like a laserknife through wood. The two guards behind Lukin tensed with hands on their weapons. The scars in the wood of the Fundament gave silent witness to the fact of past physical violence in the Council chamber.

Denmark remained standing a moment longer, his lips compressed. Yet he took his seat, growling, "I still object."

"Your objection is noted, but the motion is in order."

Franklin's heart sped. He had not known in advance of this motion and was hard put not to react with visible surprise. Censure carried heavy penalties and would make Denmark's complicated machinations more difficult. Franklin was impressed with Yang's move.

"The motion has been made and seconded," said Lukin. "Under Solity rules, censure of a director is only one step away from expulsion. While the censure is in effect, the director's actions are severely constrained. It can only be lifted by action of this Council. Discussion is now in order. Director Denmark, because you are the subject of this motion, you and your staff will stay silent."

Franklin watched with avid interest. Denmark had his eyes locked with Yang's, then took an irate breath before raising a hand in assent to Lukin's rule. Franklin remembered the many years in which Denmark had been his mentor. Once again, he learned from the man—how to accept a setback.

Director Pires of State raised her hand for recognition. With a nod from Lukin, she said, "I completely agree with this censure. I have long been irritated with Director Denmark's penchant for warmongering instead of diplomacy. If we censure him, we will have greater control over his tendencies."

Director Shanah of Technology spoke next, his factual tones at odds with the power in the room, as if he were oblivious to the extreme tension.

216

"I'm sure some of our Technology members could have helped the weapons development team, but we were never asked. I also support the motion."

Denmark was stony, but Franklin saw a curl of contempt in his lips aimed at the Director of Technology.

Franklin's mind spun. *How can I use this situation to advance my own position?* Denmark was a severe obstacle to the Lazarites, having dealt a terrible blow to their teams in Timpi yesterday. Franklin didn't know where Palatin was, but he hoped the engineer would make it to Tileus to complete Yitzak's plans. Supporting this censure could ease the pressure on Palatin and the rest of the Lazarites.

Lukin recognized Miriam Keita of Justice. She spoke with quiet confidence. "I also support censure. For too long, Director Denmark has run rough-shod over the other members of this esteemed Council. His plans have been risky with nothing more than a miniscule promise of success. Now, the risks outweigh the promises."

Denmark failed to suppress a furious glare at her.

She continued, "In addition to the problems cited by Director Yang, I understand the chief engineer of Denmark's failed weapon has fled the city. His Technology girlfriend," she glanced at Shanah in pointed accusation of his department, "was captured in Timpi this week. Yet the engineer eluded pursuit despite Guard raids here and in Timpi. I've also learned the girlfriend escaped from Guard confinement yesterday through the incompetence of General Defense agents there.

"Further, another pair of explosions occurred yesterday surrounding a different weapon development program, with the death of the famed Yitzak Goren.

"It appears Director Denmark is failing in his control of his department. Further, concerning the chief engineer, it seems likely the director personally fostered, even mentored, the career growth of a Lazarite agent into that crucial position."

"Not true, Chairman," Denmark's gruff voice inserted.

"Silence, Director!" roared Chairman Lukin, "or I will have you forcibly removed from the chamber." The posture of the two guards behind Lukin reinforced his edict.

Franklin looked at Keita with increased respect. He was open to learning, and he was astonished at how she wielded her power. Her information was achingly current and her manner was calm while she added her castigation. He noted the way she had oh-so-politely included Shanah in the culpability. He watched with awe, but he also felt a twinge of fear. *Even though Yang made the motion, Keita was probably the primary agent behind this censure. With her network of informants, she would be most likely to expose my own dual life.* The power plays involved in this room were incredible—and they acted as a warning to his own Lazarite leadership. He could not slip up in any way.

Franklin took his turn. This was his first official action as director, in a highly-charged political issue. His heart was in his throat while he spoke. "Capital also supports the censure, Chairman. The setback in our reserves will actually take two years to recover, rather than the one cited by Director Yang. We believe it unacceptable for one department to affect Solity so severely."

Further discussion was short. The Council voted unanimously—less the forced abstention of Denmark—for censure.

"Director Denmark," said Lukin, "this censure takes effect immediately. Until this Council removes it, all major actions by your department must be cleared in advance with us. One of my security officers will accompany you at all times, monitoring every action and reporting directly to me. Are you willing to accept these restrictions?"

Denmark had calmed somewhat, though his coffee eyes still blazed. "I thank my colleagues for correction. I can assure you the engineer Palatin was not part of the Lazarites when I advanced his growth. His unique knowledge was valuable to Solity. Our agents believe he was recently suborned by that Technology girlfriend," a diversion of blame to Shanah, "and we expect to recapture them both shortly. The weapon development is continuing, and I fully expect success.

"Nonetheless," he continued with a harder voice, "I find this all very suspicious. With the Tileus war looming, with the Lazarites becoming bolder every week, this is a strange time to weaken General Defense. I cannot help but wonder which of you is part of the Lazarites, that you wish to diminish us all."

Franklin's heart skipped at least one beat at the incredibly accurate indictment. He watched the other directors glance suspiciously at each other, though none seemed to focus on him. Holding his composure, he cocked his head in admiration. Denmark's response was—almost—a class act. The only improvement Franklin could envision was not to have failed in the first place.

"Appropriate words, Denmark," said the Chairman, "yet I still must insist you answer the question. Are you willing to accept these restrictions? Your alternative would be to resign."

Denmark clenched his teeth in silence, the flush rising in his face again. The long pause brought attention again to the armed guards. Finally, he answered, "Yes, Chairman, I accept."

"Thank you," said the chairman. "Done. Which brings us to our third topic for today. With the absence of Director Denmark's failed weapon, what about our negotiations with Tileus? Denmark is correct. Tileus is a threat, dangerous to us all. We've worked for thirteen years toward his goal of re-integrating them into Solity. What shall we do now?"

Franklin had little to contribute from Capital to the following discussion. Denmark managed to redeem himself somewhat with the information obtained from interrogations. Franklin listened intently, determined to know the risks to his Lazarite teams. It appeared Han Yenstil's team in Timpi was either dead or captured. Denmark had full information about the girl's cell in Oriens. The cell system continued to work, however, because the other teams in all cities had not been exposed.

The Council decided to continue toward a failed negotiation with Tileus as a basis to initiate the war they wanted. They would give all appearance of cooperation while inserting obstacles at every opportunity. This might give time for General Defense to succeed in the bomb development, and would certainly allow continued build-up of the military.

From Franklin's viewpoint, such a path also acted to the benefit of his Lazarites. The delay would allow time for Palatin to build the transpath in Tileus. *Perhaps the device can fulfill its promise to entirely change the formal negotiations, perhaps even change the world.*

❧ ✳ ☙

Overlock watched the Council proceedings with disdain. Politics was one path to power, convoluted and sneaky, not nearly as straightforward as his brand of physical persuasion. It did not give the same rush of satisfaction. He preferred to have some fragile person helpless in his capable hands. Edobar's advancement meant nothing to him, but he listened with interest to the power games over his director's censure. Denmark seemed to be on a decline, which threatened Overlock's own ability to enjoy his desires.

Overlock considered it time to activate his personal plans.

The director left immediately when the meeting closed, taking Overlock aside in the hallway.

"Damn, we've got to regain our position, Shelton. Have you found anything we can use against Keita?"

"No, sir. She plays everything very close. Even this motion today. I knew she had met with Yang, Pires and the Chairman, but I couldn't find out the topic."

"Keep trying to find something about that bitch. Talk directly to her if you need to, but be careful if you do. She's nearly psychic in her ability to read people. In the meantime, I need you to go back to Timpi and find those two. I want Palatin and his girlfriend in our hands."

"I'll do so, Director." Overlock saw one of Lukin's off-white security guards step up behind the director. *And so it begins. Denmark is diminished.*

The guard stopped next to them. "Excuse me, Director," he said, "but I have been assigned to shadow you."

Overlock watched Denmark seethe inside, nearly bursting out in rage, before the director nodded in acquiescence. Denmark rushed down the hall, the guard at his heels, before the other directors had even left the Council chambers. Overlock remained in the hallway, watching them go. He had his orders for now.

But he had his own task to pursue first.

He'd ridden Denmark's rise to power for nine years. It had worked well. The director's ruthlessness almost matched his own. The political games, silly as they were, had given him many opportunities to enjoy himself in his own unique way. He'd left a trail of delightfully destroyed bodies and broken psyches behind him. He often savored his memories, reminding himself of all the misery he'd accomplished. He thrived on the fear left behind.

Yet all in all, Denmark's situation gave him concern. With a censure in place, the director would not be as free to act as he'd been—and neither would Overlock.

When Miriam Keita came out of the Council chamber with her assistant, Overlock quietly followed her. Her Justice offices were in the same building. Their path took them away from the Council chamber and the other directors.

When they'd reached a relatively private place, Overlock approached her with proper deference. "Director Keita, may I have a private word with you?"

He had never spoken to her before. Standing close, he suppressed his own surprise at her appearance. He knew she was fifty-six years old, but she looked only thirty, a tribute to years of cosmetic treatments only available to those with power. Her silver hair flowed to her shoulders in a cascade as unusual as clarified basalt.

Her intent dark blue eyes seemed to strip away his masks. She tilted her head to one side. "Alone, Shelton?" He saw a hint of caution. He was, after all, Denmark's man—and she had just engineered a caustic condemnation of Denmark.

"Yes, ma'am. What I need to ask is private but safe."

She was famous for her ability to read people. He saw her eyes on his while he gave that assurance. She gave a small nod. "Poldar, please stand aside where you can watch but not hear," she said to her assistant, who bowed his head and complied.

"Before we talk, Shelton, I need to know," she said. "Are you speaking on behalf of Director Denmark?"

"No, ma'am. I speak for myself."

"All right, then. Proceed."

"Director," he said, "today's action has me concerned about my own position."

"You should be. Your patron is not what he once was."

"I recognize that. I'm a simple man with simple desires. I've been able to support Director Denmark with my capabilities."

She snorted in amusement. "Yes, Shelton. I do know about your...unique desires." Her pause conveyed contempt, disgust, and respect all at once.

"Director, I believe I need new opportunities. I wish to offer those capabilities to you, if you have a...unique desire...to use them."

CHAPTER 35

Who could believe it? Palatin managed to escape to Tileus, where he supposed the technology might be achieved. Rather than support and help, he immediately ran into the problems of Tileus.

—*The Making of a New Humanity* by Ellen Thranadil, Tileus Press 448 A.T.

The insipid green jail walls were driving Jake crazy with frustration. He'd heard nothing about Zofia. And his cell stank, a persistent odor wafting from the toilet in the corner. He could understand Tileus wanting to protect their borders, but he hadn't had a chance to talk with anyone yet. *A day and a half wasted. I need someone who will listen, who can help me build the transpath, or the war's going to happen anyway.*

Though they kept him isolated, he had little privacy. Guards walked by at odd intervals, day and night, though he had no way to gauge time. A camera threatened him with a constantly blinking red light.

He laid on a metal-frame bed and used a metal toilet, the cell's only furnishings, both fastened securely to the floor. He wondered with dark humor whether they were fastened to keep someone from stealing them.

His ribs still hurt every time he breathed, but not as bad as it had been. If he stayed with shallow breathing, the pain was mostly okay.

Waiting was terrible.

He worried about Zofia, whether she was alive, recovering or getting worse. They gave him no information.

They'd also confiscated what little he had, including the holochip, when they threw him in here. The chip. The single item that mattered. Without it, his knowledge would not be enough to re-create Yitzak's work. Could he even get it back?

He heard a guard approaching, probably bringing breakfast. *Time to try again. I have got to get through to these people.* He jumped to his feet, but stayed away from the bars. On previous attempts, the guards had gotten furious when he got too close.

"Officer, help me," he urged as soon as the man was visible. "I've got to speak to someone in authority."

The guard checked Jake's distance, then put the metal tray of food onto the floor outside the cell. "Just eat your food, man."

"Dammit, I brought something from Prime to prevent the war. It's that important!"

The officer shoved the tray under the cell bars and stood up. "Due time. That's all I can tell you. Eat."

"What about the girl who was brought in with me? She was badly hurt."

The officer just shook his head and walked away.

Frustrated, angry, lost, Jake stepped to the bars and rattled the door in its frame. "I've got to get out of here!"

No one listened but the echoes.

⌒ ❋ ⌒

Later in the morning, Soren Moller watched through a one-way mirror while an officer ushered Palatin into the adjacent brightly-lit interrogation room. Palatin was a tall, trim man with dark red hair. His hands were cuffed in front. Though he seemed desperate, his demeanor reeked of frustration rather than the usual perp's desperation to lie. The officer sat him in the interview chair and fastened him to the chair's cuff bar.

Soren heard everything in the room. Palatin pleaded with the officer to tell him what was going on. The officer properly said nothing and left the room.

Manny Hong came in to join Soren. "Okay, he's in place. How long do we let him stew?"

Soren shrugged. "We've already let him stew for a day while we took statements from everyone else. He should be ready by now. But we'll let him settle down for a few minutes before we start."

"What do you make of it all so far?"

Soren didn't answer yet. He sat down, still watching the suspect. Palatin looked around the bare room. Not much to see. A table, a couple of chairs, a camera—the police purposely kept interrogation rooms empty and chill so the targets wouldn't get distracted. He saw Palatin focus on the one-way mirror.

"Hey, in there," the man said. "Let's get started. I know you're watching. I need to talk with you. I need your help."

"Strange plea," said Soren to Manny. "I don't think I've heard a suspect so eager to talk." He cocked his head, puzzling over this man.

"It might fit with what we've gotten from the other interrogations."

"Yeah. Let's walk through what we know. These two came from Prime, transferred by the smuggling operation we've been trying to break. The Solity Guards were chasing them so hard they fired on their small boat in mid-transfer—"

"Those officers were practically foaming at the mouth," Manny said with amusement. "I was tickled when they demanded we turn the pair over to them. Dissidents and revolutionaries, they said. They even used the word 'dangerous.'"

"Neither of them looks dangerous to me. The girl's mind is messed up. This guy looks brainy. Both are athletic, but not hard-core buff. These two must be something special—or why would the Solity Guards risk an international incident? We're chasing a spy network, but I'm not at all sure these two are spies. I get the sense something else is going on here."

"Yeah, I agree. I'm not sure what, but this doesn't feel like spies."

"They don't look much like spies. But then, a good survival trait for a spy is not to look like one."

Soren kept watching Palatin. The man seemed to have accepted the wait. He was sitting still with his eyes on the table.

"Interviews with the *FreelyGo* and Coastal Patrol crews just gave us the facts," Soren said. "None of them knew what was going on. The cutter captain had a clear-cut case for what his ship did. The Prime police boat was in Tileus waters, firing on a Tileus boat."

"The cutter blew those suckers out of the water," Manny snorted.

"Yeah. Prime's been getting way too big for their coveralls recently. The Coastal Patrol did a great job. Good on them. But I wish they'd brought in the Prime fishermen. They could probably tell us more."

"What about that holochip?" Manny pointed at the evidence bag in front of Soren.

Soren said, "That's a biggie. We don't know what's on it. It opens to a home page, but it's got protections to get past that. We've got people who could probably bust it, but I don't know yet whether we need to."

They fell silent, watching Palatin breathe. Obviously waiting.

"Did you notice neither of them has an active implant?" Soren asked.

"Yeah, I did. And they both have recent scars on their necks."

Soren stood up and paced to the one-way mirror, eyes on Palatin. He took a deep breath while his thoughts came together. "I tell you what, Manny. I don't think they're spies." He ticked off facts on his fingers. "She's been tortured. Solity Guards are chasing them. He's been telling the jail officers he's got some sort of important information. He's got a protected holochip. And now, he seems eager to talk." He turned to face his partner. "Despite coming here through the smuggling network, these two seem more like defectors than spies."

Manny leaned against the wall. "The girl's memory might come back, but all we've got right now is whatever we can get from this Palatin guy."

"So, let's get to it. Assume he's for real, so we'll keep it soft unless he gets difficult. I'll lead."

☙ ❋ ❧

The room was cold, almost frigid, while Jake waited. With his hands cuffed, he could barely squeeze his elbows around his chest for warmth. The only noise was the susurration of the air conditioning. His mind was whirling, planning what to say and how to say it.

How can I convince these people? I've got to be friendly, cooperative. They're used to dealing with criminals, so I've got to be different. Honest answers. Talk about the war. Make it real to them. Then tell them about the transpath, get their help.

The door finally opened and two men came in, both dressed in ordinary clothes. The first was burly and short, with dark hair. Jake was struck with the intelligence in his eyes. Obviously a police detective, and likely a sharp one. The other man almost hit the door frame when he entered, a huge fellow with a build that spoke of many hours in the gym. Jake was less sure about him; from his look, the man could easily be a criminal. That seemed unlikely.

Jake spoke first. He kept his voice calm. "Can we finally talk now? I've been waiting over a day." He tugged on the cuffs. "And these really aren't necessary. I'm not going anywhere."

The immense man laughed, a deep sound that vibrated the room. "You're right at that."

The short one sat down directly across from Jake.

"My name is Soren, Mr. Palatin, and this is Manny. We're with the Tileus police forces."

"Please, call me Jake." *First names. Keep it friendly.*

Soren nodded. "Okay, Jake. Why don't you tell me what you're doing in our country?"

"I'm here to stop the war that's about to start. Verdant Prime is set to descend on Tileus with everything they've got. Troops, ships, spacecraft. Everything. Your people—your families—are going to be in a world of hurt. They're just looking for the excuse. I can stop that."

Soren cocked his head. Jake watched him and Manny trade a surprised glance. "That's quite a claim. How do you plan to do that?"

"With new technology. One of our Prime scientists developed it. I'm here to build a device to make negotiations work as they never have before in all of history. It will be impossible for the diplomats to lie."

His answer seemed to fall flat on the table, for all the reaction he got. Disbelief would have been easier to deal with than the blank stares he got.

After a pause, Soren said, "Okay, with such a good thing—why were the Solity Guards chasing you?"

Jake stayed on edge, trying to say the right things, but they'd reminded him too much of the horrible recent events. Nonetheless, he answered, "They consider me a traitor and they want me back. I don't think the Guards even know about this technology."

"But why sneak it into Tileus? Why didn't you just build it over there?"

Jake worked to keep his patience. "Because it wouldn't be allowed there. The Prime leaders—particularly Berndt Denmark—*want* a war. They want to bring Tileus and the other nations back under Solity control." He leaned forward, feeling desperate after waiting so long. "Believe me, you don't want to be under Solity control."

He finally had an audience, with some authority, who seemed to want to hear.

"For star's sake, you've got to believe me. We've been running from our own people for days, trying to get here. Zofia got captured. They tortured her, but we rescued her and got away." The images of the firefight on the water washed back into his mind. "Damn, out there on the water, I thought the Guards were going to take us back."

When he looked back up, the two were simply watching him with cold eyes. He realized from their impassive stares they had heard every improbable story the criminal mind could concoct.

Soren sprung another question while he dropped an evidence bag on the table between them. "What's on this holochip you were carrying?"

Jake had the impression Soren thought the question would be a nasty surprise. But Jake wanted to talk about exactly this.

"That's the key to it all. The plans for the transpath—the device—are on that holochip."

Soren nodded. "It wouldn't open for us. Can you open it?"

"Yes, of course. It's keyed to me."

The detective opened the bag and dropped the chip onto the table, then shoved it to Jake's side where his cuffed hands could reach it. Jake picked it up. With his eyes locked on Soren's, he pressed his thumb onto the chip. The opening holopage appeared in the air above the chip, and Jake spoke the voice-keyed password Yitzak had given him.

"Honest negotiations."

The opening page gave way to a three-dimensional network of file access containing the transpath plans and theory. Jake used voice commands to open a couple of the pages, showing the technical data, then put the chip back down. When he released it, the holo projections ceased.

"It's all there, Soren. The entire theory and plans for the device. When it's built, no one can lie to each other. Can you imagine what that'll do for diplomatic negotiations?" Jake paused and told the other side. "And can you imagine the people on both sides who will die in the war if we let it happen? Your wife and kids. All your friends."

Manny had been standing by the door. He stepped to the table and straddled the remaining chair backwards. His voice rumbled when he spoke. "And who are you, that you can do something with those plans?"

"I'm an engineer. And a scientist. I work in particle physics and systems engineering."

"But you say this transpath thing was created...by someone else?"

"Right. Yitzak Goren. You may have heard of him. He's known internationally for his work. He trusted me with the plans. He's sure I know enough to rebuild it here."

Manny continued skeptically, "And this—device—can stop war?"

Soren softened the question. "Hey, Manny, we're trying to stop the war, too. That's not a bad thing."

Manny paused, then shifted his topic. "And what about the girl? Where does she fit in?"

The question touched the fears Jake had been harboring for three days, ever since the Solity Guards had captured her back in Timpi.

"Zofia. How is she? Those monsters tortured her. Are you taking care of her?"

Manny chuckled. "I think the boy's sweet on her, Soren."

Jake felt his face flush. "Yes, I am. Please, tell me."

"She's okay," Soren said, "We're taking care of her."

Jake dropped his forehead to the icy table. "Oh, Earthfire. Please let her come back to me," he muttered. For a long moment, he let himself sink into despair. Nervous sweat had soaked his shirt, and the cold room chilled him. He didn't care. All he wanted was to prove himself to these people and get Zofia back. They didn't seem convinced yet.

Soren thumped his finger on the table. "Wake up, Palatin. Talk, not sleep."

Jake lifted his head to the hard eyes in front of him. "I wasn't sleeping."

"What about your implants?" Soren asked. "What happened to them?"

Jake sucked in a quick breath. These guys were sharp. "We cut them out. We needed to get past the surveillance in Oriens and this was the only way."

Soren raised an eyebrow. "You cut them out yourselves?"

Jake shrugged. "Well, we each cut out the other's."

"So, back to the girl. Zofia. Who is she?"

"She was my guide, to get to Tileus." He paused, considering what else he might say.

Manny leaned close across the table. "And how does she know how to get into Tileus? She's done it before?"

Jake just nodded. *Wait*, he thought. *This could be a trap.*

Manny continued with a sharp tone, "So she's been a spy in our country, right?"

"No, no. That's not it at all. She's a Lazarite. She's been here before to negotiate help from your people. Tileus traded weapons for food goods."

Soren cocked his head. "Tileus did that? The country?"

"I don't know who. But someone in this country, yes." Jake was feeling anxious again. This didn't seem to be going well.

"So, it might have been spies here in Tileus, providing those weapons?"

Jake grew increasingly desperate. "I don't know. I just don't know. But the point isn't who did what. The point is to stop the war."

"No, that's *your* mission. Ours is to find the spies who are hurting our country. It still sounds like you and your friend might be part of that."

"But that wouldn't make any sense. Great stars, why would Prime spies get weapons for the Lazarites? They'd help the authorities, not the Lazarites. If I were a spy, why would I bring new technology *to* Tileus?"

Jake's frustration boiled over into irritation. "But you're sitting here asking me questions when you could be *doing* something. I don't know your job, but you seem pretty clueless. You never heard of Yitzak Goren. You don't know who in Tileus is helping our Lazarites, and it's probably someone in your own government who's trading weapons with foreign nationals. And now, I'm sitting here telling you I can save a million lives on both sides, and you act like what I'm talking about isn't even important to you. You guys need to put me in touch with someone who knows, who can actually help."

His words rang against the empty walls. Soren and Manny just sat there. He'd no sooner said it than he wondered if he should have. *Not exactly the way to win friends. But maybe showing some frustration is necessary.*

Without answering him, Soren calmly shifted topic. "You mentioned Berndt Denmark. He's your Director of General Defense, right?"

"Yes, sir."

"How do you know what he wants or doesn't want?"

Another tough question. But honesty is still best. "I...uh, I worked for him."

Soren's eyes got narrow. "You said you're an engineer, but you worked directly for the Director of Defense? You didn't work on this transpath. What did you do?"

"I worked on—" Jake stopped, abruptly thinking hard. *Damn, I just lit into them, and now they ask this. What are they going to think if I tell them? "I created that bomb." Sure, that's going to go over well. "I worked on weapons for Prime." Damn, what can I tell them?*

He took too long. Manny suddenly cracked his heavy palm down on the table. "Don't lie to us, little man! The truth."

Jake jumped in his chair. The answer leaped out of him. "I worked for General Defense, on an antimatter bomb."

They reacted. He was suddenly looking at two pairs of raised eyebrows.

"But I hated it. I knew what it could do. I kept thinking about all the people who would die. Women. Children. Cities destroyed. Maybe the planet couldn't even recover from it. Making a bomb wasn't what I wanted to do. Solity *tells* you what to do. We have no choice. I fled Oriens because I didn't want to build a bomb. That's why I'm a...traitor."

Suddenly filled with shame at his final actions there, he whispered. "I sabotaged it before I left. The bomb went off prematurely in a test." He closed his eyes. "Innocent people were killed."

"An antimatter bomb," said Soren. "That would be huge. Where did the explosion occur?"

Jake sat still, remembering images of the damaged city and imagining the worse damage closer to the bomb. "South of Timpi."

He watched their eyes. The two looked at each other, then back at him. *Have I convinced them? What more can I say?*

Before he could think what to add, Soren took charge, saying, "So, let me see if I've got this right. You sabotaged your own project. You fled the scene. Your sabotage caused deaths and damage. Your partner was tortured by the authorities, but you rescued her. You made your way through a smuggling network here to Tileus."

Jake saw Soren's cold eyes fixed on his.

Soren continued, "And now you want us to believe you're going to build some device to keep people from lying to each other, and that it will stop war."

Put like that, it hardly seemed believable even to Jake.

The two detectives stood. Soren put the holochip back in his evidence bag.

Soren said, "We're going to put you back in your cell, Palatin, while we investigate your claims. We still have pending charges against you for espionage. We'll talk again."

"But wait—"

"No," Soren said. "Nothing further. You'll hear from us again when we're ready."

The two swept out the door.

❧ ❋ ❧

Soren went back to the monitoring room. He and Manny watched an officer release Palatin from the chair and take him back to his cell.

Soren paused in thought. "Did you believe him?"

"Hmm." The sound was a low growl. "Strangely enough, yes. He seems too innocent to create such an elaborate lie. And what would be the purpose?"

"Remember what the governor told us, about a massive explosion south of Timpi? Verdant Prime claimed a factory accident caused it, but I heard yesterday our intel network identified it as a failed test of a new bomb."

Manny cocked his head. "If that's true, it corroborates his story."

"Something big is going on. We need to check it out more. Let our military people know about this man and his claims."

CHAPTER 36

When the situation is bad, expect worse.
—*Collected Sayings of Yitzak Goren* by Ellen Thranadil, Tileus Press 439 A.T.

PLAYDAY, 7 QUINTEMBER, 416 A.T.

Shelton Overlock stood in a second-story office commanding the open plaza around the General Defense building. Low clouds made dawn a dim affair, with light gradually leaking into the world. He leaned toward the window, anticipation pounding his heart like the thunder rolling from the threatening clouds above. Lightning overrode the dim light to etch the five carved stone figures of the defense monument below.

Overlock had found an informer in the Lazarites. The man wanted a better Assignment with more perks, and he'd been willing to give up his buddies. The man told Overlock to expect the Lazarites to use the same combination of explosives and beam weapons as used on the lab building three weeks ago.

Consistency is the hobgoblin of little minds. If they were better thinkers, their plans would vary.

General Defense was a bigger building than the labs, but it could fall just as easily to the combination. The damage to Verdant Prime would be much greater.

Only that wouldn't happen. Overlock was ready.

Lightning flashed again. Suddenly, his implant filled with raucous music, overriding InfoNet access. *Right on time.* This was the Lazarites, and the attack was ready to start. He grinned and suppressed his imp input.

Surprise, maggots. Our coordination still works.

He picked up a non-InfoNet handheld radio communicator and spoke into it.

"All teams, stand by. Suppress your imps and be ready to move."

Twenty or so people in the light blue coveralls of Labor exploded from surrounding streets, running hell-bent across the gap toward the General Defense building. Most carried heavy backpacks; two had rifle-like beam weapons. Lightning again gave a clear picture; all had hoods over their heads and scarves around their necks. The pack-carriers raced toward the walls of the building while the weapon-holders stopped just into the plaza.

Overlock's heart raced. He waited for the teams to get halfway across the plaza, then gave the signal.

"Now. All teams, attack."

230

Doors crashed open all around the plaza, including the main doors of General Defense. Black figures charged out of each door, rifles at the ready, shouting over loudspeakers.

"Solity Guards. Stop where you are with your hands up."

The attack was immense, with the rush of twenty-five Guard squads converging on the pitiful gang of attackers. The two with beam weapons were right outside a couple of the sally ports. They were bowled over immediately and stripped of their weapons before they could fire. Other terrorists turned to fight, firing at the Guards. The fight became a melee, and Shelton couldn't follow it all. He saw two officers spin and fall, blood splattering from neck wounds. He shrugged. *Have to lose a few.*

Some of them kept running to place their explosive packs against the walls. Without mercy, the Guards shot and killed any who didn't raise their hands. The radicals fell in droves, their explosive packs dropped uselessly on the ground. One determined terrorist activated his pack anyway when he collapsed, in a pathetic, suicidal gesture. The explosive force did little damage in the open space. Instead of destroying the building, the explosion blasted the bomber into a thousand pieces and threw his nearest compatriots outward a dozen meters, adding to the carnage.

The clouds let loose their deluge while four aircars settled into the plaza surrounding the remaining terrorists. There were only five left alive, sodden in the downpour, including the two who had held the beam weapons.

Lightning struck the top of the Defense building, the thunder an immediate crash shaking the window in front of him. The lightning rods carried it to ground; the strike did no damage—just like the terrorists.

Overlock leaned toward the window and wet his lips. He had some survivors to interrogate.

⤳ ✳ ⤶

A few hours later, Overlock reported to Denmark's office in person. He was still officially working for Denmark, and he'd been careful to give the director no reason to suspect his new relationship with Director Keita.

Whatever Keita planned for Denmark would have to be a surprise; Overlock was looking forward to it. He particularly hoped it would involve retribution for Denmark's failures. He was discovering new-found contempt for his current boss, a kind of deceit that gave him delight.

"We got them all, Director. No damage to the building. No escapees. A perfect operation this time. Thank you for allowing me to run it."

"It's about time you had a successful action, after the Goren disaster." Denmark glared over his shoulder at the white-uniformed security officer, a constant reminder of his humiliation. "With the right direction, our Solity Guards can do the job they have to do. Keep at it. I want you to squash the entire Lazarites before we start the war."

"Yes, sir. We also captured five rebels in the action. I've started to probe what they know."

"Anything useful yet?"

"This raid was carried out by two separate cells. None of the extremists knew those in the opposite cell, only that others would take part. So far, though, it appears the leaders of each cell were among those killed, so I don't yet have intel on the higher-ups."

"Damn," Denmark said, slapping his desk. His temper was closer to the surface than it had ever been. "Get in there, Shelton. We need to know who's running these Lazarites."

Denmark's showing his desperation. That'll play into whatever Keita's planning.

"Yes, Director. I'm still looking forward to further interrogation, and perhaps these people know something they're not even aware of. I'm also pursuing other avenues, including what more I can get from the stool pigeon who gave us this raid."

Denmark leaned forward, eyes blazing. "Speaking of pigeons, have you found Palatin and his girlfriend yet?"

"No, sir." Overlock held in his anger. "I was in Timpi yesterday. The city is still disorganized. There's no sign of them."

"That's brolshit, Shelton. Do better."

"Director, I learned something. Our lieutenant tells me they've lost a Guard boat—"

"Is this related to Palatin?"

"We don't know. The boat was monitoring the fishing boats for smuggling and failed to return. The boat started to make an urgent report and was cut off. The Guards interviewed fishermen in the area, and it appears the boat was sunk by the Tileus Coastal Patrol."

Denmark pounded a fist repeatedly on the desk. "Is there nothing going right? This sounds like an act of war."

"Yes, sir—except the fishermen reported they were near to Tileus coastal waters."

Denmark got himself under control and gave a crisp nod. "Okay. What about the beam weapons you captured this morning?"

Shelton gave a slow, disbelieving shake of his head. "They're completely new, sir, as we thought. I tried out their effect; they seem to melt the bonds holding materials together. They have less effect on pure materials like metals, but they're devastating on modern composites."

"Any indication where they came from? Was it Tileus?"

"Yes, sir. They've got manufacturing marks matching known Tileus sources."

"Not good, Shelton. Our antimatter bomb isn't ready yet, and Tileus has a weapon we don't. Get them to our defense scientists. We need to reverse engineer this weapon immediately."

"Right away, Director."

"Time is a luxury we don't have, Shelton. Director Pires of State has set a date for our negotiations with Tileus, just over a month from now. We must be ready for our surprise attack on the day after diplomacy fails."

Only two days had passed since Franklin Edobar became Director of Capital. Now he sat uncomfortably in his extravagant office, faced with disaster.

Two more teams lost. And I might be exposed...again. Our Lazarite forces are badly weakened, and we don't have time to rebuild them.

The whole future of the Lazarites hinged on today's catastrophe. He didn't know whether the leaders for those two cells were still alive. *They both know who I am.* With Yitzak gone, he'd had to contact the leaders to set up the raid. As terrible as it felt, he hoped they'd been killed. If they were in Overlock's hands, then Franklin himself would be finished—and the Lazarites along with him.

How did this happen? Someone must have leaked the plan. He made a note to find that mole. Whoever did it wouldn't have been in the raid. They'd still be alive.

He thought about his remaining forces. He only had three more teams in Oriens, and they weren't strong. The best teams had been Yitzak's and these two, and they were gone. He still had teams in the other cities. Time to take the heat off Oriens. He'd start with Timpi, then launch events in Equaton and Millard as well.

He used a private code to scramble an imp call to Ariki.

"Kai? We need to talk. We've had another calamity here in Oriens."

"I just heard about it, Director. Overlock kept it very private beforehand, or I would have warned your teams off."

"We've lost everyone involved, either killed or captured. And we don't know how much they know. And now, Denmark and his people have a couple of the beam rifles."

"They'll work as fast as they can to learn how to make them."

"Right. And then they'll use them on our Lazarites even before they use them in the attack on Tileus."

"How long do we have?"

"Until the war? Negotiations are set for a month from now."

"I meant, until we can expect beam weapons used on us."

"I don't know," Franklin answered. "That depends on the engineers."

His stomach churned at the many things he didn't know, any of which could destroy him. Franklin tapped his finger on his desk. Nervous energy. Uncertainty. He had more unknowns than he had ever worked with before, and he was up against the top-notch people in Solity. At this moment, he wasn't sure he was up to the challenge—but he had no choice except to push forward.

"We need to accelerate plans everywhere, flood the Solity Guards with problems. Have your teams in Timpi take strong action. I don't need to know the details, just create chaos. I'll have the teams here in Oriens and other cities do the same."

"Yes, Director."

What else can we do? Nothing came to mind. Their goal was to destabilize Solity before the war could happen. Then it struck him; Ariki had just said it. *I'm the Director of Capital.* The idea was like an explosion of light in his head, and he ran with it.

"You can also expect problems with supply chains. I've just taken over Capital, so there's bound to be some glitches. I'll make sure there are more. Big ones. People will get dissatisfied with Solity when they can't get the things they need. They'll be ready for change." Even while he spoke, his mind played images of crowds of disgruntled people flooding distribution centers. Clothing in the wrong places, food spoiled by delays, production of the wrong items.

Of course, doing this will put me at more risk.

He could almost hear Ariki nod. "Yes, sir. I'll help that dissatisfaction by using the Guards here to bear down harder on anyone with a problem."

Franklin paused, thinking ahead. *And I've got to make plans to take over the Solity Council from Lukin. Unexpected coup from within, led by the new director. Not much time. Assassination? Or accusations? Which will work better?*

Ariki was still there. "I found something else, sir."

"What's that?"

"When we raided Han Yenstil's house, we took in a lot of goods and weapons. I've extracted one rather important item that's now 'lost' from Guard inventory. It's a holochip from the basement where Palatin and Dobrunik stayed. I can't get past the password page, but I think it might have Yitzak's technical plans for the transpath."

"Hell and damnation. Did Palatin go off without it? How can he succeed without the plans?"

"I don't know, sir, but I didn't want to leave it where some officer might discover it."

"No matter what else we do here, all of our Lazarite actions, nothing is more important than Palatin and the transpath. Without it, negotiations will certainly fail. That's the only thing that can stop this global war."

Franklin racked his brains, trying to remember what Yitzak had told him about the chip. *Damn. Even thinking about Yitzak leaves me feeling lost. I've relied on him so much, and now he's gone.* Then a memory came to him.

"I think Yitzak told me he made two. For Earth's sake, keep that one safe. We have to hope Palatin still has the other."

CHAPTER 37

Welton Moller rapidly became a key figure in the story of the transpath. Palatin had to convince Moller. Without that, Palatin would have to find a new solution all on his own.

—*The Making of a New Humanity* by Ellen Thranadil, Tileus Press 448 A.T.

Jake was getting desperate after four days in jail. He'd hoped the detectives would get back to him quickly. *Didn't they* hear *what I told them? Don't they understand the entire world is at stake?* Yet here he sat.

He spent the time organizing what he would do about the transpath. When they finally started, what would be first? Planning was difficult without the detailed designs on the chip, but he recalled enough to make general goals. One of the biggest problems would be manufacturing the micron-sized waveguides for the particle waves. The waveguides were practically whiskers, exceedingly fragile, yet had to maintain precise internal measurements. The challenge kept his mind busy and held his frustration at bay.

Shortly after breakfast, he heard the cell block door open and footsteps approaching. He jumped to his feet, and his heart leaped when he saw Soren and Manny accompanied by a uniformed officer.

"Am I free now?" he asked. "Can we start work on the transpath?"

"Yes, you can." Soren said. "Sorry to delay you, but we had to be sure. Even better, you've got our attention at the highest levels."

The officer opened the cell door.

"Thank heavens." Jake raised his hands in the air. He rushed out of the cell and pumped the hands of both detectives. Soren took it stoically, while Manny grinned.

Soren replied, "We need to straighten out your status here in Tileus, then we're having a conference with one of our national governors to work out what to do next."

"What about Zofia?"

"She's better. We're taking you to her now. She'll be part of the conference, too."

Jake clenched his eyes and fists for a moment, savoring success. "Thank you." He shook Soren's hand again. "Thank you."

The three policemen led Jake out of the cell block and down a hallway. They stopped at a windowed counter where an officer made Jake sign several holo documents: a temporary work visa, a release form, and a receipt for his "personal goods"—comprising only his useless Verdant Prime rationchip and the all-important transpath holochip.

"We're giving the holochip back to you," said Soren, "because it appears you're the only one who can do anything with it. But that's what our conference will be about."

Down another hallway, they went through a door off the main police processing area. Inside was a windowed conference room with a long table surrounded by eight chairs.

Zofia sat in a wheelchair beside the table. She came to life when they entered.

"Jake," she said, a smile crinkling the fading bruises around her eyes.

His relief was so great he melted inside. He took in every detail of her: the sunlight sparkling on her dark hair, the strange shirt and trousers she wore, bandages peering out from her collar, the slightly lost look in her eyes. *They said they were taking care of her, but she still looks pretty beat-up.* He dropped to his knees beside her wheelchair and took her hand in his.

"Thank heavens," he said. "I've been so worried about you."

"Jake," she said again, questioningly. He noticed her smile was fixed. "How are you, love?"

She paused, watching him with puzzlement. "Well, I...don't know...I'm better than I was, I think."

He cradled her face with his hands and kissed her gently. She responded, also gently, but without the fire they had known before her capture. When they pulled away, he sat next to her, not letting go of her hand.

"You're definitely better than you were. At least you know who I am."

"I'm still confused, Jake. I remember some things...I don't want to remember...and others...were you and I in the woods together?"

Jake felt his shoulders slump, but he kept a smile on his face. "Yes, we were in the woods outside Oriens."

"And I hurt, Jake. All over. Sometimes, I can't think for the pain."

Black thoughts clouded his mind. *If I could get my hands on Shelton Overlock!*

"I'm so sorry, Zofia. It's been a horrible time."

Her eyes turned dark with fear, apparently triggered by his words. He squeezed her hand, reminding her he was still here.

He added, "But it's been worth it. They're going to help us now."

Soren spoke from behind him. "I hate to break up this tender moment, but we've got that conference. All of us. There's an aircar waiting to take us to Freedom Aerie, our national government house. Tileus is taking your story seriously, and we need to move fast."

Jake nodded and stood to push Zofia's chair.

After an hour's transit from Freetown, the aircar circled the Tileus seat of government in Thad City before settling onto a second-floor terrace near the front entrance. Jake held Zofia's hand during the entire flight, while he gazed out the windows.

The buildings and architecture in Thad City were different from Oriens, with buildings rising to many different heights instead of the uniform five stories he knew. Each building was unique, and he saw several different trends—severely straight, ornate, curved—likely reflecting changing tastes in architecture. The styles were all foreign to him, highlighting the simple fact Tileus was not like Prime.

He realized he had no idea what to expect, or even how to behave.

Tileus had always been the enemy. Prime portrayed them as evil dissidents, taking away from the calmness of the world with their chaotic "democracy." History lessons in school had emphasized the war when Tileus tore itself away from Verdant's life, initiating over two hundred years of conflict. Jake's bomb development had been aimed at "correcting" Tileus.

The reality he saw from the aircar was very different from what he thought he knew.

Getting out of the aircar was a relief. Between Manny's size and Zofia's wheelchair, there hadn't been much room for Soren and Jake.

The wheelchair was still a necessity. "I get dizzy," she said. "It's part of my confuscon...confusion." Her eyebrows furrowed at her mistake.

"Don't worry, love. You will improve. You already are recovering."

They walked across the terrace toward the main doors. Jake took in a deep breath at the expansive view, a wide set of stone stairs down to a treed plaza seeming to hold at bay the tall buildings of central Thad City. People dotted the park, some hurrying while others lingered on benches around a pond. Their dress was different. Some wore long pants, some wore shorts, and there were even a few skirts and dresses. He was amazed at the variety of color and style but had no time to dwell on it.

"We go in through here," Soren said.

Jake pushed Zofia in her chair through massive doors under an arched stone portico.

Jake noticed the carved stone figures on the arch, but had no idea what they meant. Clearly, Tileus had its own history to celebrate—of which he knew nothing.

"We're going to meet with the Governor of Outside Affairs," Soren explained. "He's one of the five leaders of the country. They decide what issues are worthy of our national vote, and they manage departments to implement the results. The Governor's name is Welton Moller...and yes, he's a relative of mine. He's my uncle, which is why your story has gotten high attention so quickly."

"Quickly?" Jake snorted. "It hasn't felt quick to me."

"Or me," said Zofia.

Soren looked back at Jake with a raised eyebrow. "You've told us a rather wild tale, Jake. We couldn't take it at face value."

"I guess not."

"And then, even when we checked it out, we had to make our own plans what to do with you. Now, Welton is ready to help."

One of the top five governors? Jake was impressed. This morning he'd been twiddling his thumbs in jail; now he was meeting with one of the country's leaders. He'd hoped to meet with a competent scientist or engineer, someone who could at least fight for the necessary resources. *Good heavens, someone at the top can simply say "yes" and it'll happen.*

They took a tube to the seventh floor, the top. The wide hallway had shiny floors and carved wood trim on the walls. Jake saw one other person in the hall; the quiet was soothing. Soren opened a door with carved mullions and deep-set panels. They entered an antechamber, and Jake recognized the fresh scent of rosemary. A secretary nodded to Soren.

"Good morning, Detective. He's ready to see you all now."

"Thanks, Trish."

Soren opened carved French doors. A richly decorated, spacious office lay within. Wood paneling on the walls, a ceiling painted with a sky mural, a carpet in the blue, russet and green colors of Verdant forests. An expansive desk stood at their left. The wall opposite them was all windows, looking out on the plaza, buildings and cloud-studded sky. The office was quieter than the hallway, the hush of a highly-controlled, secure environment. Jake couldn't help but see the similarities—and contrast—to Denmark's office. Both represented the highest levels of power. While the director's office had been imposing, this office spoke of assured competence.

An older man with greying hair and a dark beard rose from behind the desk and came to greet them.

"Welcome, welcome," he said with warmth when he extended a hand. "I understand you are Jake and Zofia, right? You've come a long way and with great difficulty. I'm hoping we can help each other."

"I'm sure we can, sir," Jake responded. *Home-spun manner. Friendly voice. I already like this man.*

"Thank you, sir," Zofia said.

Welton turned to the detectives with a hearty laugh. "And you two. Only a week ago, I asked you to investigate spies for me. Unbelievably creative work. Instead of spies, you've found an opportunity. Of course, I didn't expect anything else. You two are top notch."

Manny rumbled something sounding like thanks. Soren shrugged, "Whatever, sir. I'm just glad you agree this might be important."

Welton guided them to a silver brocaded couch and chairs to their right. His sharp eyes seemed to take in every detail about his visitors.

"Jake, Soren told me about you and your...transpath, but I'd like to know more. Who are you? Why are you here? What can you do for us, and how can we help you?"

Finally, he could tell his story to someone who mattered. Jake told of his work for Berndt Denmark, about the antimatter bomb and its consequences. He told about the Lazarites and Yitzak Goren and his work in particle physics and mind waves. Very much aware he was talking to a policy-maker, not an engineer, Jake kept the technical details minimal. He did open the holochip to display the wealth of plans inside.

"I'm confident, sir, with the right resources, I can rebuild Yitzak's transpath here."

"And what would it do if you built it? Soren's told me a pretty wild tale."

Jake tapped the holochip on his chair arm, a plastic clicking promising incredible possibilities. "If we can have it available the next time Tileus and Prime sit down for negotiations, we can change the direction of the world. The device causes everyone in its empathic field to understand and feel the emotions of everyone else. Zofia and I have experienced it, and it's nothing less than miraculous. Diplomacy has always been based on secrecy and half-truths. In the transpath field, it is impossible to lie. Each participant knows exactly what the others are feeling."

His presentation had taken longer than he'd intended, but the governor had listened to it all with interest. Now, he was done. He'd given it his best. He leaned forward and waited, his heart in his throat.

Welton took a deep breath and cocked his head. "How well did you know Yitzak Goren?"

This wasn't the response Jake expected. "Uh...not well, sir. Only for two weeks, though we spent the last two days together. Zofia knew him better."

"Five years, sir," she said. "Maybe. I think it's been that long."

Welton nodded slowly, sadly. "He was well respected in the scientific community. His work was seminal. However...I am sorry to tell you...he is gone. We have a report he passed away this week."

Zofia let loose a small cry.

Jake put his hand on her shoulder. "How did it happen?" he asked. "I know he was in danger."

"Yes. It's not widely known, but our sources say he committed suicide. Violent explosions in his apartment. Apparently, he almost took Denmark's sadistic sidekick with him."

"I'm sorry he didn't, sir. But even sorrier to hear Yitzak is gone."

Zofia's hand grasped Jake's. She dropped her face into her other hand and sobbed. "He did so much for me."

Welton let the grief endure for a moment before continuing.

His voice resonated with decision and urgency. "If there is a possibility Yitzak's device can do what you say, Jake, and we can make sure the upcoming negotiations succeed, then we must try. Prime has been increasingly overbearing and is building toward a global war. It appears they are intent on bringing the other three countries back under their onerous control, and they're willing to use every weapon they have to do so."

Jake said, "Yes, sir. I've heard that goal expressed by Director Denmark himself." He closed his eyes in shame. "My own work on the antimatter bomb was part of the plan."

"We have little time remaining. Negotiations between our countries are scheduled for the nineteenth of Hexember, a bit over a month from now."

"A month?" Jake's eyes went wide. "A month? I don't think it's possible to rebuild the transpath in a month."

"And yet we must. Jake, I'll give you every resource we can." He turned to the detectives. "Soren, I want you and Manny to spearhead this project."

"You want us to be...project managers?" Manny sat up straight, shaking his head. "We don't know diddly about management."

Soren joined him in shaking his head. The two looked gob-smacked. "No, Uncle. We aren't the right people for this. We're detectives, not—"

"You're exactly the right people. You have the force of character, the drive, the determination to make it happen if anyone can. I trust you. I need someone to push people hard against their own natural resistance. You two are astonishingly good at pushing." He raised an eyebrow at his nephew. "I also know you have contacts in the darker parts of Tileus that may be essential. I'll expect you to use them."

Welton finished by waving a dismissive hand at the management issues. "I'll assign others to do the paperwork and organization. I want you to be the driving force, to push it to completion against every obstacle."

Jake's eyes bounced back and forth between the uncle and nephew. Forcefulness apparently ran in the family. Suddenly, after waiting for days, he felt swept along by a hurricane force.

Welton turned back to him. "You, Jake, are the mastermind. Yitzak chose you for a reason. I respect his choice. You decide what's needed. All you have to do is ask for it. Soren and Manny will get it. I also have a team of Tileus engineers standing by to help you. I think you'll find them capable."

He looked at Zofia, hopeful in her wheelchair. "Zofia, your job right now is to recover. That should be your only task until you're back on your feet. But in the meantime, what you *can* do is to encourage Jake while you heal. What's your expertise?"

"I'm a software technician on implants, sir." Her voice was more confident.

"Whatever you can do, please do. And we'll support you, too."

He stood. "It starts now. All of you, get out of here and get busy. Make it happen. Soren, you report daily to me."

Suddenly, a raucous alarm rang at Welton's desk. His eyebrows went up, and he rose from his chair to press a button on the desk and silence the alarm.

"Most interesting. I'm receiving a call on the international hot line..." He reached inside his desk to extract a small red box.

"...from Verdant Prime. It's Director Denmark."

CHAPTER 38

A spiritual principle underlies Berndt Denmark's influence on the new technology. No matter how hard he pushed against events, his firm negativity often seemed to foster exactly the opposite results than he intended.

—*The Making of a New Humanity* by Ellen Thranadil, Tileus Press 448 A.T.

Denmark took an aircar to a temporary building outside Oriens to see the new beam weapons they'd captured from the Lazarites. He'd demanded the scientists work through this weekend. The destruction of the laboratory building three weeks ago forced small weapons testing into this inconvenient location, and he cursed under his breath at the extra travel to reach the outlying location. Denmark intended to push the scientists and engineers to the end of their endurance, if necessary.

Pushing engineers. Damn. Two and a half weeks, and Rodrick Griffin's team still can't find what Palatin did to the antimatter bomb. They keep checking and re-checking the test data. I'll need to drive them, too.

Denmark was not in a good mood, despite the successful action against the Lazarites yesterday. That was one bright spot in a series of failures. He glared under his brows at the impassive, white-clad security man, his constant and irritating shadow.

"How often do you report to the Chairman?" he asked.

The man responded with a neutral tone, "I'm not permitted to tell you, sir."

Everywhere I go. Everything I do. What brolshit. How can I work the necessary politics with an overseer shining light into all my dark corners?

The aircar landed, and Denmark stormed into the building. He headed immediately to the small arms lab. He slammed the door open into the analysis room with his usual lack of warning. Beyond the analysis room was a window wall looking into the testing lab, where three technicians were working on the weapon.

"What have you found so far?" he demanded.

The lead scientist jumped to her feet, leaving alive a holo display she'd been studying. Denmark reluctantly credited the woman with force and aplomb; she answered immediately despite her surprise. She waved a hand toward the window wall.

"Yesterday, we catalogued the weapon's effects on different materials, sir. It varies, but seems most profound on modern composites—about eighty percent of our materials these days."

"Is there anything that stops it?"

"Nothing we've found, sir. Some things, like water, slow its effects—but it can still disintegrate the bonds." She smiled, her eyes alive with curiosity. "Strange to see the oxygen and hydrogen separate, then rejoin again in a blue spontaneous glow just outside its field."

Denmark waved a dismissive hand. "We're not here to muse over scientific imponderables. It's urgent we recreate this weapon. If we can also find a defense, that's even better."

"Yes, sir," she responded with visible embarrassment. "This morning, we're disassembling one of the two weapons to see what we can learn. The techs are just starting now."

Denmark moved to the window and watched the technician remove the screws from the casing.

A violent explosion erupted, flame and smoke hurling debris against the window. The three technicians were catapulted against the cabinets, falling to the floor like floppy toys. The concussion turned the window into a webbed network of cracks a meter from Denmark's face. Before he could react, the shattered glass flung toward him, and acrid smoke billowed into the analysis room.

❧ ✳ ☙

A half hour later, a medic was patching Denmark's face. He had instinctively closed his eyes; his vision and hearing were unimpaired. The glass wall had been designed for safety, absorbing the impact and shattering into nodules instead of shards, saving his life. Denmark combed pieces of glass out of his hair with his fingers.

The lead scientist and the security officer had been behind Denmark. Dirtied from the blast debris and smoke, they'd received only minor damage. The same couldn't be said for the technicians who had been in the lab. All three had been converted to flayed slabs of meat.

While the medic worked, Denmark was still quivering inside, and his hands shook. The explosion had frightened him, reminding him his own life was as fragile as the window wall. He'd been lucky this time, and he never wanted to rely on luck.

Beyond that, here was yet another failure. In the last month, everything was falling apart. As hard as he pushed, setbacks were compounding. The obstacles were almost too much for him to take.

In reaction to his fear, he raged.

"Damn it all to hell! Now we've lost one of the weapons, and we don't dare open the other one."

"Director, can you hold still, please?" said the medic. "I'm almost done here."

"You," he shouted. "Scientist! I don't even know your stupid name."

"Bedrank, sir."

"I don't even care. Why weren't your technicians more careful?"

"We had no idea, sir—"

"That's obvious. So, what are you going to do next? We still need to know how to build those things."

"First, I'll have to get more technicians—"

"Do it. Get them. And get it done, now."

He pushed the medic away. "I'm getting out of here. There are better things I can do than watching scientific incompetence."

He looked at the security officer, whose white coveralls were stained and blackened with soot. The man had a gash on his cheek.

"You. Get checked out by some medical help. Leave me alone." *Maybe I can get something* done *with him gone.*

The man firmly shook his head. "Can't do that, sir. I've got my orders." He followed Denmark out the door.

"Orders," Denmark echoed in a sarcastic tone, mostly to himself. "I'm a damned director, and I can't tell this man what to do."

Back in the aircar, Denmark calmed himself and put in a secure imp call to Chairman Lukin.

"We've had another setback, Chairman."

"Yes. I heard from my officer. Your people exploded one of the beam weapons."

Denmark's jaw tightened at the assignment of blame. "We still have the other weapon, sir. Now we know they're set to explode, our technicians will probe it more carefully."

"A wise move, I think." The Chair's tone of voice was almost condescending.

"I'd like to propose another avenue, sir. Something to shake up the relationship with Tileus."

"And that would be?"

"We have evidence of two acts of war by Tileus. One is the smuggling of these new weapons to our Lazarites. From the production marks, they obviously came from Tileus. The other is their sinking of our Guard boat in the Vissensee Channel."

"Yes?"

"I'd like to call Governor Moller again in Thad City and see if I can shake loose other information. At the very least, we'll lay the groundwork for the negotiations next month to fail."

Lukin took a long pause on the other end.

Denmark couldn't tell what Lukin might be thinking, but he waited. It galled him to have to ask permission like a schoolchild having to go to the bathroom. Before his censure, he had the authority to just *do* something like this. The damned security officer witnessed his helplessness day in and day out. *I may have to move on Lukin earlier than I'd planned, just to end this censure. First, I've got to rebuild my support from the other directors.*

Finally, the Chairman spoke again. "Okay, Director. I'll authorize it. You've used that channel effectively in the past. Do so again."

"Thank you, sir."

"And Director...I know how much it bothers you to have to ask for approval this way."

Denmark ground his teeth again. *Someday, I won't have any teeth left.* "Yes, sir."

"Remember you brought it on yourself." Chairman Lukin ended the call.

❧ ✳ ☙

Jake's heart raced while he watched Governor Moller pick up the red box from the desk. *Director Denmark?* He felt sweat bloom on his forehead.

"You have a hot line to Director Denmark?" he asked, and glanced at Zofia. "We can't have him see us here."

Welton waved a calming hand in the air. "Don't worry. He won't see you; the holo field will only show him my image. The rest of you just need to sit still and be quiet." He moved the red box to a table in the middle of the chairs where they sat, orienting it to face his own chair. He activated it, and a live holo of Director Denmark appeared above it

"Good morning, Director. This is Welton Moller."

"Good morning, Governor."

Welton leaned forward toward the holo, concern on his face. "Director, you look like you've been cut about the face. Are you well?"

Denmark seemed momentarily taken aback by the concern. "As well as needs be, sir."

"Alright, then. If you're calling on the hot line, there must be something urgent on your mind. Go ahead."

Visceral fear swept through Jake like a convulsion. In the last month, Denmark had come to symbolize everything wrong and fearful about Solity. Seeing his holo image so close, Jake wanted to run and hide. He reached out to hold Zofia's hand.

Denmark pressed on. "Yes, indeed, Governor. We've had a couple of incidents here in Prime we are struggling to understand as anything other than acts of war."

Jake saw Soren's eyebrows rise at the claim. The detective leaned forward almost imperceptibly.

Welton's reaction was more subtle; he tilted his chin. "What? Acts of war? You'll have to expand on that, please."

"I will, sir. I'm hoping you can explain them as something else." Denmark took a harsh breath. "First, as you know, we've had our own problems with a resistance movement calling itself the Lazarites. I spoke with you last month about whether you had operatives in Prime supporting them."

"Yes, you almost made that accusation."

"In another incident we crushed yesterday, we captured two uniquely destructive beam weapons of a type we've never seen. Those weapons carry production marks from Tileus. It appears, as I suggested last month, your government is supplying weapons to the insurgents in our country."

Welton hardly reacted. Jake was astonished he could stay impassive, because both Jake and Zofia knew Tileus was indeed supplying weapons.

Welton responded, "Do you have any confirmation of that claim, Director? I doubt proof would be possible."

"What more proof do we need, than to know the weapons were manufactured there, Governor?" Denmark said, with his temper rising. "And you haven't answered my question."

"You haven't asked a question, sir."

Denmark leaned forward, eyes intense. "Are you supplying weapons to the Lazarite faction? Are you interfering in our internal affairs?"

"That's two questions, sir. The answer to both is no."

Jake watched Soren sit up straight in his chair, his eyes wide. He and Manny traded a searching look. Manny opened his mouth to say something, and Soren quickly raised a hand to stop him, shaking his head. Zofia squeezed Jake's hand.

Denmark huffed, his features hard. "That's not the answer I expected, sir. Every indication we have is these weapons came from you."

"I suggest, Director, the 'proof' you've offered so far would be insufficient in the impartial courts we have in Tileus. You've shown the weapons were manufactured here. You have not shown Tileus is supplying them to your insurgents. We have a free market economy here, and anyone can purchase whatever they wish."

"I know about your so-called 'free' economy, Governor, and how the value of your 'money' changes weekly, manipulated by your Governor of Finance. What I don't understand is why your citizens put up with it."

"It's called freedom, sir, something we prize greatly."

"Then perhaps, *sir*, if these weapons are something you manufacture so freely, you could help us by providing the technology for them? Freely."

Welton gave a dry smile. "I think not, Director. We value our freedom more than that."

"And are your Coastal Patrol ships also 'free,' sir, to fire on our boats? The second act of war I want to bring up is the sinking of one of our Guard boats by a Tileus hovership."

"Ah, Director, I *am* familiar with this incident. Please confirm you are referring to the action just off the coast of Freetown this past weekend?"

"That is the one, yes."

"If so, then perhaps it should be *me* taking *you* to task. Our navigational records show your Guard boat entered our territorial waters and fired on a Tileus small craft. *We* should be complaining about *your* act of war. Do you really expect our Coastal Patrol *not* to engage when your boat violates our international agreements?"

"The Guard was in hot pursuit of smuggling activities, Governor. I would expect your Coastal Patrol to *assist* in such a case."

Jake was astonished at the vitriol being thrown back and forth. He had never worked at this level of politics, and the electric tension suffocated like toxic gas. Trying to ease his own fears, he looked at Zofia. He saw to his shock she was disappearing into post-traumatic fear. He put his right arm around her shoulders to comfort her, still holding her hand with his left.

Welton continued, now pressing harder. "Our ships might assist—*if they were asked*, Director. By the way, we rescued two of your Guards. A third unfortunately died as the result of his actions. Our people are working with yours to arrange their return."

Jake saw Denmark had changed in these weeks. The director he knew had always been in control with an edge of anger. Now he seemed to be losing it, his reactions more mercurial, less appropriate. He wondered what stresses Denmark was under to change him so much.

Welton had paused long enough to change subject. "But so long as we are talking of assistance and weapons, perhaps you can assist us by identifying what you were doing detonating an antimatter bomb in the mountains south of Timpi? What the *hell* are you people thinking, to create such a device in the first place?"

For just a moment, Denmark looked like a boy caught with his hand in a cookie jar. "Who told you we had an antimatter bomb, sir?"

"Our scientists are not fools, Director. They can assemble the evidence."

Denmark suddenly sat up straight, a new idea apparently striking him. "Or did you perhaps have help, Governor? Perhaps that smuggling incident was something more? Rescue of a dissident?"

He leaned forward in the holo frame to bark a question. "Do you have our engineer, sir?"

Jake nearly jumped out of his skin. Both Soren and Manny had their eyes on him. Soren pushed his palms downward: *calm down, calm down.* Even Welton was surprised enough his eyes flashed over to Jake.

Denmark saw the flicker and went into rage. "He's right there, isn't he? *We demand his return.* Palatin, if you're there, we will get you back. You may think yourself safe, but you are not."

Welton immediately fired back. "Are you admitting you have agents operating inside Tileus, Director? We will certainly take that into account in preparing for negotiations. This conversation is over. Such accusations as you've made are not appreciated."

Welton cut the line.

The residual tension hanging in the room felt to Jake like strangle-vines encasing his chest. He squeezed Zofia's shaking hand and checked her again. The intense anxiety of the call had driven her back into herself. Her eyes were hooded and darting around the room in fear. Jake gently squeezed her shoulder.

"It's okay, love. We're safe." He leaned over to her with his forehead, whispering repeatedly, "Safe. We're safe." He could feel her trembling subside.

"Safe," she said in a weak voice. "*He* was there, too."

Soren broke the tension with a dry chuckle. "Well, uncle, that was extreme. Manny and I have done criminal interrogations like that. Never knew you did the same in international politics."

Welton snorted. "All in a day's work, son."

Jake felt the anxiety recede. "What do we do now, sir?"

"No change to our plans, Jake. The four of you get cracking on the transpath."

CHAPTER 39

We can't understand complexity. We break a complex system into parts we can grasp, but our misunderstandings always come back when we assemble those parts into the system. If there's a deadline, count on discovering extra problems.

—*Collected Sayings of Yitzak Goren* by Ellen Thranadil, Tileus Press 439 A.T.

THRUDAY, 23 QUINTEMBER, 416 A.T.

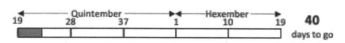

"These just aren't good enough, Soren," Jake said. He waved his hand at the latest coil of waveguides, looking like thin insulated wire but far more specialized. His voice shook with frustration.

Soren was calm and business-like. "I don't know anything about the technical stuff, so I take your word for it. Unfortunately, I've pushed the manufacturer to the wall on this. They say it's the absolute best they can do."

"Earthfire, we've got to do better—and faster. We've got forty days left until the negotiations, and I've *never* seen a complex technical development done in such a short time."

They'd accomplished amazing things in a week and a half, but the pressure weighed heavily on Jake. Welton Moller's influence worked miracles. People jumped to help. Jake already had a spacious lab with multiple workbenches and an array of computers for analysis and design. A team of eight highly competent engineers and technicians was already hard at work in the open space, sharing information daily. Jake had slipped back into his team leadership role with hardly a glitch. Soren had manufacturers supporting them, building rapid prototypes of the waveguides, antennas, and controllers. Jake's biggest problem was staying ahead of the team, creating the ideas and plans others could implement.

Manny had found a black-market source for nano-processors used to defeat surveillance systems. The simple computers were so tiny they floated invisibly in the air like dust. They communicated with each other to implement network computing. Threatening the company with prosecution, he'd strong-armed them into building flocks of the devices. Jake wasn't sure yet how to use them, but he'd assigned one of the engineers to explore the possibilities. They were one example of several technologies available here in Tileus he hadn't seen in Prime.

The original transpath plans from Yitzak were displayed in the lab's large holo, but Jake had been modifying them daily.

"The problem we've got," he explained to Soren, "is Yitzak's design is too large and too limited. It worked for his fifteen square meters of lab space, but the negotiation chamber is over a hundred square meters. These waveguides have to carry our signals up to ten meters from signal driver to antenna. We tested them today. There's too much signal loss, and they put delays into the transmission. They won't work."

"I didn't understand all of that, but I've got the concept. What do the manufacturers need to do, Jake?"

"They've got to improve their quality control. The waveguides must maintain precise micron-level interior dimensions in their entire length, even when curved."

Soren nodded understanding. "I'll go back to them this morning and tell them. They'll need to talk with you or one of your engineers."

"We can do better than that. Take Emigan with you. He understands the waveguides."

Soren snagged Emigan from his workbench, and the two left.

One more solution in process. How will we get it all done?

Zofia put her arm around Jake's waist and hugged him. The scars on her face were healing. She was getting stronger every day and no longer needed the wheelchair. Stronger, but not yet ready for stress. Welton had told her to be emotional support for Jake, and the role was helping both of them.

"You've been at this for fifteen days now, Jake, without a break. You've hardly been outside the lab except to sleep. You look pale and nervous. I'm worried about you."

Jake took a deep breath and gave her a frustrated smile. Even while she supported him, he also felt the need to strengthen her. Her voice had wavered, and he didn't want her to trigger again into post-traumatic fear. She was still fragile and had suffered an incident yesterday.

He tried to ease her apprehension. "I'm okay. I worked with this kind of pressure under Denmark. It's just there's so much to do. Yitzak had this working, but it won't do what we need without significant change. I have to make it work. You should relax as much as you can."

I wish I could give myself the same advice.

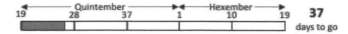

"Smaller, Jake? You need it smaller?" Bendel was the antenna expert on the team, the best in Tileus.

Jake watched him shake his head in disbelief.

Bendel was a rather strange fellow, with a pointy nose and darting eyes, his hair always in disarray. His annoying voice was intense and whiney. He hardly seemed to talk with the other team members. Sometimes he had a nervous tic that made him duck his head. The man seemed to have private pressures way beyond the needs of the project. But with all, he was brilliant. His contributions were significant.

"Yes, dammit. Size is key for portability. We can't ring the negotiation room with two-meter antennas and tangles of prototype wire; the diplomats will balk at being part of an experiment. The antennas need to be unobtrusive." Jake's throat was raw, and he heard it in his own voice. He spent most of his time talking to the team members, giving direction and answering questions. Each day seemed to stretch him like bread dough on kneading hooks. They had four weeks to go.

"How many antennas?" Bendel asked.

"That depends on the range and power you can achieve with each one. We have to fill the room with signal. I'm hoping we can do it with eight, but sixteen would be okay. For heaven's sake, Bendel, we're talking about tiny wavelengths here. Particle-sized wavelengths." Jake held his thumb and finger apart by a fraction of a millimeter. "The wavelengths are miniscule, and antenna size is related to wavelength. Yitzak used an array, but they shouldn't need to be so big."

"Okay," Bendel huffed, twitching. "I'll work on it. When can I have some signal to push through the antennas for testing? I'll need data as soon as possible."

Jake's frustration crested. He waved his hands in the air. "I don't know yet. Mos is working on a signal driver. Every part of this development has problems."

Bendel backed away from him, his tic active and head twitching, patting the air with his hands. "It's okay, Jake. We're doing everything we can." Despite his attempt to reassure, his voice grated on Jake's anxieties.

Jake pounded the table with a fist. "It's not enough yet," he shouted. Everyone in the lab stopped and looked at him.

"Good heavens, people. We've got to get it all together at the same time," he yelled at the whole team. "We're never going to feel the transpath effect unless we can..." he started counting on his fingers. "One: generate the signal with Mos's drivers. Two: get the signal from the drivers to Bendel's antennas through good waveguides. Three: fill the room with signal. And Four: have it all synchronized in micron-sized phase. *It's all got to work.*"

He felt Manny's heavy hand on his shoulder. "Keep it cool, boss. We'll get there." Manny gave a reassuring squeeze to ease Jake's anxiety while also making his collarbone crunch. "Maybe you need to take a little time off and let people work."

Zofia came up on his other side. "You bet, Jake. It's the weekend. Let's go to lunch for an hour. Leave everyone alone to do their work."

His first impulse was to bark at her. A large part of him wanted to decline the offer, to keep working, to *make it happen.*

"Come on, love," she said while she slid an arm around him and leaned into him. "Let's have a nice lunch, okay? Get away from it for a bit? We can talk about how you'll lose at zero-G next time."

Jake crumpled and nodded. "You're right. I can't think straight right now."

He turned to the door and heard applause behind him. Jake turned back to see everyone in the lab grinning at him while they clapped.

Jake shook his head and laughed. "Okay, okay, everyone. I get the message. You all keep working, and I'll go de-stress for a while. But...I'll be back in an hour."

PLAYDAY, 34 QUINTEMBER 416 A.T.

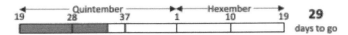

"Soren, have you spoken with your uncle in the last few days?" Jake asked. "I'm getting concerned about what might be going on in Prime. I get the news on my new implant, and it doesn't look good."

Soren grunted. "Hmph. Yeah, I report to him every day. Every. Single. Day." He shook his head in irritation. "Manny thinks having a governor for an uncle gives me an advantage. I think it's a pain in the neck."

Jake snorted. "I can understand that. Working for Denmark was like that, too. Has our deadline eased at all?"

"Still the same, twenty-nine days from now; the date for negotiations hasn't changed. The stakes keep getting higher, though. Uncle Welt had another phone confrontation yesterday with Denmark. Accusations flying back and forth. Denmark now knows you're here. He demands your return. Uncle Welt ignores his demand and has never confirmed your presence. Verdant Prime keeps adding on more demands, making them sound like ultimatums. Now they want Tileus to phase down our military and disable our weapons, all supposedly in the name of peace. It's becoming crystal clear Prime has no intention for the negotiations to succeed."

"That's their strategy. Has been all along."

253

"Yeah, but it's not very—"

Soren suddenly stopped talking. He blinked, and his eyes filled with wonder.

Jake was looking at him when it happened. He felt Soren's bewilderment. Not just saw it in his eyes, but felt the man's emotion deep in Jake's own awareness. He also sensed Soren's intelligence and competence at everything he did, the gruff confidence from inside Soren's soul instead of just perceiving it by his actions. The connection filled Jake with a deep trust in the detective's contributions.

He'd felt this before. It dawned on him what was happening.

"The transpath signal," he whispered to himself, smiling broadly.

Jake spun around to look at the others in the lab. Every person had stopped what they were doing. When he looked from one to another, he felt the individual sensations from each. He looked at Mos and felt his wonder, dedication, fear. Shifting his eyes to Emigan, he sensed the man's pleasure and curiosity—and also some deep suspicion at the strange sensations. What he perceived changed with whom he observed, the feelings specific to each person. Manny seemed filled with delight and surprise, with a tinge of apprehension. The combination from everyone was almost overwhelming. This was humanity at its best, connecting in ways people had never known before. Each transmitted emotion brought a level of trust with it, a knowledge that Jake perceived them fully and could rely on what he felt from them. If Jake hadn't felt it before, in Yitzak's lab, he'd be as baffled as all the others.

He looked at Zofia. She was grinning, almost laughing in joy. She was coming alive again after so many weeks, and the transpath allowed him to feel her growing assurance of her own capabilities. She pumped her fists— success—and gave a little jump of elation. He also felt her pride in him, her love for him. His smile joined hers, the shared emotions enhancing each of them. For the first time in weeks, Jake felt satisfaction in their success.

Zofia was the first to speak, her voice cutting through the awed silence in the lab. "This is it, buckos. What you're feeling is what we've been trying to make happen. Imagine what it will be like when our diplomats meet with this mutual understanding."

Soren turned to look at Jake. "You were telling us about this when you first arrived, Jake, but we couldn't believe it." Jake sensed admiration and chagrin in the detective that bolstered his words. "I admit it. You were right all along."

"Who did it," said Jake. "What did someone just turn on?"

When he said it, the feelings died again. Bendel turned from his workbench, his nervousness making his head twitch. "Uh...boss...I think I did. It's the new antenna. I just connected it to Mos's signal driver." He nearly blushed in embarrassment. "I just turned it off again."

"Well, whatever you did…it worked," Jake enthused. "Congratulations. This is a major success. And, by the way, that means your new antenna works. Which version did you use?"

Bendel held up a prototype antenna array hardly larger than his palm, with a whisker waveguide trailing down to his bench. "This one. You think this will be small enough?"

"Small enough?" Jake said. "That's fantastic, to get such a strong signal out of something so small. Yitzak Goren—our genius—did it with two-meter antennas. You've taken it down to five centimeters. What range will it have?"

"Not much. About three meters, just enough to hit all of us here in the lab."

Jake thought it through and his smile faded. "Okay. As great as it is, we're not done yet, folks. This is a marvelous first test, but it won't fill the negotiation room with valid signal. We can put Bendel's antennas in every corner of the conference room, but we've still got to have good waveguides to get signals to each antenna—and if they aren't synchronized, it won't work."

His words dampened the enthusiasm while everyone pondered the remaining difficulty.

Nonetheless…" He grinned again and clapped his hands. "Great success. For Bendel's antenna and for Mos and his signal driver." He glanced at the calendar display, with big red Xs marking off the days. "We've got twenty-nine days remaining. We can come back to this tomorrow, but let's call the rest of today a celebration. Let's party!"

The team cheered.

჻ ✳ ჻

An hour later at a nearby easygo, Soren had a beer in his hand like everyone else. They had pitchers on the table, flowing freely. Even Jake looked relaxed.

Soren, though, was watching Manny with caution. *What's going on with him?* His partner was usually the first to laugh at a party, but Manny looked serious. He stared across the table at Bendel in the same way he watched a perp. When Bendel left his beer and got up from the table to go to the bar, Manny leaned over to whisper.

"Soren, I think we've got a problem."

"What's that?"

"My detective alarm bells went off when Bendel flipped the switch off. I happened to be watching him at the moment. He nearly jumped out of his skin, and it looked to me like guilt." Manny paused. "And that's what I felt from him through the transpath, until he turned it off."

Soren watched Bendel.

"By the way," said Manny. "We gotta get this transpath thing for our police interrogations. It really works."

Bendel didn't order anything at the bar. After a couple of minutes of nervous agitation, he sidled toward the exit door.

Soren's bells went off, too. "Follow him, Manny. Let me know what happens."

Manny left, and Soren returned his attention to the party. Just like Manny, he couldn't help being a detective. He watched everyone, and he saw their reactions through their nonverbals even without a transpath.

Why would an engineer feel guilty when what he put together worked? The question played in Soren's mind. He waited and watched the others.

Jake had come down from his emotional high and was explaining to Mos, Emigan and Zofia about the synchronization issue. Soren hardly understood it, but the engineers did. *Jake's a good team leader. He brings out the best in his people.*

His imp dinged with an incoming call from Manny.

"It's as bad as I thought," his partner said. "Looks like we've got a mole on the team. Bendel just made a drop in a trash can. I've got a surveillance team inbound to capture whoever picks it up. I think Bendel's on his way back to you. I'll let you know when to grab him."

"Right." Soren slumped in his chair. He always liked to believe the good in people, but police work kept smashing the idea. He hated it when his suspicions were right.

"And next time, partner," Manny added, "you get to follow the target. It's raining out here. Hard. You owe me a laundry bill."

A few minutes more, and Bendel came back into the easygo and rejoined the team. He was sopping wet, dripping on the floor. He twitched so much he sloshed his beer when he sat down. Jake and the other engineers were deep in tech talk and didn't even notice the water dripping from the man's sleeve. Bendel didn't talk. It looked like he was practicing deep breathing exercises—and losing.

Ten minutes later, Manny called again.

"Got the pick-up woman, Soren, along with the drop. Damn, but it's wet out here. Bendel tried to deliver one of his new antennas. There's also a holochip with what looks like all the technical data he could seize. Looks like we've finally got two of those spies your uncle told us to nail. Take him in."

Business. Always business. Damn people anyway. Soren rose from his chair and walked around the table to behind Bendel. He gripped the man's shoulders.

"Bendel, stand up. You're under arrest for espionage."

Soren had tried to do it quietly, but Bendel jumped to his feet, head jerking and eyes wide. He spilled his beer all the way across the table.

"What? No. You can't. I didn't—"

"Hands behind your back, Bendel."

All the conversation stopped. The whole team was watching. Even the rest of the easygo quieted, with heads turning to them.

Jake said into the sudden silence, "What's going on, Soren?"

"Sorry to say it, Jake, but this man's been spying on the team and passing information to someone. We just caught him making a drop." Soren snagged Bendel's hands in a tanglecuff and turned to walk him to the door.

"But..." Jake sounded shocked. "But...great stars, he's my antenna engineer. How will we get things synchronized without him?"

CHAPTER 40

Secrecy was as much a part of human existence as water, fostered by the competition of each person's striving for personal goals. Intrigue followed secrecy like a vulf pack after prey.

—*The Making of a New Humanity* by Ellen Thranadil, Tileus Press 448 A.T.

THRUDAY, 41 QUINTEMBER, 416 A.T.

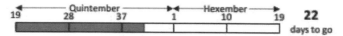

Franklin Edobar played a dangerous game, balancing his duties as Director of Capital with his underhanded sabotage of the distribution networks under his authority. He gave subtly conflicting direction to different branches of his organization, resulting in disasters of major magnitude.

Electrical distribution to Equaton got cross-connected with Oriens. A four-hour blackout happened in the afternoon heat of a near-summer day.

Vehicle fuel intended for Timpi never left Oriens. Farmers trying to recover from the antimatter explosion could not run their equipment.

Food sent to Millard was divided up in small towns along the way. The towns had splendid parties. Riots happened in Millard.

Through it all, Franklin kept his hand hidden. He made the incidents appear to be the accidental consequences of the antimatter explosion and his predecessor's senility.

At the same time, his Lazarite cadre was more exposed than ever due to the General Defense actions. Every cell was under suspicion. Franklin fielded a call from Kai Ariki, whom he had raised to his primary deputy in place of Yitzak Goren.

"Director, I'm having to dance on pins here in Timpi. Overlock is getting too close. He seems to know about Palatin's departure, and he's investigating our Solity Guard forces. It won't be long before he discovers my part. I'm worried he'll expose me. And now, I know too much about you."

Ariki was usually calm and in control; today, Franklin heard his agitation.

"What could help you, Kai? What can I do?"

"I need a distraction, something to withdraw his heat while we plant different evidence. Can you create events that would be more important to Overlock than tracking down Palatin?"

"That's difficult. I know Denmark is pushing him to solve that mystery. Overlock is like a kincat on the scent. I can't think of anything to cause Denmark to divert him to another task." Franklin felt his own nervous sweat.

"Perhaps we could sidetrack him with accusations. Could we put him on defense instead of offense?"

Franklin looked up at the ceiling. "That's a good idea, Kai. I could accuse him of interference in a way that shifts blame from us to him. I can perhaps solve two problems with one action. Let's see what I can do with that."

Franklin laid out a plan of attack in the next hour, ready to spring at the Solity Council meeting this afternoon. He made private calls in advance to Pires and Yang seeking support, laying groundwork for a Council vote. Perhaps he could even take Denmark's censure to the final step.

જ⁂ৎ

The Council chamber reverberated with power, each of the directors working toward their own goals. There seemed to be a sense in the air—for unknown reasons—Chairman Lukin might be fading, might be vulnerable. The others were circling like tsifta in a pool of feedfish. Keita and Denmark, in particular, were pushing hard.

Franklin pushed back, working to establish himself as a potential contender for the Chair. Though newest to the council, he believed he had sufficient force of character to succeed. He had support from Pires and could get it from Shanah and Kerr. It remained to be seen whether he had sufficient dirt on Denmark and Keita to sway the vote when it happened. His action today would help. At a break in the agenda, he took the floor.

"Chairman, I have a problem I'd like to bring to the Council."

Lukin nodded to him. "We have time, Director Edobar. Please go on."

"Thank you, sir. Since my taking leadership of Capital, I've seen multiple puzzling incidents of distribution problems—"

"Yes, Director, we're aware of those. Several have led to unfortunate reactions, even riots. Do you now have explanations?"

The Chair's pointed near-accusation had focused all attention on Franklin. A lesser man might have quailed at such attentiveness from this crowd of hungry carnivores. Franklin, however, was ready.

"Yes, Chairman, I do. I've had people examine each of these incidents, and I find a common thread: interference from outside the Capital department."

He heard a suppressed gasp from Kerr, Director of Development, the one Council member least able to handle the intense politics, but Franklin ignored it.

"Either before or after each incident, my people have documentation Director Denmark's subordinate Overlock was actively in the area." The room erupted in surprised muttering, and Franklin raised his voice to override the noise. "We believe General Defense, and Overlock in particular, have been sabotaging our distribution channels."

Denmark slapped his heavy hand on the table. "That's a lie, Chairman. These incidents look like sabotage, but we don't yet know how they're happening. I've personally sent Overlock to *investigate* the sabotage, not to create it. You've got an overbearing security officer watching everything I do. Check with your white-coated snoops for the truth."

The current security officer stood behind Denmark, impassive as usual. Overlock sat beside him. Franklin glanced at Overlock, who leaned forward, his eyes glittering with eager interest and a smirk on his face. Rather than taking umbrage, the man seemed to preen at the attention, looking forward to the quarrel.

"Chairman," Franklin replied, riding over Denmark's interjection. "Look at the man. Overlock obviously enjoys creating conflict, and we know he works under Denmark's close direction. The director could easily have other instructions to Overlock, either preceding his censure, or involving coded messages undetectable by your security officers. I move—"

"You don't get to move anything about me, Edobar," barked Denmark. "You're the junior member here, without—"

"Enough!" shouted the Chairman, cracking his gavel on the table. "Both of you, stop now. We *will* handle this in a composed manner."

Still fuming, Denmark quieted.

Having made his point, Franklin was willing to be silent. His heart pounding, he kept his face calm.

Director Pires of State calmly raised her hand. Chairman Lukin pointed a finger to recognize her.

"Chairman, I also have some knowledge of this. I can affirm Overlock has indeed been in the vicinity of the incidents."

Franklin still kept his face impassive. He congratulated himself for having called Pires earlier to give her the information. He waited for the expected support from Yang, also.

Unexpectedly, Director Keita lifted her hand for recognition.

"Chairman, I beg to differ."

Franklin had a hard time not showing his surprise. Keita was powerful, perhaps second to Lukin. This was bad.

"I have also had agents investigating these incidents, seeking evidence for Justice actions concerning the riots. I can affirm Overlock was there, but my agents are certain the problems source solely within Capital." When she finished the sentence, her eyes went directly to Franklin's.

Franklin was momentarily in shock at the direct contradiction, but recovered quickly. "Of course, that is the impression Overlock would seek to convey."

Before he could expand on his statement, he received an illicit text from Keita in his imp, appearing in his retina. Solity Council had a firm rule directors did *not* send surreptitious messages during the meeting; Keita apparently considered this issue important enough to break the rule.

The text in his imp said, **Back off, Edobar; go further, and your own hidden connections will surface.**

All this, in the moment of eye contact while Franklin spoke and Denmark stormed. Franklin dropped his gaze to the table to hide his reactions.

Great stars. What does Keita know?

Before he could act on the thought, Keita followed up with a second text. One word.

Lazarite.

He sat in shock and fear, not knowing what to do next. This was a disaster; he'd used everything he could to keep his resistance leadership secret. Obviously, he could not oppose Keita. He'd have to come to terms with her somehow.

Franklin looked to the Chairman and spoke again.

"Chairman, on further thought, I am willing to trust Director Keita's information. Perhaps I need to send my investigators back into my own department."

"Perhaps you should, *Director*," Denmark hissed.

Lukin said, "Do that, Director Edobar, and get back to us with answers. We'll set aside any accusations until we have more information." He turned to Denmark. "In the meantime, Director Denmark, please maintain a positive control on your staff, particularly on Overlock."

Franklin's heart still pounded. Exposure here in the Council of his Lazarite leadership was what he had feared most. Now he faced the reality. Given Denmark's censure, Keita was the most powerful in the room second to Lukin. What would she do to him?

A third text surprised him with the answer.

Support me for Chairman, and we can use your network.

He'd been thoroughly outmaneuvered. Keeping his face impassive, he thought it through. If she wanted to expose him, she could, but instead she was offering compromise. It would mean giving up on his personal aspirations, but her text seemed to offer support for his Lazarite work. Who knew when Lukin would be gone? Anything could happen, and he could wait.

He looked across the table to Keita and gave a small nod. They'd have to talk later.

261

Meanwhile, the accusation he'd made about Overlock—even if not confirmed—might have diverted Overlock for now, putting him on the defensive.

The Chair continued, "We have two and half weeks before our negotiations with Tileus. Most of our plans are in place, to guide those negotiations to failure. General Defense is ready," he nodded to Denmark, "to launch our offensive immediately afterwards."

"Yes, we are, sir," said Denmark.

"Director Pires of State is our ostensible leader for the negotiations—"

"Yes, Chairman, I am," she said.

"—but with our objective of an immediate attack, I want Director Denmark to guide the proceedings. Director Pires, you should take real-time direction from Denmark during the meetings."

Pires set her jaw in irritation, while Denmark nodded with forceful satisfaction.

"You two work together to lay out plans, alternatives, and contingencies for what might happen at the meeting. We want no surprises."

CHAPTER 41

Whatever can go wrong, will. Everything takes longer than you think. (But these aren't my sayings. They come from some pre-colonization Earth person named Murphy.)

—*Collected Sayings of Yitzak Goren* by Ellen Thranadil, Tileus Press 439 A.T.

Weeks of recovery had raised Zofia's spirits. She hadn't had a full-blown PTSD incident in ten days. Supporting Jake in his work had given her purpose when she felt vulnerable and useless, but now she was recovering enough to get involved. *I should thank Governor Moller for givin' me the task to support Jake; he understood what I needed.*

Now they had just two weeks remaining.

She joined the team to install the transpath equipment in the negotiation room on the seventh floor of Freedom Aerie. She was impressed with the room. Beautiful marble floors matched inlaid marble panels in wood-framed wainscoting. A glistening conference table for twenty filled the room with a pair of sprawling stained-glass chandeliers hanging above. Around the walls were chairs for another forty. The scene out the windows took her breath away, an expansive view across the varied buildings of Thad City.

While Jake and the technical team worked with the equipment, Zofia asked Manny what had happened to Bendel.

"We kept him alone for a day before interrogating him. In the meantime, we'd gotten most of the information from his pick-up man. When we talked to Bendel, he was ready to spill."

"What made him do it?"

Manny shook his head sadly. "Strange little man. He had gambling debts in the black market, and his contact promised enough money to pay them off. He'll be convicted, but they'll probably give him probation."

"It's a shame. Bendel's technical work was brilliant. We're still usin' his antennas for today's test."

Zofia helped Emigan install the dozen antennas at the edge of the ceiling. It took an entire day. Mos's signal driver was a half-meter box temporarily sitting on a side table along the wall. Zofia and Emigan completed the transpath system by hooking hair-thin waveguides between the signal driver and each antenna. The configuration filled the room like a spiderweb with the signal driver as the spider.

When they were done, the team was quiet.

Jake smiled to Zofia, then said to the team, "Cross your fingers."

Zofia grinned and held up both hands with fingers crossed. Inside, her heart skipped in anticipation. She wanted this to succeed on two levels. She'd worked for years for the Lazarite political goals, and this was a major result. But now, she also wanted success for Jake, for her man. She held her breath.

Jake sat in a chair by the driver and picked up the small remote control they'd made. He closed his eyes with his finger above the power control. He tapped it on.

Nothing happened. Her hopes fell flat on the carpeted floor.

Zofia glanced at each person in the room. No one reacted. *Oh, no. It's not workin'.* Her shoulders slumped.

Jake opened his eyes and she saw his disappointment. He looked at the green power light on the signal driver.

Then Jake wilted, too. "It's not working, folks."

His tone was as dead as the system. He turned it off again.

"Earthfire!" Jake exploded. "Now we're really short on time." His head hung low.

He needed her. Zofia put her arm around his shoulders. She squeezed hard until he looked at her. Then she kissed him.

"We'll find it, Jake. We know it worked in the lab last week."

She helped them trouble-shoot the rest of the day, trying different combinations. Swapping waveguides. Two antennas instead of twelve. Each antenna alone. Each configuration raised her hopes, then dashed them again with no perceptible emotional signal. Finally, they returned it to the same configuration they had in the lab, by cutting a waveguide down to a one-meter length and hooking up only one antenna.

When Jake turned it on, the transpath flooded Zofia's head with the fear, concern, and relief from the others. She felt an immense release coming from Jake, and she hugged him again.

He turned to the team. "There it is," he said. "It still works—just like it did in the lab. But this room is too big, and the configuration we planned isn't going to work here."

Through the system, Zofia felt the frustration from each member.

Emigan shook his head. "It's got to be my waveguides. Despite all the work we've done, they still lose too much power and slow down the signal. It only works if the antenna is within a meter of the driver."

Jake turned the system off again.

The situation niggled in Zofia's head. As an implant technician, she had years of experience debugging problems. This was just another one, only bigger. She smiled, realizing she'd recovered enough she could face a challenge.

NEWDAY, 1 HEXEMBER 416 A.T.

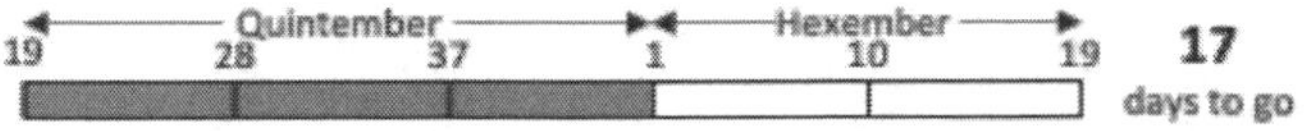

Two days later, Zofia arrived to see the calendar display had flipped over to a new month—*the* month. The team had moved back down to the lab so the conference room could be used by others. They still had no solution how to get the particle-wave signal synchronized to each antenna with sufficient strength.

She had stopped on the way and carried in coffee and doughnuts for the team. She felt good, because she had an idea. *Maybe this can work.*

"Breakfast," she called out when she set it down. "Sugar and caffeine to stimulate thought. Get your chemical high here."

"Yay," said Mos. "Just what I needed."

Jake took her hand. "You're doing much better, love. You look cheerful today. Your wounds are healing, and your emotions and mind are healing, too."

"Better, yah." She snorted. "Sometimes I wish I could erase from memory all the things Overlock did to me. But my mind is workin' again. Being in Tileus feels light and free. Just knowin' Solity is no longer watching every single thing we do..."

"I feel that, too. But we have to get the transpath working, or Solity—I fear they'll take over here."

Soren added, "That's something none of us want. Everything I hear about that Denmark man makes me shudder."

Jake nodded. "Oh, yeah. He's a piece of work. And you should meet his assistant Overlock; he's even worse."

She jumped when Jake said the name.

He noticed and squeezed her hand. "Oh, I'm sorry, love. I didn't mean to bring him to your mind."

"It's okay, Jake. I'm getting' past it, and we have to get this workin'." She paused to gain courage to put forth her idea. "I've been thinkin'. Does it have to be one signal driver? Couldn't we put a driver next to each antenna?"

Jake shook his head, doubt causing him to wince. "I don't know how we'd get the signals synchronized from multiple drivers. The timing has to be precise."

"I have a possibility," she said.

When he looked up, she was grinning. He cocked his head with interest.

"Manny got these nano-processors," she continued. "They're so small they float in the air like dust. Each one hasn't much capability, but they're incredibly fast. Can we turn them into a literal cloud of computing? Not like 'cloud computing' on the InfoNet, but a real cloud. Imagine the air filled with tiny processors that make up one big timin' coordinator."

She watched Jake stop in mid-bite on his doughnut, which now hung in his hand near his open mouth. As she'd expected, he hadn't really thought of her as part of his technical team. She chortled inside. *I'm more than a pretty face and a sexy zero-G opponent, my love.*

She explained, "The tiny processors would have to calculate distances to get the timin' right. It's a complex programming job, but it's possible. Each of a dozen signal drivers can receive a synchronized timin' pulse, even though the processors are floatin' randomly in the air."

Zofia finished with a grin. "I can do that. Programmin' is my thing."

FRIDAY, 6 HEXEMBER 416 A.T.

Zofia buried herself in difficult programming for five days while the team built another eleven signal drivers. She found the problem to be a delight. It took her back to secondary school, when she'd won prizes for creative programming. She hadn't used these skills since, except when she'd spoofed the Prime implants for the Lazarites; repairing implants just wasn't the same.

The team came together again in the negotiation room with only a week and a half to go. It seemed she had her fingers crossed ninety percent of the time.

The spider web of waveguides was gone. Now a dozen antennas and a dozen signal drivers were mounted in the negotiation room, short waveguides connecting each pair. Mos had modified the drivers to receive a sync pulse from the nano-processors. Tiny green lights glowed on all the drivers, but nothing was happening yet.

The team stood in the room. Hope was in the air.

Jake said, "Okay, Zofia. This is your show."

She nodded and took a deep breath. Her confidence was high, but she still had a serious doubt feeding her fears. *I know my programmin' is solid, but what if...* She shook off the thought and opened a glass bottle filled with a hazy mist of nano-processors. She waved it in the air, and the mist dispersed.

Everyone held their breath, Zofia most of all, while the motes spread.

At first, she perceived no change.

266

Then she felt it happening. She looked at Jake and his triumph swept directly into her mind with the power of the transpath. He threw an arm around her shoulder and they turned to face the others.

She grinned so wide it felt her cheeks would meet her ears. Her programming worked.

But then her breath caught, because something still jarred. The emotions from those across the room were fragmented and tenuous, even confused. She saw delight on Manny's face, but the transpath instead gave her confusion from his mind. She looked at Mos, whose expression was one of surprise, but got a sense of irritation from him through the transpath.

The feelings didn't match the facial expressions.

"It's still not right," Jake said with a low voice.

She agreed, while she saw and felt everyone else come to the same conclusion. "It seems to work close up, but not across the room. What's going on?"

Jake collapsed into one of the conference chairs and put his face in one hand. "A week and a half to go, and it *Still. Doesn't. Work.*" He pounded a fist on the table to punctuate the last three words. His voice rang with desperation. "We have got to get this working, or Prime will get everything they want in the negotiations. Global war is next."

Zofia laid her hands on his shoulders and her cheek beside his. She was as devastated as the waves she felt from him. What more could she do?

Five days later, Zofia and Mos rushed across the lab from where they'd been working together. When she crossed the lab, she slam-dunked a broken part into the trash can with a grin.

"We've got it, Jake," Mos shouted. "The problem was in the drivers, not the cloud computing."

Jake looked up. "We've got seven days left. Can we fix it in time?" A tinge of hope colored his voice.

Mos nodded enthusiastically. "I just have to add an incoming address to each driver."

Zofia bounced from foot to foot. "And I'll add specific addressin' to the cloud software, so the drivers know which pulse is for which."

Mos said, "It'll just take a few days to modify it all."

"Good, good," said Jake. "Do it, right away."

Jake's shoulder and back muscles were cramped with tension. *He's so tight.* Without asking, she started massaging his neck. She reached around with one hand and tapped his nose with a twinkle.

"Relax, Jake," she said. "Move by move, we're getting' closer to the goal. We'll get it this time."

"But what will be next?" he moaned. "It's been one problem after another. Can we get it all soon enough?"

This latest solution had her hopes higher than high. "We have to, love. The whole world depends on it."

"Great." He gave her a weak smile. "Just what we need: more pressure."

This was great. She was amazed to use her skills to solve problems of the world—even of humanity. What a change from fixing complaints about implants. But she also knew the Tileus leadership was counting on them. And so far, they hadn't delivered.

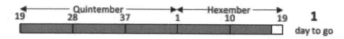

"Are we ready?" Jake asked the team. "Is it going to work?"

Zofia's heart pounded. She glanced around the negotiation table to see nervous energy in every face. In six days, they'd reconfigured the drivers and tested them individually, but this was the first full-system test of the new configuration.

They'd decided to use this test also to demonstrate the capability to Governor Moller. No time remained. If it worked, they'd be heroes. Her solution would have worked. They might literally save Verdant from destruction. If not...she stopped herself from thinking what a disaster it would be. Global war. They had no idea whether Denmark's new team had succeeded with the antimatter bomb, and it was only one of the world-shattering weapons possessed by Prime and Tileus.

Negotiations were a day and a half away.

The equipment was installed and unobtrusive. The antennas at the edge of the ceiling looked like fire suppression nozzles. The signal drivers were hidden in the ceiling above each antenna. The room air was replete with invisible nano motes to do the computing and control.

Zofia sat beside Jake and nudged him with her shoulder for mutual support. She'd made the imp call to Welton Moller a few minutes ago, and the governor was now on his way up from his sixth-floor office. She was still surprised every time she used the new, richer interface of the Tileus implants. It startled her to make a call and find herself virtually inside the governor's office with sight, sound, and even scent. Prime didn't have that technology.

The door opened and Moller entered.

"Glad you could join us today, Governor," Jake said.

"We'll do the negotiations with or without your transpath, Jake, but I'm hoping for success. You folks have certainly given it your best effort."

"I hope so, too. We've corrected from last week, and we believe it'll work."

"What'll it be like?"

Zofia grinned, thinking of the amazing surprise the governor was about to experience—she hoped.

Jake glanced at the team. "We've all felt it, sir, in our successes so far." Nods around the table confirmed it. "I really can't describe it, but I believe you'll find it nearly miraculous."

The governor looked at Soren. "You've felt this, too?"

"I have, Uncle. When Jake first described the transpath, I thought it all deception, a ruse to justify spying. Now, I'm amazed. I look forward to seeing what will happen."

"Then let's do it." Moller sat down at the center chair of the table.

Jake said, "I'm giving Zofia the honor of control today. Her software solution saved our bacon." He handed the remote to her and nodded permission for her to turn it on. She answered with a wink, her pride soaring.

"I'm goin' to turn it up gradually, see," she said, "like we plan to do durin' the negotiations."

She tapped the control on and slid the power bar up a fraction. The indicator rose from zero. Jake reached out to hold her hand, showed her the crossed fingers on his other hand. She flicked her eyes from person to person, looking for reactions.

Manny was first. His head cocked up and a broad smile came on his face. He nodded.

Then Zofia felt it, sets of emotions tingling at the edges of awareness. Looking at Soren, she felt a slight sense of his satisfaction. Mos had a little smile, too, and from across the room Zofia felt a twinge of his pleasure.

The governor said, "I'm feeling something here. Very strange."

Zofia looked at him and sensed a touch of Moller's caution and hope.

Jake said, "Turn it up some more, Zofia."

She kept watching the governor while she slid the control up. What had been a slight twinge became a broad sense of connection. She felt astonishment radiating from Moller. The man's eyebrows went up and he gasped. Hope rode fast on the heels of the surprise, touched with some fear. Moller shifted his gaze to Zofia, and she felt the man's compassion, satisfaction, and joy in whatever he sensed from her. The governor looked at Soren, and Zofia experienced Moller's pride in his nephew.

"This...is...incredible," said the governor, while he continued to look at each individual and sample their emotions. "Even when you told me about it, I never believed such a thing was possible. The diplomats are given a new tool—hell, *humanity* is being given a new tool—for understanding, for connection, for peace." He turned again to Jake, and Zofia felt hope surge in the governor when he said, "This will work."

At his words, the empathic feedback from the entire group overwhelmed her with their pride and positivity, a sense the world—at least, that portion of it here in this room—would be as right as trees in a sunny forest. Jake laughed out loud, and he was joined by everyone.

Zofia bubbled along with them. She'd been a simple technician, doing her job to solve people's technical problems. Now, she'd contributed a key solution to the transpath. What a change. She'd redeemed herself, grown out of her torture, and done something significant for humanity. She felt about ready to burst with joy at what she'd accomplished.

She suspected, through the transpath, she glowed like a bright beacon to the others. That made her laugh out loud.

Jake interrupted her thoughts. "Zofia, where do you have it set?" He was looking at her quizzically, likely wondering what was so gratifying to her.

"About eighty percent."

Jake chuckled, "We can take cues from Governor Moller during the negotiations, but I'm thinking we won't need any more than this."

Moller laughed out loud again. "You've got that right, my boy. This will definitely enhance the negotiations. The only question we have now is how it will affect Directors Pires and Denmark. What will it reveal in them? And how will they react?"

CHAPTER 42

In the decades since that eventful day, many have second-guessed the occasion. One frequent outrage concerns the way Tileus kept the transpath hidden from the Prime negotiators. Critics still claim the meeting would have gone better had the technology been open and acknowledged. Others demur, saying Berndt Denmark would likely have refused to take part in the negotiations. I was there, and can affirm the decision was seriously considered. The results surprised nearly all of us.

—*An Annotated History of Verdant* by Ellen Thranadil, Tileus Press 442 A.T.

Governor Ellen Thranadil strode from her preparation meetings to the negotiation room, her head held high. Three assistants trailed her. Her confidence for the meeting soared, a complete turn-around from her expectations a week ago. These negotiations could be the capstone of her long career; she looked forward to a second career writing about politics. The polished stone floor reflected the sunlight from the end of the hall, the brightness matching her own hope for success.

The transpath would make all the difference.

She had experienced it herself yesterday. Welton Moller's technical team had last-minute success on the device. The entire Tileus delegation gathered to experience the transpath so they would know what to expect. Ellen and Welton were the Tileus principals: Governor of Commerce and Technology, and Governor of External Affairs. By arrangement with Verdant Prime, they were allowed six assistants, one of whom would be Jacoby Palatin to run the device.

Yesterday, Ellen had been nervous. Welton told her it would be remarkable, but she still feared exposure of her emotions to others. As a long-time politician and leader, she knew the power of inscrutability and of separating emotions from facts. She knew how often she found it necessary to keep reactions hidden.

When Palatin turned on the device, Ellen became an astonished convert. It completely revised her concepts of what it meant to negotiate. She knew immediately this technology would change humanity.

Today, she led her team into the room, past the security guards at the door, and around the table to their places. She and Welton would be side-

271

by-side in the center of the table. Each had a primary assistant beside them, with the other four seated under the windows behind them.

The Prime delegation had not yet arrived. Their lead delegate was supposedly Director of State Calie Pires, with Denmark supporting her. However, Ellen had intel reports the real power in the room would be wielded by Denmark.

Ellen nodded and smiled at Palatin against the window. He looked nervous. She took her seat.

"Good morning, Welton. Are we ready?" Her voice was easy, but always slightly hoarse from a throat surgery long ago. She had found in years of negotiation the timbre of her voice often led opponents to underestimate her.

Welton chuckled, his easy humor apparent even in a time of tension. "If we're not, it's too late to do anything about it. I think our carrot-and-stick approach, coupled with the transpath, will work."

"Well, I've got the carrot," she said with a smile. "Keeping the peace lets us engage in trade so they can get our technologies."

"And I've got the stick: our military and its advanced weapons."

"Hopefully, Directors Pires and Denmark can be brought to see reason."

"Perhaps," Welton added, "we can offer the transpath itself. It might even soften Prime's rigid hold on its own people."

Ellen turned to Palatin. "You've created something that will go far. After today, I'd like to talk with you about business matters."

"Yes, ma'am." He looked surprised at the offer. "But I didn't create it. I'm only the engineer who made it work here. Yitzak Goren was the inventor."

She smiled at him. "That may be, but I think you have a great business opportunity."

Welton's eyes unfocused for a second while he received an imp message. "The Prime contingent has entered Freedom Aerie. They'll be here in a few minutes."

Ellen turned back to the table and arranged her materials and her thoughts. Welton was their lead; her job was to support him.

☙ ✳ ❧

Jake's nerves settled while he thought about Governor Thranadil's offer. The technical work was done, other than adaptations. Perhaps Jake could tackle the challenge of whatever Tileus called "business." He barely understood yet how "money" worked, but he knew they were related.

First, they had to discover whether the political part of this gambit would forestall the war. Governor Moller had chosen to surprise the Prime negotiators with the transpath. Jake had some fear about how Denmark would react. The man was volatile even at his calmest. Under the pressure of negotiations, what might he do?

Governor Moller had told Jake only yesterday to be in the room and control the transpath during the meeting.

"Sir, do you think it's a good idea for Director Denmark to see me in the room?"

"I think it's an excellent idea, my boy. That's my reason to have you there. It'll unbalance Denmark, which is part of my strategy. I want the man to be out of his comfort zone."

"I'm very uncomfortable with the idea, sir."

"Of course you are, but you'll do a fine job." Moller had paused before continuing. "You've not been part of our planning for this meeting, because of your demanding technical work. You haven't missed anything you need to know. We know we can negotiate with Pires. Denmark is the problem. So, you should know our strategy is to irritate him to the point where his thinking is not clear. Then we'll be able to push him in the direction we want.

"Just be ready for my signals. We'll do it in stages. At my first signal, bring the transpath up to barely perceptible. At my second signal, advance it to the full setting."

"Yes, sir."

Now Jake sat under the window waiting nervously for Denmark to arrive. The simple transpath control sat on the low table beside him. One touch turned it on, a slide adjusted its intensity. Anyone could run it. Yet he looked forward to seeing the final result of his work—and wondered what it would do to Denmark.

When Governor Moller said Denmark and his team were on the way, Jake's heart pounded. He shook his head.

Can't let Denmark get to me. I've found a new life here, where they value what I do. He no longer controls me.

❧ ❈ ❧

Denmark's stride was firm when he entered the Tileus house of government, Pires beside him matching his pace. A properly obsequious host led the way. Their assistants followed in a pack. None spoke. Their heels clip-clopped on the shiny floor in ragged rhythm, the sound echoing from the walls.

Denmark was ready. He had amassed damning data on Tileus' interference in Prime, and he intended to use it to gain concessions from Governors Moller and Thranadil. He also intended those concessions to be insufficient. Pires would lead off with the soft approach of diplomacy before he hammered home the ultimatums.

After some consideration, he had decided not to bring Overlock. The man comported himself well in high-powered meetings, but he was too well-known for his violent practices. He'd left him in Prime, tracking down Lazarite cells.

Pires spoke when they reached the lift tube. "Berndt, I'm thinking of reversing the order—"

He raised a hand to stop her. "Not here, Calie. I'm sure we're under surveillance. And don't change our plan." He coupled his gruff voice with piercing eyes to emphasize his command.

Damned soft woman. Always trying to avoid the difficult path. Good thing the Chairman told her to follow my lead. This is the culmination of my thirteen-year plan. When these negotiations fall apart today, we'll launch our full-scale attack tomorrow.

Minutes later, they swept into the negotiation room. Always aware of appearances, Denmark allowed Pires to precede him, but he made sure his entrance was forceful. He took in the arrangement of the room the instant they entered, picked the center seat across from Welton Moller, and moved there rapidly with firm poise.

Moller and Thranadil rose from their seats, as did their assistants. Denmark had never met Thranadil, though they'd spoken on an audio line. From her raw-sounding voice, he had pictured her as dumpy and old. He was surprised to see she was tall and slim with an athletic build. Her hair was grey, long and lustrous, a striking combination, almost aristocratic.

The table was too wide to allow handshakes, but they all greeted with nods and formality.

Moller had the first words. "Welcome, Director Pires. Welcome, Director Denmark. Thank you for coming." Thranadil echoed him.

"Glad to be here, Governor Moller," Pires responded. "Governor Thranadil."

Denmark added, "We hope to have fruitful discussions today." He smiled inside. *Don't ask me to define what "fruitful" means.*

All the cordial formalities felt slightly bizarre, almost as if the angry hot line calls with Moller had never happened. While Denmark took his seat, his eyes ran over the other participants in the room. With a start, he recognized Palatin. He glanced at Moller in time to see the corner of Moller's mouth twitch in a slight smile. Moller had been watching for his surprise. *Sneaky tactic. Palatin's been here all along; I was right, damn it. But what's he doing in this meeting? He's certainly no diplomat. Should I object to his presence? Claim sabotage? Use him as a bargaining tool?* The alternatives flashed quickly through his head, and he decided his best approach was to take it in stride. *I'll save any accusations for later, when I need them.*

He nodded to the engineer. "Good morning, Palatin. Hmph. No longer…lying about your presence here, I see." The pause spoke full paragraphs of unsaid words.

That'll challenge him, being solicitous after chasing him all over Creation. Make him worry.

Then he added, "How's Ms. Dobrunik?"

274

He watched Jake take in a shallow breath and sit up straighter, his eyes holding a spark of belligerence.

"Are you asking for yourself, Director...or for Overlock?"

Palatin's snarky tone showed Denmark's barb had sunk true.

Moller leaned back to place a calming hand on Jake's arm.

Having used him effectively for now, Denmark dismissed the man from his concerns.

❧ ❋ ❦

Jake's ire jumped up at Denmark's solicitous banality. Jake set his lips in a thin line. *Now I'm really looking forward to his defeat. Arrogant bastard.*

Jake watched the principals, wondering how this kind of meeting went.

Moller gestured to Thranadil to begin.

She activated a holo display at one end of the table. It showed two parallel lists. "Very well, Directors. Here are the lists we traded prior to the meeting, containing our concerns—"

"Demands," inserted Denmark.

"—our *concerns* about the international relations. We've rearranged our two lists side-by-side, matching items where they fit."

Jake kept still, but he was astonished at how quickly the knives were coming out.

Denmark tapped the table next to Pires, some sort of signal on their side.

"I can summarize our *demands*," Pires said, her experience in international relations showing in the way she smoothly inserted her control. "They fall into three major categories. First, Tileus must stop inserting provocative agents—spies—into Prime. Second, Tileus must make available to us the new technologies you seem to hoard. And third, Tileus should stand down and de-fang its military to reduce tensions. There are further issues, but these three must happen if we are to come to any agreement at all."

Jake saw minimal reactions from the Tileus side. The delegates had already seen the lists, so Pires' words were no surprise to them. Jake jerked slightly in surprise, particularly at the demand to reduce Tileus military. He caught Denmark watching his motion and knew the reaction had been a mistake; he'd given Denmark information. *New rules, Jake. Keep a poker face.*

Thranadil responded smoothly. "We acknowledge your concerns in these areas. As you can see in the parallel lists, the top three Tileus concerns dovetail nicely with yours, though some are more difficult than others. First, we request Prime to cease its saber-rattling, to tone down the war rhetoric not only against us but also against the countries of Rathas and Winter. Your aggression destabilizes the entire world. Second, we ask Prime agents operating in Tileus be explicitly identified rather than covert. And finally, we thoroughly welcome new opportunities to trade with Prime."

Moller added, "When I look at the top three items of the two lists, I see room for much agreement. I'd like us to work toward that instead of making...demands."

Jake was not skilled in reading body language, but this was a good opportunity to practice. These four were accomplished diplomats and showed little. Yet he saw a slight tic in Thranadil speaking of nervousness. *Perhaps she's wondering what the transpath will do.* Moller stayed consistent with his hearty hail-fellow-well-met bravado, but even Jake saw through it to the steel he had experienced in their meetings. Pires's eyes kept flitting back and forth between the Tileus delegates, occasionally also taking in the assistants. Jake couldn't tell what she was learning. As for Denmark—Jake knew the director well enough to see the bluster rising.

"There may be room for compromise on some lesser items," Denmark said, his voice rock solid, "but the top three Director Pires has cited are non-negotiable."

"Non-negotiable?" asked Moller. "Then why are you here at these negotiations? Do you view this meeting as just another way to rattle your sabers? We're here to find common ground, ways *not* to end up in war."

Jake knew the accusation was close enough to truth to get under Denmark's skin.

Denmark's voice became more strident. "We're not here to 'rattle sabers,' Governor. We're here to gain your concessions on these major points, and we're willing to work with you on others. To be honest, I'm not convinced we should be here at all, that this meeting is worth our time. Your side wanted this. I counseled against it."

Jake had seen this before. Denmark was still fully in control of himself, using the apparent rise in anger as a way to push the others. And he was lying; Jake knew failed negotiations were a part of Denmark's plan.

"So, is it your goal," Moller asked, "to decimate Tileus' ability to defend ourselves, even while you develop new weapons like your antimatter bomb? That seems rather one-sided."

Moller seemed to be purposefully goading him, touching the most sensitive points. Jake saw Denmark's face flush, and Jake was hard put not to react with a raised eyebrow. Moller had just gotten under his skin, and Denmark was no longer quite in control of himself. Pires put a hand on Denmark's elbow, but he shook it off.

Denmark sneered, "If we need to be one-sided to protect ourselves and the planet, we'll certainly do so."

Pires took back the lead, saying, "Perhaps we can start by discussing the least controversial of the three main issues: technology trades."

Thranadil agreed. "You do know, Directors, Tileus has many technologies Prime does not."

"Hoarded technologies," Denmark muttered, his face still red. Now, Jake wasn't sure what Denmark was doing. Was he really angry, or was it a ruse? He'd seen the director use his blazing anger effectively, even when he was not completely in control.

"For instance," Thranadil continued, ignoring his remark, "we have capabilities in our implants you do not, such as full video display from sender to receiver, rather than audio and text only. We also have sensory connections to hearing, smell, and taste. Our citizens use these capabilities daily, but Prime has never bought them for your implants."

"You also have a demolecular beam technology," added Pires. "We'd be interested in exploring its use in production facilities."

Jake saw Denmark's lips curl into a smile. Something sneaky hid behind Pires' request. Then it came to Jake: Pires was talking about the beam weapons, not manufacturing tools.

"Yes, we do," agreed Thranadil, "and more. We can give you a list of technologies we believe you don't have."

"And what would you want in return for these?" asked Pires. This was the key question.

"We can explore concessions in the other major areas as a trade-off," said Thranadil, a transparently soft way of referring to Prime's militarism. "We would also be interested in greater import of your farming produce during winter months. If, that is, it has not been badly damaged by your antimatter explosion."

Denmark slammed a fist on the table. "I've told Governor Moller before, we are *not* pursuing antimatter technology. The explosion outside Timpi was a factory failure."

The sickeningly obvious lie caught Jake by surprise. Knowing the man as he did, Jake saw the outburst had even embarrassed Denmark himself. Against all protocol, Jake was startled into speaking directly to Denmark.

"Excuse me, Director, but have you forgotten I was the team leader for your antimatter weapon?"

Before anyone else could react to the shock of his interruption, Denmark exploded.

"No, Palatin, your treachery will *never* be forgotten in Prime. The penalty for treason is death, and it has no expiration date. Ever. Just in case you should contemplate a visit to the country you betrayed." He was spraying spittle by the end.

Moller used the interaction to benefit. "He's here now, Director, and he'll remain."

Denmark stormed, "Then perhaps we need to talk about *your* agents in *our* country, and how much damage they do."

Jake sat stony-faced while Denmark launched into an angry recitation of incriminatory data, obviously prepared in advance. Denmark laid out facts his team had gathered about Tileus spies and their connections to the Lazarites. He kept indignation close to the surface and used self-righteousness to give weight and impact to his evidence. Thranadil tried to insert a word here and there. Each time, Denmark raised his voice to cover hers. It appeared he was trying to put the Tileus team on the defensive before making his primary demands again. Clearly, he was working himself up into pure wrath, whether manufactured or real.

In the middle of the tirade, Jake saw Moller tap his cheekbone. The signal. Jake reached for the transpath control.

CHAPTER 43

Emotions are not obstacles to successful negotiations. When they are exposed and honest, they become the core of agreement.

—*A Practical Guide to Negotiation* by Ellen Thranadil, Tileus Press 426 A.T.

Denmark was finishing his planned harangue. He knew he'd done well, raising the rhetoric to stratospheric levels while never—quite—stepping over into rage. Not that rage wasn't there. He'd been caught in the embarrassing lie about the antimatter bomb. He hated that.

Denmark was about to return to his demands when a motion caught his eye. Palatin looked down and did something to a little box on the low table beside him. Then he looked up boldly, directly at Denmark. The engineer seemed to be watching for something. The sheen of sweat worried Palatin's forehead.

It might have been innocent, but Denmark didn't buy it. *What is that devious little traitor up to now?* Glaring at Palatin, the distraction caused the smooth flow of Denmark's words to stumble like a torrent around boulders.

Denmark tapped the table for Pires to take over. He needed to think. Figure out what was going on here.

Pires took the cue and said, "With all the facts Director Denmark has given us, it's time to address this issue of spies in each other's countries. Prime wants Tileus to stop inserting agents, and you want ours to be identified. These seem to be compatible. We may be able to come to agreement."

While she spoke, Denmark felt...uneasy. A strange sense of discomfort steadily increased. He had a vague awareness of earnest honesty warring inside him against his firm goal to make the negotiations fail. The sense seemed to come from Pires' words, and it did not at all reflect the position they had agreed to present. Moller, across the table, was watching Denmark intently. Now, Denmark felt a touch of curiosity—and perhaps triumph— that irritated him further.

He overrode Pires' ongoing speech. "I'm not confident agreement is possible, even on this point. We want Tileus agents out of Prime, yes. That's because your agents are provocateurs, actually aiding and abetting the insurgent Lazarites. Such interference is damnably close to an act of war. The few people we have in Tileus are doing nothing of the same sort."

The odd feelings stirring within him seemed to change when he looked at different people. The sentiments were coloring his own thoughts with unwelcome tones. He spoke louder, trying to shut out the intrusion.

"For instance, we have documented instances of Tileus technology being used by the Lazarites, technology that doesn't otherwise exist in Prime." He ticked off instances on his fingers. "Last month, our InfoNet was disrupted prior to and during a resistance action, preventing Solity Guards from quelling the disturbance. That happened twice more, once during a street riot and once during the bombing of a major defense laboratory—"

"Good heavens, man, you have some significant uprisings going on," said Moller, raising Denmark's anger more.

"It's not about the uprisings, sir, it's about your participation in them!" He added another finger. "During one Lazarite action, we captured beam weapons of a type we've never seen—with production marks from here in Tileus." And another finger. "And now you are obviously suborning our own citizens, like this traitor Palatin."

Denmark planted a fist on the table, his voice rising to a bellow. "This is unacceptable, Governors. Damn it, Tileus is interfering in our country. You are taking actions leading directly to war, actions against all the international agreements. We need more than just passive correction; we also need an apology—and retributions."

No matter how strident his words, though, Denmark could not shake the sense of unease inside himself. When he looked at Moller, his own determination was colored by an unaccountable triumph.

Moller said, in words conciliatory but tinged with disdain. "What sort of retributions are you imagining, sir? We're here to negotiate. Make your requests clear, please."

Denmark was beginning to mistrust his own feelings. *What's happening to me? Why am I losing control? I've got...feelings...getting in my way. Pull it together, man. Get back to your power base.*

"Requests?" Denmark barked. "Requests? We're not here to pussyfoot around with give-and-take. We're here with demands." He looked at Thranadil and suddenly felt curiosity. It befuddled his words. "This isn't a chance to satisfy idle curiosity—" *Where did that word come from? Curiosity? What the Hell?* "—No, stop these warlike acts in our country."

He began to sense these emotions were not his, that they were being planted into him from outside. *That "curiosity" came from Thranadil, I'm certain.*

He finished by roaring his demand, "It's not enough just to have the agents identified. We want them out. Your aid to the Lazarites must stop."

He looked to Pires for back-up. She was reaching out a hand, trying to calm him. Instead of support, he felt a trace of sorrow and contempt, and it enraged him further.

"And more," Denmark continued, seemingly unable to stop, "we want you to stop hiding technology from us. We have every right to the same advances you have. You send your beam technology into our country to destabilize us, and yet you won't let us buy it from you. Your implants are doing things we can only dream of. It isn't right. It's not fair."

Oh, damn, I have to stop. I sound like a petulant child in a tantrum at the teacher.

He forced himself to stop talking, his hands clenching and unclenching under the table. Looking again at Pires, he felt her contempt like a tidal wave rushing at him.

No one can treat me with contempt, he thought, and thinking it confirmed the emotion was actually coming from Pires. *Have I lost control of my own mind?* He kept looking at the people around the table, his mind affected by each one. He shook his head like a brol in heat, trying to clear it. *I'm losing control of this meeting.*

He saw Moller tap his cheek. Palatin manipulated the device at his side again, and overwhelming emotions assaulted Denmark like a fist in the face. Sorrow and pity. *What? Where is this coming from?* He was shocked to his core and felt certain these feelings were being pushed into his mind from the man he was watching, Palatin.

"What's going on here?" Denmark raged. "Damn it, you people are doing something to me!"

He looked at Pires, who was watching Moller, and his feelings changed again. From her, he felt wonderment, fear, reserve, hope. She shifted her gaze from Moller to him, and Denmark felt her change to shock, disgust, even pity.

In the midst of his confusion, Denmark had a revelation. *I've felt this damnable sensation before.* Denmark jumped to his feet, shouting, "I know what this is. It's Yitzak Goren's mind control, that's what it is." He aimed an accusatory finger at Palatin. "You, Palatin. Turn it off, now."

Palatin glanced at Moller, who shook his head, denying.

Denmark felt sensations crowding in on him from every direction. Earnestness, alarm, anger, elation, concern. His mind whirled.

He shook a fist toward Moller across the table. "You're trying to sabotage these negotiations. I won't put up with it." His voice rose to a roar. "I don't know what you're doing—or how you're doing it—but turn it off. Turn it off now, or we're leaving."

He could hardly think his own thoughts now, for all the intrusive emotions.

Pires turned to him from her chair. "Director, please sit down. I'm astonished at what I'm feeling, and it gives me hope I haven't had in years." Her back was straight, in a determination he'd never before seen in her. "I'm the lead for these negotiations, and I'm not leaving."

Denmark directed his uncontrolled rage and contempt at her. "Brolshit. You're only the lead in name, Pires. You're nobody, a convenience, not a leader. That's why the chairman told you to follow my direction. Damn it, you're being manipulated. Don't you recognize it?"

Even while he asked, though, he felt in her the hope she talked about, girded by steel he'd never known was in the woman.

Moller said, his words filled with the solidity of granite, "Director Denmark, if you walk out of here you will be the only one. Regardless of what you might say afterwards—whatever false accusations you choose to make—your departure will reflect only on you. It's widely known you've squandered your trust in Prime. You've even been censured by your own council. Win here, at this table, and you might return to a restored favor. Leave, and you will be returning as a minority of one to a reception prepared by your opponents. Your abdication of responsibility will be known by all."

In the midst of the tangled emotions that were not his, Denmark recognized the truth of Moller's words. He dropped his gaze to the table. *Thirteen years of work toward this goal, today. Damned if I leave. Failed if I stay. How can I think with all this garbage stuffed into my head?*

Denmark was more confused than he could ever remember.

If I walk out, I'll never again have a chance to carry through my plan for re-integration of the planet. This would be the defining failure of my life.

Yet if I stay—the feelings impinging in his head made it hard to think this through—if he stayed, he was subject to this constant assault on his senses. Far worse, Denmark understood everyone else in the room had the same access to his head as he did to theirs. *Mind control! Are they reading my thoughts? But I can't read theirs.* They seemed to believe this to be a good thing. *They welcome this unwarranted invasion! How can I hold power if they see inside me? That would sabotage my goal just as surely as walking out.*

Damned if I leave. Failed if I stay.

Denmark looked up again at the others. He saw their responses to him in what he felt from them. From Moller, he felt triumph and pity. From Thranadil, he sensed regret, embarrassment, sadness—and pity. From Pires, whom he expected to support his goals, he felt relief, uncertainty, tinged with both scorn and hope—and pity.

Each of them seemed to be reacting to what they sensed in him, and the combination from all boiled down to a condemnation—of him. He felt each of them responding to his rage, his determination to drive things, his desire to control, his lonely hatred and contempt for others.

And they knew all of these came out of his own fear of failure.

Even Palatin. This puny engineer radiated self-confidence, security, peace—and pity.

Too much. Way too much. Wrath consumed him, and he lost all sense of diplomatic control.

"Stop it, all of you. Take your pity and contempt, and shove it up your asses."

He whirled on Palatin. "You in particular, boy. I gave you opportunities, and you betrayed me. Your project failed, and you failed. You're a traitor. But you're not safe. We can reach you and your low-class Dobrunik wench, even here. In fact, I can reach you, right now."

Denmark was beyond thinking. He merely acted in his rage. His hand shook when he pulled a needle gun out of his pocket and aimed it at Palatin. The room erupted in chaos.

ờ ❋ ઉ

Jake's anger flashed at Denmark's insult to Zofia. When he saw the gun, he reacted without thought. All the action he'd been through prepared him for this moment.

Jake sprang across the slick table surface, like zero-G racquetball without the zero-G.

Commotion erupted all around. People scrambled in panic. Chairs slid and crashed to the floor. Shouts of "No." The spit of the needle gun, several times. Something stung his shoulder.

Jake's vigorous slide took him across the table and into Denmark's midriff. He wrapped his arms around the director.

Momentum flung Denmark backward, toppling over the chairs and onto the floor. He spat obscenities and flechettes. Jake and Denmark wrestled together on the floor. Another body crashed on top of Jake, taking his breath away. A struggle for the gun went on next to Jake's head, the spit of each trigger-pull loud in his ear. The hard gun hilt rapped his skull several times.

Then it was over.

The security guards pinned Denmark down, the gun now in a guard's hand.

The guards let Jake rise to his feet. He felt shaky. His shoulder throbbed, and blood on his sleeve showed he'd been hit.

Blood had sprayed elsewhere in the room. None of the principal delegates were hurt, but Thranadil had blood on her face. The blood wasn't hers; two of the Tileus assistants were down under the windows. The medics were working hard on one, pounding his chest.

Jake's eyes went back to Denmark. The director was on his back, held down by two guards. Denmark had stopped raging and was still.

Someone came to Jake, a medic.

"Stay still, sir. Let me examine this."

Looking past the medic, Jake saw the guards lift Denmark to his feet. They held him rigidly in place, though he kept struggling to break free. His words were incoherent now, filled with untampered frenzy.

"What do we do with him, sir?" a guard asked of Moller.

The governor took the time for several deep breaths. "He's still a diplomat. Hold him here while we think. Keep him restrained."

The medic had bandaged Jake's arm. "You'll be fine, sir. Just surface damage. I need to help with the other two, by the window."

Jake saw another pair of medics carry one of the assistants out on a stretcher. Someone badly hurt. The sight of such misery put him over the top.

Completely breaking protocol, Jake faced his prior boss and said, "Director Denmark, this is despicable. You son of a bitch, you've turned an opportunity for international accord into a sick target shoot. What you've done is beneath the dignity of your office."

Moller turned to watch Jake but did not stop him.

Denmark shouted in answer, "What you've done is worse, Palatin. Treason. Betrayal. You think Tileus is better than Prime? These people live in chaos! Bedlam. Anarchy. You'll find out."

The guards held him in place. He shook with fury and still struggled to free himself, unable to speak, shivering with rampant fears.

Jake had always known the director's moods flashed into rage in an instant. Now, Jake could feel inside Denmark at one of those moments. The sense was a stinking abscess of obsession, contempt, arrogance, and defensiveness, all driven by a basic fear of failure.

The director's weaknesses were fully exposed. Jake was astonished such a twisted specimen of broken humanity had somehow risen to the highest level in Solity.

That fact alone was an indictment of Solity.

Jake paused to regain some control. "Great stars, I feel your fears, Director, every one of them. Yes, you were right. What you feel is the transpath Yitzak Goren created for you. It's not mind control. No, it's an accurate transmission of each person's emotions to you. And from you to us."

Jake looked at each participant, all of whom were focused on Denmark. Shock, disgust, anger, wariness, disbelief—the emotions from each battered at Jake. Most of all, he felt pity coming clearly from each person, overwhelming in its unanimity. Pity that would destroy a prideful man.

Jake turned back to Denmark, and he saw that prideful man in transition. He felt Denmark taking in the pity from the others. Denmark's eyes flicked from one person to another. His transmitted emotions raced from fear to contempt to determination, ultimately to desperation, flashing back and forth in attempted self-defense. He cringed, trying to hide himself from the glaring truth he sensed in each person.

Jake continued relentlessly, yet with a touch of compassion entering, "What we see in you, sir, is a hollow soul with no real power at all. You feel pity from us, because none of us had any idea one person contained such pain."

Jake surprised himself with the ability to speak this truth to the man who had dominated his life for years.

The director seemed unable to speak, unable to encompass the enormity of what he sensed from them all. Perhaps a rational man might have recovered. Denmark, however, pinged his gaze frantically around the room, out the windows, apparently seeking some escape. The emotions in him settled down into enduring fear, a mortal fright like that of a child in a borrowed home living a borrowed life.

Denmark was frozen. His face was empty, impassive. He looked as sadly damaged as a costly figurine with a crack through its heart, ready to collapse at the slightest touch.

Jake brushed himself off and walked around the table back to his seat. He knew he would never again be cowed by Denmark.

Moller said to the guards. "Help Director Denmark back to his seat. But keep him restrained. The rest of you, please sit down and compose yourselves. We're going to do this."

In measured motion, Denmark slowly sat down, his head lowered, his emotions jangling, guilt and fear foremost. His entire demeanor changed toward a traumatized humility completely foreign to him. Jake sensed the man give in, surrendering himself to a knowledge too dark to contain.

Jake was unclear whether Denmark would ever recover.

At the same time, Jake's heart pounded in freedom and compassion and awe.

๛ ✳ ๖

Calie Pires had watched Denmark's dissolution with consternation. She had instructions to follow his lead, but Denmark remained silent, unresponsive. The Verdant Prime side of the negotiations was now completely up to her. She looked around at the rest of the room and felt the emotions. Unlike Denmark, her heart soared. Pires saw, in this transpath field, an opportunity for diplomacy never afforded before: parties to the negotiation could know each other without secrecy. She saw honesty and knew it for itself. There would be no lies, no half-truths. It raised hopes for success she had abandoned forever in Denmark's shadow.

"We are still here, and I would like to continue." She paused, waiting for whatever squelch might come from Denmark. None came. "Let us see if we can come to agreement."

"We'd like that," said Moller.

Through the transpath, Pires also felt Moller's hope, his honest desire to treat them fairly, mixed with uncertainty about what might happen with Denmark. She looked to Thranadil and felt the woman's integrity.

"Perhaps we can resume," said Pires, "with trade negotiations. Your technologies for our foodstuffs can be a very good trade basis. We'd like to add this transpath to the list of technologies. Later, we can move back to the issues of inter-country agents and military reductions."

Denmark remained silent, his head lowered, to all appearances a shattered man.

Pires took part in the remainder of the day in amazement. She and Moller decided to reduce both country's militaries. Agents from each country would be explicitly identified, with roles and limitations known. She worked new trade opportunities with Thranadil. They even discussed their mutual relations with Rathas and Winter, coming to understandings about how to approach those countries. In the end, all four diplomats—Denmark included—signed the agreement.

CHAPTER 44

Success also has its consequences.

—*Collected Sayings of Yitzak Goren* by Ellen Thranadil, Tileus Press 439 A.T.

After the close of the conference, Jake met with his team in their lab to let them know of the success. When he stepped through the door, Zofia's eyes went wide at the sight of blood on his sleeve.

"Damn, Jake, what happened to you?" She rushed to him to touch the bandage on his arm. "You look like you've been shot."

"I was," he said with a shrug, "but it only grazed me."

The others crowded around: Soren, Manny, Mos, Emigan, their two technicians. Everyone expressed alarm.

"At a diplomatic meeting?"

"Why was there shooting?"

And the key question: "Did the transpath work?"

Jake laughed, nodding. "You bet it did. I'll tell you everything, but the governors now have a treaty between Tileus and Prime that solves everything. The transpath worked."

"So, bucko," Zofia said, while she bumped his hip, "how did you get shot?"

He ducked his head. "Well, that's the scary part. Director Denmark couldn't handle the emotions. He went crazy, and things got wild. He pulled out a gun, for star's sake—"

"A gun?" shouted Emigan.

Manny let loose a booming laugh.

Jake nodded. "Yeah, he aimed at me, first. Accused me of being a traitor. Needles were flying everywhere, into the walls, the windows, just missing the diplomats. He was a terrible shot, but he kept pulling the trigger. Only grazed me, but a couple of the assistants under the windows were hit. One of them died, the other's in surgery. The diplomats are all okay."

He gave a helpless shrug. "I...uh...tackled Denmark from across the table to stop him."

"You what?" echoed several.

Jake grinned self-consciously. "Yeah, I did sort of a zero-G racquetball move. I slid over the table to tackle him, then the security guards piled on and took away his gun."

"I wish I'd been there to see that." Zofia said, her eyes sparkling. "That son of a bitch needed to get what was comin' to him."

"Yeah. I called him that, too."

"To his face?" Zofia looked delighted.

Jake shrugged, grinning. "Well, you know, the transpath? The feelings were already there."

He shifted to thoughtfulness. "I don't know, Zofia. As much as I've hated Director Denmark, I felt pity for him, to see him break down that way."

She shrugged. "Maybe so. But what he had Overlock do to me..." Her face turned dark when she had another thought. She touched the scars on her throat. "I'd love to get Shelton Overlock somehow."

Soren said, "The point, though, is we won. We got the transpath working, and it made the difference. The negotiations were successful."

"So, what do we do now?" asked Mos.

"We've got a bright future," Jake answered. "Governor Thranadil approached me about keeping this team together, if you all agree. She thinks the transpath can be the core of a good business. We can make it portable. Make it available to everyone. People won't have to rely on secrecy anymore.

"It sometimes seems as if all human problems boil down to differences. Ellen hopes the transpath can bridge those gaps."

ஒ ✳ ஒ

WENTDAY, 21 HEXEMBER, 416 A.T.

Two days later, Director Denmark was still reeling from his humiliation. Two security guards met him on his return to Prime. They informed him Chairman Lukin summoned him to a special meeting of the Solity Council tomorrow to address the serious complaints from Tileus about his actions. His authority as director was revoked.

His embarrassment had fully transitioned back into hate: of Jacoby Palatin, of the Tileus governors, of Director Pires, of Director Keita. The more he thought, the more people he found to blame for his situation. He sat in the fifth-floor office that would shortly no longer be his. The bright sun outside did nothing to lighten his mood. The council hadn't even seen fit to continue his security monitoring.

In a perfunctory mood, Denmark went through the records of the last few days. He couldn't see any way to recoup his loss. One of the items in his holo was a report from Shelton Overlock about a successful raid on Lazarites in Equaton. It hardly mattered.

The report, however, got him thinking about Overlock. Yes, he had another person to blame for his failure. He'd told Overlock to recapture Palatin. Overlock even had the girlfriend in his hands and lost her again. At every step, Overlock's failure to capture Palatin drove the engineer further and further away. If Overlock had done his job, Palatin never would have ended up in Tileus with that working transpath.

That's the real blame. Overlock and his overeager incompetence. I'll have to do something about him. So. What's he been doing while I've been gone? Has he done anything worthwhile? Denmark called up the records of Overlock's implant calls. Connections to subordinates in Timpi, Equaton, Oriens. Incoming calls from informants, other subordinates.

And two incoming calls from Director Miriam Keita. One yesterday, one this morning.

What the hell is Overlock doing with Keita? I told him to find dirt on her, but why would she be calling him?

All of Denmark's anger focused on this. He couldn't touch the other directors, or the Tileus governors, or even that traitor engineer, but if Overlock had something going on with Keita, a desperate wrong was happening. Denmark's rage overflowed. *Overlock's been behind this failure all along. I can do something after all. I can't let him get away with this.*

Denmark retrieved a needle gun from his desk and put in a call to Overlock.

"Meet me downstairs right away, Shelton. In your basement chamber. I've got something to show you."

☙ ✳ ❧

Minutes later, Denmark keyed the security lock on the basement room where Overlock did his worst. He and Overlock were the only two with access to the room but Denmark rarely came down here. Wet work made him uncomfortable; he preferred psychological domination as his weapon of choice. The last time he'd been here was shortly after the destruction of the lab building, when Overlock had a dying Lazarite in a chair.

Denmark's thoughts still whirled around his failure. *Even after death, Goren got his revenge on me. Yet another way Overlock failed; Goren killed himself instead of suffering.* He ground his teeth again, determined to win something out of all this.

The torture chamber was empty. The malicious equipment sparkled with cleanliness; the slick floor shone all the way to the drain. Ominous implements to inflict pain hung in their places along the wall. Blades glinted. In surprise, he stopped just inside the door. *What? Is the man going to ignore my summons?*

"Shelton?" he asked the empty space, irritation rising. "Are you here?"

Overlock's sibilant voice sounded just behind Denmark. He'd been behind the door.

"Certainly here, Director, staying alert for you."

When Denmark whirled around in exasperation, he felt a prick behind his elbow, the jab of a needle.

"What are you doing?" he shouted.

Overlock stood with his trademark thin smile, his pale blue eyes watching Denmark's reactions, a hypodermic in his hand. Denmark knew that look; he'd seen it whenever Overlock had a victim available.

No hesitation, just rage. Denmark swung a fist. He wasn't as tall as Overlock, but he carried more mass, solidly packed into his short frame. He connected with Overlock's jaw, driving the man back. Denmark swung again, his other fist, but fell off-target. He only grazed Overlock's chin. Denmark's head whirled with strange fuzziness. *What did he inject?*

"You failed, Director," said Overlock. "I can't be working for a failure, so I've found a new sponsor. Director Keita asked me to send her regards."

Overlock put down the hypodermic and picked up a scalpel, grinning again. "She's willing for me to do it my way."

Denmark's head was starting to spin. *Not much time before this drug takes over.* He lifted the needle gun out of his pocket and fired. His aim was terrible, even at close range, so he fired again and again. And again. Until the magazine was empty. Denmark's confusion grew. His eyesight blurred. He fell to the floor, his body weakening. The room spun around him.

He no longer saw Overlock standing where he'd been. *Oh, there he is. On the floor.* Overlock was down, covered in blood. *Must have hit him.*

Denmark couldn't move, his head still turned to one side. *Paralytic. But I'm still breathing. Overlock wouldn't want to kill me immediately.* The thoughts didn't change anything; he still couldn't move. *This helplessness will pass, and I got him.*

Then he watched Overlock start to move. Crawling toward him, leaving a trail of blood. The scalpel still in his hand.

∽✳∽

FRIDAY, 24 HEXEMBER, 416 A.T. ·

Jake and Zofia had a busy week working with Ellen to get their business started. Five days later, Jake met Zofia for lunch at a seafood restaurant in downtown Thad City. He smiled to remember their first dinner together at the Tangled Tackle in Oriens. Their friends had accused them of breaking the Verdant Prime fraternization laws. No such laws here in Tileus.

They got a sidewalk table, enjoying the bright, warm day. Summer was here. He wondered if summer would be cooler here, further north than Oriens.

"Hi, love," he said, and greeted her with a kiss while she sat. Kissing in public. "Did you have any luck getting those parts for Mos's new design?"

She grazed a hand across the side of his neck and smiled. "You bet. The supplier is all on board. Everyone's heard about what the transpath did. They're eager to be part of it."

"I think I found us a permanent location for our lab and manufacturing. It's not large, but it doesn't need to be yet. Still, it's big enough to provide the company room to grow. And it fits within the budget we've created."

"I'm glad Ellen Thranadil found a business consultant for us. He's been really helpful in the plannin'."

Jake shook his head gently. "I'm still amazed at where we're going. In Prime, all we had to look forward to was doing the same Assignment year after year. Here, our technical skills, with some added business knowledge, give us no limit at all. We can create something to spread through all three human worlds—and beyond, if people start colonizing again. And it'll be ours, not owned by the state. It's very different here in Tileus—all a big risk. We could fail and have nothing. Or we may end up living very well."

She laughed. "Better than Director Denmark and his big office?"

Jake turned serious. "You haven't heard?"

She shook her head.

"I had a conversation this morning with Welton Moller. His contacts in Prime—"

"Spies," she corrected with a twinkle in her eye.

Jake smiled. "Yes, spies. Some big changes have happened this week down in Prime."

"Like what?"

"Chairman Lukin of the Solity Council had a heart attack. Director Keita is the new chairman."

"Keita? Not Denmark?"

"No." He paused. "The word is Denmark's dead."

She sat up straight, sucking in breath through her open mouth. "No."

"Yes. He was found with Overlock in the basement of the General Defense building. Apparently killed each other."

She slumped, looking down at the table. Jake reached out a hand to touch her arm.

When she looked up again, she had fire in her eyes. "I want to know more," she said. "I want to know they suffered."

Jake nodded. "Well, yes. One of Governor Moller's moles actually saw the scene afterwards. They were both on the floor. Overlock was shot repeatedly and bled out. Before he died, though, he apparently sliced up Denmark with a scalpel. He must have injected Denmark with a paralytic."

"Wow. That sounds like quite a blow-out battle."

"Yeah, it does. Just right for the two of them."

She held his hand tightly. "I'm glad. We don't have to worry about either of them ever again."

Jake reached out with his other hand to hold both of hers. "We don't. Never again."

They made their orders through the on-table menu, then talked about their business plans. Setting aside the darkness that had ruled their lives for so long, dinner was easy and long.

At a break in the conversation, Jake reached out to hold her hands again. He chuckled deep in his throat. "But I've got something else to bring up, too. Something much more positive."

She cocked her head with a grin.

"You know we're no longer in Prime."

"Of course, you idiot." She swatted one of his hands gently.

"There are no laws here about fraternization. No DNA breeding program. Right?"

Her face turned serious, and he saw her catch a breath.

"I was thinking, Zofia, maybe we should be together in everything—not just in business."

She paused, waiting, her eyebrows puzzling.

"Uh...Jake? Love? Was that a proposal for marriage?"

He blushed.

"If it was, that was probably the lamest excuse for a proposal I've ever heard of. Get it right, bucko. Try it again, and maybe I'll say, 'yes.'"

This time, he got on his knees and pulled out a ring.

Acknowledgements

No novel happens by the author's efforts alone. Looking back on it, my first draft of every single chapter had weaknesses that took away from the purpose of that chapter. Thankfully, I've had people to straighten me out.

Every chapter went through a two-stage review by my local group, the Working Writers' Workshop led by Phil Walker (*The Scroll* and seventeen other books). In a single week, the chapter got written critiques (and changes) from all members. Then, after revision, I'd read the chapter aloud while they marked up hard copies with further critiques (and changes). The process not only improved the book immensely, but had a great positive impact on my writing as a whole. The members included Keith Abbott (*Lights Out*), Cris Brizuela, Aubrey Cross, Susan DeLay, Paul Eberz (the acclaimed *Smoke* series), Rich Friedman, Leon Gottlieb, Shelley Jones, Jack O'Brien (*The Roundabout Way*), and Carey Winters. I thank each and every one of them for their many insights.

Some of the material about Verdant also got critiques from the online Other Worlds Writers' Workshop run by Michele Combs and including Jason Andress, Wendy Edsall-Kerwin, Irene Fields, Meaghan Haughian, Jessica Hawkins, Emily Renk Hawthorne, EJ Heijnis, Gregg Jansen, and Harry Whomersley. Of all the OWWW friends, however, my special thanks go to Clark Sodersten, who gave me extensive help on the entire novel as well as critiquing everything I've posted there.

I've been amazed at the help offered by Mark Newhouse (the award-winning *Devil's Bookkeepers* trilogy), who taught me more about tightening and editing than I could often take in.

But of course, my greatest gratitude of all goes to my wife Beth, who supported me and put up with all those hours when I was buried in the computer.

About the Author

Iconoclast, polymath, and author, Doc Honour has been a US Navy pilot, an international leader in systems engineering, and a successful entrepreneur. He holds a PhD from the University of South Australia in systems engineering. Doc has led teams of up to 50 people to build complex systems; the system integration problem sequences in this book reflect his real-life experience. He has taught nearly 500 short courses to help others learn to do what he has done. Doc Honour's short story Fishing Hands won a top (Gold) award in the 2022 Royal Palm Literary Awards of the Florida Writers Association. Born on Guam, he's lived in 34 different places. These days, he lives in Florida with his wife and a rather willful Australian Shepherd named Chip.

Find out more at DocHonourBooks.com.

Made in the USA
Columbia, SC
12 January 2023

10151884R00181